WELL-BEHAVED CHILDREN SELDOM MAKE HISTORY

WELL-BEHAVED CHILDREN SELDOM MAKE HISTORY

A FUNDERBURKE AND KAIMING MYSTERY

CHRIS CHAN

LEVEL
BEST BOOKS

Once more, to my parents, Drs. Carlyle and Patricia Chan
And to my Aunt Cheryl and Uncle Raynold

Contents

Introduction

In our two previous books, we both told the story of a case on our own. In our third book-length account of one of our investigations, we're going to trade off narration duties. As we're both juggling work and family duties, this makes the task of writing a lot easier.

For the benefit of individuals who aren't familiar with our careers, we both work for Cuthbertson Hall, a K-12 school in Milwaukee, Wisconsin. We went to high school there together, reconnected years after graduating, and began dating. Funderburke is a lawyer who got ostracized from the profession after getting a lot of corrupt attorneys disbarred, and he became a private investigator and later the Student Advocate at Cuthbertson, protecting the rights of kids in trouble. Nerissa is a history teacher and the head of a fund that helps teenaged mothers finish their education, and is also a private investigator in her own right.

Funderburke is the child of a messy divorce, and from the age of thirteen onward his relationship with his mother, the sharpest divorce attorney in Milwaukee, was highly strained. Nerissa spent a difficult childhood raised by a depressed single mother. At a very young age, Nerissa became the mother of a daughter named Toby (this was before she met Funderburke), and she moved to Milwaukee in the hopes that a relative could help her get a proper education. Eventually, Nerissa and Toby were adopted by Keith Kaiming (and also by his wife Midge when they married a few years later) and life improved exponentially for them.

When we were trying to decide which case to write about next, we chose the Berchtwelt case in light of a new documentary recently released on a streaming service that argues that Benek Berchtwelt was indeed guilty. This documentary was based on a highly inaccurate book written by the prosecutor of the case, Tatum Sangster. At the request of Benek's family members, we have written this book to correct the record. At the request of several other people involved in the case, we have not used their real names.

—Isaiah Funderburke and Nerissa Kaiming Funderburke

Prologue: Killing the Boogeyman

The most important person in eleven-year-old Volker Berchtwelt's life was his older brother Benek. He loved his grandfather, Otto, but despite his grandfather's many virtues, they never shared the same easy camaraderie that the brothers did. Volker was mildly fond of his largely absent father, and as for his mother, she was practically dead to him. He had never forgiven her for abandoning the family nine years earlier, and she had never tried to make amends or even maintain a presence in his life, except for calls on his birthday and Christmas. So as far as Volker was concerned, she could stay in Boston or Providence or wherever she was living with her latest in a long string of boyfriends. As long as he had Benek, Volker reasoned, he'd be all right.

As close as the siblings were, their differences were stark and obvious. A little over six years separated the two. Benek was six foot three, slim, and athletic. Volker was small for his age, solidly built, and had no talent for sports. Benek's hair and complexion were far fairer than his brother's. Volker was an excellent student, Benek scraped by with middling grades. The elder was popular amongst his peers, the younger had no friends aside from his sibling, and he was fine with that.

Volker had always admired his brother, but it was when he was six years old that he really began to idolize his brother, even worship him. Their grandfather's bungalow was nearly a century old, and their home creaked and groaned throughout the night, especially as the autumn progressed and the temperatures dropped. Young Volker was convinced that the noises were the sound of the Bogeyman, who crept through the shadows, and was prepared to devour him as soon as he fell asleep.

Grandpa had told him that there was no Bogeyman, and to stop being silly and close his eyes and keep them shut. But six-year-old Volker was appalled at his grandfather's lack of belief, and insisted that a hideous monster stalked their home.

He confided in Benek, who nodded sympathetically, and repeated that the noises came from the shifting joists of the house.

"*Some* of the noises may be the house," Volker conceded, "but not all of them. I know the Bogeyman exists! I've seen him."

"What does he look like?" There was no incredulity in Benek's face, just warm understanding.

"I can't see in the dark. He's just big and spooky and terrifying."

"All right." Benek rummaged through a drawer, found a flashlight, and handed it to his brother. "The next time you see the Bogeyman, turn this on and point this at him. The Bogeyman hates the light. It makes his flesh burn. Shine the light on him, and he'll run away. And if he gives you any more trouble, call for me." At the time, their grandfather worked from nine P.M. to six A.M. as a night watchman for a local strip mall, so it was just the two of them most weeknights.

That night, ten minutes after he'd turned out the light to his room, Volker thought he'd heard the Bogeyman crawling on the floor beneath his bed. He grabbed the flashlight, bounced the beam across his bedroom, and found nothing. Eventually, he gave up looking, collapsed back onto his bed, and soon drifted off to dreamland. Three hours later, he sat up with his heart racing. Seizing the flashlight, he pointed towards the far corner of the room, and through his bleary eyes, was sure that he saw a tentacle pass through the beam.

So he screamed. He filled his little lungs with air and yelled until Benek ran into the room. Benek flicked on the lights, performed a quick search, and assured Volker that the Bogeyman was not there. The same series of events repeated for five consecutive nights, at which point Volker noticed that his brother wasn't quite so sympathetic and obliging as he had been earlier in the week.

On the sixth night, right around midnight, Volker once again awakened, convinced that the Bogeyman was scratching on the inside of his closet door.

He yelled, but this time it wasn't Benek who rushed into the room, Volker turned the flashlight towards the entryway, and his voice froze as he gazed upon a hideous, gray-green face, a body covered with similarly colored fur, and curving claws at the ends of his enormous hands.

The Bogeyman took two lurching steps toward the bed, uttered an inhuman growl, and Volker was a moment from leaping out of bed and flinging his diminutive body through the window when Benek's voice, threatening and authoritative despite the awkward squeaks of puberty, bellowed, "Keep away from my brother!"

Benek rushed into the room, wielding his baseball bat. The Bogeyman whirled around, and Benek swung low and struck the monster in the left knee, causing the Bogeyman to topple forward to the ground. Benek swiftly delivered five quick blows to the creature's head before kneeling down and taking the Bogeyman's pulse.

"The Bogeyman is dead," Benek informed Volker with self-satisfied triumph. "He won't be bothering you again."

Volker's mind reeled, and he managed to choke out the words, "Are you sure?"

"Positive. He's dead."

"There could be another one."

"Unlikely. Bogeymen are very rare, and they never visit the homes where other Bogeymen have hunted. They're oddly territorial that way. The body releases pheromones that only other Bogeymen can smell, and they warn their fellow creatures away. No, once a Bogeyman dies in a house, no other Bogeyman will ever come to that place again. Nor any other kind of monster, they're afraid of making an enemy of the Bogeymen. Relax. Go back to sleep. I'm going to drag the body down to the alley on the next block and toss him in the dumpster. I'll be back in five minutes."

It took Volker three hours to fall asleep again, and then he slept until one-thirty in the afternoon. Thankfully, it was a Saturday. Time passed, and Volker's rest was no longer troubled by fear of monsters. This continued until just over two years after that memorable night, Volker walked home from school with Benek by his side, and froze. A pop-up Halloween supply shop had taken out a one-month lease in a recently-closed mattress store, and standing prominently in the plate-glass window was the Bogeyman.

Even though the autumn light was waning at three-thirty in the afternoon, Volker could tell at once that the figure in the window was not an actual monster. It was an inexpensive costume that was still quite capable of being fear-inducing under the right circumstances.

Volker's mind, remarkably nimble and perceptive for his age, performed the calculations swiftly. "Who was that in the Bogeyman costume two years ago?"

"Alfie." Alfie Witteveen was Benek's best friend since childhood. He lived a quarter of a mile down the street and was always hanging out at their house.

"He gave a nice performance."

"That he did. I wasn't half-bad either, you know."

"Yeah, you were pretty great in your role as the Bogeyman Killer. How much did the Bogeyman costume cost?"

"Didn't cost us a dime. Alfie's dad wore it at a Halloween party the previous year, and it was stuffed in a cardboard box in their basement." After a pause, Benek asked, "Are you upset about our little deception?"

Grinning, Volker replied. "Nope. Not one bit."

Volker stopped believing in the Bogeyman that afternoon. But from that moment forward, his faith in his brother was unassailable. How many older siblings would go through an elaborate ruse like that just to help his sibling sleep securely? Though he had no evidence to back up his estimate, Volker was sure that the number was minimal. Benek had come up with a dramatic plan to cure his night-time fears, and all Volker felt was admiration for his brother.

Two years later, Volker was ten and Benek was one of the best-liked students in his high school junior class. He was co-captain of the cross-country, basketball, and baseball teams. With his little brother's help, he was maintaining a B-minus average. After a few years of dating a new girl every month, he was going steady with a remarkably beautiful young woman named Lada Casagrande, the Prom Queen and co-captain of the volleyball team. She led a volunteer group at her local soup kitchen, and she was fond of vampire teen romances. Volker didn't particularly like or dislike Lada, and even though she was often at their house, they had little interaction with each other.

The relationship continued, and around Easter, an uncharacteristically nervous Benek was sitting in a corner of the living room, looking like he was about to be violently ill.

"What's wrong?" Volker asked.

"Nothing," Benek answered. After two seconds of attempting to repress the next words from exiting his lips, he blurted out, "You're going to be an uncle."

The next few months were awkward. Benek wasn't himself, and Volker did his best to keep up his brother's spirits. In August, Lada gave birth to a healthy baby girl and named her Aurelia. Benek returned to his stellar athletic career and his mediocre academic career, and was elected Homecoming King. Lada withdrew from their local school, started taking classes online, and visited the Berchtwelt home a few times each week with baby Aurelia.

At the start of October, Lada stopped coming to their house. Volker knew that Benek had argued with her, but his older brother refused to share the details. One clear, balmy Friday night, Benek came home from cross-country practice, and the two siblings spent the evening eating a frozen pizza and watching *South Park* episodes. Volker reluctantly went to bed just after eleven, but he was awakened the following morning at dawn when the police arrived at their home. They told Benek to stay in his room, but the walls of the bungalow were thin, and he could hear everything if he pressed his ear to the ventilation shaft.

In the gentlest possible manner, the detectives informed Benek that Lada had been murdered the previous night, and after a few comforting words, they asked him where he'd been during the hours of eight and ten. Benek explained that he'd spent the entire night at home, hanging out with his brother. When the police finished their questions and had a brief talk with Volker in his grandfather's presence, Volker confirmed his brother's alibi, assuring the police that aside from a couple of two-minute bathroom breaks, he could account for every second of Benek's time from six until eleven that night.

The police thanked them and went on their way. A few days later, the brothers and their grandfather attended Lada's funeral, where Lada's mother informed them that she would be caring for Aurelia for the time being. Mrs. Casagrande was frigid towards Benek, and backed out of his hug as quickly as possible.

After another week, the police showed up at Benek's cross-country tournament and arrested him immediately after he'd finished his race. He was not given the opportunity to receive his blue ribbon.

Volker's emotions were dominated by confusion and agitation. "But he *couldn't* have done it!" he informed Benek's public defender, Naeem Popoola. "He was with me the whole time. It had to have been someone else."

Their public defender was very kind, and he repeatedly assured Volker that the police had made a mistake, and that the trial would clarify the matter. All Volker had to do was put on a suit, tell his story, and the jury should see immediately that he was telling the truth. "Reasonable doubt," the lawyer informed him. "Just tell them what happened and all will be well."

So Volker's grandfather bought him the cheapest suit they could find, and Volker rehearsed his story dozens of times with the public defender, and when the big day finally came, Volker told the court that his brother had been with him for the entire evening of the murder. Afterwards, the Assistant District Attorney, Tatum Sangster, peppered him with questions. She'd been very polite, almost sisterly, but the implication in her words was clear. Volker didn't care for the gleam in her eyes as she interrogated him.

"You love your brother very much, don't you, Volker?"

"Yes, I do."

"You'd do anything for him, wouldn't you?"

"He'd do anything for me."

"You'd even lie for him, wouldn't you?"

"No!"

"Are you sure that you're telling the truth, Volker?"

"Yes!"

"Isn't it possible that you might have gotten a little mixed up? Perhaps you're thinking of the wrong night. Isn't it possible, Volker, that the night you ate frozen pizza and watched *South Park* with your brother was actually the *previous* evening?"

"No! Benek was with me every second the night Lada was killed!"

The questioning continued for a little while longer, and then Benek's attorney asked a few questions on redirect to make it clear that Volker was sure of his statements and was being totally honest.

Volker was the star witness for the defense. A few of Benek's coaches testified as character witnesses, and after closing arguments, the case went to the jury.

"They'll believe me," Volker said to himself repeatedly. "They know that Benek was with me the whole time and that he couldn't have done it. Then he can finally come home."

Volker kept telling himself that for four days while the jury deliberated. When they announced their verdict, Volker's mouth was bone dry, but he clung to the hope that the jury could tell he was telling the truth.

And then the jury found Benek guilty.

Chapter One: Disagreeing with Ed McBain

FUNDERBURKE

Mrs. Gastrell looked as if she expected no dissent, so I decided to argue with her, no matter what she was going to suggest. "Of course, I don't think anybody will object to the revocation of Volker Berchtwelt's scholarship," she declared.

"Why should we do that?" I had no idea who Volker was at that time, but I was not about to have Mrs. Gastrell, a professional Concerned Parent™ who believed that the combined wealth of her and her husband allowed her to waltz into a meeting of the Cuthbertson Hall Trustees and expect that the school accept her dictates without question.

She turned to me and, with a level of hauteur that would have made Queen Victoria look like a cast member of *Jersey Shore*, declared, "We cannot have the brother of a convicted murderer, and a perjurer himself, attending Middle School with our children. Surely, you can't allow such an undesirable influence amongst us."

"I agree," Dr. Tidwell nodded. "It's just not a good idea."

The Berchtwelt trial hadn't gotten much in-depth coverage in the media. I knew that a high school student had been tried and convicted of the murder of his girlfriend, but as I hadn't been introduced to Volker, who was completing his first year as a Cuthbertson scholarship student, I didn't make the connection. Volker was a total stranger to me, but I wasn't about to let a seventh-grader be expelled on Mrs. Gastrell's say-so. "As Student Advocate, it is my job to look after the rights of any Cuthbertson student accused of wrongdoing, and therefore, I cannot allow this young man to have his scholarship stripped from him without due process. Has he done anything to warrant expulsion?"

"His brother is a convicted murderer," Mrs. Gastrell repeated with the same level of icy disdain one might give a dog who, after five years of training, had never quite managed to master housebreaking.

"That means nothing. Half of our scholarship students have relatives with criminal records. That's one of the reasons we give them scholarships. To provide them with educational opportunities that they might otherwise not have, and therefore avoid a life of crime themselves."

"I can't say I'm happy about those students, either," Mrs. Gastrell admitted.

"But most of those students' relatives aren't murderers," Dr. Tidwell noted.

With a vigorous nod, Mrs. Gastrell added, "And they aren't perjurers, either."

"Has Volker been convicted of perjury? Or even charged with that crime?"

Both of them seemed astounded by my question. "Well, no. Not as far as we know."

Not bothering to mute my triumph one scintilla, I continued. "Then, if the authorities do not see fit to charge young Volker with a crime, we can hardly take it upon ourselves to find him unworthy of attending our school without a proper investigation."

"This is outrageous!" Mrs. Gastrell's face was turning the color of a Barbie's Malibu Dreamhouse, and I was loving it.

"No, it's the presumption of innocence. The cornerstone of our judicial system. Besides, you don't want to expose the school to a lawsuit, do you? You don't want the school smeared by all the news outlets who love to see the city's most prestigious prep school dragged through the mud, do you?"

Dr. Keith Kaiming, chair of the History Department and my girlfriend Nerissa's adoptive father, was clearly enjoying this as much as I was, but he masked his emotions better. Not completely, but better. "I think,

Funderburke, that you should look into this matter and get back to us. No sense moving forward without a thorough knowledge of all the facts."

After a murmur of agreement from slightly over half of the meeting's attendees, it was decided that I should put my private investigator skills to good use, and that the matter would be addressed at the next month's meeting, the day after Memorial Day. These meetings are always held on Tuesday afternoons. On her way out, Mrs. Gastrell shot me the same glare that freshly minted brides bestow upon the fellows who spill a glass of red wine all over their wedding dresses at the reception, and I took a moment to bask in my triumph before realizing that I had best have a conversation with Volker the very next day.

I phoned Volker's homeroom teacher later that evening, brushed up on the online news coverage of the case, and the following morning, Nerissa and I took Volker out of his first-period independent reading for an introductory conversation. We introduced ourselves, explained the situation, and the first words out of Volker's mouth were, "I wasn't lying!"

"We didn't say you were." Nerissa can have a very soothing effect on people, and her words sparked an immediate reaction in Volker.

He took a few breaths, ran his hands through his hair, and then looked up at us with tiny tears in the corners of his eyes. "I don't think that anybody really believes me. Not the police, not anybody in the courtroom, not even Grandpa. But you just met me, and you're on my side?" He made a little noise that an uncharitable person might describe as a derisive scoff.

I decided that blunt honesty was the only way to move forward, and I informed him, "We're neutral right now. We're going to look into this with an open mind, and we'll make our decision based on the evidence. And right now, we'll listen to what you're saying without any preconceived notions. If we believe you, we'll go all out for you. You have my word on that."

He looked at me, then turned to Nerissa, then sighed. "What do you want to know?"

"Start with the beginning of your brother's relationship with Miss Castagrande."

And he did, spending several minutes outlining the first months that the

3

pair dated, then moved on to her pregnancy, then their estrangement right before her death. "I didn't learn until much later what was really going on with that."

"What do you mean?"

"A couple of my brother's friends told him that he should get a blood test done to confirm that Aurelia was really his. He laughed them off at first, telling them that Lada was totally faithful to him, but they kept nagging him, and they mentioned some rumors they heard, so eventually, he got some kind of samples together—I'm not sure exactly how it worked."

"And then?"

"Aurelia isn't my niece."

I'm not proud of this, but that little twist made me much more interested in the case. I leaned forward. "Do you know who her father is?"

"No. No one does, as far as I know. But Lada refused to admit anything. It really ticks me off how she kept doubling and tripling down on her lies. She just kept saying, "She's yours! Of course, she's yours!" So she had another test done, and they got exactly the same result, and then she just kept insisting that it simply had to be some kind of mistake, because Benek had to be Aurelia's father, and there were a lot of arguments..."

"How bad were these fights?" Nerissa asked.

"They never got physical! That girl Maia lied!"

"Back up a sec. Maia, who?"

"Maia Landeen. She was in their class. She says she saw Benek choking Lada during an argument, but that never happened!"

Neither of us said anything for a moment, and then Volker looked at the ground. "You think he did it now, don't you?"

"I told you two minutes ago. We never make a decision before we hear all the evidence," I assured him. "Please keep going."

He led us through the night of the murder, repeatedly emphasizing that his brother never left the house. He then led his way through the trial, the verdict, and the aftermath. "His lawyer filed a Notice of Appeal several days after the verdict, and the hearing at the District Court of Appeals is a week from Friday. Today's Wednesday, that means there's only nine days to go.

Just eight full days."

"What were the grounds for review?" I asked.

"I don't know. I'm not sure what you mean by that."

"That's fine. I'll need the name of your brother's attorney. I'd like a word with him."

Volker looked me straight in the eyes. "Are you saying you're going to investigate?"

"Yes, I am."

"Do you believe me?"

My gut told me that Volker was being totally honest, but I deferred judgment to Nerissa, who can read people more perceptively than anybody else I've ever met. "What do you say, Nerissa?"

"I believe him completely. So that means we're looking at a wrongful conviction here."

Hope flashed across Volker's eyes. "What are you going to do now?"

I pulled a little notebook out of my coat pocket. "I'm going to ask you a few more questions, and then I'm going to start my own investigation."

I'm going to go on a little digression here, but I promise I'll get to the point swiftly. Ed McBain, for anybody who's not familiar with his work, was a prolific and successful American crime writer. He wrote dozens of books in multiple series, but his most famous works are the 87th Precinct novels, published over nearly fifty years, from 1956 to 2004. These novels are leading examples of police procedural novels, and I'm a big fan of them. I do not, however, agree with all of McBain's personal opinions, including his views on realism and the role of private detectives in the criminal justice system.

In one interview, McBain said, "I write police procedure and not detective novels because they are more true to life. Private detectives don't solve crimes. They spend their time spying on husbands and wives." That confident pronouncement has some truth to it, but it's also a crock of falsehoods as well. As in so much of life, broad brushstrokes tend to blur more than elucidate. A lot of private detectives never investigate crimes. Many, perhaps most of them, earn their bread and cheese by photographing adulterers. The vast majority of murders are solved by dogged members of the official police force, and a whole lot of them deserve respect for the effort and tenacity they put into their investigations, all for precious little money and thanks.

But mistakes get made all the time, and innocent people get caught up in the justice system woodchipper. And that's where a certain group of specialist private detectives enter the picture. Take a look at almost any prominent firm of defense lawyers, and in addition to their personal assistants and their paralegals and their receptionists, there's another category of professionals who are almost invariably on the firm's payroll. *Private investigators.* That's because any lawyer with a grain of sense knows not to rely solely on the facts the official police provide to them. Even the most dedicated detective can overlook a witness, or a lab technician can add the wrong chemical to a test tube, or someone can leave out a critical word when a report is typed.

So if an innocent person is accused of murder, and that person can afford a top-notch attorney (and granted, those two categories don't overlap a lot), the defense lawyers will make sure they've got their best private eyes on the case, questioning witnesses to see if there's the slightest detail they've forgotten, digging into the science journals to see if the forensic evidence is reliable, constructing alternative theories of the crime and running them down to see if they'll hold enough water for reasonable doubt.

And every so often, the private investigator finds out what really happened. An overlooked detail is unearthed, a lie is checked against new evidence and caught, a contradiction is unearthed, a technical mistake is called to the court's attention. Whatever happens, it leads to clearing an innocent person and the arrest of the true perpetrator. Yes, these cases are rare, but so are African forest elephants, and no sensible person believes the world's a better place without them.

I want to make it undeniably clear that I believe that guilty murderers need to be shoved into a cell and left there. But nothing makes the bile rise to my throat like an innocent person getting railroaded. Everybody accused of a crime in America can get a public defender to represent them in court, with the taxpayers picking up the bill. This is because the legal system is a labyrinth, and without a proper guide to lead you through, people are not just liable to get hopelessly lost, but they could lose everything as well. And aside from a particularly prosperous few, not many people who can afford a skilled lawyer at the start of a trial would be able to hire that same lawyer again by the ordeal's end, whatever the verdict.

But an overworked, low-paid public defender will only help you in the courtroom, and there's no provision for the person on trial to get a private investigator on their side as well. And while no one's more disgusted than I am by the imaginative and innovative ways that the government finds to flush taxpayer funds down the toilet, I'd be willing to back the use of public funds to allow defendants the services of a private detective in order to dig around, though with the proviso that if the P.I. happens to find strong evidence of guilt, that it must be submitted to the authorities as well.

And the more I dug into the news coverage of the case, the more convinced I was that Benek Berchtwelt had needed a first-class private eye on his team. But, an experienced investigator only uses the media accounts as a start. You need to go to the sources for first-hand information.

So that's why, after a bit of phone tag, Benek's lawyer, Naeem Popoola, accepted my invitation to come to dinner at Nerissa's family's house that night in order to discuss the case. Nerissa's adoptive mother, Midge, had gone all out, making her signature chicken marsala with three kinds of mushrooms and garlic mashed potatoes, and the elder set of triplets had joined forces to make a chocolate and strawberry tartuffo. As might be expected when the dessert was made by six-year-olds, it looked messy but tasted amazing.

I think Naeem was a little nonplussed by the Kaiming family home, which rarely holds fewer than fifteen family members, friends, and neighbors around their dinner table on any given night, and usually several more than that, but the kids were on their best behavior, and little Bernard, the eldest of Nerissa's younger siblings, had monopolized most of Naeem's conversation by lecturing him on a book he'd recently finished reading on the history of *Sesame Street*. We'd agreed to wait until after we'd finished eating to discuss the case, as the topic might have spoiled the food.

After we'd had our fill, Keith, Midge, and Midge's younger sister Rally took care of the dishes, Nerissa's daughter Toby retreated to her room to do her homework, and the elder members of the family looked after the smaller kids. Nerissa and Naeem took cups of coffee into Nerissa's little study, and Naeem took the chair at her desk while the two of us curled up next to each other on the window seat.

"Well, where should we start?" Naeem asked.

Nerissa's nothing if not direct. "Do you think he did it or not?"

Naeem didn't hesitate. "No. I'm going mainly on instinct here, but I'd bet my car—which admittedly isn't a very large wager—that Benek is completely innocent. But I couldn't get the jury to look past all the evidence."

"There was a lot of proof against him?" I asked.

"Mainly circumstantial. I thought his little brother would make for a convincing alibi, but the jury must have believed the Kasprzaks instead."

"Who are they?"

"A seventy-something couple who live across the street from the victim. They swear that they saw Benek entering her house on the night of the murder, even though Benek insisted he hadn't been there since the previous evening. They were adamant that Benek pulled up in front of Lada's house around eight P.M. on his bike. They'd seen him several times before; he'd helped them out once when Mrs. Kasprzak dropped her keys and accidentally kicked them underneath the car. So that made it two against one regarding the alibi, and the jury figured Volker was the one lying."

"Is there any reason at all why the Kasprzaks might have tried to frame Benek?" I asked.

"None that I know. They barely knew him and had no reason to send him to prison."

"How good is their eyesight?"

"Good enough for the two of them to regularly take trips to Lake Geneva to stay with Mr. Kasprzak's brother. They prefer to drive at night because the streets are less crowded. They claim they saw Benek while they were loading up their car, left the house at 8:15, and arrived at the brother's house about an hour and ten minutes later for a week's stay."

"Did the police go to Lake Geneva to interview them?"

"Uh...no. I believe they weren't questioned until they got back home."

"So it was at least a week since they claim to have seen him." I knew from experience that prolonged delays between events and questioning can lead to major discrepancies.

"That's right. I couldn't shake either of them on the stand. They were positive they saw him on Friday night. And I didn't think they were lying, either. Maybe they got mixed up, but I don't know how."

"And the victim—Lada—was strangled?" I asked.

"Yes. She was found in her room, face-down on the bed. She was killed with a pair of her own jeans, taken from the hamper full of clothes to be washed."

"Was Lada alone in the house at the time?" Nerissa wondered.

"Yes. Her mother took the baby to visit her sister. Mrs. Casagrande's sister, I mean. Mr. Casagrande died from an undiagnosed heart problem three years ago, their elder son is married and lives in Green Bay. I think he and his wife have adopted Aurelia now. Anyway, it was just the three of them—Mrs. Casagrande, Lada, and Aurelia—living there at the time. Mrs. Casagrande got back home at just a few minutes after ten-thirty."

"And what time did she leave the house?"

"Before six. Lada was on the phone with three friends between six and eight, with gaps of several minutes in-between. Besides the aunt's testimony, there were neighbors who stopped by, and the forensic evidence saying Lada was dead a half-hour before her mother came home, there's no way Mrs. Casagrande could have harmed her daughter."

Nerissa ran her hand through her hair. "Do you have any theories over who *could* have killed her, if not Benek or her mother?"

He shook his head. "If I knew of anybody who might make for a viable suspect, I would have brought that person up as an alternative perpetrator at the trial. That was the major stumbling block. If not Benek, then who? Apparently, everybody loved Lada. No one had any motive aside from Benek—the prosecution's theory was that she humiliated him by cheating

9

on him and bearing another man's child, and he mulled over it for a while, snapped, and killed her."

"Of course, there *is* another suspect based on that theory," Nerissa noted. "The real father of the child. Someone who didn't want the world to know about his relationship with her."

Naeem nodded. "Yeah, that possibility crossed my mind. That suggests a married man, maybe a teacher, perhaps a neighbor. Possibly someone else with a reputation to lose, probably an older guy who could go to prison. I don't know, but without any leads, I couldn't just suggest some nameless sperm donor. If only I'd known who it was, that could've been a game-changer. As it was, the jury only had one suspect put before them—Benek. And they thought he had a history of violence."

"Do you believe that?" I asked.

"Benek swore up and down that he'd never struck or choked Lada, and I believed him. But Maia—that's the girl who swore she saw him the day before the murder, choking Lada in the parking lot of the custard stand that was a popular hangout spot for the high school crowd—she was very convincing. I don't want to call her a liar. I hate to think that a young woman would make something like that up, but if Benek didn't...I can only assume that there was some kind of mistaken identity situation going on here. Maybe it was someone who looked a lot like Benek."

"Do you know of anybody who resembled him?" I asked.

"No. I did have the bright idea that maybe Maia saw him from behind, and misread the number on his letterman jacket or something. He was number eighteen, and I wondered if it was really sixteen or nineteen or something like that, but...I checked the rosters at the high school, and the guys with those numbers all have much different hair from Benek, and are different ethnicities, so it's unlikely that any of them could have been mistaken."

"What supposedly happened with the assault?" Nerissa asked.

"All right. The Shining Star Custard Stand is two and a half blocks down the street from the high school. It's next to a little park that's about a quarter of a city block—just a bunch of benches and picnic tables and a few clusters of trees. Maia says she was just leaving the custard stand restroom when she heard a scream coming from the park. She ran over there, not bothering to think about her own safety, and when she got there, she saw Benek and Lada behind a trio of very large trees. Benek had his hands around her throat, and Lada kneed him in the groin and ran away. Maia caught up with her and asked her if she should call the police, but Lada insisted it was nothing and that she should drop it. And then Benek grabbed his bike and rode away."

We mulled over this for a moment. "So, we have one witness who saw him attack the victim the afternoon before the murder, and two witnesses who say he was there the night of the murder. What was the other evidence against him?" I asked.

"His fingerprints were all over the scene of the crime, but he visited the Casagrande home all the time, so that could all be explained away. The bite mark evidence couldn't be."

"Can you describe that, please?"

"There were teeth marks on her left shoulder. The bite mark analyst at the trial said they were a match for Benek's teeth. He said that Benek must have bitten her as she struggled with her."

"Wait a minute." Nerissa hurried out of the room and returned a moment later with Midge. "Mom, weren't you telling us about the unreliability of bite mark evidence on our double date a few months ago?" Midge specializes in legal medicine, and she runs a consultation business. She's our go-to resource for anything connected to forensic science.

Midge pushed her glasses back and pursed her lips. "It's garbage and should never be allowed inside a courtroom."

"You're sure?"

"Back in the 1990s, bite mark evidence was being touted as the greatest innovation in forensic science since fingerprints."

"What about DNA?" I asked.

"Try to nitpick less, Funderburke. Careers were made with individuals rebranding themselves as "forensic dentists," testifying that they could swear beyond the slightest doubt that the defendant's teeth marks were on a victim's skin. But their conclusions weren't based on rigorous testing. There's no proof that each person's teeth are unique and distinctive, like fingerprints. Bites don't leave consistent imprints, skin is a malleable object that can distort imprints, and even a brief amount of time can heal and distort wounds. Dozens of innocent people have been shoved into jail because misguided hacks got up on the stand and swore that the defendant's mouths caused scars and wounds." Midge turned to Naeem. "Was part of the evidence presented against your client bite marks?"

"Yes."

"Who testified against him?"

"Dr. Albion Suco."

Midge made the same face the younger set of triplets did when they tried pureed broccoli for the first time. "I know him."

"You don't respect his work?"

"I've consulted on two cases in the past three years where Suco has testified on bite marks. In one case, the marks were caused by severe scabies, not a human mouth. The only reason that man should be in a courtroom is if he were a defendant. I know of at least one more person who went to jail based on his testimony where exonerating DNA evidence was uncovered five years after the conviction, but the appeal is still crawling its way through the system, so an innocent man is still in prison, and the authorities don't want to prosecute the real murderer until the first guy has been officially cleared, so Suco is a moron and a monster, and I said so in court in a different case, though not using those words."

"What happened?"

"My innocent client got acquitted, and Suco threatened to sue me. His lawyer sent me a letter demanding a public apology and a hundred grand or he'd take me to court, and I compiled a dossier of Suco's misguided pronouncements and a stack of letters from actual scientists calling him a quack in legally acceptable language, sent them to the lawyer, and I never heard another word back."

For the first time, I saw something resembling hope in Naeem's eyes. "Can I get a copy of that dossier?"

"Yes, if you send me copies of the medical reports as well."

"I'll email you them as soon as I get home."

"And I can send you a copy of my files now."

Naeem hesitated. "I don't think I can pay you your standard rates."

"Funderburke and Nerissa get the one hundred percent family discount. Which, quite frankly, they use pretty often, but it's all in the interests of justice."

Midge left to unearth her anti-Suco file on her computer, and Naeem leaned back in the chair. "If only I'd known about you people a few months ago."

"Better late than never," Nerissa shrugged.

"Is there any other evidence we should know about?" I asked.

"Not really, and that's something that I find particularly frustrating. The evidence against him was circumstantial and scanty. There were the witness statements putting him at the scene of the crime on the night of the murder, contradicting his statements and his brother's corroboration. The fingerprints at the scene, as I said, were easily explained away. It was the two witnesses who really won over the jury. Maia Landeen convinced them that he was violent, and Albion Suco was one of the most confident men I've ever seen on the stand. So the jury swallowed the bite mark evidence and the testimony of his history of abuse."

"How long did they deliberate?" I asked.

"Over a week, actually. When I polled the jury, I could tell there was a pretty wide spectrum of thoughts on the verdict. Half of them seemed pretty confident, a few seemed mildly sure, and I'd say three were very reluctant to vote "guilty," but I think they felt pressured by the others and went against their consciences. Don't quote me on that." He glanced at Nerissa's desk clock. "I'm going to need to get back soon. I have court in the morning, and I need to go over my notes. Thank you for the dinner. This was the first home-cooked meal I've had in months. Normally, I just pick up something from the Milwaukee Public Market on my way home."

We shook hands with him. "Can you send me all the information you have when you send the autopsy report and bite mark evidence to Midge, please?"

"Of course." Naeem said his goodbyes and thanks to the rest of the family before leaving.

As she locked the door behind him, Nerissa asked, "What do you think?"

I folded my arms. "Your mom will take care of the bite mark evidence, and in an ideal world, that'd be enough to get the conviction tossed, but there's no guarantee the courts will be willing to reject bite mark pseudoscience. That means I need to do more digging. I believe Volker, which means that the witnesses who claimed he was there that night would have to be lying or mistaken, and since I can't think of a reason for them lying, I need to find out how they could have either misidentified the person they saw that night or gotten mixed up about the day. If the testimony about Benek choking Lada was true, that proves he was an abuser, though that's not direct evidence of murder. I need to check that as well. I should also hunt around to see if I can find any procedural errors that might cause a reversal."

Nodding, Nerissa said, "I'd like to talk to some of Lada's female friends. They'd be more willing to talk to me than you, especially if Lada confided to them about any domestic violence she may have suffered."

"And now there's just eight full days before Naeem has to present his case for a new trial.... That's not much time, especially considering all of the regular work we both have to do...." If I could devote my total attention to Benek's case, nine days would be ample. But, given the fact that I had eighteen open cases to look into involving other students, three background checks on prospective employees to complete, and classes to substitute teach, I was worried that I wouldn't have time to dig up much helpful information for Benek's case.

The next day was Thursday. After another chat with Volker first thing that morning, I received the contact information for Benek's best friend, Alfie. He was the only one of Benek's close pals who wasn't in Illinois for the rest of that week for a baseball tournament. As there wasn't much time before the appeal, I figured I should conduct as many interviews as possible. Once the school authorities cleared me, I was able to speak with Alfie during his lunch, which consisted of a soggy grilled cheese sandwich made with a single slice of processed American and pasty white factory-baked bread and a bowlful of canned pears in syrup that appeared to made of sugar and

14

just barely enough water to create a liquid. It didn't come close to the meals served at Cuthbertson, but I didn't voice this comparison aloud.

I felt sorry for Alfie the moment I first saw him. He had one of the worst cases of adolescent acne vulgaris I'd ever seen, and from the size of the pustules and the redness of the blotches covering most of his face, I knew at once he'd had to put up with more than his share of cruel taunts. He was about five foot eight, but looked a bit taller due to his extreme skinniness. His hair was cropped close, and even though he was barely eighteen, I could see his scalp coverage was already starting to recede at the temples and the crown. When he smiled at our first meeting, his braces twinkled in the fluorescent cafeteria light.

"It's so great that you're doing this," he told me as he poked his pears with a plastic fork. "I just know you're going to get Benek out of prison."

"So you're sure he's innocent?"

"Absolutely. No way he did it. He loved Lada, even if she did cheat on him."

"Do you have any idea who the father of her child might have been?"

Alfie choked down a bite of his sandwich. "I don't want to speak ill of the dead."

"Do you want Benek cleared or not?"

"You're right. His freedom's worth more than Lada's reputation."

"So, do you have a name?"

"A lot of them, actually. Lada was a flirt. She really liked athletic guys, the taller and buffer the better. Look, she was maybe the hottest girl in school, you know? Just smoking gorgeous. Amazing face, mind-blowing body, at least until she got knocked up. And she wanted her boyfriends to be at her level. There are a bunch of good-looking guys who play sports."

"Which ones?"

He shrugged. "She dated Lucien Claverhouse right before Benek. And Dalton Blencowe before him. Now, I don't know for sure, but according to the rumors…." A few seconds of hesitation, and he continued. "She cheated on all her boyfriends. I wouldn't call her a…I forget the word. It's not nincompoop…"

15

"Nymphomaniac?"

"That's it. I wouldn't say she was a sex addict or anything like that, but the girl had no self-control when it came to guys."

"Did you ever talk to Benek about this?"

"I thought about it, but one of our mutual friends brought it up one time, and Benek started screaming at him. He called the other guy a liar. Benek would never allow anybody to say one word against her, so I figured I'd just keep my mouth shut unless I could present him with rock-solid proof. I know she was seeing someone else on the down-low. I just don't know for sure who. You know the high school rumor mill. So many names get floated around..."

"I understand. It can be nearly impossible to sort truth from lies. So, no other definite names?"

He looked around, and whispered in my ear. "Her volleyball coach. Coach Shencrowe. And her Spanish teacher. Señor Zhrzan."

"You know this for a fact?"

"No, but I've seen the way they looked at her. It was creepy, especially as they're both in their thirties."

"Do you think that anything that might have happened...do you think that forcible compulsion might have been involved?"

Alfie hesitated and his shoulders raised and fell a couple of times. "I don't know. Everything I've heard is just word of mouth."

"Hmm.... Have you reported this to anybody else?"

"The school doesn't like to hear about things like that. They prefer to believe it doesn't happen. But it does. All the time."

"Do you have any specific names? Any leads for any proof that could be used to start an investigation?

"What? No! Do you really think that anybody would care about that? Trust me, at this school, nobody gives a damn about this sort of thing."

"You might be surprised." I pulled out my phone, checked my contacts list, and scribbled a couple of names and numbers onto my notepad. "These are police officers I trust and respect and a very principled private investigation firm. If you ever come across anything solid, or find anybody who is willing to report improper behavior, then please, call at least one of these numbers yourself, or get the victim to call a number. Or you can always call or email me." I scrawled my own contact information at the bottom of the paper, tore off the page, and handed it to him.

He stared at it for a moment. "I can't read cursive."

I forced myself to say nothing as I rewrote the names in all caps, and returned the paper to him.

Alfie nodded absently. "Are you all right?" I asked.

"Yeah. I just got some bad news about my grandmother. She's got a heart problem, and she's not going to last much longer."

"I'm so sorry."

"That's all right. She's ninety. She's had a good run." Pocketing my notes, Alfie nodded, wolfed down the remains of his meal in two massive bites, wiped his mouth on the back of his hand, and rose. "I have to get back to class."

"Of course. Thank you for your time."

"Just promise me something." It looked like little tears were forming in the corners of Alfie's eyes. "Please, do whatever you possibly can to clear Benek's name and get him out of prison. I know he's innocent. Will you do whatever you can?"

"I'm going to try to figure out the truth of this matter." I was purposely non-committal because, at that moment, I still wasn't sure what to think about Benek. I thought that Volker's alibi was genuine, but I also thought it was very possible that Benek had been abusive toward Lada, so I wasn't fully aboard the Benek train yet.

I thanked him for his time, and I wandered through the school's halls, which were completely decorated in gray and tan, with windows parceled out as if glass was tightly rationed, and I thought to myself that attending this high school was pretty good preparation for prison. After stopping by the administrative offices to thank them for letting me speak to Alfie during school hours, I stepped out into the parking lot to find a young woman leaning against the wall, arms folded and looking straight at me. She was about five foot one and very thin, with dark brown hair just skimming her shoulders and clad in double denim.

She stuck her hands in her pockets and walked up to me. "You're that detective, Funderburke." It wasn't a question.

"Yes. Who are you?"

"Bex Juaquin. Lada was one of my best friends."

"I see." From the glare she was shooting me, I didn't think saying "I'm sorry for your loss" was going to go over well, so I decided to try a different approach. "I want to find out the truth about her murder, whatever that truth is. Do you think that Benek Berchtwelt killed her?"

The daggers in her eyes blunted a bit. "So you're not trying to get him out of prison?"

"Benek isn't my client." I chose not to inform her that I was looking out for the interests of his little brother. "I'm here for the truth. If I find more proof of Benek's guilt, I'll turn it in to the authorities, and he'll stay in prison. Now I answered your question, would you please be kind enough to answer mine? In your opinion, is Benek guilty?"

"Definitely."

"Please tell me why you're sure of this."

"Did you hear the evidence at the trial? People saw him that night. He bit her. That's pretty solid proof."

Now was not the time to bring up Midge's thoughts on bite mark evidence. "How long did you know Lada?"

Her face softened. "We've known each other since we were in daycare together. She's been my rock my whole life. When my parents split up, she helped me through everything. When my grandmother died, I stayed at her house for a week, and she never got upset with me for waking her up four times a night with my crying. When my loser boyfriend cheated on me and gave me the clap, she went with me to all my doctor's appointments until I got the all-clear. She was the giver in this friendship. I was the taker. Over seventeen years, I racked up a lot of debts to her I can never pay back. The least I can do is keep her killer rotting behind bars."

"Were you acquainted with Benek?"

"Yeah. He was my friend, too. Was."

18

"Did you have any reason to think that he'd ever be violent towards her?" She started to speak, then stopped and sighed. "No. That's why Maia's statement took me completely by surprise. He worshiped her. She was crazy about him. A lot of the couples here, they know it's just a high school relationship. They know it's not going to last, they figure teen dating is nothing more than practice for real life. Most of the long-term puppy love pairings here, they shoot each other goo-goo eyes and say they're going to be together forever, and everybody else wants to scream, "No. You're not." But if anybody at our school was going to make it for the long run, I would have said it would have been Lada and Benek. Especially after the baby."

"Miss Juaquin, I don't want to cast any aspersions or say anything remotely negative about Lada. I simply need to make sense of everything. You say the two of them were deeply in love. But then how do you explain…"

"The baby not being Benek's? Look, she didn't know it wasn't Benek's. I talked to her when they got the results. She was blindsided. She said it had to be some sort of lab error. And that's what I say happened. The kid is definitely Benek's. I think there must have been some mix-up on the part of the scientists or something."

"They ran two tests."

"Then they made the same mistake twice. She told me that she'd never cheated on Benek, and I believe her. She would have told me right away if she had."

"Did she ever tell you about Benek being physically abusive to her?"

"No. She was always telling me how great he was and telling me that she wished I had as good a relationship." She shrugged. "The boyfriend I mentioned earlier, the cheater? After I kicked his diseased butt to the curb, he made a pass at Lada."

"So you never saw any bruises or scratches or anything like that on Lada?"

"I didn't say that. She was an athlete. We both got tons of little injuries. Nothing serious. But none of them from Benek."

"So when Maia said she saw him choking Lada—"

"That must've been the first time. He just snapped because of the whole paternity thing. He must've gone crazy. Psychotic break, I guess." She looked at her feet and dragged her right toe on the pavement. "I was sick that day, you know? I went home early with a stomach bug. Maybe it was food poisoning. The food here is awful."

"I saw it. I smelled it." Thankfully, I didn't taste it.

"Anyway, I left early the day she died, and I was in bed, half-delirious that night. I got a text from her around five, telling me she thought she knew what happened with the whole paternity test thing, but I was in no condition to respond or call her. The next morning I was a lot better and I texted her back, but it was too late." A tear ran down her face. "I gotta go. Remember, Benek's guilty." She hurried back into the school, and I processed what she told me for a minute before heading back to my car, wrapping my leather coat around me to block the chill of the late April wind.

Unless I'm substitute teaching, I have a lot of flexibility in how I manage my time when I'm investigating. Often, my work consists of background checks on prospective employees, but when a student comes to me with a problem, my plans get a bit more varied and interesting. The Cuthbertson lunch staff knew to set aside a meal for me for whenever I returned. As long as I was on this side of town, I might as well see if I could work in a little more face-to-face interviewing.

My phone rang just as I reached my car. The caller ID informed me that it was Clotilde Casagrande, Lada's mother. "Mrs. Casagrande?"

"Yes, Mr. Funderburke. I'm returning your call."

"Thank you. I—"

"I do not wish to speak to you at the present. I hope that you will understand."

I was disappointed, but I was not about to push a grieving parent. No good could come from trying to force an interview. "Of course. I realize that this is difficult for you in a way I can't possibly begin to comprehend. I just want to thank you for taking the time to return my call. I really do appreciate that level of courtesy, Mrs. Casagrande, and I hope that I have not upset you in any way." I felt like I was laying it on a little thick, but I hoped it might leave the door ajar a little bit in the future.

"Thank you, Mr. Funderburke." There was a two-second pause that felt four times longer, and I was ninety percent certain the next sounds I would hear would be her saying "Goodbye" and then hanging up, but I heard her slight intake of breath, and I knew there was a chance. A moment later, she continued, saying, "The message you left me was very respectful. You explained your intentions well. All this time, I hadn't thought about how this whole ordeal might be affecting little Volker."

I pumped my fist, and immediately was glad that there were so few windows in the school, so no one was likely to have seen me. After a silent *Thank you, Mister God*, I told her, "Yes, he's insisting he was telling the truth, and it's breaking his heart that no one believed him."

"I can imagine. The odd thing is, Mr. Funderburke, I know children, and when I saw Volker on the witness stand, I believed him. Or at least, I was certain he believed what he was saying. But then, how can you explain all of that other evidence?" She sighed. "I don't know. I'm sorry. I can't talk about this anymore. When I'm ready, I'll call you. Goodbye." As she hung up, I knew that I hadn't made an enemy out of the victim's mother. Aside from not wanting to cause her any further distress, I needed to avoid any potential adverse publicity about a big, bad P.I. harassing the mother of a murder victim.

But she had a good point about "all of that other evidence," so I decided to interview the witnesses who had seen Benek the night of the crime. I hadn't been able to reach the Kasprzaks by phone, so I drove to their home in the Polonia area of Milwaukee. It's a long, thin section of the South Side. As the name suggests, it was known for being an enclave for people with Polish heritage, though the last couple of decades, the Hispanic portion of the population has risen substantially, and it's common to see signs in English, Spanish, and to a much lesser extent, Polish. I drove past St. Stanislaus Church, and a couple of minutes later, I was on the Kasprzaks' block.

It was a pleasant neighborhood with a canopy of trees covering the street, but the level of care and maintenance put into the properties varied drastically. Half the houses and lots were kept in excellent condition, a quarter of the homes were a little scruffy and needed a bit of work here and there, and a quarter of the properties looked battered, and clearly no landscaper had visited these latter domiciles in at least a decade. Three of the homes had happy-looking dogs behind the fences, barking at me in the friendliest possible manner. I helped an equally friendly Mexican woman in her mid-sixties lift her pushcart full of groceries out of a pothole, and she thanked me and complimented me on my coat. A dead-eyed teenager with skin the color of milk shuffled down the street and tossed a plastic soda cup onto the lawn of a house where the front window had been replaced with a flimsy-looking piece of plywood. Judging from the litter intermittently scattered along the street, I figured that a lot of passersby treated the ground as their wastebasket, and only the homeowners who cared took the time to pick up the trash.

I parked on the street in front of the Kasprzaks' home. I knew that the Casagrande home was directly opposite theirs. The shades were drawn, and there was no car in the lot, so Mrs. Casagrande was probably away at work, which was fortunate, as I didn't want to sour the amicable note we'd finished our conversation on by having her think I was coming to her house to pester her after she'd specifically requested that I leave her alone until she was ready. The Casagrande home was immaculate, at least on the outside. As for the Kasprzak house, it was just barely on the scruffy side. The house was in pretty good shape aside from a single missing shingle on the roof, and the lawn hadn't received its first mowing of the spring yet, though, as we'd had a couple of inches of snow the second week of April, the plant life hadn't really started to return yet.

I could see a gray-haired man through the window, watching a forty-inch television, so I hadn't made the trip in vain. I climbed the steep, slightly chipped cement staircase up the hill to their front door, and after I pressed the bell, I heard a man's voice shout, "Honey? Can you get that?"

A woman replied, "Isn't your back better yet?"

"No! I can't get up. My legs spasm when I try."

"Fine!" A few moments later, a woman with a mass of white curls on her head appeared in the front door window. "We're not interested in buying anything!"

"I'm not here to—"

"Wait! Haven't I seen you on the news? You're that private detective, aren't you? The one who works for that fancy-schmancy prep school? Culverston?"

"Cuthbertson Hall, yes."

"Wait…didn't that Benek boy have a brother who goes there? Are you here to ask us questions about that?"

"Yes. I don't want to take up—"

"Come in, come in." She pulled open the door and gestured me inside. "We don't get a lot of visitors, especially not handsome young men." It's an odd fact that women my age almost never consider me good-looking, aside from Nerissa. But once they hit sixty-five or so, suddenly, the ladies take a liking to my face. "My, aren't you big and strong," Mrs. Kasprzak murmured, passing a hand back and forth over my back. "I just love your coat. It's so buttery-soft."

"Er…Thank you." I wasn't quite uncomfortable at that point, but another comment or two like that would get me there.

"Come in, come in." Mrs. Kasprzak ushered me into the living room. "Do you mind if I don't offer to take your coat? I quite like seeing you in it."

I supposed this conversation could be going a lot worse. "Not at all."

Mr. Kasprzak glanced up at me for about a quarter-second before returning his attention to ESPN. He didn't look the least bit surprised to see I'd been allowed inside the house, nor did he appear to have any interest in asking me what I was doing. "Hey."

"Hello. Nice to meet you, Mr. Kasprzak."

"Uh-huh." I had no way of knowing if he'd actually heard anything I'd said, but I knew better than to interrupt a man in the middle of his sports programming.

"Can I get you something nice?" Mrs. Kasprzak asked me. "A soda or a piece of cake? It's not homemade, it's frozen, but it's good. Or do you not eat sugar?" She patted my stomach. "You've got abs there, don't you? I can feel them. We've got seltzer water and some orange slices. I keep preparing them for my husband, hoping he'll snack on something other than chips, but her never touches them."

"Umm...the seltzer and orange slices, please."

"Of course. Just a moment." She led me into a corduroy-covered recliner that looked as if it was twice as old as I was, yet it appeared to be immaculately clean and smelled of pine air freshener. Apparently, she thought my knees were in much worse shape than they actually were, because she placed an arm around my shoulders for some unnecessary support while I lowered myself into the chair. The stuffing had been unevenly distributed through decades of use, but it was remarkably comfortable, and the back support was superb. "Don't be shy, pull the lever, put your feet up," Mrs. Kasprzak informed me. I didn't need much convincing on that point.

She was back with my refreshments in less than a minute, and she pulled an ornately carved wooden chair next to me. It didn't look nearly as pleasant a place to sit as my corduroy recliner, but I figured she had her reasons for what she was doing, and I didn't want to waste a question asking her if she'd rather sit somewhere else.

After eating a segment of one of the sweetest oranges I'd even eaten, and wiping my fingers on a paper napkin left over from Christmas, I asked her if she'd mind telling me what she'd seen the night of the murder. I can summarize the content of the ensuing conversation is a twentieth of the time she used. Mr. Kasprzak's brother had recently had a stroke, and they'd agreed to spend a week with him, leaving Friday and returning the following Friday. As they were loading up the car, they'd seen Benek, who came over to visit his girlfriend multiple times a week.

"And you'd actually spoken to him in the past?"

"Yes. One time, he helped us after our keys fell under the car, and once, he helped me move a heavy plant from the front stoop to the back porch." Mrs. Kasprzak sighed. "He was such a strong, fit, young man. So attractive."

"Uh...huh. Did you actually speak to him on the night of the murder?"

"No. I said hello when he arrived just before eight, but it was a blustery evening, so the wind might have carried my words away. Or perhaps his mind was elsewhere, or he had those tiny little headphones in her ears or something like that. I don't know. Anyway, we didn't have any time to talk. We wanted to get there before nine-thirty. That's my brother-in-law's usual bedtime."

"Wasn't that a bit late to start a long drive?"

"Oh, no. I do the driving these days, and I actually prefer the roads at night because there aren't nearly so many other people on the highway."

"I see."

"Actually, I had planned to leave around seven, right after we finished dinner, but I almost forgot. I got my days mixed up. We would've left a day late if I hadn't checked my watch and saw it was Friday."

A little electrical current started twitching in my cut and spread throughout the rest of my body. I didn't want to be overly optimistic, but I was sure that this was a point that needed to be explored further. "This watch...is that the one you're wearing?"

"Oh, no. It was my old watch. I inherited it from my mother a decade ago; it wasn't very comfortable. It was too heavy on my wrist, and the edges of the clasp kept nicking my skin. I used my old digital watch for a while, but the last couple of years, I've been wearing a newer, better watch that I bought myself for our fiftieth wedding anniversary after my husband forgot all about it." She sighed. "Such a lovely watch. It was twenty-two karat gold, you know, and had this very attractive pattern of flowers on the band. If only I'd remembered to put it back on after doing the lunch dishes."

"Why? What happened to it?"

"Well, I left it on the side of the sink while I was scrubbing the frying pan I used to make my husband's Monte Cristo sandwich, and then I had to run some errands, and my husband had to come with me, because I can't lift some of the heavier items, like the twenty-four packs of his favorite soda, which I buy because they're quite a bit cheaper per can than the six and twelve-packs. So we were out of the house for about two and a half hours, and when we got back around five, we noticed—or rather, *I* noticed, my husband wouldn't notice if the house was on fire, that the rear door was unlocked. And then I looked around and saw that a number of items were missing. My watch. All of the good sterling silverware. The smaller TV in the kitchen. An antique clock, a couple of silver candlesticks. I realized that we'd been robbed by the burglar who'd been terrorizing our neighborhood for the past couple of months."

"This is the first I've heard about this burglar. Did the police ever catch him?"

"No, unfortunately not. From late August to mid-October, about ten percent of the houses in this area were broken into at one point or another. Whoever did it was very skilled, and knew how to pick the lock to a door without causing any damage, or at least found a house where somebody didn't secure the place properly. Actually, we don't know for sure it was just one person, but whoever it was came at all times of the day. One home down the street, the man living there left for work first thing in the morning, and when he came back later to retrieve the laptop he'd forgotten, he found that the laptop and quite a few other valuables around the house were gone. Other robberies happened during the afternoon or evening, but always when no one was home. You're making a very interesting face, young man. Do you think you know who this mysterious burglar is?"

"No, I'm sorry, but I definitely don't. But I am just getting the first whiff of an alternative theory of the crime. Do you know more or less when the burglaries stopped?"

"Middle of October, as I said."

"Around the time of the murder?"

"Thereabouts, I'd say. Wait, you don't think...that *Lada* was the burglar? No, you're wrong there. She would never have done such a thing, especially not to us. She was like a granddaughter to us. Whenever I couldn't read the tiny print on my medicine instructions or something like that, she'd hop across the street and tell me what it said."

I shook my head. "No, that's not what I was thinking at all. I was wondering if the burglar might have been responsible for the murder."

"Oh..." Mrs. Kasprzak's forehead creased a couple of times. "*Oh!* But Benek was there the night of the murder. You can't deny that."

"Well, that's why I need to ask you some more questions, please." I looked down at her wrist. "You're wearing a digital watch now."

"Yes, I told you, my mother's watch was just too heavy. After a couple of days of feeling that my hand was going to break off, I went down to Target and bought myself a seventeen-dollar digital one. It's not nearly as pretty, but it tells me what I need to know."

"Do you happen to have your mother's watch handy?"

"Why, yes. It's in a lockbox I bought after the robbery. Would you like to see it?"

"Please. I'd be very grateful."

Three minutes later, she placed her mother's silver wristwatch in my hand. "It's very nice, isn't it?"

I nodded. "Yes, it is." It was a fairly large piece, nearly the same size as my grandfather's old watch on my wrist. The hands were larger than average, which made for easier reading, but it was the date dials that caught my attention. "Mrs. Kasprzak, are you aware that this watch is a day ahead?"

"What? How did that happen? Is it running fast?"

"The actual time is correct–you're just a minute behind me, and I checked my watch time against my cell phone time this morning. When was the last time you used this watch before October?"

"Well…I don't know. It may have been a while…"

"Was it before the most recent Leap Year?"

"I suppose it could have. Why do you ask?"

"The date dials on watches like this don't have a setting for leap years. That means that every four years, when it's February 29th, the watch doesn't state that's the day—it just assumes it's a twenty-eight-day February, and it reads March 1st. And the mechanism on a watch like this can run for a long time before stopping. Years, maybe."

Mrs. Kasprzak thought about this for a minute, and her face turned the same color as her hair. "But that means, when I saw Benek…"

"It was really Thursday evening. The night *before* the murder, when Benek admitted being there. Although that raises a question. Why didn't you know it was Thursday? Wasn't there a newspaper or a television program or something to help you know what day it is?"

"We canceled the newspaper four years ago when we couldn't read the tiny print anymore. We're retired, and we don't do anything regularly during the week. I don't watch TV at all. I read and work on jigsaw puzzles. Large piece puzzles. All my husband watches is sports, mostly football, and whenever it's not Sunday, the days just run together on me. That night, I was thinking about how we'd have to drive to Lake Geneva the next evening—I'd already packed that afternoon to save time—and I looked down at my watch and saw it was Friday, and I thought I was having the worst senior moment yet—I'd actually missed a whole day! But this means..."

I pulled out my phone. "Mrs. Kasprzak, may I start recording this, please? I'm going to need a statement from both of you."

"Yes, of course. May I ask you one question first, please?"

"Of course, Mrs. Kasprzak. What do you want to know?"

"If you don't mind my asking, what is your ethnicity, dear? You have that exotic, ambiguous look, and it's got me wondering."

After I navigated through that personal and, frankly, rather sensitive question, given the fact that I don't know my father's identity, I got the statements I needed, though I needed to wait for three commercial breaks to get Mr. Kasprzak to make his statement, which basically boiled down to that now he was retired, the only day of the week that mattered to him was Packer Sunday, unless of course they played on Monday Night Football. As for everything else in his life, he did what his wife told him when she told him. He found it made his existence significantly easier.

By the time I was finished with them, it was a quarter to three, and my stomach was growling so loudly I thought a feral dog had climbed into my car. I considered stopping somewhere, but I remembered that it was baked chicken tenders with macaroni and cheese day at Cuthbertson, so the seltzer and orange segments held me over for the forty-minute drive. The lunch staff had left for the day, but I had a master key, and in the staff refrigerator in the corner, I found a covered plate with "FUNDERBURKE" written on a Post-It upon it, piled high with food, including far more peas than I wanted. A couple of minutes in the microwave, and I tucked in and replenished my strength, finishing everything, including the peas. After my after-school meeting with the rest of the security staff, I changed and worked out in the Cuthbertson weight room. A little after five-fifteen, while I was in the middle of my kettlebell swings, Nerissa came in, wearing her black and magenta tracksuit.

"Hey," I greeted her. "How was soccer practice?"

"It's weird. Some of those girls act like they think the ball's a land mine. They kick it real lightly and run away from it, instead of punting it or keeping up with it. I don't know how I'm going to break them of that habit. Did you find out anything useful?"

"I did." I started telling Nerissa about what I'd learned over the course of the afternoon, and as she listened, she picked up a kettlebell twenty-five pounds lighter than mine and started doing swings along with me. We switched to other exercises midway through my report, but the whole summary took only ten minutes.

"Good work today, Funderburke." Nerissa placed her kettlebell back on the shelves and started stretching her arms. "In related news, I scheduled video chats with five more of Lada's female friends and a few of her teachers tonight and tomorrow. I don't know if I'll unearth anything useful, but we'll see. By the way, I asked Naeem to come over to the house for dinner Wednesday, a week from yesterday."

"That's two days before the hearing. Couldn't he come Thursday, so I have another day to investigate?"

"I figured that he'd need a little extra time to go over any new facts we find. I did talk to two of Lada's friends during my free period this afternoon. They didn't have anything we could bring into court, but both of them claimed that they never knew Benek to be violent. They did add that they had no idea how finding out he wasn't the baby's father would affect him. So you found out more useful information than I did today."

"We're collaborating, not competing."

"It's sweet that you think that way." Nerissa walked over to the bubbler and took a long drink. Dabbing her lips with a tissue, she said, "I've got to get home. See you at dinner."

Later that night, as I drew up my plans for the next few days, I thought to myself that there was another recurring message in Ed McBain's 87th Precinct novels that did not match with my personal experience. In most of his books, at some point, one of the police detectives, usually his most prominent character, Steve Carella, self-assuredly declares, "There are no mysteries, only crimes, and the people who commit them." Whenever I read that line, or a reasonably close variant of it, I invariably think to myself, "What the heck does that even mean?" I usually have to stop reading the novel and play a conversation in my head.

> ME. What do you mean, you hate mysteries? You've built your whole career around solving mysteries.
>
> 87th PRECINCT COP. No, we don't solve mysteries. We investigate crimes. When we figure out how it happened, we generally know who committed it.
>
> ME. So when you go to work, there's a crime, like a murder, a theft, something like that?
>
> 87th PRECINCT COP. Yes.
>
> ME. And you don't know who committed it?
>
> 87th PRECINCT COP. Right.
>
> ME. And your goal is to find out the facts by asking questions, analyzing evidence, and so forth?
>
> 87th PRECINCT COP. Yes.
>
> ME. Essentially, you're trying to find out something you don't know about who committed a crime?
>
> 87th PRECINCT COP. Yes.
>
> ME. THAT'S A MYSTERY! (*Exasperated sigh.*) You're turning me into Mandy Patinkin here. When you say "mystery," I think, "You keep using that word. I do not think it means what you think it means."

My best guess is that when McBain started his research on police procedure, some detective he was talking to told him that line, and McBain liked it so much he repeated it *ad nauseum* in his works and was so preoccupied jotting his notes down that he forgot to ask just what in the name of Ned the officer meant by it. I'm sure that there's some level of nuance behind that line that McBain never got around to explaining in sixty years of writing, but in my world as a private detective, my work is full of mysteries. I'm surrounded by contradictory information and points that don't make sense, and I have to find out the truth. To me, my job, heck, all of *life*, is practically nothing *but* mysteries. If you asked me to define mysteries, I would say that they were "unanswered questions or situations that you can't explain, but really want to understand. Maybe the police officers in the 87th Precinct have a radically different definition. I don't know, they've never bothered to define their terms. But whenever I read Steve Carella grousing about how much he hates mysteries and how they don't exist in police work, I keep thinking it's a lot like saying, "Carella hated sandwiches. In real lunches, Carella knew that there were no sandwiches, just meat and cheese stuck between two slices of bread, and the people who ate them." And don't get me started on the not-quite-as-often-repeated-but-still-said-all-the-time line in McBain novels about how, in the light of modern psychological analysis, the officers knew that there "were no villains in the world, only disturbed people." To be fair, McBain often follows that up with a comment that shows how certain characters find the "no villains" worldview ridiculous, but frankly, personal experience and reading history have taught me that way too many people make a conscious choice to do evil, and you can't blame it all on mental illness. Villains are real.

I'm rambling. I do that sometimes, especially when I have an ideological difference of opinion with somebody. There are reasons why I don't get invited to many parties. But I do want to stress that I really enjoy McBain's novels. I've read them all at least three times. But sometimes, I get hung up on little points that don't make sense to me, just like in the *mysteries* I investigate *and frequently solve*.

For example, I realized that one of the main reasons that Benek was convicted is because the witness, Maia Landeen, claimed that she'd seen him choking Lada. As I saw it, there were four possible explanations for her testimony.

1. It was completely true, and Benek had the disgusting habit of physically abusing his girlfriend.

2. It was true, but the strangling incident Maia witnessed was the first time Benek had become physically violent towards Lada.

3. It was false, and she told a lie for unknown reasons.

4. It was false, and she was somehow horribly mistaken.

If #1 was the case, then I thought that Benek was right where he belonged in prison, and even if he hadn't killed Lada, I wasn't in any hurry to get him out, unless doing so would put the real killer, who, for all I knew was poised to murder someone else, in the penitentiary sooner. But as Nerissa told me later that night, none of Lada's friends had ever seen any signs of abuse, nor had Lada confided in any of them about being attacked in any manner. Plus, Volker was adamant that his brother would never have raised a hand against his girlfriend, though his bias was obvious.

"There's something else in the police report that makes me wonder," Nerissa told me as we were washing that night's dishes.

"What's that?"

"They catalogued a lot of the items in Lada's room. That includes the makeup. There were at least sixty items on the list. Mascara, eyebrow pencils, twenty-four bottles of eighteen shades of nail polish, twenty-five tubes of ten shades of lipstick…. Hey!" She snapped her fingers twice in front of my face. "Funderburke, your eyes are glazing again. You're making the 'I'm so bored I think I'm gonna die look' you always make when I start talking about how frustrated I am that my foot problems mean that I can't wear the heels that caught my eye."

"I don't—"

"It's okay, I get it. You're a guy, and makeup, hair, and wardrobe are of zero interest to you. I understand. To be fair, I'm not always giving you one hundred percent of my attention when you start giving me your theories on the best way to win game shows, like your thoughts on winning Master Key on *The Price is Right* by sniffing the keys, because the keys that open the locks for prizes work through magnets, and because the tip of the human nose is sensitive to magnetism, theoretically the key that provokes the strongest tingling sensation from your nose is the one that will win you all three prizes."

"So you *were* paying attention when I told you that tonight."

"Yes. I don't particularly *care*, but I do listen. So because this is important to the case, would you please listen to me and try not to think about the best ways to improve your odds of snagging a Daily Double on *Jeopardy!*? Please?"

"I will. Go on, if you are so inclined."

"Thanks. So, I also noticed that Lada had two different prescriptions for anti-acne medication, and all of her facial cleansers were for sensitive skin. And I also checked the social media accounts of her and her friends, and noticed over the past two years, even when she was pregnant, her outfits tended to be on the skimpy side." Nerissa grimaced. She hates revealing clothing. Most of her garments may have started out in a tannery, but she keeps it modest, elegant, and classy. "Now, when I looked at her makeup list, I realized right away what *wasn't* there. No foundation. No concealer. No blush. Not one item of any of those products. I bet she broke out in pimples whenever she dusted makeup on her cheeks. Do you see where I'm going here?"

I didn't. I held up a finger to tell her to let me think, and by the time I'd scraped the last of the baked-on manicotti from the pan, I knew what Nerissa was trying to tell me. "She didn't have any makeup that could cover bruises or other wounds."

"Exactly! And believe me, I know from helping my birth mother cover up her black eyes just what products you need to disguise a nasty shiner. Lada didn't have the makeup table of a regularly abused woman trying to hide evidence of her violent mistreatment from the world, and she didn't wear the outfits to cover up bruises on her arms or legs, either."

I thought about it for another minute and shook my head. "It's indicative that the first possibility isn't true, but that doesn't disprove the second possibility, as he could've snapped due to the whole paternity situation or something like that."

Nerissa nodded. "Also, this is just a random theory with no evidence, but Benek's an athlete. What if he took some performance-enhancing drugs that gave him an uncharacteristic burst of temper?"

"Roid rage? I don't know. I'll ask Volker, but the police searched the Berchtwelt house, as well as both of Biden's lockers at school, and there isn't any mention of steroids in their reports."

"Well, that was just an idea that popped into my head."

"And it wasn't a bad one. But there's also the third and fourth possibilities to discuss."

Nerissa placed the last glass into the dishwasher, added the detergent, and started the wash cycle. "I don't like the thought of a young woman making up something like that, but all of the girls I talked to tonight said that they didn't believe it, that such violence was totally out of character for Benek. But only two of them came straight out and called Maia a liar."

"And Maia hasn't responded to you yet?"

"Her father called me back and told me never to try to speak to her again. He said she already had to change schools due to the backlash from her testimony, and he won't have me traumatizing her further. I can see his point, but it doesn't help the investigation any."

"No, it doesn't." I slid the cleaned pan onto the drying rack. "And as for the fourth possibility, well, anybody can make an honest mistake."

The following morning was Friday. Six days to go before Naeem got my report. I decided to do a bit of armchair investigating. I shut the door to my office and turned on my little television to *The Price is Right*. I'd watched the show sporadically when I was home sick growing up, but it wasn't until I had a few months of unemployment after getting fired from what used to be one of Milwaukee's most prestigious law firms that I got addicted. Long story short, as a freshly minted lawyer with too many principles to stay in the profession, I discovered the corruption going on in the family law division, and wound up getting blacklisted after my whistleblowing drove the firm into bankruptcy. During the next few months, I scratched out a living as a barista until a customer recruited me to join his private detection firm, and since my shift didn't start until noon, I never missed an episode of *The Price is Right*, and I don't intend to break the habit anytime soon, although more often than not, I have to record it and watch it in the evenings, but being occasionally able to indulge in one of my beloved game shows at work is one of the many perks of my job.

A little time with one of the more popular search engines, and I found the custard stand and the park where the altercation between Benek and Lada allegedly happened. The park was in the middle of a commercial district, and I estimated that there was a one in a thousand chance that one of the shops overlooking the park had a security camera pointed towards the park, and if, by some miracle, such a video camera existed, there was an approximately one in ten million chance that any recording from six months ago still existed. I called the stores with a view of the park in order, west to east, and the uniform store, stationery shop, and bakery told me that they didn't have any video footage of the park. I thought the jewelry store was my best shot, but they informed me that they didn't save any recordings older than two weeks. The spice shop didn't answer my call, but when I started talking to the proprietor of a gaming store, I turned my eyes heavenward, realizing that the age of miracles had not yet passed.

"I wondered if somebody like you'd call me," the owner, Mats, told me. "I thought it was funny that I wasn't called to the trial to authenticate the video."

"Excuse me, please. What video are you referring to here?"

"The video of the defendant and the victim. Didn't you get it?"

"No. At least, there's no record of it in Naeem Popoola's notes. Just what kind of video are you referring to here?"

Mats shook my eardrums with a particularly guttural cough and then commenced his explanation. "Okay, about two years ago, I installed a video security system because kids were vandalizing the shop. Spray painting "NERDS" on the plate glass window, drawing anatomical pictures on the door with markers, that sort of thing. So when the police suggested I install the system to catch them in the act, I bought this top-of-the-line system with enough memory in the hard drive for at least six months of storage. Pretty nice, huh?"

"Definitely. Does your camera have a view of the park across the street?"

"A great one, yeah. Anyway, the vandalism has gone down a lot since the last kids to scrawl obscenities on my wall were caught and punished, so I haven't had to check out the security footage that often. But during the trial—I'm a huge news junkie, by the way, I always read the paper cover to cover and watch four different channels of local coverage over the course of the day—I saw that girl, Maia something, talking about witnessing an altercation back in October, and I thought, "Whoa, that probably happened right outside my store. So I figured out which afternoon it had to be, started looking through the footage, and after a couple of minutes, I found it."

"The altercation between Benek Berchtwelt and Lada Casagrande?"

"Well...I wouldn't call it an altercation. You'd probably want to see it for yourself."

"I'll be at your store in forty minutes." Secure in the knowledge that *The Price of Right* was recording, I slipped into my walking coat, left a note on my door saying I'd be back in the afternoon, and tried my darnedest to keep under the speed limit on my way across town.

When I arrived at the shop, I was stunned. It didn't look like much from the outside, just another little cube in an evenly divided series of stores, all part of a Cream City brick box. For any non-Milwaukeeans, the nickname comes from the light tan color of the bricks used to build a lot of buildings around here. I'm not in the habit of being blown away by interior decorating, but as soon as I stepped through the door, I was impressed. The walls were painted with various landscapes from classic fantasy series, with suits of armor flanking the doors, and swords and battle-axes spaced out on the wooden panels. The shelves were filled with role-playing tabletop games that I personally am not particularly interested in, but I certainly don't look down on anybody who does choose to engage in such forms of entertainment.

"Funderburke, right? I saw your picture in the paper a few months ago."

I didn't notice Mats at first. He was seated behind a glass case, but an enormous fiberglass dragon behind him caught my eye first, leaving this nondescript yet friendly-looking man well-camouflaged. After the preliminary greetings and handshake, he pulled a DVD out of a drawer and pushed it towards me. "That's your copy. The relevant portion is at the seven-hour and twelve-minute mark. Here it is on my hard drive. I've got it cued up for you."

He tapped his laptop keys and spun the computer around. I immediately recognized Benek and Lada, and after watching it for two minutes, I asked Mats to rewind it so I could watch it again. Two minutes later, I asked to see it one more time. Two minutes after that, I was shaking Mats' hand with both of mine, informing him that he had just made a friend for life, and if he ever needed the services of a private detective, I would be more than happy to provide my help gratis.

I realize that I'm withholding information here, but to streamline and clarify the narrative, I'm going to wait just a little bit for the big reveal, not for some cheap dramatic twist, but to keep from repeating myself and to present my findings in a clearer way.

Feeling obligated to buy something, I scanned the discount shelf and saw a replica of the Isle of Lewis chessman, marked seventy-five percent off because the chessboard had cracked down the center. I actually thought it looked cooler that way, so I eschewed the credit card Cuthbertson provides me with for expenses, and bought it with my own money. I took a couple of large print crossword puzzle books as well, as my former third-grade teacher and current landlady, Mrs. Zwidecker, is an avid fan of them. At the moment, I wasn't aware of anybody in my social circle who was into role-playing tabletop games, but as soon as I met someone who was enthusiastic about them, I vowed that I would steer them towards Mat's shop, because I believe in supporting small local businesses, and by golly, after viewing that security footage, I couldn't think of a Milwaukee merchant who deserved patronage more.

When I got back to Cuthbertson, Nerissa was in the middle of that day's pre-lunch free period. I rushed to her office to tell her about my latest discovery, but she beat me to the punch. As I stepped through the door, she leapt out of her chair, skipped up to me, kicked the door shut, and gave me a kiss that nearly knocked me off my feet.

"You'll never believe the conversation I just had with one of Lada's friends," she told me.

Deciding my news could wait, I asked for details.

"I started asking her friends for the names of other friends who might be willing to talk to me, and they referred me to this one girl, Consuela, who was a year ahead of Lada and is attending Alverno College now. She still lives with her parents, just three blocks north of Lada's house, so they still hung out all the time before she was killed. The last time Lada came to visit was two days before she was killed. They had lunch before Consuela left for her afternoon classes. By the way, Consuela's convinced that Benek's guilty. She never knew him to be violent, but she's sure based on her gut feeling. But that's not the important point. You see, Consuela has a cat. A Siamese. And when Lada came to visit, it was in heat and acting crazy. The cat had climbed up on the china cupboard, and without warning, while the two girls were talking...." Nerissa paused for dramatic effect, for about three seconds too long. "The cat *jumped down from the cupboard, landed in Lada's arms, and bit her on the shoulder through her sweater!*" Nerissa jumped up and down so much the collar of her red leather blazer popped up, making her hair shake. "Consuela didn't follow the news of the trial closely because she found it too upsetting, but that's how Lada got the bite! Mom was right! The forensic dentist couldn't tell the difference between Benek's teeth marks and a cat's!"

I didn't think Nerissa could become any more excited without physically exploding. Then I showed her the surveillance footage, and was proven wrong.

The next day was Saturday. That afternoon, aside from my usual weekend activities of spending time with Nerissa, swimming, Mass, and catching up on my reading and recorded episodes of *Jeopardy!* and *Wheel of Fortune*, I ran a few background checks on everybody connected with the trial. The judge, the prosecutor, the witnesses, and the jurors. There's always a chance that a little digging will turn up something that could be grounds for a retrial, like some sort of familial or business relationship between two parties. I was so busy with my other work, I didn't have much time for too much more investigating Benek's case Sunday through Tuesday.

By Wednesday, I had compiled a moderately extensive dossier of the various people involved in the trial, and I spent the afternoon preparing for Naeem to join us for dinner. After we'd finished our salmon and twice-baked sweet potatoes, Nerissa, Midge, and I returned to Nerissa's study in order to present our case for Benek's appeal.

"Can we start with the bite mark evidence?" Naeem asked. "I think that's our strongest grounds, and since I'm running on four hours of sleep, I need to get home sooner rather than later to hit the sack."

Midge provided a set of bullet points explaining how new research had determined that bite mark evidence was no longer considered reliable, and handed Naeem a short stack of letters from colleagues of hers who had reviewed the bite on Lada's body, and found that there was impossible to defend the claim that it was inflicted by Benek.

"Unfortunately," Midge concluded, "judges are notoriously impossible to predict when it comes to controversies amongst forensic experts. When two scientists disagree on a matter that will affect an appeal, sometimes they'll just side with whichever person they like more, rather than thoroughly analyzing the varying arguments for the evidence's validity. Sometimes, a little bit of controversy amongst scientists is enough to make the judges decide not to decide. This one time a few years ago, a judge out east rejected my conclusions that a certain knife couldn't possibly have caused the fatal wounds, because the other side's so-called expert kept batting her eyelashes at him. It was disgusting, but the judge was smitten. And an innocent man was stuck in prison for another two years until the real killer struck again, caught using the same weapon that still had traces of the original victim's blood on it. And that hack with the eyelashes got tenure at an Ivy League university." Midge made no attempt to hide the disgust in her voice.

"Well, thank you," Naeem told her. "This is just what it need."

"Oh, there's more." Nerissa revealed how she'd learned about the bite being caused by a cat, and I handed Naeem a notarized statement from Consuela confirming the story.

Naeem's eyes widened, and for the first time in our acquaintance, he actually beamed at us. "This is brilliant. I think this will get us a favorable ruling."

"Ha! We're not finished yet," I informed him. Not nearly as concisely as I probably could have, I described my interview with Mr. and Mrs. Kasprzak (actually, mostly Mrs. Kasprzak), and explained how they'd gotten mixed up about the day they'd seen him. I handed him a signed statement from the Kasprzaks, also notarized.

"If you'd been here to help at the original trial, I don't think Benek would've been convicted," Naeem told us. "His case probably wouldn't have even come to trial."

"And that, Mr. Ed McBain," I thought to myself, *"is why private detectives do indeed have a critical role in investigating crimes."*

Aloud, I said, "Oh, I'm not done yet." I'd made about a dozen backup copies of the surveillance footage just in case of disaster, and I played one of them for Naeem, popping it into Nerissa's laptop. "Take a look." After putting the video into context, I pointed at the screen. "That's Benek and Lada, walking down to that isolated grove of trees. They look pretty friendly and civil together, don't they? He doesn't look like he's seething with rage, right?"

After Naeem murmured his agreement, we watched the two teens talking for a few moments, until Lada burst into tears. "Watch Benek's hands closely," I told Naeem.

Naeem squinted. "It looks like he's comforting her. He's putting his hands on her shoulders. Not her throat. And she's shaking because she's crying."

A minute later, Lada straightened up, fished in her pocket for a tissue, and wiped her eyes. Then, without warning, she ran away. Benek called out to her, and then he jogged in her direction, out of view of the camera.

After slowly turning around in his chair, the distance between Naeem's jaw and his chest swiftly narrowed. "He didn't strangle her."

"Nope."

"Then Maia Landeen—"

"I don't think she lied," Nerissa interrupted. "Not deliberately, that is. I think that Maia witnessed the two of them from a distance and misinterpreted it. Or maybe her eyesight isn't great. Whatever she thought she saw, when she heard the next day that Lada had been strangled, Maia unconsciously rewrote what she saw in her mind, and she convinced herself that she'd seen Benek choking Lada. The video in her head moved Benek's hands from Lada's shoulders to her throat. She wasn't lying; she just committed a bit of mental editing based on events."

"She was very convincing on the stand," Naeem recalled.

"That's because she genuinely believed what she was saying," Midge explained. "I've lost count of the miscarriages of justice that have arisen because a witness misremembers something, but is so dead certain about being right that there's no way counsel can shake them, even when they're confronted with photographic or videographic proof their memories were inaccurate. If juries knew just how easy it is for witnesses to touch up their memories unknowingly with mental Photoshop, they would never convict someone based solely on one person's eyewitness testimony again."

"Maia torpedoed our defense," Naeem murmured. "From the moment she started speaking, there was no way that the jury would see Benek as anything but an abusive boyfriend."

"And you've never seen this video before?" I asked him.

"Of course not. I would have shown it to the jury to rebut Maia's testimony if I had."

"That's very interesting. Because the man who gave me this footage claims that he turned it in to the prosecutor in charge of the case."

"ADA Tatum Sangster?"

"That's right. She never passed it on to you?"

"No...." There was a glint in Naeem's eye that lawyers get when they suddenly see the legal tide turning in their favor. "She was required to provide me with any evidence that challenged her case as part of discovery. That's further grounds for reversal."

"Well, Christmas came early this year," I informed him. "Because I've got one more weapon for your legal arsenal." I pulled out my background reports. "I dug into the pasts of everybody involved in the case, including the jury. Nothing potentially problematic, except for Juror #6. The retired welder."

"I remember him. What's wrong with him? He seemed like a nice old guy."

"He was admitted into a nursing home last week. It appears that he's battling progressively worsening dementia."

"Where did you get that information?" A bit of nervousness crept into

Naeem's eyes. "You didn't hack into confidential medical files, did you?"

"Of course not. I checked his daughter's social media pages. They threw a party for him two days after the verdict. The get-together was meant to mark his moving into assisted living. If you take a look at her posts, she mentions how her father got his diagnosis three years ago, and how they made the "difficult decision" to begin the transition to assisted living. If you check this printout—" I handed a sheet of paper to him. "—you'll see that in her caption to a collection of photographs from the last twelve months, she talks about how her father "wanted to make a positive contribution to society during his last year of independence," including ladling out meals for homeless people, giving away a bunch of his possessions to people who could use them, picking up trash along the side of the highway, and...doing his civic duty as a juror."

Naeem stared at the paper for a moment. "I didn't notice anything amiss."

"If you look at this social media post..." I handed him another printout. "You'll see that a couple of months ago, his daughter vented about some of the inconveniences he caused her when he was "sundowning." It seems like he does pretty well in the mornings and early afternoons, but once it starts getting dark, he struggles. As I said, this is preliminary, and I don't know anything for certain, but if these posts are true, and I have no reason to think that his daughter would just make up something like this, then one of the jurors had Alzheimer's."

"What does that mean?" We all whirled around and saw that Nerissa's little brother Bernard had wandered into the room.

"Bernard," Midge said with only a touch of sternness, "We're talking about important trial issues here."

"I know, Mom. That's why I wanted to listen to what you were saying. It's very interesting."

I figured this was a teachable moment for the kid, so before anybody could tell him to go, I explained, "Bernard, in the American legal system, people are entitled to representation and a jury of twelve of their peers. If a lawyer falls asleep during the trial, and the defendant is convicted, that can be cause to have the verdict overturned. The same issue applies if the lawyer is affected

42

by alcohol or drugs."

"Of course, that doesn't mean an automatic reversal," Midge added. "Some judges will argue that there's insufficient evidence that the lawyer was actually sleeping, and others will claim that the dozing off only matters if it was during a supposedly "pivotal" point in the trial. And of course, "pivotal" often means what the judge says it means. And if a lawyer prefers not to get disbarred, the defendant's own attorney may deny being anything other than sharp and alert the whole time. In any case, any judge worthy of the black robe ought to notice if a lawyer's fallen asleep and wake up that attorney."

"And the same principle applies to jurors," I informed Bernard. "A sleeping juror might be grounds for a mistrial, though once again, it depends on the judge and why the other jurors or the judge didn't notice the drifting off and take steps to correct it. It ought to be obvious to everybody when someone's sleeping. But what isn't as obvious is when a juror has Alzheimer's or something similar. What if a defendant was denied access to twelve jurors who were fully capable of listening to all of the evidence, remembering it properly, and then analyzing everything thoroughly?"

"I'd say that the defendant was entitled to a new trial," Bernard told me.

"We think alike," I replied.

"Has there ever been a case where a defendant's conviction has been overturned because one juror had Alzheimer's?" Nerissa asked.

"I haven't found anything yet," I admitted, "but there *have* been cases where a judge has developed dementia, and all of that judge's cases over a certain period of time were reviewed, but once again, there's nothing automatic. We could be moving into uncharted territory here."

"And that's risky," Naeem said. "But now we've got four causes for reversal. The forensic bite mark evidence is challenged. The newly uncovered video evidence contradicts the witness testimony of a fight. The witnesses who claim he was there at the time of the crime have recanted and explained why they're mistaken. The prosecutor had the video and didn't turn it over to me. And finally, we have reason to believe that a juror was not performing his civic duty at full capacity. If I had just one of those, I'd say we had a fifty-fifty shot at best. But with all of this...I don't want to raise my hopes too high, but...." He smiled. "It's rare that there's a slam-dunk at getting a conviction overturned, unless the real killer confesses and there's a mountain of new evidence proving it. Of course, you can never tell if a judge is going to take a bad day out on you, but...I'm pretty optimistic. And without the witnesses placing him there and the bite mark evidence in doubt...they probably won't even bother to try him again."

The following morning, Nerissa and I gave Volker an update on our investigation and Naeem's assessment of our chances. Volker was so excited he started quivering. "You did it! He's coming home!"

"Hold it, don't get excited," Nerissa cautioned him. "It may be a while before the court announces its decision, and even then, they may not release him right away. It's possible that they'll hold him for a new trial, though personally, I don't think there's enough evidence.to warrant that."

"And there's something else," I added. "Even if he's released, unless Lada's real killer is caught, there's always going to be a cloud of suspicion over Benek. He may not be able to return to his old high school, and his future career opportunities may be threatened."

Volker waved his hand, as if these were trifling matters of no consequence to him. "It'll work out all right. But who do you think really killed Lada?"

I shrugged. "I don't know. There were suggestions that a couple of her ex-boyfriends or a couple of the adult men at her school might have been involved, but that was just unverified speculation. No evidence whatsoever. Personally, I'm leaning towards the burglar theory. The guy who'd been breaking into houses in the neighborhood went into Lara's home, thinking there was no one there. She caught him, he panicked."

"But there's no proof it was a burglar," Volker said.

"Actually, there's the fingerprint evidence."

Nerissa's eyebrows twitched. "There weren't any unidentified fingerprints at the crime scene."

"Exactly. The fingerprints of Lada, her mother, and Benek were all over the place. No evidence that anything was wiped clean."

"So how does that..." I saw the light dawning in Nerissa's eyes. "Oh..."

44

"What?" Volker asked. "The killer wore gloves?"

"That's very likely."

"So what does that mean?"

"I checked the weather report for the night of the murder," I explained. "It was a warm night. The pre-midnight low was sixty degrees. So it's unlikely the killer was wearing gloves, though I suppose it's possible that he had them in his pocket, but then he wouldn't have been wearing them the whole time. The fact that the murder weapon was a pair of dirty jeans indicates that it was a spur-of-the-moment, unpremeditated crime. So if the killer was a visitor who was let inside the house and wasn't planning murder when he arrived, why would he be wearing gloves every second?"

I could see the gears turning in Volker's head. "But a burglar would have been wearing gloves."

"Exactly."

Perhaps it was my vanity, but I thought that I saw a spark of admiration in Volker's eyes. "Where did you learn how to be a private detective?"

"I had guidance from a guy who'd been in the business for over thirty years. He was never particularly successful financially, but he was great at his job. He wrote and self-published a manual on how to teach yourself to become a private eye. It sold maybe twenty copies, and after he died, I sent most of the remaining stock to libraries around Wisconsin."

Volker was practically dancing in his chair; he looked so happy. "But everything's looking up for Benek, right?"

"I hope so."

"What should I do while we wait?"

"Just hope and pray for the best," I replied.

"My family's nonreligious."

Nerissa shrugged. "Then we'll do the praying, and you just get your brother's room all cleaned up and ready for him to return."

Volker leapt up and shook both of our hands. "Mr. Funderburke, Miss Kaiming, thank you. I don't have a lot of respect for a lot of adults, but you two have really come through for me." A big smile spread across his face. "And everything is going to work out great! I know it!"

Chapter Two: Adoption Day

NERISSA

Though I love celebrating Christmas, Easter, Halloween, the Fourth of July, and Thanksgiving, none of them are my favorite holiday. For me, the best day of the year is Adoption Day, a holiday celebrated only in the Kaiming household. At least our version of it, other families who've adopted kids may have their own take on it. The first Adoption Day was in May of my freshman year of high school, when it looked like Toby and I were about to be unceremoniously tossed into the foster care system. Dad stepped up and took us in, and for that, I'm eternally grateful.

We started our own traditions that year. Every Adoption Day begins with breakfast at one of our local hangouts just down the road. Later in the afternoon we go to a movie, followed by frozen custard. If there's a conflict, like a soccer game or something like that, we see the movie on Adoption Day Observed that coming weekend. Dinner is always pizza. As much of the extended family as possible attends at least one of the events. When Mom and Dad got married over Spring Break of my senior year, I made her wait two months to sign the adoption papers so it would be on the same day. Every year, I buy Dad a leather jacket that I have to nag and cajole him to wear in public. Mom doesn't need that kind of encouragement with hers. Every year, they buy books for me and Toby, which I always read within a week of receiving them. I'm not sure about Toby.

This year, Adoption Day fell on a Saturday. I don't know why I get as excited as I do, but that day, I woke up an hour before I usually do on the weekend and couldn't fall back. Mom was also up after comforting my fussy youngest sibling, so the two of us went out for a quick five-mile run around Lake Park. After we returned home, I showered, then donned the outfit I'd finally decided on after a week of pondering. Indulging in my fondness for metallic colors, I pulled on my sparkling gold polyester sweater, my gold lambskin maxi skirt and matching short trench coat, and a golden pair of ballet slippers. Deciding to wear my hair down with a gold silk headband, I looked myself over in the full-length mirror, liked what I saw, and practically danced out of my room, nearly bumping into Toby, who was sporting her favorite baggy sweater and one of the sweatskirts she always wears. I couldn't tell whether she'd brushed her hair or not.

"Happy Adoption Day!"

"Happy Adoption Day!" I threw my arms around her and tried not to feel hurt when I felt her cringe at my touch.

I grabbed her hand and hurried down the corridor into the younger triplets' nursery. Dad had just finished dressing them, and I rushed in for a hug. He was wearing a wine-colored dress shirt and dark blue slacks, and I knew he hadn't put more than a quarter-second's thought into selecting the day's outfit. After the "Happy Adoption Day!" exchange, I asked him, "Ready for presents?"

"If we have to." Dad's resigned tone indicated that he still hadn't gotten over the crimson moto jacket I'd found at my favorite thrift shop last year for five bucks. I think it was worth every penny.

"Meet me downstairs." I rushed back to my room and grabbed the wrapped boxes off my bureau. When I reached the bottom of the staircase, Mom and Dad were standing off to the side, strapping the younger triplets into their carriers. Four gifts that were obviously books were on the coffee table.

"You two first." Mom said. I admit I didn't pay much attention to what Toby received. They always give her something from her favorite genre—manga—and the fact that I'm not more interested in that is often a point of contention between us. Dad gave me a copy of Robert Caro's *The Power*

Broker, and Mom's present was Volume Nine of *The History of Middle-Earth: Sauron Defeated*. Tolkien is her favorite writer.

I handed Dad his present, and he unwrapped it with the face of a man marching to the firing squad. "Is this Funderburke's coat?" he asked as he held up the black lambskin walking coat.

"It's similar, but it's a different designer. And before you ask, I found it online and negotiated the seller down to thirty bucks. It was only worn once, and I had it cleaned. I wanted my guys to match. Go on, try it on."

It fit him perfectly, so he didn't have the excuse he had three years ago when the sleeves of the gray suede blazer were an inch and a half too short. "Do I have to wear this today?"

I doubled the size of my eyes. "I'll cry if you don't, Daddy."

"I think you look very handsome." Mom looked fantastic in her rich chocolate-brown trench, which paired beautifully with her sapphire cotton dress. Dad's eyes said, "Et tu, Midge?" and after the elder triplets, Bernard, Eleanor, and Amara, ran downstairs, we piled into our cars and drove to breakfast.

Half an hour later, I was surprised that Funderburke hadn't shown up yet, as he's almost never late. We're well-known at the restaurant, and the manager set the special party room in the back aside for us. With my parents, Toby, all six of my siblings, Dad's grandparents (both his father's parents and his mother's mother), Mom's grandmother, Mom's aunt and uncle who raised her, Mom's two younger siblings, Dad's parents and his younger brother, one of Mom's cousins, his wife, and three of their kids, it was a moderately-sized family gathering. After the third text to Funderburke asking him where he was, I started to think he'd overslept, but then I realized that as his landlady, Mrs. Zwidecker, was coming too, she would have made sure he was awake.

As the kids were getting antsy, we placed our orders. Midway through, Funderburke texted me back: BE THERE IN TEN MINUTES. ORDER FOR US PLEASE. I used my best judgment in telling the waiter what to bring, and just as we were all being served, Funderburke arrived with Mrs. Zwidecker and my Great-Aunt Scholastica.

Funderburke didn't look well. His eyes were smoldering, and not in a sexy way. His expression seemed to be equal parts seething and sick. I hurried up to them, said my greetings, and took a closer look at Funderburke. My first reaction was to be a little hurt that he hadn't worn one of the suits I bought him—he was wearing a black T-shirt and track pants under his coat. Then I realized that whatever had happened, he'd had good reason for being too distracted to dress up for the party. His shaving was perfunctory. It looked like he'd dragged his electric razor over his face a few times and only clipped two-thirds of his morning stubble. Unlike Toby, I was pretty certain he hadn't brushed his hair.

"You want to talk about whatever's bothering you?" I asked him.

"Not in front of the kids. C'mon." Funderburke led me outside, and I saw Mom and Dad rising from the table.

"I ordered you your usual, an egg white scramble with one yolk, grilled chicken, mushrooms, olives, spinach, and a little feta, with whole wheat popovers and fruit salad. I also ordered you your favorite, double chocolate chip pancakes with strawberries, as it's a special occasion. You can eat what you want and bring the rest home."

"I don't think I can eat anything right now." Now, I knew that something was deeply wrong. Funderburke's always hungry.

"You're scaring me now," I informed him as we passed through the front vestibule. "What happened? Did something happen to a student?"

He turned to me, ran his hands through his hair, and after long enough of a pause to get me shaking with impatience, said, "It's Benek Berchtwelt."

"What? Did they deny his appeal? On a Saturday?"

"No, it's not that." Funderburke appeared to be fighting the urge to shout, but though he was clearly angry, it obviously wasn't at me. "He's fighting for his life."

"What–" I didn't finish the question. I took a millisecond to think, and then asked, "Was he attacked by another inmate?"

"From what I heard, it was six other inmates. Members of some prison gang, they're not telling me who yet. I don't have all the details, just that first thing this morning, they cornered him and beat him up." He shuddered.

49

"Oh no." I turned around and saw Mom and Dad behind us. After taking a few seconds to bring them up to speed, Funderburke said, "I got the call from Volker an hour ago. He phoned me right after the prison authorities gave him and his grandfather the news. He begged me to come over to his house, and he obviously needed moral support. You stay here."

"No, I'm coming with you."

"I know how important Adoption Day is to you. I don't want to spoil it. Any more than I have so far, I mean."

Grabbing his hands, I told him. "Something like this, we do together. C'mon."

"Funderburke, you know you shouldn't drive angry or hungry. Remember the time you crashed into the snowman?" Mom told him.

"That wasn't my fault."

"Take five minutes and eat something. Then go to Volker."

When Funderburke's mad, he gets argumentative, so I silenced his objections with a kiss and pulled him back into the restaurant. Bernard took one look at his face and asked him what was wrong. I told Bernard that I appreciated his concern, but there was a problem with a student, and Funderburke just needed a little quiet time to process it.

"Is it that about the guy who went to prison for a murder he didn't commit?" Bernard asked.

Honestly, we try to keep all the details about violent crimes as far from the kids as possible, but sometimes I think that Bernard's the best detective in the family, because when anything happens in our house, he hears about it. If that kid had been around in the 1940s, we could have taught him German and set him loose in Berlin. Forty-eight hours later, he'd have gathered up enough intelligence to bring the Nazis to their knees. It would've ended the war a lot sooner and saved a lot of innocent lives.

Everybody at the table tried to avoid looking at Funderburke's thundercloud-like face, and I let Bernard control the conversation with me while I ate my avocado toast and poached eggs as quickly as possible. After three minutes, Funderburke's phone rang, and I informed two of my sisters that it was an emergency when they reminded him about the "no phones at

50

the table" rule.

"I'm on my way," Funderburke said right before he ended the call. After dabbing his mouth with his napkin and folding it up on the table, he rose and wished everybody well. I followed him, waiting until we were out of the restaurant to ask what he'd heard.

"Benek died."

Neither of us said another word for the entire drive. We pulled into the Berchtwelt driveway, and I wondered how long the obscene graffiti attacking Benek had been spray-painted upon their garage door. After I got out of the car, I smelled the paint fumes, so I figured that it was fairly fresh.

Otto Berchtwelt, Volker's grandfather, opened the door. He was a formidable-looking man holding a very heavy cane, and he appeared to be a few years short of seventy. Though I didn't want to stare, I was pretty sure he had a prosthetic foot. I could see the bottom of an insulin pump just under the sleeve of his T-shirt, so I guessed that he'd lost the foot to diabetes.

"You're from Cuthbertson?" Mr. Berchtwelt asked.

"Yes. I'm Isaiah Funderburke, and this is Nerissa Kaiming. We're so sorry."

"Why are you sorry? You're the only ones who've done a damn to help us, aside from that hapless public defender." He waved us into the house and led us to a door in the back of the house. "This is his room." He tapped the door with his cane. "Volker? Your teachers are here."

The boy who answered the door was not the same kid who we'd talked to earlier that week. Every childhood ends, but it's usually a gradual process that happens a little at a time over months or years. For the fortunate, it's just the maturity that comes with the dawn of adolescence. For Funderburke, it started when his parents divorced when he was in the third grade, and culminated in the death of his best friend in seventh grade. In my case, it began with my birth mother's downward spiral of depression and promiscuity, and reached its apogee with the arrival of Toby.

I knew that in Volker's case, his childhood started to crumble with his brother's arrest and conviction, but today's news had forever changed him. His eyes were harder than they'd been previously, and his face was even angrier than Funderburke's.

51

"Thanks for coming." His voice hadn't changed in terms of pitch, but it was unsettling hearing so much fury coming from a little kid's mouth.

After hearing Mr. Berchtwelt's response, I figured "We're sorry for your loss" wasn't going to cut it. "We're here for you," I told him. "Please let us know if there's something specific we can do in order to give you the support you need."

Volker stared at me without moving. Finally, he asked, "Can you make sure the prisoners who killed my brother get the death penalty?"

A couple of moments passed, and Funderburke explained, "Wisconsin doesn't have the death penalty."

"There's got to be a way to make their punishment worse. Is there a less humane prison they can go to? Maybe somewhere that Amnesty International is trying to close down?"

I was a little taken aback by the ferocity of his anger, but I understood. I've been in similar positions, like with Toby's father, who was left permanently more dead than alive after he was the victim of a terrible violent crime. I told Volker the story, hoping it would help somehow.

He looked up at me. "Were you in love with him?"

The blunt question surprised me, but I didn't need long to answer. "No. But he was a friend, and I cared about him."

"I'm sorry for the guy. But it's not the same."

I couldn't argue with the kid. "No, it's not. But I'm trying to help."

"Punishing the people responsible is the only way to help the situation."

"The authorities will investigate," I told him.

"Do not ask me to put my faith in the justice system right now."

That was fair. "Have you had anything to eat this morning?" I asked.

"I'm not hungry."

"I understand that, but maybe having a little food could help a bit." I wished that I'd thought to bring something from the restaurant. "Let me make you something."

"I don't want anything."

"Please let me do something." I motioned him towards the kitchen. "Maybe some eggs?"

For the first time, there was a flicker of something in Benek's eyes other than rage. "I don't think we have any eggs in the house."

It was true. At my home, the challenge is to find enough space to squeeze everything into the refrigerator. At the Berchtwelt house, the refrigerator held half a six-pack of beer, a gallon jug of milk with about an inch remaining in it, an opened pack of hot dogs, and a few sodas. I didn't see any fresh produce anywhere.

"What do you usually have for breakfast?" I asked, making a mental note to buy groceries for them.

"Cereal. The chocolate one."

The shelf had three open boxes of breakfast food with plenty of sugar and the bare minimum of nutritional benefits in them. I poured a little into a bowl and added milk. One whiff told me that the milk was one day away from spoiling. Volker ate a few spoonfuls in silence. Just as I was about to ask him if he wanted anything else, there was a thump at the door. Funderburke crossed over, as several identical thumps followed.

"What was that?" I asked.

"Well…they have eggs now…" Funderburke muttered. He whipped out his phone and started recording the vandals—three teenagers—through the window. When they saw him through the window, they sprinted away, holding up their middle fingers as they ran.

Volker and his father joined us. "Do you know them?" Funderburke asked.

"Yeah. They went to high school with Benek. They're a couple years behind him."

"I'll get the mop and bucket," Otto muttered.

"Why should you clean this up?" Funderburke asked.

"I can't afford a cleaning service."

"That's not what I meant. Volker, can you give me their names? I need to have a talk with their parents."

At first, the parents in question acted as if Funderburke was insane for thinking that their dear little darlings ought to be punished for their vandalism, but when he calmly yet aggressively told them that he had video evidence of their actions, and that he had some friends on the police force that would be very interested in seeing it, they started to become less defiant. Two of the parents informed Funderburke that they'd send their kids back to the Berchtwelt house to clean up the mess, though the first mother Funderburke talked to hung up the phone and refused to answer his repeated calls.

Midway through Funderburke's conversations, I heard a crash from the kitchen. I rushed in and found Volker standing over his cereal bowl. It was plastic, so it hadn't broken, but milk and cereal were everywhere. I unrolled some paper towels and started to kneel down, but Volker insisted he would wipe up the spill. "I knocked it over, why should you have to do anything?"

It took him about a minute, and when he tried to dispose of the paper towels, he found that the garbage can was overflowing. He had to struggle, due to his small size, but he managed to pull out the stuffed-to-bursting bag, refusing my help. He did allow me to line the bin with a fresh bag. Volker dragged the garbage out through the side door, shuffled through a tiny garage, jumped up to push back the can's lid, and tried to lift it up and put it inside, but when he tried to lift it over his head, it slipped out of his hands and fell upon the ground. The plastic tore, and I insisted that Volker let me help him, otherwise the mess would spread all over the place. We managed to get the garbage back inside the bin without any of the contents spilling. On our way back in, Volker picked up a baseball bat standing in the corner. "This was Benek's."

I didn't know what to say, and then, without warning, Volker whirled around and turned towards a sack of salt for icing the walkways in winter. He raised the bat above his head and struck the bag over and over again, hitting harder every time. After four minutes of hammering the salt, he collapsed on the ground from exhaustion. I saw tears rolling down his reddened face. When I tried to hand him a tissue, he smacked it out of my hand, then apologized and asked for another.

"I don't know why I did that," he said as he dabbed his eyes.

"You needed to vent your anger," I told him. "Bags of salt can't get hurt."

"Not the salt bag. Knocking away the tissue you tried to give me." He picked up the tissue that had floated away from my smacked hand and crumpled it up with the other one. "You've been kind, and you've gone the extra mile to help. Actual help. Giving him a real defense. Not just vague expressions of support. You and Funderburke did a great job. A really great job. And I just know it would have worked out. Maybe it would've taken another trial, but he would have been acquitted eventually. If you kept investigating, you could probably have caught the guy who really did it and cleared his name. That would've been great. Everybody who had a hand in smearing him and sending him to a cell would've had to eat excrement. They would've had to get down on their knees and beg for forgiveness. And I probably would've given it to them. Eventually. After a lot of groveling I could've forgiven them, after they'd been properly shamed and forced to wallow in just a tiny fraction of the humiliation that we've had to endure for the last few months. I would've made the kids who egged and spray-painted our house lick it clean with their tongues. They would have had to fling themselves down into the mud and cry that they were wracked with guilt. The policemen who built the case against Benek and arrested him would suffer. So would the bite mark witness, the judge, the prosecutor, the jury. All the neighbors and classmates who've treated us like we're radioactive. If they'd admitted they were wrong, and I could see just a shred, a tiny shred of remorse in their eyes, I could have stopped hating them. Eventually, I would have stopped being mad. I could have moved on and been happy. I wouldn't have forgotten what happened, but I could have moved forward. As long as Benek was free and able to live his life, it would have been all right. But now, nothing is ever going to be all right ever again."

I tried to say something, but I couldn't. I knew from looking at him that no amount of platitudes or attempts at comfort would do anything to blunt his fury. I've seen a lot of angry teens in my time. When I was thirteen, I had so much rage at me, mostly directed at my birth mother and her endless chain of sleazy paramours, that if some enterprising engineer had found a way to strap some sort of suction cup to my head and extract all the fury from my body, the energy from my emotion could've powered all of Rhode Island for a week. A lot of the girls that I mentor didn't become teen mothers due to any fault or failure of their own. They were sinned against rather than sinning themselves. And they have a lot of justified resentment against the adults in their lives who were supposed to look out for them, and instead exploited and betrayed them.

But I'd never seen a teenager with so much seething anger as Volker. Not in a thirteen-year-old who looked like he was ten and was barely five foot two. On reflection, I hadn't seen anybody of any age with that much wrath, and I knew all that emotion was going to come out somehow, and wondering how that was going to happen scared me.

After a couple of minutes of standing in silence, I heard Funderburke's and Naeem's voices coming from inside the house, so I walked towards them. I was kind of in a haze, so I didn't quite realize that Volker was right behind me.

I stopped at the doorway of the living room. Otto was sitting in a tattered recliner with his head in his hands. Funderburke was standing next to Naeem, who looked absolutely crushed. Neither of them could see me from the way they were positioned.

"So they know who beat and killed him?" Funderburke asked.

"Yes," Naeem nodded. "Not that they needed much of an investigation. They were members of one of the nastiest prison gangs in the place. They caught them in the act, all splattered with blood. No question they have the guys involved in the attack."

"They'll charge them for his murder, right?" Otto sounded like he had been completely gutted.

"I don't know. From what I hear, the perpetrators were already going to spend the rest of their lives in prison. It's early days yet. We'll see what happens."

"Was he in pain?" Otto asked.

"No, they knocked him unconscious, he didn't feel anything after the first few seconds..." It was such an obvious lie on Naeem's part that both Funderburke and Otto stared at him, fully aware that he was sugar-coating the truth in the hopes of sparing Otto's feelings." Naeem couldn't commit to the fib. "Yes. Yes, they gave him anesthetic when they got him to the infirmary, but he was in a great deal of pain. I'm sorry."

"There's something else, isn't there, Naeem?" Funderburke stared at Naeem, wordlessly ordering him to tell everything, no matter how painful it would be to hear.

"What do you mean?" Naeem dissembled.

"I can see it in your face. There's more that you don't want to tell us."

Naeem flinched, and I knew Funderburke was on the right scent.

"I…don't know what you're talking about."

"Oh, dear Lord." Funderburke ran the back of his hand over his forehead. "They didn't just beat him, did they? There was…further abuse, wasn't there, of a sexual nature?"

After quivering for a few seconds, Naeem nodded.

We all jumped as a primal scream of pain emanated from Volker. It lasted for a full ten seconds. Funderburke whirled around and looked horrified. He'd never have asked that question if he'd known that Volker was there.

A frigid, clammy sensation passed through my entire body as Volker's eyes grew even harder and fiercer. "I will make everybody who played a role in sending Benek to prison and getting him killed pay. All of them. They'll beg for mercy, and I will never, ever let their suffering end."

Chapter Three: A Dozen Smug Idiots

FUNDERBURKE

I have always hated funerals. I don't care if you call them "memorial services" or "celebrations of life," they're always terrible. People say that "funerals are for the living," but for my money, they're just stealing from what remains of other people's lives. When I die, I don't want a big funeral. Don't bother with embalming or anything, just say the prayers and bury me. I want a quiet Mass with immediate family only sending me off, and I want the cheapest possible coffin because money is for people who need it. And the coffin should be closed, too, because I don't want anybody who cares about me being forced to stare at my corpse.

The Berchtwelts didn't have any choice about keeping Benek's casket closed. His body was in no condition to be displayed.

Otto was afraid that any funeral they held might be protested, so there was no formal gathering. The Friday evening after he died, Benek was buried on the far edge of a scruffy cemetery by the side of the highway. We asked Alfie to tell as many of Benek's friends as he thought would come, but to wait until a few hours before the event. Alfie and about thirty-five teammates of Benek's from all three sports he played arrived. Aside from Nerissa and Midge, there were no females present. Naeem was also in attendance. A disheveled-looking man showed up just a few minutes before everybody started to leave. He spoke to Otto and Volker briefly and hurried away. I learned later that the man was Volker and Benek's father, Erich, but he was gone before I could speak to him.

There was no reception afterwards. Benek's classmates went their separate ways after they each tossed a little soil into the open grave, and when we asked the remaining members of the Berchtwelt family if they wanted us to come back to their house, they both informed us that they'd rather be alone for a while. "We've got plenty of food thanks to you," Volker told us. "We're eating better and healthier than we have in a long time. Right now, I just want to sit in front of the TV and watch *South Park* DVDs and plot vengeance."

I said the usual warnings against revenge that everybody's always heard before. I can't say that my heart was one hundred percent into it, and if I was being totally honest, a significant percentage of me was mirroring Volker at that moment. My late mentor, who taught me the ropes about the private detection business before alcoholic hepatitis took him away from us far too soon, told me to never get emotionally involved in an investigation. That is one of the few rules of his that I've occasionally been unable to follow. Darn it, I was proud of my work in this case. I thought I'd built a pretty near bulletproof case for Benek's appeal. If I'd been around during the initial trial, there's no way he would've been convicted. There's a fair chance it wouldn't have come to trial at all, or at least the charges could've been dismissed right after the prosecution rested its case. But I wasn't involved until too late, the appeals process took too long, and the prison was too dangerous.

The next night, Naeem came to dinner again. The chicken meatball stroganoff was pretty great, but with my mind on other matters, I wasn't able to enjoy it at the level it deserved. This time, Naeem had asked if he could come over to talk to us, and I knew at once it was for more than trying to cadge a free home-cooked meal.

Once again, we gathered in Nerissa's study after tapioca with raspberries, and after I made sure that none of the kids were hiding in the room, Naeem looked at us with apprehension. "I think I may have made a mistake."

"At the trial?" Nerissa asked.

"No. With the file you gave me."

I had no idea what sort of mistake he might have made with my research, and asked him to explain.

"The afternoon before the funeral, I left it on my desk, but then I had to rush to the bathroom. Ever since what happened to Benek, my stomach's been going crazy."

"Understandable." I hoped he wouldn't go into more details.

"Volker and his grandfather were scheduled to meet with me that afternoon, to talk about the possibility of getting Benek's conviction overturned posthumously. Apparently, Otto couldn't find a parking space, so he dropped Volker off while he drove around the area. Volker was alone at my desk for a while...I didn't notice anything while I was talking to them, but once they left, I realized that your file was out of order."

"I told you to be careful with it. There's some sensitive information there." I regretted the recriminations as soon as I said them. Naeem was clearly distraught, and I felt sympathy towards him rather than annoyance.

"I know, I know, I'm sorry. I was supposed to keep it locked up, and I just forgot. My mind has been everywhere by where it's supposed to be."

"And Volker saw it," Nerissa concluded.

"That's what I'm guessing," Naeem agreed. "He was only alone with it for about fifteen minutes, so I don't know how much of it he could've read."

"He has Benek's old phone," I reminded him. "He could have photographed the entire file in a fraction of that time."

That possibility hadn't occurred to Naeem. "What do we do?"

"Tomorrow, right after church, we'll go over to the Berchtwelt house and talk to them," Nerissa said.

And we did. We sat with Volker at his kitchen table, and I decided the best approach was the direct approach. "Volker," I said, "Naeem thinks you might have read the file I compiled on everybody connected to the trial."

"He's right, I did."

"That was supposed to be for his eyes only."

"I didn't see a note telling me not to read it."

"Fair enough. Did you photograph it?"

Volker's mouth tightened. "Why do you ask that?"

The dissembling told me the answer just as clearly as if he'd said "Yes."

"Because if you did, I'd like you to delete it, please."

"And why should I do that? Not that I'm admitting anything, by the way."

"Because aside from the fact that not everything in that file is age-appropriate for you, that file contains a lot of personal information on the jurors."

"So what?"

I sighed. "Volker, you haven't known me for all that long, but I think you know me well enough to know that I have a lot of strong opinions about the justice system. And one of them is that our system of trial by jury only works if certain measures are taken to protect the jurors. They should be able to maintain their anonymity unless they choose to reveal their participation after the conclusion of a trial without being influenced, threatened, shamed, or in any way harmed. Their decisions have to be based on the facts rather than on any outside pressures. No jurors should ever have any fears that their verdicts will cast any shadows on their lives after performing their civic duties. We have enough people struggling to get out of jury duty as is. Don't get me wrong, I know that those jurors made a horrific error in Benek's case, and I'm angry at them, too. And I heard what you said about wanting revenge on everybody who put Benek in prison. I hope that the relevant officials look into the case and see if any repercussions should hit the detectives who investigated the case, and the forensic dentist who misidentified the cat bite. If we're right in thinking that the prosecutor deliberately withheld the video evidence, she should be disbarred. The judge, though, I think, was just overseeing the case and didn't make any glaring lapses or mistakes, and Maia Landeen mistook what she saw, but she didn't deliberately lie. The Kasprzaks made a terrible error, but it wasn't out of malice. As for the jurors...they analyzed the evidence, and they reached the wrong conclusion. I think they're going to have to live with the consequences of that decision, but that's where the matter must rest. Please, leave them to their consciences."

Volker made what he thought was an innocent face, but it didn't look the least bit cherubic. "You think that feeling a little guilty is enough punishment for those jurors?"

"It has to be."

"You believe that losing a few minutes of sleep once in a while is all they deserve?"

"Sometimes you just have to leave it to God."

"I don't believe in God. So, you're saying that if a jury comes to a wrong conclusion, and an innocent person suffers, that they should walk away with no consequences whatsoever?"

"Unless it's incontrovertibly proven that a juror took a bribe or something like that, the potential repercussions of punishing jurors could lead to all kinds of complications. Fears of punishments or lawsuits would mean that the public would be even less willing to serve than they are now."

"So the jury gets away with it? Their role in killing Benek? Slandering me? Letting the real killer walk free?" Volker didn't wait for us to respond. He shook his head with such force I thought he might give himself whiplash. "No. I don't accept that."

"This is the way the justice system has to work, Volker," Nerissa spoke gently, but a bit of the stern teacher tone everybody has to develop if they want to survive as educators crept into her voice.

"If a doctor tells you your symptoms are all in your head, and refuses to give you the medicine you need, and you have a stroke and wind up in a wheelchair, you sue him for malpractice. When a lawyer doesn't pay attention to your instructions and doesn't file your motion on time, and you lose a lawsuit and your house, you sue him to get your money back. Why should being a juror be any different? This is about more than making a mistake. Those jurors had a choice. Let's skip over all the other testimony, forget whether it was deliberate lies or accidental untruths for a minute or two. Let's just think about what would have happened if they believed me. Even if they thought he bit her, he could have done it hours earlier. Maybe they thought he was an abuser. But if they'd accepted my testimony, *there was no way he could have done it.* They would have *had* to have acquitted him. Instead, they said, "This boy's testimony is a lie. We give it no credence. He is covering for his brother, and if they so choose, the authorities could prosecute him for perjury and being an accessory after the fact." It's only because the D.A.'s office didn't get around to slapping handcuffs on me that I'm not in the slammer myself. Why? Why did they do that?" Tears started welling up in Volker's eyes. "How could they look at me and believe I was lying? Why wasn't my testimony good enough for reasonable doubt?"

Neither Nerissa nor I had a ready reply to this. "We don't know," I admitted. "I think that there are a lot of adults who simply discount everything said by a kid automatically."

"And I'm sure it was obvious that you loved your brother," Nerissa added, "Which means—highly unfairly, I know—they thought you had a motive to lie. And they didn't see any reason why the other witnesses would perjure themselves. They just assumed, influenced by all of the other evidence. It wasn't fair; it wasn't right. But that's what they did."

"And you think that we should just leave it alone?" Volker asked.

"I think our best course of action is to work on a publicity campaign to tell the world that Benek was innocent," I told him. "We'll do a little more research, present our case, work with the local media, and maybe we'll start changing minds. Then the jurors will come across the story, and they'll realize their error, and then they'll have to deal with their consciences."

Volker slumped back in his chair and folded his arms. "They'll know, but I don't think the world will believe it. Grandpa and I have been subjected to so much hate because of this. People think they're standing up for a murdered girl by chucking eggs at our house and spraying paint on our garage. Even if every news station in the state announces that Benek didn't do it, will that make up for all the damage, all the humiliation, all the vitriol hurled in our direction? No. No. No. When a restaurant gives you crummy food, it is perfectly socially acceptable to go on the Internet, go on a reviewing website, and tell the world that the establishment's products are not fit to eat. The same goes for humans. When they mess up badly, the world should be aware that their judgment isn't to be trusted. The first juror was an assistant principal—"

"So you did read the file?" I asked.

"I was there for *voir dire*," he snapped. "Why would we trust her judgment about the people she hires to be around children? A woman who doesn't believe an honest boy could hire perverts and drug dealers because she doesn't know who's lying to her face. What right does she have to be in a position of authority? Everybody should know she can't be trusted. Or how about the engineer? If you can't trust his judgment at a trial, why should you trust his ability to build a bridge for you? Assuming he's the kind of engineer who builds bridges, I don't know. But you get the idea. The fact of the matter is, if you knew your mechanic made mistakes, you'd warn other people so they didn't go to him and get their brakes messed up, because if they or anybody else got into a car crash, you'd feel terrible because you could have said something but you didn't. Well, why shouldn't the world know that these people can't tell an honest kid from a couple of old people who can't tell what day it is? The way I see it, they were given a civics test on jury duty. Weigh the evidence and make a judgment. And they failed. They flunked the test; they got an "F." Why shouldn't their ineptitude be made known to the world? Every aspect of their judgment should be put under scrutiny. You fail your driver's test, you can't legally get behind the wheel of a car. You fail your civics test, you should lose some of the privileges of citizenship. They shouldn't get to vote anymore, not after convicting an innocent man. The older ones, I don't see why they should get Social Security benefits anymore. Those are for citizens; they shouldn't see a dime as punishment. Or better yet, shouldn't Grandpa and I get their Social Security money as reparations? It's only fair. You can't send a man to prison based on mistaken witnesses and quack doctors, and say, "Oops, my bad," and expect that to be the end of that. The jurors sat in that deliberation room, and they passed judgment on my brother, and they passed judgment on me, because by finding him guilty, they made it clear that my testimony meant nothing to them. So the twelve of them put their tiny heads together—a dozen smug idiots—and they didn't know the truth from lies. They can't get away with it. It's just wrong. I won't pretend the right thing to do is to just let it go."

He stopped for breath, not exactly hyperventilating, but inhaling and exhaling a bit more rapidly than normal. During the silence, he didn't break eye contact with us. If I read the expression in his eyes correctly, he was begging for our approval, waiting for us to tell him that we agreed with him one hundred percent and that he was totally right to feel as he did and do whatever he wanted to do. I got the sense that every second we didn't say that, we were letting him down.

And if I'm being honest, I was in the awkward position of *half* agreeing with him. What happened was a terrible miscarriage of justice, and I thought that there had to be some sort of reckoning, something more than just some quiet settlement paid for out of the taxpayer's wallet, that would get a two-paragraph mention in some double-digit page of the newspaper and then never be mentioned again.

If I'd been on that jury, I would have believed Volker and concluded that his testimony warranted reasonable doubt. But I'm wired to believe kids, and most adults have developed a prejudice against children when their word is up against an adult's. In this case, *two* adults. Of course, I would have been more suspicious of the bite mark evidence than ninety-nine-point-nine percent of the population, too. So I was in the position of judging the jurors by believing that I would have come to a different conclusion than they did, and once I was convinced there was reasonable doubt, Henry Fonda would've had nothing on me in that jury room.

Nerissa was the first to speak. "Volker, what do you think would happen if everybody who went into a courtroom and didn't get the verdict they wanted tried to get revenge on the jury? Can you imagine how guilty criminals might intimidate future juries by attacking the jurors who ruled against them?"

"I'm not going to *hurt* anybody," Volker assured her. "Look at me. I'm too little to intimidate anybody. At least I'm not going to hurt them *physically*. I just want to embarrass them like they humiliated me. They called me a liar in their arrogance, and now I want to humble them."

For a lot of kids, this would've just been talk. They would've vented, then slunk off to the sofa to play video games, and then never actually acted to get their revenge. But I could hear the gears turning in his brain.

"Don't worry." If Volker wanted his expression and tone to be reassuring, he failed miserably. "I'm not going to kill anybody. I'm not going to break any laws. I'm not going to risk going to jail or juvie. If Benek couldn't defend himself there, I wouldn't survive a day. So I'm not going to risk my life and freedom for revenge. But I need to teach a lot of lessons." He looked up at us and smiled. "You two did everything you could for me, and I'll love you both forever because of that. But everything went wrong, and now I have to make some sense out of this crazy world."

The phone rang. Otto answered it, grunted, and then hobbled over to Volker and handed it to him. "It's your mother."

"I don't want to talk to her. I have no mother."

"Please, Volker," Nerissa's voice broke a little. "You just buried your brother. You don't have much family left; don't throw any of what's remaining away."

"Do you have any idea what her leaving did to us?"

"I can guess. But do you know what she might do in the future now that she's lost a child? If there's any possibility that some good might come out of this, please don't risk missing it. My birth mother wore out my patience with her antics., and I never did anything to reconcile with her before it was too late." Nerissa leaned forward. "It haunts me. Please don't make my mistake."

Volker took the phone. "Fine. But I don't want you to hear what I have to say. Please go home, and I'll talk to you on Monday. And I promise not to do anything you wouldn't approve of before then."

I was quasi-comforted. Still, my powers of observation caught the proviso that he wouldn't do anything *before Monday*. As Otto ushered us out the door in a friendly yet firm manner, I started to wonder about what—if anything—he was planning for Tuesday.

Nerissa phoned her family to tell them we'd be late for dinner and that they should start without us. After she hung up, she turned to me and asked me if I thought we should warn everybody on Volker's excrement list.

My response came about half a minute later, as I had to navigate through some spring road construction on the way to the highway. "First of all, Volker is a client and is entitled to his confidentiality rights. Second, Volker specifically said that he was not planning any physical harm towards those individuals involved in his brother's conviction. If he's going to criticize them verbally, he enjoys the same First Amendment rights as anybody else. Of course, the usual slander risks apply, and it's never a good idea to antagonize a judge or a prosecutor, because you never know how the power of their office might rebound upon you."

"I'm aware of all that. But if anything goes wrong, the powers that be might blame you and go after your license. Or maybe Maia Landeen will file a defamation lawsuit. Yeah, we're just trying to give Benek his constitutionally allowed defense posthumously..." Nerissa sighed and pushed a stray strand of hair out of her face. "Maybe I'm overreacting. I don't believe that kid is homicidal. He's not going to get a gun and start firing it at the jury members. But if he took it into his mind to chuck a banana cream pie at the judge's face..."

"That's a waste of a good pie."

She rolled her eyes at me in the way that only a loving and annoyed girlfriend can. "Be serious, Funderburke. Volker is not going to drop this matter. I don't know what he has planned, but it's going to be a mess to clean up after it."

"Is it going to be our responsibility to clean up any hypothetical mess?"

"He's one of our students. He's a client."

"He's not our son, and he has a moral right to be upset."

Nerissa started to say something, changed her mind after a couple of syllables, and then said, "I wonder if those twelve members of the jury have any premonition of what's coming their way."

I thought back on the twelve jurors. Most of my research was Internet-based, though a few phone calls filled out some basic gaps for me. I should stress that the level of reconnaissance I was able to do wasn't enough to tell anything about the individuals in question were really like. All I could get was some basic details about their lives.

I need to point out that I'm not being coy or anything by referring to the jurors by their numbers. After what happened over the next couple months, all of them, or their family members, decided that they didn't want to be publicly linked with Benek's conviction, so to respect their desire for anonymity and to prevent people from tracking them down and expressing negative opinions in their general directions, no proper names will be used.

Juror #1. Female. Assistant principal in the Milwaukee Public School system and the foreperson of the jury. Negligible social media presence, very unpopular amongst students, according to an online rating site for school officials. Divorced, one son.

Juror #2. Male. Engineer at a small local company. Member of Mensa, frequent blogger, vlogger, and social media poster. Very outspoken, has opinions on every conceivable topic. Divorced, one daughter who lives in Florida.

Juror #3. Male. Master builder, skilled craftsman specializing in home remodeling. Three children, wife of thirty-six years dealing with unknown health problems.

Juror #4. Female. Last known member of a once-prominent Milwaukee family of manufacturers who sold their businesses thirty-five years earlier. Their family name can be found all over the city, having donated tons of money to numerous arts venues and colleges. Married once, no children, separated for over two decades, estranged husband currently living in Costa Rica with a mistress forty years his junior and their three small kids.

Juror #5. Female. Waitress. Never married, two small children.

Juror #6. Male. This is the man mentioned earlier who had dementia. Worked as a custodian, groundskeeper, and handyman before settling into a career as a welder. Recently placed into a nursing home. Widower, a daughter, and a son. Four grandchildren, two with each of his children. Three dogs, now living with the son.

Juror #7. Female. Supermarket employee. Divorced, one son. Deceased— a month earlier she was killed in an accident when a palette of tin cans fell off a high shelf upon her in the warehouse area. Family currently suing.

Juror #8. Male. Salesman. Separated, currently in the middle of a divorce, two kids, a son and a daughter. Based on the location of his current apartment, his financial situation isn't affected too negatively by the divorce at present.

Juror #9. Female. Independent small businesswoman with a shop promoting health and wellness. Married, no children. Enjoys hiking, kayaking, fine wine, and cat pictures, based on her social media accounts.

Juror #10. Female. Earned her Ph.D. in behavioral science with an emphasis on gender. She matriculated from a California university twenty-seven months earlier, spent a year teaching in Italy, worked as a visiting assistant professor at a Milwaukee college for three years, accepted a tenure-track job offer at a prominent though not Ivy League university in New England, set to begin teaching in the fall. Won her university's top grad student award for her dissertation.

Juror #11. Female. Homemaker. Married for fifty-one years, recently widowed. One daughter, deceased from ovarian cancer. Owns a Persian cat. Currently dealing with health problems, possibly cancer.

Juror #12. Male. College student set to graduate at the end of May. Very active in student groups and political causes. Parents are upper-middle-class or lower-upper-class. Journalist at multiple small local newspapers and websites. Highly vocal about his opinions on social media. Describes himself as "first and foremost an activist."

They came from twelve different Milwaukee neighborhoods, all over the city. Five were white, four were Black, one Native American, one Hispanic, and one Middle Eastern. Three were Catholic, four were Protestants of various denominations, one was Muslim, one was Jewish, one was an atheist, one was an agnostic, one was nothing in particular. Their incomes ranged from subsisting on Social Security to over three hundred thousand dollars a year, though most were on the lower end of the income spectrum. Their ages ranged from twenty-two to seventy-six, their heights from five foot three to six foot five, and I'm pretty sure they wouldn't want me talking about their weights. And due to their requests for anonymity, I'm not going to tell which juror fell into which category. But I'd be interested to hear people's best guesses.

I thought about these people, and I wondered what their reasoning had been in the jury deliberation room. Had any of them had any doubts at all about Benek's guilt? How had they felt about being jurors? What went through their minds when they found Benek guilty? Had they heard about his death? If so, how did they respond to the news? Had they thought about Benek at all after the verdict?

I thought about these questions for a few moments, and then realized that

I distracting myself from the question that was really bothering me. What did Volker plan to do now?

Chapter Four: Beyond Hats and Superglue

NERISSA

"No, Mrs. Gastrell, we've decided that Volker Berchtwelt will keep his scholarship."

She clearly did not like what I had just told her, but I didn't care.

"I doubt that the rest of the trustees will support this decision," she huffed.

"Actually, I've spoken with all the other trustees, and once they were informed of all of the facts, they agreed that Volker should stay." I quickly told her about our investigation and the exonerating information. She was not convinced.

"Benek Berchtwelt is still a convicted murderer."

"Perhaps not for long. As he died before the appeals process was completed, and in light of the new evidence, the verdict is likely to be overturned. And that, from a legal perspective, wipes out the reasons for expelling Volker. You don't want to expose the school to a lawsuit, do you? Volker's a top student, and he can't be removed from the school without grounds."

Mrs. Gastrell mumbled in what she probably hoped was an intimidating manner, and I gave her a polite smile. My lips said "have a good day," but my heart said, "screw you." I turned, flicked a thread off of my dark cherry suede power suit, and headed for the parking lot without looking back at her. Toby and Dad were waiting for me outside my car. As confident as I had been in defending Benek in front of Mrs. Gastrell, I still couldn't shake the feeling that Volker was planning something with the potential to blow up his future.

But warnings and platitudes weren't going to cool down Volker. If we were going to convince him that steps were being taken to correct the injustice against Benek, he would actually have to see the process of the justice system in action. So, once again, the Kaiming household was going to be the location of a peace summit of sorts. As this was a potentially delicate matter, Great-Uncle Harvey and Great-Aunt Yvonne had taken over the kitchen. Mom's aunt and uncle had raised her and her siblings after their parents died when Mom was in her early teens. Great-Uncle Harvey was a longtime ADA before his retirement several years earlier, Great-Aunt Yvonne was a forensic pathologist who used to work for the Milwaukee County Medical Examiner's Office, and they were both very close friends with the current DA, So Great-Uncle Harvey and Great-Aunt Yvonne were joining us at the table, along with the DA and Tatum Sangster, the prosecutor who'd handled Benek's case. Volker and Otto would be joining us as well. As this was a potentially delicate matter, Great-Uncle Harvey and Great-Aunt Yvonne had taken over the kitchen. Great-Uncle Harvey prided himself on his grilling, and he knew the DA was as partial to red meat as he was, so he was preparing a personal favorite of both of theirs—lamb chops with a mustard sauce. ADA Sangster was a vegetarian, so Great-Aunt Yvonne was making manicotti and a couple of vegetable side dishes. She kept asking Great-Uncle Harvey to taste her spring peas and turnip mash, and he kept sniping the same way he always did when she pressured him to eat vegetables, and then she brought up his cholesterol. They've had the same conversation so many times it's more banter than argument. But for some reason, their food is always better when they're arguing, so I figured it was a good sign. Meanwhile, Mom had prepared a chocolate mousse pie earlier in the day before turning to some blood tests (connected to a murder, not cholesterol), and it (the pie, not the blood tests) was waiting for us in the fridge. Actually, the blood tests were in the basement refrigerator.

Tonight, the kids and Ted, excluding Volker, were eating in another room with Rally and Mom's grandmother, as some of the dinner-table conversation was going to be a bit sensitive for young ears.

I think we managed to get the tone exactly right for the DA, though I didn't think that anything could have made Sangster happy that night. I wasn't sure what to make of her. Her pantsuit was a bit more expensive than I thought an ADA's price range could reach, but it wasn't the best quality—I could see the stitching already starting to fray—and she hadn't had it tailored to fit her perfectly. It seemed like a waste of money to me, and I couldn't understand how she didn't notice it. I tried to bring up the topic of high-quality bargain clothes shopping with her, but she was unreceptive to my conversation starters.

Great-Uncle Harvey and the DA were chatting it up and laughing, and it was obvious to everyone, including Volker, who was gripping his knife and fork a bit too tightly for my tastes, that our charm offensive was working on him. As for Tatum, she abandoned the manicotti after two bites, saying it was "too much cheese" for her, though she had seconds on the turnip mash. She'd declined the chocolate mousse pie, sniping about the amount of sugar the average American eats. From the expression on Funderburke's face when he heard her speak, I knew that if he and Sangster had ever been set up on a blind date, it wouldn't have continued past the appetizers. Anyway, she definitely wasn't Funderburke's type. She was curt and dismissive whenever we tried to speak to her before we finally gave up, and I could tell that she was chafing Funderburke, who likes his women warm and friendly.

After three helpings of the manicotti and lamb chops and a single portion each of both vegetables, the DA was in a particularly amicable mood as he ate his wedge of chocolate mousse pie and sipped his espresso. Very little of the conversation had been devoted to Benek's case. Indeed, Great-Uncle Harvey and Great-Aunt Yvonne had been the DA's main talking partners. Most of the rest of us just chatted quietly in groups of two or three, except for Tatum and Volker. Neither spoke more than a few words. Tatum just picked at her food and shot annoyed side-eye to most of the people at the table every so often, and Volker just glared at Tatum for the majority of the meal.

Right after Volker swallowed his last bite of pie, the pressure building up inside him was finally released. "So, when are you going to vacate my brother's wrongful conviction?"

I could have told him that he should have left it to my family. My great-uncle and great-aunt knew how to butter up their friends in high places. The DA trusted their judgment as friends and colleagues, and if anybody could convince him to start the process, which was likely to leave the authorities with massive quantities of egg on their faces, it was them.

"Your brother was guilty!" Tatum snapped.

Well, that tore it good and proper. The resulting verbal explosion from Volker left no eardrum unshaken, and pretty soon, we were witnessing a professional woman in her late twenties in a shouting match with a thirteen-year-old boy, with both pounding the table and using language that made us all glad that the kids were in another room. After a minute or so, it was clear that neither one was going to cool down anytime soon or listen to our entreaties, so Funderburke and I both took one of his arms and hustled him to my study. A moment later, Funderburke returned to the dining room, retrieved the rest of his pie, and then reentered my study and shut the door tightly.

Volker glared at us, not as fiercely as he had at ADA Sangster, but still pretty sharply. "Don't ask me to apologize for that."

Funderburke raised his right index finger. "Volker. There are a lot of people who deserve your rage. But don't ever disrespect the Kaimings by throwing a fit at their dinner table again."

I saw something that I chose to view as shame in Volker's eyes. There was a different tone in his voice as he reflected on his behavior. "Are you going to give ADA Sangster the same lecture?" Volker asked.

"I have a feeling she's going to get a comparable dressing-down from someone else," I told him. "You don't yell like that in front of your boss without repercussions."

Funderburke sighed. "Nerissa, I know you don't like it when I'm cynical, but I believe she's reasonably well-connected. Without indulging in unfounded speculation, her parents have been known to cut substantial checks to a bunch of local political campaigns."

I pondered this for a moment. Her family had money. That could explain the pricey clothes, but I wondered why she had a lack of sartorial discernment. Before I could mull on this subject much longer, Funderburke continued. "I think that she may be afforded a certain degree of leniency that people of less adroitly-positioned backgrounds would not be able to exploit."

Volker mulled over this for a few seconds and then slammed his little fist upon my desk. "Did that help? Do you think beating up my chair will help you feel better?" I quipped.

"I'm just so angry," he muttered.

"And you have every right to be," Funderburke replied, "but you have to find constructive ways of dealing with it. When I was a little older than you, I started taking up swimming. The physical activity helped me release a lot of frustration."

"Didn't you just say that I had to find a constructive way of releasing the anger?" Volker asked. "How the hell is splashing water in a pool going to be constructive? How is the backstroke going to make the world a better place? This whole system is messed up, and if I don't step up and make it right, I'll be betraying my brother. I need to make sure that nothing like this ever happens to another innocent teenager again."

"And how are you going to do that?" I asked. "Are you going go to law school, become a prosecutor, and take over the DA's office?"

"That'll take too long. I need to do something right now. In a year, everybody involved in the trial except me will forget all about him. I need to make sure the jury and prosecutor and witnesses and everybody else realize what they've done and learn a lesson that they'll remember for the rest of their lives."

When he said "the rest of their lives," I relaxed a bit, because that confirmed that he wasn't actively planning their deaths. But it wasn't clear just what he did have in mind. Before I could ask, Funderburke beat me to it and point-blank asked Volker what sort of lessons he intended to teach.

"*Matilda* lessons," Volker replied.

"What, you mean Roald Dahl?" Funderburke asked.

"That's right. That was my favorite book growing up."

"One of mine, too," I added.

"And mine," Funderburke said. "Though *The BFG* just edges out *Matilda* as my favorite Dahl novel."

"Well, if you know the book, then you know what Matilda does to teach her awful parents a lesson. When her dad's beastly to her, she puts superglue in his hat so it sticks to his head. Or she slips peroxide in his hair tonic and bleaches it. Little ways of getting back at the adults who wronged her."

Funderburke shifted from one foot to the other. "Volker, as much as I love Dahl's take on kid vigilante justice, I have to tell you, in real life, that could get you tossed into juvie lightning fast. Think about it. If you slipped superglue into ADA Sangster's three-inch high heels, and her feet got stuck, that could be considered intentional causation of bodily harm, and you could be prosecuted for it. Trust me, just because of what happened to your brother, that doesn't mean that the authorities wouldn't think twice about throwing the book at you."

"In *Matilda*, when she wants to teach her mother a lesson, she hides a talking parrot in the house and freaks out the rest of her family."

Funderburke reflected on that for a few moments. "Something like that might be okay if you didn't cross certain lines. I mean, you can't break into people's houses, and there are disturbing the peace issues and treatment of animals concerns, and I don't know how long after a trial prohibitions against intimidating a jury are—"

I don't often have to use the "warning tone" to Funderburke, but I slipped it into my voice at that moment. "Funderburke..."

Volker seemed interested. "I still have my First Amendment rights, don't I?"

"Last time I checked, this was still America," Funderburke replied.

"So what if I tell my story? Can't I just tell the truth about what happened? Can I tell as many people as possible that Benek couldn't have done it?"

Now, that was a plan I could get behind. "Yes. You can definitely explain that Benek had an alibi and that the authorities didn't listen to you. I'm just trying to think of the best way to tell your story. I've got some friends in Milwaukee's media, and they might be able to get your story out on a talk show a radio program, or a feature article on you. That would work. You have to be prepared to expect a certain level of backlash, but I think you'd be smart to approach that tactic."

Nodding, Volker gave me a little smile. "Would you help me with that? If I were to write up what really happened, would you look over my essay and help me from there?"

"Absolutely." A little alarm bell went off in my head as I said that, as I realized that I was still behind schedule on my dissertation work, and I had a veritable avalanche of term papers barreling down in my direction, plus a couple of the girls in my scholarship program needed me to help them set up restraining orders against their former partners, but I rationalized that one more item on my to-do list wouldn't break me. After all, Volker wasn't going to write a book, probably just a thousand words tops.

"Good, good." He nodded, staring out into the near-darkness outside my window. Then, the little knot in my stomach started twisting again. I know when kids are holding out on me, and Volker wasn't going to be content with a little article on page sixteen of the *Milwaukee Journal Sentinel*. He was looking for a full-court-press publicity blitzkrieg, changing hearts and minds about his brother. He probably had his eye on a streaming series based on the case, not for the money, but for justice.

And that unnerved me, because Volker was furious at the jury members who had convicted his brother without considering the possibility that the alibi he had provided was genuine. But now, he had appointed himself judge and jury against everybody who'd wronged him, and he wasn't interested in hearing any defense they might offer. A fleeting thought made me return to wondering if Volker had considered taking the job of executioner as well, but I forced that thought from my mind, because I wanted so badly to believe that violence was a line he wasn't going to cross. Vengeful mischief, maybe, but not actual bodily harm. I hoped.

At this point, Funderburke, who had taken a break from the conversation in order to devote his attention to the remains of his pie, put down his fork and moved his chair closer to Volker. My first instinct was to be a bit annoyed that my boyfriend had put dessert over trying to quell the kid's rancor, but when I saw the refreshed light in his eyes, I realized that he'd just needed a quick break to refresh his mind and clear his thoughts. I reminded myself that I should always give people who've earned my trust the benefit of the doubt.

Funderburke met Volker's gaze for five seconds before speaking in a tone so calm and reasonable that it came off as mildly forced. "Volker, if you work with us on the media campaign, we'll be with you one hundred percent all the way. But we work for your school and we have other responsibilities, both work and moral, and there are lines that not only can we not cross, but we actively have to prevent our students from crossing, as well. So, when you consider the possibility of going to war against everybody who you totally justifiably resent, you have to ask yourself this question: can you win these battles on your own? You're trying to avenge yourself against well over a dozen people, individuals who are older, wealthier, and have a great deal more to lose than you, which means they may be pretty desperate to defend what they have. Before you pick up a torch and set fire to everything you don't like, I think you have to consider just how much fuel you have in your tank. How much time and effort are you willing to put into this, and how long will this last? The kind of revenge you're looking for isn't going to happen overnight. You need to be aware of how hard and how far you'll have to push yourself, and not only will you have to plan a massive offensive, but you'll have to develop a comparably skillful defense as well. If you put superglue in someone's hat, don't be surprised if they come after you twice as hard. You're going to come across people who are desperate to protect their reputations and will not take kindly to being told that they have blood on their hands. What happens if they come after you? We've already fought off an attempt to get you expelled. That was all us; you weren't directly involved in that kerfuffle. What if they go after your grandfather? If they get him fired, what will that mean for your family's finances? What if they sue for perceived mental distress? You can't afford the legal fees; they'd take your house and your grandfather's car and kick you out onto the curb. If you take up arms against everybody you're angry at, you're one against twenty. If they want to crush you in retaliation, it's twenty against one. Don't try to win a war with peroxide and superglue when the other side is arming itself with lawyers and the power of the establishment."

From the expression on Volker's face, I could tell that he hadn't considered the possibility that the people he targeted might retaliate. Maybe he'd been watching too many television shows and movies where one character goes off on a rant to another character, rattling off a massive "Here are the reasons why you suck" speech, and the recipient of the tirade simply cringes meekly and accepts the criticism without a word of self-defense. I don't know what sort of real-world experience those screenwriters have, but based on every argument I've ever had, including two weeks earlier, when I confronted the parents of one of my scholarship students who had left her and her three siblings alone at home with no food or money while they went down to Chicago and got high, I've never known a person to just buckle under an onslaught of denunciation. It's much more likely to produce a popular obscenity or a counter-attack of equal intensity albeit lesser justification. The addict parents who abandoned their kids didn't express the slightest touch of guilt or self-reflection. They just lashed out at me, sneering at my attitude, my career choices, my daughter, my face, my clothes, and even my hair. Then and now, they saw themselves as victims, and I was an uppity lump of pond scum for getting their children put into a protective foster home. It's often the most miserable excuse for human beings that are the fiercest at defending themselves.

After a knock on my door, I called out, "Come in," and momentarily, Dad stepped into the room, shutting the door behind him.

"What's going on?" I asked.

"ADA Sangster has left. She declined our offer of leftovers to take home. The DA's still here. He's in the living room with Aunt Yvonne and Uncle Harvey, drinking coffee. They're all having a grand old time catching up. The DA is very interested in working with us to overturn Benek's conviction posthumously, though right before she headed home, ADA Sangster made it clear she is somewhat less than receptive to that proposal."

"Why not?" The fire returned to Volker's eyes.

Leaning against my bookcase, Dad explained, "ADA Sangster has a personal investment in seeing the conviction upheld. How much do you know about her personal life and family?"

"I was just talking about how her parents are well-known as donors to a bunch of prominent political causes," Funderburke replied.

"True enough. But did you know that she has political ambitions of her own?"

I shook my head, as did Funderburke. "I wasn't aware of that," he said, "but I'm not surprised."

Dad nodded. "Uncle Harvey was a career prosecutor. Tatum Sangster sees her job as a stepping stone to her preferred career in politics. There's a congressional seat opening up in the near future. She wants it."

"How do you know about this?" I asked.

"Yeh-Yeh.[1] You know what a political animal he is. He was talking with some of his friends with ties to the regional political machines, and one of the hot topics of discussion is how many people want that seat in the House of Representatives. There's Sangster, there's a former classmate of hers, there's your old pal Tyler Coquina—"

"There's no way he could ever get more than twenty people to vote for him," I shuddered, thinking of how that repellant wannabe political superstar had been rebuffed by voters so many times over the last few years.

"Well, if anybody's told him that, he didn't listen. Plus, there's that seventy-year-old alderman who believes that he deserves a place in Congress as a reward for all of the money he's funneled to his backers over the years. There's a lot of people who want to go to Washington. Based on some comments she made to Mom earlier, she has some very fierce political opinions and wants to turn them into national policy. ADA Sangster is part of a long line of young up-and-comers with the same career plan. College, law school, a job in local government, then an elected position, possibly in the state congress but preferably federal, then after a bit, a Senate seat or a governor's mansion, followed by a run for the presidency or at least the VP slot."

"Does she think that my brother's case is going to take her all the way to the White House?" Volker asked.

"At least, she believes that overturning the conviction could scuttle all of her political ambitions. Volker, I don't know if you realized it, but your brother's case became more than just an ordinary trial. ADA Sangster and her consulting team sought to turn it into the cornerstone of her public image for her political campaign. She wanted to present herself as the vanquisher of an abusive and jealous boyfriend. I would not be surprised if she had a ghostwriter and an agent lined up to turn the case into a book and then a movie, with the goal of placing herself in the central role and winning the actress playing her the Oscar. If Benek's exonerated, then ADA Sangster becomes the woman who sent an innocent teenager to be beaten, raped, and murdered in prison. Put that in the hands of an opposing political campaign, and she can say goodbye to any chance of holding elected office."

Volker mulled over this for a moment. "So what it boils down to is, she's more concerned about her own political ambitions than my brother's reputation and the integrity of the justice system?"

"Those are your words, not mine, but I'm not going to argue with you."

"Has she given any thought as to what might happen if Lada's real killer goes free and strikes again? What kind of defender of the innocent and abused will she be then?" Volker asked.

Dad sighed. "Great questions, and ones that should be directed towards her. Although I'm quite sure she won't respond well to such inquiries."

Volker swore, and when I chastised him, he didn't respond. After a bit of prodding, he very quietly asked, "Could I be alone for a while, please?"

We agreed and left him in my study. As soon as the door was shut, I asked Dad, "But the exoneration process is going to continue, isn't it?"

"Considering how convinced the DA was when Uncle Harvey and Aunt Yvonne explained your findings, I'm sure it will. But if there's any way the ADA can throw a monkey wrench into the process, it's probably going to happen."

We crossed into the living room to see if we could have a word with the

WELL-BEHAVED CHILDREN SELDOM MAKE HISTORY

DA, only to learn that he had left a minute earlier. Great-Uncle Harvey and Great-Aunt Yvonne assured us that he was on our side now and that we had no reason to worry.

"That's good...." I stopped talking as I heard faint whimpering. "What's that? It sounds like an injured dog."

"I don't think it's an animal," Funderburke replied. "It sounds more human to me." We followed the sound into Mom and Dad's study, and after a few seconds of looking around, Funderburke and I found Toby underneath Dad's desk, holding her knees, shaking, and crying. "Toby? What's wrong?"

"I don't like it when strangers come to dinner, and I hate it when there's yelling."

Funderburke pulled a couple of tissues from the box atop Mom's desk and handed them to her. "Thanks, Dad." She started calling Funderburke "Dad" a while back. That makes me inexplicably but extremely happy.

"Don't you have algebra homework to finish? It's getting late." Toby sniffled in response to my question, but she nodded and crawled like a crab out from under the desk, wiped her eyes again, and hurried up to her room without another word.

"That was weird," I whispered to Funderburke.

"She's done that before," he told me. "Don't you remember how last month they found her in the back of the Middle School Library, curled up on an empty bottom shelf and crying?"

I was genuinely embarrassed to have only a faint memory of that. At the time, I'd been busy helping one of my scholarship girls file a restraining order against her mentally unstable ex, and I'd only heard about the incident second-hand from Funderburke, and in conjunction with a couple of other student crises, it just hadn't registered the way it ought to have. "Funderburke, I want you to answer me without any sugarcoating. Do you think that I pay too much attention to my scholarship girls and not enough to my own daughter?"

He didn't hesitate for a second. "No. You're a great mother and a devoted teacher. I think that Toby's starting to go through adolescence, so the chemicals in her brain are causing all sorts of havoc, so I think she's going to need some extra love and care in the months to come."

I mulled over that as I ran my hands through my hair. "I'm afraid she's going to grow up and resent me. It's not easy being my daughter. I hear the whispering people do behind our backs."

Funderburke took me in his arms. "Nerissa, I say this with love. Stop talking nonsense."

"She's been acting so strangely lately. Is this puberty or something else?"

"I don't know. Did you want to go up and talk with her?"

"Yes, but let me make a couple of calls first. I want to see if I can reach my friends before they go to bed." I flopped down into Dad's chair and called some reporter friends of mine, working in the local newspaper, magazine, radio, and television industries. I pitched the story of a wrongful conviction, a tragedy, and the little brother determined to prove to the world what really happened, and at the risk of sounding immodest, I think that I sold the narrative quite well. I could've gone into public relations if the thought of that career path didn't make me cringe. I didn't realize that I'd been talking to various members of the media for over forty minutes by the time I was finished. Funderburke had wandered out of the room by this time, and I soon found him in the kitchen, helping Mom and Dad with the last of the dishes. I tapped him on the shoulder as he rearranged the contents of the refrigerator, making room for all of the leftovers.

"Got enough space?" I asked.

"I do now. I told you that all those hours playing Tetris would pay off someday." He pushed a sealed container of manicotti into a slot in the front of the middle shelf, straightened up, and closed the doors. "It's getting late. I need to head back."

"Have Volker and Otto left yet?"

"No," Mom informed me. "Otto's dozing in front of the television next to Grandma. As far as I know, Volker's still in your study."

Funderburke and I walked down the corridor and opened the door, where I found Yeh-Yeh talking to Volker. "–and as long as you're careful in public, they can't prove what you're thinking in private." Yeh-Yeh didn't hear us entering the room, but Volker looked slightly alarmed when he saw us, and he gestured rather dramatically in order to silence Yeh-Yeh.

Yeh-Yeh rose from the chair with a bit of difficulty, and made a show of relying heavily on his cane as he hobbled towards the door. He always acts more decrepit than he really is when he's up to something.

"What were you two talking about?" I asked.

"Oh, just shooting the breeze." From the expressions on both of their faces, I knew that we weren't going to get a straight answer about what they'd been discussing, but I was willing to bet my clothing budget for the next month that Yeh-Yeh was providing tips for getting revenge without getting caught. Yeh-Yeh fancies himself a rabble-rouser, and ever since his retirement from teaching Global History at Cuthbertson, he's devoted an unsettling amount of spare time to voicing his grievances against people at the universities he taught at before coming to Milwaukee who he thinks held him back professionally. With an exaggerated yawn, Yeh-Yeh announced he was turning in for the night, which I knew at once was a crock. He's never in bed until two in the morning at the earliest.

Once he was out of earshot, I asked Volker, "You want to tell me what he was saying to you?"

"No."

I could've interrogated him further, but Funderburke's expression indicated that he thought further questioning would be useless, so I made the choice to let the matter drop for the night. Instead, I informed Volker that he should be prepared for some interviews with the news media the next day, right after school. His enthusiasm glowed like a thousand suns.

And the following afternoon, at three-thirty, Volker, hair freshly brushed, sat on a bench in front of the Lower School playground and answered a college pal of mine's questions in front of the camera for the evening news. I had to leave for soccer practice after that, but Funderburke stayed for the interviews with the newspaper and a local weekly magazine. Afterwards, Otto picked up Volker and drove him to a little radio station six miles from their house for a five-thirty interview.

I rejoined Funderburke in the Cuthbertson weight room after practice ended at five, and we wrapped up our workout in time to catch Volker's radio interview. As he told his story, I thought to myself, *This kid is good. He's ready for primetime.* My opinions were reinforced as I caught his interview on the ten o'clock news, and the following morning, when I read the front-page, below-the-fold newspaper article titled 13-YEAR-OLD BOY CLAIMS BROTHER WRONGLY CONVICTED, I patted myself on the back, telling myself that telling his story to the media would defuse Volker's anger.

I admit it. I was wrong.

[1] * Chinese for "paternal grandfather."

Chapter Five: You Know, I Learned Something Today...

FUNDERBURKE

If you spend any amount of time working with members of the legal profession, you'll notice that an obscenely large number of people in that field believe that they can dictate scheduling for everybody else. So when Tatum Sangster phoned me at seven-forty-five AM, while I was rushing to prepare for work, and she ordered me to, "Come to my office downtown this afternoon at four-fifteen," she seemed absolutely flabbergasted when I told her, "No, that just won't do."

"I beg your pardon?" she asked.

"I have a very busy schedule and that time does not work for me. In fact, this entire afternoon and evening are booked solid for me." Technically, I didn't have any plans that couldn't be delayed or rearranged, but I was in no mood to be amenable to her.

"Can you take off of work and stop by at ten-thirty this morning?" she asked after a few moments.

I did have that period free that day, but I wasn't going to miss *The Price is Right* for the likes of her. "Oooooh, that's not going to be manageable. But how about this? Tomorrow, I'll be at Cuthbertson late for Nerissa's soccer game. Why don't you come here at, say, six-fifteen? The game should be finished by then, unless they go into overtime."

"This can't wait!"

I savored her annoyance like chocolate ice cream. "Well, I suppose I could squeeze in time for a phone call. I think I can talk at ten tonight."

"We'll talk now."

"No, I'm getting ready for work. Send me an email at your earliest convenience, and we'll confirm a time later today." I disconnected the call in the middle of her splutter, and whistled a little bit as I buttoned up my shirt.

I ignored the two incoming calls from Sangster during my drive to work with Mrs. Zwidecker. Once she had been safely dropped off at the Lower School main door and I'd parked in the faculty lot, I ran into the headmaster's administrative assistant just as I was about to reach the main doors of the Upper School.

"Funderburke, I'm so glad I caught you," she said. "We've been getting a barrage of calls from the District Attorney's office. They want to speak to you about the Berchtwelt case."

Realizing that I could duck her calls no more, I phoned her as soon as I reached my office. In my most pleasant and melodious voice, I wished her an excellent morning and hoped that her work was going well.

She did not reciprocate my salutations. "I watched Volker Berchtwelt's interview on the news last night, and I read the newspaper article about him this morning."

"Did you listen to his radio broadcast yesterday evening?" I inquired. "It was excellent. That kid has a knack for interacting with the media."

"I thought you'd like to know that I plan to rebut Volker's allegations. There was evidence against his brother, who never made it into the courtroom for various legal reasons. Not only that, but I can prove that I gave a copy of that tape—which, incidentally, doesn't show everything that happened between Benek and Lada at that park—to Naeem Popoola. I just thought you'd like to be aware of this so you can take the opportunity to disassociate yourself with the Berchtwelts. I know that you like to attach yourself to various causes, but this one is going to backfire on you. As a professional courtesy, I'm giving you the chance to protect your reputation. Otherwise, you might have to suffer some serious embarrassment, and that would be a shame. I had an internship with your mother, and I feel like I owe some special treatment to her eldest son."

My relationship with my mother is notoriously strained, so ADA Sangster wasn't winning me over to side by name-checking her. Now, I'm always willing to admit that I may have missed something with my investigations. I was willing to concede that I might have missed something important, but I was still a complete believer in the validity of Volker's alibi, and that meant that whatever evidence might point in Benek's direction, he still was an innocent man, and certainly didn't deserve what had happened to him.

I am also fully aware of the importance of bluffing. She shouldn't have mentioned my mother's name. I learned early in life that the lawyers at my mother's law firm are trained to act like they're holding four aces when they only have a pair of deuces. There's a mantra in legal circles, "When the law is on your side, pound the law. When the facts are on your side, pound the facts. When the law and the facts are both against you, pound the table." In other words, when you're in a tough spot, make a fuss and try to intimidate the opposition. And though Nerissa is the one with a preternatural ability for sniffing out the effluence of male bovines, I wasn't about to fold before calling.

"Could you please send me copies of the information that *allegedly—*" I spaced out every syllable—"proves Benek's guilt? Also the documentation that Naeem received a copy of the security footage? If you can have a messenger run that over ASAP, I'll look over it and consult with my client."

The four-second pause confirmed my suspicions. "That's confidential information."

"No, it isn't. The defense has a right to discovery—"

"Benek is dead, and the evidence wasn't introduced in court."

"Sangster, I believe that Volker was telling the truth and not mistaken. *Ergo*, any supposed evidence against Benek is either incomplete, spurious, or misinterpreted. What have you got to lose by my scrutiny of it?"

"It's what *you* have to lose? Do you want to look like a fool?"

"I definitely don't want to look like a coward who backs down at the slightest unverified challenge."

"Then you face public humiliation. Do you think your fragile male ego can handle that?"

That clinched it for me. Sangster didn't even have two deuces. She had no matching cards. I thanked her for her concern, and asked her to let me know, and where to view her media appearances. She wished me good day in a particular terse manner, and our conversation ended on a rather ominous note, as she expressed her hope that I would find her upcoming interviews enlightening.

The more I mulled over our conversation, the surer I was that she was bluffing. Given everything that Keith had told us two nights previously, she was fighting for her political life, and I was going to view any evidence she brought up at this late date with the same scrutiny that I applied to the original case against Benek. With Benek's conviction almost guaranteed to be overturned due to the support of the DA and Benek's death before the appeals process had been exhausted, it seemed like Sangster was calculating that her best chance of protecting her reputation was to convince as many people as possible that her case against Benek had been righteous.

In the meantime, I had more pressing problems. Nerissa's birthday was coming up at the end of the month, and I didn't have a clue what I was going to get for her present.

May is a busy birthday month for the Kaimings. Keith and his grandfather share a birthday, and it's easy to buy presents for them—a gift card to the local bookstore is always appreciated. Toby's birthday a week later was only slightly more challenging—a complete series DVD boxset of a murder mystery anime that she'd been wanting to see, and after I'd done my due diligence to confirm that the show was age-appropriate for her, I managed to find a reasonably-priced all-region set on eBay that could to be shipped from Malaysia to Milwaukee within two weeks for minimal shipping fees. The elder set of triplets, a few days later, were more than satisfied with a collection of board games, puzzles, an Aerobie, and a few classic children's books. I don't profess to have a fraction of Nerissa's ability to read people with a bit of visual scrutiny and close attention to what they say, but I can tell when people are genuinely delighted to discover what's under the wrapping paper and when the "gee...*thanks*" coupled with a barely disguised grimace is a signal that you might as well have placed your hard-earned cash in an ashtray and set it on fire.

Now, Nerissa's gifts to me are usually hit-or-miss. She usually gives me two separate gifts. One is always clothing that matches her own personal style preferences rather than my own. Prior to dating Nerissa, if someone had told me that I would be the owner of a non-zero number of pairs of snakeskin slacks, I would have laughed directly in that person's face. Yet life, and my girlfriend, always find ways to surprise me. But in addition to the clothing, she invariably finds something else amazing, such as a sword from the Civil War or a signed Erle Stanley Gardner first edition. So, while I never buy Nerissa clothes, I'm often at a loss to find something that matches the quality of her better gifts. And I'm only two days older than Nerissa, so when she gives me something awesome, the pressure gets turned up to maximum level to match it.

I was scribbling out a list of Nerissa's favorite things—fashion, American history, Broadway musicals, soccer, and so forth, when my office phone rang.

"Funderburke? This is Paxton at the front desk."

"Hi! How are you?"

"Not bad. There's a guy here who wants to see you." He told me the name of my guest, and I recognized it as the real name of Juror #8, the salesman who was getting divorced.

"I'll be right over. Thanks!" As a security precaution, it isn't wise to allow a stranger to wander the halls of Cuthbertson unsupervised, so I made my way across the school as quickly as possible to greet him.

I'd only seen him in photos, so when I saw him for the first time in person, it was a bit of a shock. The pictures I'd found of Juror #8 online were almost two years old, and judging by his appearance, the last twenty-four months had been rough on him. His previously dark hair now had copious amounts of gray, with numerous silver stands crisscrossing the top of his head. He'd been reasonably thin in his photographs, but he'd dropped at least fifteen pounds and was now gaunt. Throw in some dark circles under his eyes, and this was a man who looked like he'd been under a crushing amount of stress.

We shook hands, and I tried not to recoil at how cold and clammy his palm was. We exchanged small talk as I led him back to my office, and as soon as I'd shut the door and showed him to a comfortable chair, I suggested that he tell me why he'd come for an unannounced visit.

He stammered for a bit, and after a little spluttering, he burst into a coughing fit. I handed him a can of lime seltzer water from my mini-fridge and patiently waited for him to finish.

Squeezing the empty can between his hands, he looked at me with the expression of an injured puppy. "I'm responsible for that boy's death, aren't I? I killed Benek Berchtwelt by voting "guilty.""

As my visitor provoked feelings of pity in me more than anything else, I was inclined to be delicate in my response. "Have you seen the recent news coverage about the case?"

"Yeah, I saw it on the news last night." Juror #8 tried to take another sip of seltzer, found the can was empty, and declined my offer of a second beverage. "I was flipping through channels, and I recognized Volker Berchtwelt right away. When he testified, I believed him. I told myself, "That kid's telling the truth. His brother was there with him that night."

Taking a moment to choose my words, I asked, "So if you believed his testimony, that meant that Benek had an alibi. Why didn't you vote "not guilty" then?"

"I wanted to. I tried to. But the others were so certain he did it...I...I guess I just caved."

"Are you saying it was an eleven-to-one case?" If that was so, then this guy was no Henry Fonda.

"No, there was another."

"Another person who was inclined to vote "not guilty?" Just the one?"

"Yes. Juror #11." That was the elderly widow with a Persian cat and health issues. "We both thought that Volker was a reliable witness, so we figured that was reasonable doubt."

After he stayed quiet for a little bit, I prompted him with a "But the other ten jurors were so certain of his guilt that you deferred to their opinions?'

"Yes! I tried to explain why I thought he had to be innocent, but Jurors #1 and #2 and #9 and #10 were adamant." Those were the assistant principal, the engineer, the small businesswoman, and the academic. Juror #8's voice raised to a plaintive whine. "Juror #1 kept snapping at me, saying I was being ridiculous for ignoring the forensic and other witness evidence. Juror #2 was so mean; he kept sneering and mocking me in front of everybody. And Juror #9 and #10 just sat there with their arms folded and made it clear that they were one hundred percent convinced of Benek's guilt, and no amount of discussion would make them shift an inch. I tried to tell them I thought the little brother was telling the truth, and they said I was gullible, that I was an idiot, that anybody could tell the kid was just covering up to protect his guilty brother. I held out for a while, but I just couldn't take it any longer. I started thinking they must know better than I did, so...I caved. I didn't want to convict him, but after four days, I was so tired, I just couldn't take it anymore. I changed my vote to "guilty." I was exhausted. I wanted the whole thing to be over. You understand, right?" Maybe my face didn't reassure him, because he winced and then added, "As soon as I walked out of the courthouse and onto the street after the verdict, I wanted to take back my vote. I thought that I should turn around, run back to the courtroom, and tell the judge I'd made a mistake. But I didn't. I had to go across town to my old house for my daughter's birthday. I couldn't miss that. Do you understand?"

I did. This guy was clearly wracked with guilt. He'd had a reasonable doubt regarding Benek, and he'd allowed himself to be talked into voting against his conscience. He'd been distracted by his attempts to maintain his connection with his fracturing family. So he'd been a party to a verdict he didn't believe in, because he wanted to go back to what was left of his life. Personally, I held no rancor towards the guy.

But I couldn't say the same for Volker.

"Could you please take me to Volker?" Juror #8 begged me. "I want to talk to him. I need to apologize. Maybe he'll forgive me."

I leaned forward, trying to make my expression and voice as kind as possible. "I understand your feelings, and I applaud your effort to make amends. But I don't think that you're going to be able to fix the situation. Volker's been hurt very deeply, and if you speak to him, I have my doubts that the interaction will be a healing one for you."

He stared at me for a few moments, and then burst into tears. He pressed his palms against his eyes so tightly he couldn't see me pass the tissue box towards him, and he was so distracted by his own guilt that he didn't notice as I gently prodded him with the corner of the box or heard me when I offered him tissues. Eventually, I managed to get through to him, and after some more attempts to persuade him that a face-to-face conversation might be a combustible situation, he continued to insist. Against my better judgment, I agreed, and I called the secretary at the Middle School and asked her to summon Volker to my office as soon as recess started in twenty minutes' time.

I used the waiting time to help Juror #8 pull himself together, and he used about half the tissues in the box drying his eyes. "Feeling better?" I asked once his tears had finally slowed to a trickle.

"No."

"This is about more than the trial, isn't it?" I asked him. "This divorce is taking a lot out of you, isn't it?"

The tears started again. "Uh-huh."

"Do you still have feelings for your estranged wife?"

He nodded, then grabbed another handful of tissues. "I love her so much."

"Then you don't want the divorce?"

"No. She says she's not having an affair, but she's just...bored. She says that we stopped being lovers and became friends a long time ago, and I just don't understand why she feels that way..." The sobs came more frequently and heavier, and my questions about his kids and how they were handling everything only received perfunctory responses.

He was bawling harder than ever when my phone rang. "Mr. Funder-burke?" Volker asked. "What's going on?"

I explained the situation, but before I could finish, Volker said, "I'll be there in two minutes," and slammed down the receiver without any consideration whatsoever for my eardrums.

Stepping outside my office, I closed the door behind me and waited for Volker to arrive. I didn't have long to wait. He was out of breath, and he obviously ignored the school prohibition about running in the halls.

"Let me talk to him, please."

"Volker, I need you to promise that you're going to keep your emotions under control when you talk to him. Please, don't let this turn into a screaming match."

He looked up at me for a few moments. Finally, he said, "I regret to say that, in good conscience, I cannot make that promise." As I took a moment to think about how to respond to that, Volker's face softened. "You're a great guy, Mr. Funderburke. You're looking out for me, and I appreciate that. But no good is going to come from preventing or delaying this. I've spent months thinking about what I'd say to a member of the jury, and if I don't get the chance to talk to him right now, I'm going to explode. I'm not going to punch him or throw anything at him. I'm just going to tell him how I feel. I'll try to modulate my volume, but there's only so much I can do."

I'd been there. From personal experience, I knew that telling a thirteen-year-old how to express his complex emotions is like telling a river to reverse its flow. I let him in my office, preparing for an outburst that could blow my door off its hinges.

Juror #8 was dabbing at his eyes. "Do...do you recognize me?"

"I'll never forget your face. You're a member of the jury who sent my innocent brother to prison to be raped and murdered. And now you want to talk to me?"

"I...I had to apologize. I made a mistake. I'm so sorry."

"Listen! Did you hear that?" Volker cupped a hand to his ear. "Can you hear what's happening now?"

"What? No, what is it?"

"It's a miracle! When you said "I'm so sorry," it magically made my brother Benek come back to life! He's okay! He's outside the office right now!" Volker grabbed the knob and pulled the door open. "Oh, wait. That's not true. He's not there. He's in the ground. His battered, violated corpse is stuck in a cheap box and there's a lot of dirt piled on top of it. We're never going to sit on the couch and watch TV and eat pizza together again. We're never going to play video games again, he's never going to play the sports he loved again. He's dead." Volker slammed the door shut. "And no matter how many tears you shed, no matter how many times you say sorry, nothing's going to change the fact that you didn't believe me, and by assuming I was a liar, you took my brother's freedom, and then you took his life."

"I *did* believe you!" Juror #8 stammered. "When I heard you on the stand, I knew you were telling the truth. But the others on the jury, they were the ones who didn't. They were the ones who yelled at me and mocked me and criticized me. They kept putting pressure on me until I finally broke down and voted the way they said I should. But I never thought you lied."

What followed was the kind of quiet that precedes a thunderstorm. Volker drew himself up to his full yet admittedly diminutive height, and took two slow steps towards Juror #8. "So you believed me. You knew that if I was telling the truth, that meant that Benek couldn't have done it. And you sent him up the river anyway?"

Juror #8 didn't say anything. He just managed a tiny little nod. This was the spark that set off the conflagration. "Well, that makes you worst of all, doesn't it? The other members of the jury, at least they believed in their verdict. They were wrong—as horrifically mistaken as you can possibly get—but they genuinely were convinced that Benek did it. That makes them stupid and wrongheaded and unworthy of trust and respect, but you…you didn't have the courage of your convictions. All it took was some fools sneering at you, and you folded to peer pressure. When you were placed on that jury, you accepted a sacred trust that society places upon you. You took an oath that you'd give the defendant the benefit of any reasonable doubt. YOU LIED!" Volker's voice made all the objects on my desk shake. "You took an oath to the court and any God you might believe in, and when the chips were down, your poor widdle feelings couldn't take a little criticism. The reputation and life of an innocent teenager meant *nothing* to you. All that mattered was that you got away from the big, bad bullies. No wonder your wife kicked you out. She realized she wasn't living with a man, but with a worm. A spineless, slimy worm who couldn't be trusted. She knew her kids weren't safe with an invertebrate like you—NO! Don't try to silence me!" Volker snapped at my attempts to calm him down. "I don't know why you came here. Maybe you thought you were going to get forgiveness or absolution. You're not. You're going to crawl home to whatever hole you live in, and you're going to wallow in the knowledge that you've failed as a human being, you've failed as a citizen, and there's no way you can ever make it right. It's too late. My brother's gone, and no matter what you're going through now, he had it a thousand times worse because you folded as easily as one of those dozens of tissues you're surrounded by here. So keep crying, because that's the one thing you can do right. You make me wish I believed in hell, because then you could go there. But I don't, so all I can do is hope you have some insight as to just how weak and cowardly you really are. I hope that every time you try to sleep, you have nightmares of what was done to my brother during his final moments, and you wake up alone and screaming."

With that, Volker whirled around, flung open the door, and stormed out, stomping down the corridor. I didn't think I should go after him, and I hoped that this outburst had helped him in some way.

As for Juror #8, he looked like a husk of a human being. He had stopped crying, but any trace of light had faded from his eyes. My imagination ran away from me and made me wonder if Volker's tirade had made Juror #8's soul flee his body. He said nothing to me, but he stood up with the face of a man who has lost more than he thought he had, and shuffled out of my office, providing no answer to my questions.

I didn't know what to do, so I looked up his estranged wife's phone number. When she answered my call, I briefly introduced myself and asked her, for the sake of their children and any affection she might have had for him in the past, to please do a wellness check on him, because I was concerned. I don't know what I was expecting her to be like, but she seemed very nice, and she assured me that she would check on him as soon as she got off from work.

At the start of the day, I'd expected everything to be slow and typical. After *The Price is Right*, I would've had a quick meeting with Cuthbertson's tech support over our plans to prevent a cyberattack, and after lunch, I had a study hall to proctor, but otherwise, my schedule was clear. But it's often when I expect life to be the calmest when the metaphor tornados touch down, and my phone rang moments after I finished my call with the soon-to-be-ex-Mrs. Juror #8. Mrs. Clotilde Casagrande was on the line.

"Mr. Funderburke?"

"Mrs. Casagrande? How are you?"

"Not well, but please don't ask me for details at the moment. I have a few questions for you, and I'd like you to answer them with as few words as possible, please."

"Okay…" I couldn't tell from her voice how she was feeling towards me at the moment. The terseness of her tone indicated that she was a hair's breadth away from chewing me out, but the wavering in her voice indicated that she wasn't committed to being angry.

"I received a call from the prosecutor who handled my daughter's case. Tatum Sangster. She phoned me ten minutes ago and told me that she wanted me to do a press conference with her this afternoon."

"*Told* you. Not *asked* you?"

"She…yes, I suppose "told" is the best way to describe it. She was most insistent that I stand beside her when she spoke to the media today."

"Did she tell you how to dress?"

"Well, yes, she did…Mr. Funderburke, I called to ask *you* questions."

"That's true. Please, ask them."

Mrs. Casagrande took a deep breath and asked, "Do you believe that Benek was innocent?"

"Yes."

"I hear that his brother was on the news last night. I didn't watch it. Did you know about this?"

"Yes."

"Did you help him prepare for that?"

"Yes."

"Didn't you think it would have been considerate to let me know ahead of time that you were going to tell the city that my daughter's killer is still out there?"

We had reached the point in our conversation where I needed more than a one-word answer. "Mrs. Casagrande, the last time we spoke, you told me that you did not want me to speak to you until you were ready. I was trying to respect your wishes."

"Benek is dead. You can't do him any good right now. Didn't you think it might be better to wait a while before you started shouting your theories to the world, and let grieving people have a chance to get a handle on their emotions?"

I counted to ten very rapidly in order to process my thoughts properly and find the best tone for responding to her. "Volker Berchtwelt is also grieving, Mrs. Casagrande, and he's in torment because the justice system told him he lied when he gave his brother an alibi. He's one of two people in the world who knows for an absolute fact that Benek did not take your daughter's life. The other is the real killer. And it's very possible that the person who really murdered your daughter may attack someone else. The sooner the police realize they arrested the wrong man and start looking for the real murderer, the safer Milwaukee will be. I don't think you want another parent to go through what you have endured, Mrs. Casagrande."

Several seconds passed, and then she spoke. "I told you, I haven't watched the news, and I haven't read the paper. Could you please tell me what evidence you've found that makes you take Volker's word over everything that was brought into the courtroom?"

I ran through the results of my investigation as quickly and concisely as possible. I managed to tell the whole story in just over seven minutes, and she didn't make a sound until I had finished. "Well," she finally replied. "I don't know how to respond to that right now."

"Please, take all the time you need."

She sighed again. "I never liked that woman. The prosecutor, I mean. I never got the sense she really cared about Lada. I told myself that was all for the best, that she wouldn't be bogged down by emotional issues, that she'd be able to focus on the case and get the job done. Are you quite sure that she deliberately withheld that surveillance footage from Benek's lawyer?"

"He's adamant on that point. However, ADA Sangster disputes that, and I haven't heard her side of the story yet, so I'm willing to wait until I hear what she has to say. She just called me this morning to tell me that she has evidence that brings my findings into question, but she has provided no information to substantiate her claims."

"You sound skeptical that such evidence exists."

"Well, I'm sure that she can find a couple of supposed experts who will place their hands on their hearts and swear that the bite mark evidence is good as gold, but I believe Volker, and I don't see how Benek can be anything other than innocent."

There was another long pause. Mrs. Casagrande's voice was very soft now. I knew that there was little chance of her chastising me. "I told you, I always liked Benek. At least, until…But that raises another question. Who do you think really killed her?"

I hadn't mentioned my burglar hypothesis earlier, so I explained it now.

"So that's your theory, then?" Mrs. Casagrande asked. "I suppose that's possible…"

I could tell at once that her suspicions were elsewhere. "Do you have another suspect?"

After a few moments hesitation, she told me, "I have no proof. If he's innocent, I wouldn't want him to get into trouble."

"Of course, of course," I told her, trying not to sound too anxious to hear who was at the top of her list of potential stranglers. "But just between us, if you did want someone investigated, what name would you mention, please?"

She wrestled over deciding to speak or stay silent for a while, and finally spat out the name, "Dalton Blencowe."

"I've heard of him. Your daughter dated him prior to Lucien Claverhouse, right?"

"Yes. I don't think Lucien would have done it. Not because I like him. I don't. But he never really cared about Lada. Lucien wanted a very pretty girlfriend, and once they broke up, he went straight to someone else who was easy on the eyes. She didn't mean enough to him to drive him to murder."

"But Dalton is a different matter?"

"Yes. Lada was the first serious girlfriend he ever had. And…he became obsessed. He called her a dozen times a night, but he'd want to know exactly what she was doing. He liked her to dress…a certain way when she went out with him, but he wanted her to put on baggy clothes when she was with her friends and to not wear makeup, so boys wouldn't look at her then. When she was with him, that was a different story. There were other things I won't go into now, but it finally got to be much too much, and when she broke up with him…it was incendiary. He kept pressuring her to come back to him, and thankfully, she held firm. I was proud of her for cutting all ties with Dalton. She never even looked at him again if she could help it. But…since the breakup, I saw him driving by our house really slowly, at least a couple of times a week. This was while she was dating Lucien, and while she was with Benek, as well. If I had to suggest anybody as a suspect, well…"

I provided her with profuse thanks, and asked her if she'd had any reason to suspect an adult teacher or coach at her school.

"What? Certainly not! My daughter was not the sort of girl who would do that, Mr. Funderburke."

Quickly pouring oil on the waters, I assured her, "Of course not. But that doesn't mean a creepy older man wouldn't develop his own messed-up obsession without any encouragement from her."

This appeased her. "Yes, I see your point. No, she never mentioned anything about a teacher or a coach, but one never knows with middle-aged men…"

"If you don't mind my asking, Mrs. Casagrande, have you ever dated anybody who you later suspected was using you as a means of getting to your daughter?"

"I have not dated at all since my husband died, Mr. Funderburke." There was stiffness in her tone, but no chilliness. As I rapidly weighed my options for how to best keep this conversation cordial, she asked me, "So, you're convinced that Benek was innocent?"

"I am, Mrs. Casagrande. I know what that means to you and what you've been through, and you don't deserve to go through any more agony, but I really believe that this was a miscarriage of justice."

"Very well. I shall call the prosecutor and tell her that I will not be joining her at her press conference. I'd better do that quickly, if you'll excuse me. I feel a migraine coming on, and I want to make my next call as quickly as possible. Goodbye, Mr. Funderburke."

Over lunch, I told Nerissa everything that had happened that morning. After school ended, I went down the road with the Kaiming family to the retirement home where they often attend Mass in the afternoon, and then after we returned to Cuthbertson, I hit the weight room while Nerissa coached soccer practice. I kept my eye on the television in the corner while I exercised, and towards the end of the five o'clock news broadcast, I saw Tatum Sangster's familiar face.

The coverage of her press conference was brief and heavily edited. It boiled down to three basic talking points.

1. Benek was guilty as hell.
2. An unnamed private detective was causing a lot of pain by stirring up this closed case.
3. Anybody who distrusted bite mark evidence was a fool who hated science.

I had no idea who this unnamed private detective was, but he sounded incredibly handsome to me.

As I put down the dumbbells and walked over to the elliptical machine, I wondered just how many people were watching this broadcast and believing everything that was being said. I didn't spend that much time lost in thought, because right after the commercial break, the news anchor was back with a special interview. She had moved from her desk to a small, paneled room, and she was seated in front of six people, sitting on chairs on a two-level platform, three to a row. I recognized their faces immediately, as Jurors #1, #2, #3, #4, #9, and #12. The three men were seated behind the women. Jurors #1, #2, #4, and #9 were dressed in semi-formal attire. #3 and #12 were wearing casual button-down shirts and jeans.

The news anchor turned her makeup-slathered face towards the camera and made an expression that she thought resembled a serious newsperson. Frankly, her supposedly somber and intelligent countenance didn't give me the sense that she was aspiring to be the next Walter Cronkite so much as she'd eaten too many beans and Brussels sprouts before going on the air, but perhaps my general cynicism towards the news media tainted my reaction a bit. Her turquoise eye shadow didn't do her any favors, either. I asked one of the track and field players who was standing next to the television to turn it up a bit, and turned all of my attention to the interview.

SUPPOSEDLY SERIOUS NEWS ANCHOR. Welcome back. You just saw some of the press conference held by ADA Tatum Sangster in response to the movement to overturn the conviction of convicted murderer Benek Berchtwelt, a high school student who was found guilty of the brutal murder of his girlfriend, Lada Casagrande. Casagrande had recently given birth to a baby that Berchtwelt thought was his, but DNA evidence proved that he was not the father. The prosecution argued that Berchtwelt's rage over his girlfriend cheating on him led him to become violent. The case became a *cause celebre* and invigorated local movements to battle domestic violence. Berchtwelt recently was killed in a prison fight, and now his attorney and an infamous private investigator are trying to clear his name. You've just heard ADA Sangster's explanation of why she believes the jury got the verdict right. Here now, we have six members of the jury that convicted Benek Berchtwelt, who want to explain why they believe they convicted a guilty man. Thank you all for joining us here tonight.

(General chorus of responses.) Let's start with you *(Turns to Juror #1.)* As forewoman of the jury, how certain are you that you Berchtwelt was guilty?

JUROR #1. One hundred percent.

SUPPOSEDLY SERIOUS NEWS ANCHOR. You're absolutely positive?

JUROR #1. There is no doubt in my mind that he killed that

poor girl. Over the course of the trial, I became convinced that he was an angry, violent, possessive young man who lashed out at his girlfriend because she refused to let him dominate her life. The evidence was convincing, and I looked into his eyes several times over the course of the trial. What I saw frightened me, and I don't scare easily.

SUPPOSEDLY SERIOUS NEWS ANCHOR. Hmm, very disturbing. And you, sir. *(Turns to Juror #2.)* Do you believe that you came to a just verdict?

JUROR #2. I do. It was the bite mark evidence that convinced me. I'm a practical man, I believe in science, and I thought that the bite was proof positive that Berchtwelt was not just violent, but savage, almost feral. I'm very proud that I was able to play a part in keeping a clearly psychotic young man off the streets where he couldn't harm any more innocent girls.

SUPPOSEDLY SERIOUS NEWS ANCHOR. Powerful emotions, thank you. *(Turns to JUROR #3.)* And you, sir? Do you have any doubts about your verdict?

JUROR #3. *(Tugs at his collar.)* Well...I didn't at the time, but when I read that story in the newspaper this morning, for the first time, I started to wonder. At the trial, I had no doubt at all what happened. If I got it wrong, well, I'll have to live with that for the rest of my life. But I'm not ready to flip my opinion just because of one shady P.I.'s say-so. I have to wait and see.

SUPPOSEDLY SERIOUS NEWS ANCHOR. Hmm, and for the benefit of those just turning in, it's likely that Berchtwelt's conviction will be overturned simply because he died before the appeals process finished. *(Turns to JUROR #4.)* Does that sound fair to you?

JUROR #4. Certainly not! We took a lot of time out of our busy lives to attend the trial and deliver a just verdict. Overturning it is a slap in all of our faces. It turns all of our sacrifices into a waste of effort. They should show a little decency to that girl's family and just let his conviction stand.

SUPPOSEDLY SERIOUS NEWS ANCHOR. Thank you. Strong emotions for an unusual situation. *(Turns to JUROR #9.)* What are your thoughts?

JUROR #9. I'm mad. I'm really angry that the verdict we worked so hard at reaching is being overturned. I'm a businesswoman. I lost a hundred-thousand-dollar deal because I was stuck in the jury room all that time. I'm not going to get recompensed for that. And now it's all for nothing? That's not right. I'm furious about that.

SUPPOSEDLY SERIOUS NEWS ANCHOR. It seems that a lot of you are upset by the attempt to overturn the verdict. What about you, sir? *(Turns to JUROR #12.)*

JUROR #12. Listen, our justice system is hopelessly outdated and needs serious reform. A lot of people are languishing in prison because of draconian drug laws and institutional racism that punishes some groups and gives others a slap on the wrist. We should be focusing on freeing the people who are currently in prison, rather than trying to clear the name of a guilty boy. It's just not a smart use of resources. Focus on the living, not the dead.

SUPPOSEDLY SERIOUS NEWS ANCHOR. I see. Well, thank you all for your thoughts. We've just heard the opinions of the jurors who convicted Benek Berchtwelt. Please stay tuned. Sports is up next.

I wondered if Volker was watching this. I hoped not—he was angry enough already. None of the six jurors, with the possible exception of #3, who was willing to consider the possibility of Benek's innocence, had said anything to make Volker feel the least bit sympathetic towards them. However, his use of the word "shady" didn't do anything to make me warm towards him. And I didn't know where the Supposedly Serious News Anchor got off using the word "infamous," either.

But none of this situation was really about me, and instead, I chose to focus on what this interview would mean for Volker's state of mind. I had a certain level of sympathy with the jurors. When the local government informs you that you have to put your normal life on hold and haul your rear end downtown at the crack of dawn to sit in a government building surrounded by strangers, it's certainly natural to be a bit peeved when you're told not only was it all for naught, but also that you had one job—to see that justice was done—and you failed miserably.

The million-dollar question for me was, how many members of the jury genuinely still believed that Benek was guilty, and how many were doubling down on their verdict because they couldn't handle the moral responsibility of a wrong decision and whatever culpability they bore for Benek's fate? For Volker, I was pretty sure that whichever option was closer to the truth, it didn't matter. Their names were written on his excrement list with indelible ink.

After I finished my run, I ran into Nerissa in the hall and brought her up to speed. After I cleaned up and changed, I discovered a text Volker had sent me during the news broadcast: HALF THE JURY'S ON THE NEWS RIGHT NOW. I called him immediately and told him I'd seen everything.

"Mr. Funderburke, I know you've done a lot for us and I know you don't need me putting more on your plate, but could you please come down to my house? Things are getting kind of crazy here. There are reporters, and protesters, and..." He didn't finish his thought, and even though driving across town didn't hold much attraction for me, I definitely wasn't going to say "no."

So I caught Nerissa on the way to her car and told her I'd be late for dinner that night, and luckily I thought to check the traffic on my phone, because an evening baseball game and the end of the work day meant that rush hour was worse than usual on the freeway, so I took a longer route that still saved me a lot of time that evening.

I had to park half a block from the Berchtwelt home because most of the street was filled with cars and news vans. A trio of young women who looked like college students were holding signs saying "JUSTICE FOR LADA," and a reporter I didn't recognize was standing on the sidewalk, talking into the camera about the rising controversy over the case. Another reporter I did recognize was doing the same thing from a different angle, and I briefly considered taking a circuitous route to avoid walking into the path of the cameras before deciding the heck with it—the shortest distance between two points is a straight line, and I had already gotten my exercise for the day.

The reporters asked me questions, and I answered in Latin, provoking some facial expressions that I would've liked to have photographed. I nearly tripped over the bicycle that had been padlocked to the porch, but I made it to the door with my dignity and bones intact. Otto was waiting for me, and he opened the door just wide enough to for me to slip through, grateful that I hadn't had my dinner yet. Once inside, I saw Volker and Alfie sitting on the couch and walked up to them.

Volker smiled. "Thanks for coming."

"It's all part of my job as the Student Advocate. If those reporters and protestors behave themselves, their First Amendment rights will protect them, but the moment they start trampling your lawn or your neighbors' flower beds, you can ask them to call the police."

"We're...not on the best of terms with our neighbors," Otto explained. "For obvious reasons."

"I understand. Have you had any more problems with vandalism?"

Otto sighed. "A bag of garbage was thrown on our lawn this morning. It burst all over the place. When I tried to clean it up, I lost my balance and nearly split my head open on the sidewalk. I'm all right, just mad."

From the look on Volker's face, he was equally enraged. Only Alfie looked fairly relaxed. In response to my inquiry as to what he was doing there, he explained that his mother sent him over with some of her beef stew and biscuits as a show of support. "And I wanted to come, to see if there's anything I could do to help. You know, respect Benek's memory. I've been doing what I can at school. Whenever I hear somebody gossiping, talking smack about him, I always tell them they don't know what they're talking about. That Benek was wrongly convicted, and they're smearing a really great guy."

"Are you getting any flack over standing by your friend?" I asked him.

"A little. It cost me my date to the graduation dance, but she's not worth it, anyway. Loyalty's important to me. Benny always stood up for me when other kids bullied me, and now that he's...gone, I'm doing what I can to pay him back."

"We really appreciate it," Otto informed him.

"Hey, you two are family to me. Benek was my brother, too. Not by blood, but, you know. And I've always seen you as my little brother, too, Volker."

Volker smiled. "I feel the same way. When almost all of Milwaukee turned against us, you were there, and I'm never going to forget that."

Alfie said his goodbyes, explaining that he had to get back to study for his final exams. I wished him luck as he strapped on his helmet and pulled on his cycling gloves, and Otto once again opened the door, the bare minimum possible, to allow Alfie to exit.

As soon as the door shut, Volker asked, "What did you think of the interview with the jurors?"

I took a breath to choose my words carefully, and then said, "The media was heavily biased against your brother, and if they admit they were wrong, their credibility will take a major hit. So it's in their interest to keep pressing the narrative that the jury got it right."

Volker nodded. "I agree with you." He paused. "Do you watch *South Park*?"

"No. I don't have cable."

"Well, there's a recurring gag that I think reflects my feelings right now. At the end of some episodes, one of the characters says, "You know, I learned something today," and that leads into a little speech about the moral learned from that episode's adventures. Sometimes the moral is obvious, often it's kind of twisted, or it's a parody of the traditional forced lesson tacked onto a show, and it's often told with piano music playing in the background. You don't need to know much more than that. All I'm saying is...You know, I learned something today." He took a deep breath before continuing. "Adults hate being wrong. Given the choice between admitting their terrible mistakes and the horrible consequences they have unleashed upon the world, they will double down and triple down and quadruple down on insisting that they were right, and they'll slander you if they think it'll protect their precious, precious reputations. See, doing the right thing doesn't matter. Listening to your conscience is for suckers. Morality and ethics can fall by the wayside, because there's just one thing that really matters: saving face. All six of those jurors on the news tonight, they were entrenching themselves in their cursed verdict in order to save face. And they don't deserve their dignity. They should be losing face like the Nazis at the end of *Raiders of the Lost Ark*. And since the powers at be will never so much as whisper "shame on you" in their ears, I am going to have to take matters into my own hands."

I started feeling my intestines tying themselves into a knot. "Volker, I really think you need to—"

"Don't. Just don't." He pounded his fist against the sofa cushions. "Mr. Funderburke, I really, really respect you. But you're telling me to be a good little boy and just let the system screw me over, and I know that's not really what you're saying, but it's how I'm feeling, and I've had enough. I've talked it over with Grandpa and Alfie, and they're going to help me."

"Volker, I can't—"

"I know. You have to hold onto your traditional ethics in order to keep your license. I get it. You believe the criminal justice system is flawed, but it's the only system we have, and we need to hold ourselves to the highest possible standards. But I don't believe that. I don't believe that an old man in the sky is going to punish the wicked and reward the virtuous, and I definitely don't believe that a bunch of civil servants who are worried about their pensions and future political careers can be trusted to do the right thing when it's so much easier to cover up their mistakes. Maybe I'm cynical, but nothing will change until people are shamed and forced into doing the right thing. And I'm never going to rest until everybody who bears a portion of the responsibility for Benek's death has made it right."

"Volker, I have to—"

"I'll stop you right there. I know that you have a responsibility to report any breaches of the law. So, I'm not confessing to planning anything illegal or physically harmful to anybody. They threw my brother in prison to be raped and beaten to death. I'm not going to let this happen to me. And I'm not going to put you in an ethically gray area. For all you know, I'm just going to pray for all their souls and for God to change their hearts."

I arched an eyebrow. "Even though you've made it abundantly clear that you don't believe in that at all?"

"Maybe I'm a cafeteria atheist. Every now and then I'm willing to try something I find ridiculous if there's any chance I can use it to smite my enemies. But today, something broke inside me. Here's a couple of things you don't know. Did you know they're not planning to prosecute Benek's killers? They called us today and told us that since the prison gang that did the unspeakable to him are all going to rot in jail for the rest of their lives already, they're not going to charge them. They said it would be a waste of resources."

I could see the logic in that, but I didn't approve of this pragmatism, and I said so.

"There's something else," Volker added. "My long-divorced parents, who turned us over to Grandpa long ago and abandoned us to pursue their own pleasures, are suing. They haven't seen each other in years, but a couple of slick lawyers approached them and told them they could make millions suing the state of Wisconsin over what happened to their son. They couldn't make five minutes for him when he was alive, but now that he's dead and there's money on the table, they want to stuff their wallets. They make me sick. The jury makes me sick. The prosecutor and the expert witness on bit marks, and the media and the protestors on our lawn...They all sicken me. So now, I need to make some sense out of this messed-up world."

"Volker, I can't let you destroy yourself in your search for revenge."

"You're a good guy, Mr. Funderburke, but you're not my guardian. Anyway, remember what I told you about Roald Dahl's *Matilda*. No one ever punished Matilda for spiking hair tonic with peroxide or putting superglue in hats. No one even suspected her." He smiled, and it was the most ominous grin I'd ever seen. "I'm going to follow in her footsteps."

Chapter Six: Vera Pelle is Not a Fashion Designer

NERISSA

I think that I need to make it clear that I've been heavily oversimplifying my life when I wrote this manuscript. For the purposes of brevity, Funderburke and I have largely focused on the Berchtwelt family case, and I've made a conscious decision to cut out most of the other aspects of my life that aren't germane to Volker. Discussing my research for my dissertation would be a distracting tangent, and if I were to include all the time I devote to helping my scholarship girls juggle coursework with motherhood, ignore public disapproval, and deal with deadbeat and abusive ex-boyfriends, as well as other predatory family members, this chapter alone would be half a million words long. So focus is the key here.

But I do think I need to convey just how much I had on my plate at this time, especially to describe my emotions during this busy weekend. Contrary to the impression I may have created so far, Volker was not my top priority at this time. He was not one of my ten top priorities. Between family and work issues, on an average day, I probably devoted three percent of my daily thoughts to Volker and his family drama, four percent at the most.

So to provide a more accurate picture of what life was really like, I'm going to make a reference to *The Muppet Show*. When Jim Henson and the other writers were crafting episodes of the series, they had a dictum. At the end of every show, the "final score" had to be Chaos 99, Kermit 100. Kermit would always triumph over the bedlam that the other Muppets brought to every show, but just barely, and there would always be a LOT of weirdness and pandemonium at play. Most of the time, I think my daily final score is Chaos 80, Nerissa 100.

But over the next few weeks, there were several days where I lost in a blowout. Chaos 200, Nerissa 50. Sometimes the score was even more lopsided. And even though it was in no way my fault, I felt like I had disappointed myself by failing to control the chaos properly. Funderburke sweetly told me not to be ridiculous, that I'd handled everything brilliantly. I knew he was being sincere, I just didn't agree with him. The end of the school year was a really rough patch.

Funderburke's birthday fell on a Saturday that year. He could think of no better way to enjoy the day than by sleeping through most of it. It had been a long, stressful week, and the poor lamb was only averaging seven hours of sleep a night, which is about three hours less than what he needs to function at peak condition. Incidentally, that week, I was lucky to squeeze in four and a half hours of shuteye a night. I drink a lot of coffee. So Funderburke slept until two in the afternoon and enjoyed fourteen hours of recharging, and I picked him up at two-fifteen and took him this great little gyro and falafel place for lunch—actually, breakfast, for him. Afterwards, we stopped by an arcade and played skee-ball for about twenty minutes before driving down to Sts. Crispin and Crispinian's On-the-Lake to meet the rest of the family for Saturday afternoon Mass.

As we were filing out of the church, Funderburke's uncle, Father Francis, asked Funderburke to stay behind and he'd speak to him momentarily. The rest of the family headed home while the two of us chatted in Fr. Francis' office. We were waiting for about fifteen minutes. When Fr. Francis returned, he apologized for the delay, explaining that some of his parishioners had needed to speak to him, and we assured him we didn't mind. He wished Funderburke a happy birthday and handed him a gift wrapped in blue paper. It was obviously a book, and when Funderburke said he'd open it at dinner, his uncle informed him that he wouldn't be able to attend the party, as a parishioner with longtime health problems had taken a steep downturn and was not expected to make it to morning, so as soon as we were done talking, he'd be heading to the hospice to provide some solace in the man's final hours.

"There is one rather sensitive issue that I needed to speak to you about, Isaiah," Fr. Francis told him. "It's about your mother."

Funderburke's entire body stiffened, as it often does when his mother is mentioned. The two of them had been estranged since his early adolescence as a result of her being completely hypnotized by her diabolic second husband, who had committed horrific acts and convinced her that Funderburke was responsible. Even Funderburke's innocence being incontrovertibly proven hadn't led to an apology or even an attempt at reconciliation for many years. Over the past several months, the two of them had taken baby steps towards repairing their relationship, but their detente had been hit with some major setbacks in the wake of the two of them being on opposite sides of a case. As mentioned earlier, Funderburke's mother is one of the most successful divorce lawyers in Milwaukee, and Funderburke, having endured his parents' particularly virulent divorce during his formative years (at least, the divorce of his mother and the man he thought at the time was his father), is a vocal critic of the divorce industry and a tireless proponent of the rights of children during divorces. Funderburke's mother, Michelle Lilith, represented the mother of the family, and was going for full custody and pretty much every asset of value. The father in the case had hired his own pit bull, and wanted his soon-to-be ex-wife to spend the rest of her days begging on the street, wrapping herself in used garbage bags to cover her nakedness. Both of these supposed adults had taken up with new partners. Funderburke, at the kids' request to help defuse the situation, had wound up finding evidence that the mother had lost all of her own money in a bad investment, and she and her boyfriend had cleaned out a small inheritance that the kids' late grandfather had left them, held in trust. Not only that, but Funderburke discovered that the father's new fiancée had a criminal background that meant that she should never be left around young children, or have her teaching license reinstated. Ms. Lilith had tried to protect her client from any legal repercussions, attempting to place all the blame on the boyfriend, and Funderburke was having none of it.

The end result was that instead of Ms. Lilith's law firm raking in hundreds of thousands of dollars in legal fees, they had an estate tied up in a criminal investigation, the IRS had seen fit to insert itself into the melee, assets were frozen, and all of those beautiful billable hours that were supposed to send Ms. Lilith and her colleagues to Tahiti for the winter evaporated into a valueless waste of time. So, mother and son were back on the outs, and they hadn't spoken since a particularly explosive confrontation at her office a couple of weeks earlier.

"Is she going to sue me to recoup her losses?" Funderburke asked.

"Isaiah, she's not doing well. It's obvious she's desperate if she's turning to me for help. She called me this morning and begged me to convince you to call her soon."

Funderburke's face turned to granite. "Thank you for relaying that message to me."

"Are you going to speak to her?"

"Maybe next week. Today's my birthday and I want to enjoy it."

"Isaiah…" Fr. Francis adjusted his glasses. "I'm genuinely worried about her. I've never heard her sound so despondent before."

After a few moments of wrestling with his emotions, Funderburke asked, "How's this?" and tapped out a text on his phone: SPOKE TO UNCLE FRANCIS. WILL CALL SOMETIME IN THE NEXT FEW DAYS.

"Do you promise to call her sooner rather than later?"

"Yes. I'll make that promise to you, Uncle Francis." Funderburke rose. "You'd better get to your dying parishioner. He's the one who needs immediate attention." Funderburke was about to head for the door, when, at my reminder, he tore off the wrapping to reveal a Walker Percy novel. After thanking him, the two of us headed home for his party.

The Kaiming family was all there, along with Mrs. Zwidecker and a few of our friends from Cuthbertson. Funderburke had asked for various kinds of pizza, from Milwaukee thin crust to Chicago deep dish to Detroit style, so when we arrived home we found two delivery cars blocking the driveway.

Once inside, I ran upstairs to change my clothes. I think that Funderburke has made his love for *The Price is Right* abundantly clear, but what he may be too embarrassed to admit is that he has a thing for women who dress like the models on the show, namely shiny dresses in bright colors. While rummaging through a local thrift shop the other day, I'd found a gorgeous magenta satin one-shoulder gown that shone like a gemstone. The leg slits on the side went a little higher than I liked, but after trying it on, I knew that it was meant for me, or at least, for Funderburke. When I descended the staircase and caught Funderburke's eye, I knew that the dress was worth every cent of the eighteen bucks I paid for it.

I won't go into too many details about the party. I will mention that Dad's younger brother asked to leave an hour after he arrived, and when his parents told him he needed to stay, he slipped down to the basement to be by himself. Around seven o'clock, the landline rang, and after Dad answered it, he handed the portable phone to Funderburke. "It's ADA Sangster," he informed him.

Funderburke took the call in my study, and I joined him. Putting the phone on speaker, he greeted her with an airy, "Hello, Tatum. Have you called to wish me a happy birthday?"

"I had no idea it was your birthday," she replied. I expected at least a perfunctory well-wishing after that, but she immediately segued into the reason for her call. "You haven't been answering your phone."

"I'm enjoying the evening with friends and family and unlike some people, I prefer to keep my electronic devices off when I'm trying to spend time with people I care about, and I'd like to get back to them, please."

"You need to come to the Eternal Rest Cemetery immediately," Sangster said.

"No, I don't."

"I beg your pardon?"

"As I have already informed you, I am not at your beck and call. If I want to spend the evening eating pizza with people whose company I enjoy, I will not interrupt the gathering to cater to your whims. Unless you have a court order, you cannot compel me to travel halfway across town–"

114

"Your little client Volker is going to be arrested," she informed him.

"On what charge?"

"Vandalism. Take a look at your phone."

Funderburke did so, and he showed me a photograph that had been texted to him. It was a picture of the gravestone of Juror #7, the supermarket stocker who'd been killed in a tragic accident. Underneath her name and date of birth and death, there was a square brass plaque that obviously hadn't been part of the original design of the headstone. It read:

SHE SENT AN INNOCENT MAN, BENEK BERCHTWELT, TO HIS DEATH.

HE SUFFERED HORRIBLY DUE TO HER FAILURE AS A JUROR.

MAY SHE REST IN TORMENT.

"Do you see that?" Sangster asked.

"I do."

"That was glued on with powerful epoxy. It can't be removed without damaging the headstone. Her mother is extremely distressed over this. If Volker apologizes, I might be persuaded to ask the judge to—"

"Did anybody see him paste this plaque onto the headstone?" Funderburke asked. After a few moments, Funderburke replied, "From your silence, I'm going to guess that you have no witnesses. He didn't engrave the metal himself. Do you have any idea who prepared that plaque? Because I should tell you, those things aren't cheap, and the Berchtwelts are very short of money. They barely have enough to keep the lights on and the refrigerator stocked. So I'd like to know where you think Volker got the cash to pay for it, and the glue for that matter. If you have anything other than wild accusations—"

"Name one other person who could have done this!" she snapped.

"I don't have to. That is not my responsibility. If you're going to file charges, the Constitution of the United States of America requires—"

"Don't lecture me about the Constitution, you washout lawyer!"

115

"We'll discuss your poor choice of words another day. Bottom line, do you have a single atom of hard evidence that can tie Volker to this plaque? No? If and when you do, call me. Until then, I'm going back to my pizza before it gets cold." With that, he disconnected the call. "Another slice, and then I'll call Volker," he informed me. He had two before picking up his phone again.

When he finally reached Volker, the kid's voice was all saccharine innocence. "Dear me," Volker said. "Who on earth would have done such a thing?"

"Are you saying you have no knowledge about this?" Funderburke asked.

"Why would you think I did?" It was obvious that Volker was evading the question, but neither of us felt like calling him out at that moment.

"Have the police come to question you?"

"No, Mr. Funderburke. Should I expect them?"

"Probably. If they do—"

"I'll invoke my right to remain silent. They won't even be allowed inside the house without a warrant. I'll refer them to you. Sound good?" Funderburke agreed, and Volker wished him a happy birthday before hanging up the phone.

"Of course he did it," I told Funderburke.

"We don't know that."

"He's the one who talked about getting revenge with super glue."

"Only with hats. He never said anything about defacing a gravestone."

"Funderburke, do you really think anybody else would have done this?"

He sighed. "I'll admit that he has to be at the top of the suspect list. But let's consider all the possibilities here. What if someone wanted to discredit him?"

"Why would someone do that?"

"Perhaps Sangster thinks that's the key to protecting her political career? Maybe the bean counters in the local government decided that they'd frame him, and offer to drop the charges if the Berchtwelt family withdrew the pending lawsuit?"

I hadn't thought of those possibilities. I didn't particularly believe in them, but Funderburke had provided me with reasonable doubt. Reasonable-ish doubt, at least.

It's possible that I could have simply shoved the matter out of my mind and resumed celebrating Funderburke's birthday. But a nagging thought prevented me from relaxing: *If Volker was involved in vandalizing the gravestone, then it wasn't going to stop there. After all, why target the one juror who's beyond all guilt?*

I also was a little concerned about Funderburke's cavalier attitude towards the possibility of Volker being involved in the vandalism. I knew that part of it was due to the fact that he was talking to ADA Sangster—she'd tried to get high-handed with him, and he'd balked. But I'd seen a few of those lawful/neutral/chaotic good/evil memes lately, and they'd made me think about where my family members fell on that alignment. Mom and Dad are really straitlaced and pretty rigid in their moral codes. I'd rank them as Lawful Good. Given my feelings regarding helping girls in situations similar to mine while flaunting conventions I think are stupid, I'd call myself Neutral Good.

But more and more, I have the feeling that Funderburke could be classified as Chaotic Good. He listens to the dictates of his conscience and he doesn't give a toss for anybody who disagrees with him, and he has no patience for anybody who might try to rein in his exuberance for people he feels are causing harm to others. Honestly, his moral compass is one of the attributes that I find most attractive about him, but I had the sense that if Volker launched a full-scale campaign of revenge, Funderburke would be rooting for him. He wouldn't actually help him glue plaques to gravestones or anything like that, but he would do everything in his power to shield Volker from the consequences of his actions, much like he had on the phone a few minutes earlier.

My mind was distracted the rest of the evening. The guests were all gone by nine, and even though many of them had taken food home with them, there was still enough pizza in the refrigerator to cover the next night's dinner. I'd left my own phone in my room, as my new dress didn't have any pockets, but when I checked it, I found a message from ADA Sangster, saying, PERHAPS YOU SHOULD TELL YOUR BOYFRIEND TO REIN

IN HIS CLIENT. Attached to the text were a couple of links to a website that printed crowd-sourced reviews, and clicking on the first link led me to a review page that I quickly realized was for Juror #3's home remodeling company. The second review page was for Juror #9's business, addressing her organic baked goods and sustainable foods and ethically made beauty products.

Both websites had been inundated with one-star reviews. In the past several hours, users had written brief yet devastating takedowns of both businesses. Juror #3's remodeling company was accused of failing to show up when they promised, of performing shoddy work where tiles fell off the walls, pipes sprung leaks, new paneling developed mold within weeks, and electronics and jewelry disappeared mysteriously from homes where his team worked. In a similar vein, Juror #9's business was accused of being neither as healthy nor as conducive to promoting wellness as Juror #9 wished her clients to believe. The lotions and soaps were accused of provoking allergic reactions, the food was not only said to be unpalatable, but also not truly organic, according to a user describing herself as a former employee turned whistleblower. Furthermore, various forms of vermin were reportedly seen scuttling around the shop, and three of the store's patrons had bitten into muffins or rolls and found repulsive surprises inside.

As all of the negative reviews had appeared in such a brief time frame, it seemed fairly obvious that this was not the result of years of terrible service, but instead was a recent and well-coordinated effort to bombard these companies with negative publicity. And though I didn't have any evidence to support this conclusion, I couldn't help but concur with ADA Sangster and place Volker at the top of my list of suspects for who was behind this.

I showed all of this to Funderburke, and though he didn't say anything, it was clear by his facial expressions that he was certain that Volker was the mastermind behind this review bombing, but he wasn't going to express these opinions.

"How do you think we should proceed?" I asked.

He sighed, started to say something, and then changed his mind, took a few moments to compose his thoughts, and then said. "I say we wait until tomorrow to address the situation. I'm having a nice birthday and I think that I deserve a little time off. I'm just going to go home, read a little bit, and get a solid night's rest."

Normally, I never put off until tomorrow what I can do today, because otherwise, the pending task looms in my mind and leaves me incapable of enjoying the moment, but I saw the justice in his remark, and I decided to let the matter rest. Volker ought to be in bed anyway. It wasn't the duty of a teacher to wake up a thirteen-year-old student on a Saturday night and chastise him for seeking revenge.

I did, however, wonder how ADA Sangster had learned about the online review bombing. The defaced gravestone might have been in some police report that made its way to her desk, but a bunch of negative comments on a random corner of the Internet weren't likely to have come to her attention unaided.

I didn't know, but I theorized. At first, I wondered if Volker somehow told her, probably anonymously, because he wanted her to know what he was doing. Then I realized that one of the jurors targeted by the review bombing had probably called ADA Sangster to complain.

Funderburke loaded his presents into his car, mostly books and gift cards. I carried the presents I gave him. "Do you like your gifts?" I asked.

"The dinosaur egg is amazing!" His face lit up like the Las Vegas Strip. I'd spent the last month looking for something cool for him, and finally, I'd seen an article describing the recently acquired items at a shop in Cedarburg. One of them was a fossilized dinosaur egg in a little wood and glass case. It seemed unusual and interesting, which is right up Funderburke's alley.

"How about your second present?" His face fell at my question. I don't know why I asked. I knew that he never responds well to new clothes, especially those that I select for him because they match my own personal style preferences. I'm always poring over discount clothing websites, and when I saw a black lambskin business suit for sale in Funderburke's size for thirty-nine dollars, I couldn't resist buying it for him, even though I knew deep in my heart that it would take all of my feminine wiles—and by "wiles," I mean "nagging"—to get him to wear it, knowing that the only reason

119

why he'd put it on would be to please me, and I loved him for constantly humoring my whims.

"Promise me you'll wear it for my birthday Monday?"

He gave his word, and we kissed good night. Before I went back inside the house, I did a little walk around his car—which was far from new—and mimicked a *Price is Right* model's gestures as I did so. Funderburke seemed to appreciate my little performance.

The next morning, after the family went to Sunday morning Mass, we were back home and finishing a breakfast of scrambled eggs, waffles, and fruit salad, when Funderburke's phone rang. He followed the family rule about not answering it during mealtimes, but several minutes later, after we'd cleared the table, he checked his voicemail.

"That was ADA Sangster again. She says that a few of the jurors want to talk to me."

"About what?"

"She claims that Volker's allegedly been harassing them. At least, that's what she says. She didn't provide me with any evidence."

I had hoped to spend the afternoon grading quizzes, but Volker's crusade to make the people who had wronged him pay took precedence. Sangster had provided him with the contact information for three of the jurors, and Funderburke called them and made appointments to talk to them over the next few hours.

Juror #11 was the first person on our schedule. After a twenty-five-minute drive to a medium-priced hospice care facility, we were shown inside and led down a corridor lit with harsh fluorescent light until we reached Juror #11's room.

It was clear at a glance that she was a seriously ill woman. Her emaciated frame and the turban around her head were clear signs that she was fighting a particularly nasty battle with cancer. Juror #11 greeted us warmly, and asked us to sit in two scuffed plastic chairs that were placed beside her hospital bed.

"Thank you for coming," she said in a raspy croak.

"Of course," I said. "Do you need anything before we talk?'"

"Water, please." I picked up a carafe from the bedside table, and Funder-burke handed me a glass from the tray covering her lap and handed it to me. After I filled the glass, I handed it to Juror #11, who had difficulty holding it. Funderburke helped her take a few sips, and once she had rehydrated, she turned to us.

"So decent of you two to come to me," she whispered. A little water dribbled down her chin. Funderburke plucked a tissue from a box on the table next to her and gently wiped her face. Thanking him, she informed us, "I have a wide range in my quality of life. Just yesterday, I was able to drive down the street to meet a friend for coffee. I must have used up all my energy, because I can't even stand up today." After coughing heavily, she continued. "I doubt I'll be able to speak for very long, so I hope you'll understand if I make this as quick as possible. I hope you won't resent me too much for making you come all this way for a five-minute conversation." Another cough, this one sharper and more guttural than the last. "I should have just spoken to you over the phone. Selfish of me, really. I don't get many visitors, and I do like talking to people face to face. The nurses here mean well, but they're overworked and understaffed, and they haven't got the energy for a proper conversation." She sighed. "Neither do I, much as I hate to admit it."

We hastened to reassure her that we didn't mind coming to visit her, and she waved away our words before informing us that she'd best get to the point. "The woman who prosecuted the case called me. She told me that the boy—the little brother of the young man we convicted—was clearly deranged, that he was going after the members of the jury, trying to punish them for sending his brother to prison." More coughing. "I told her that there was very little he could do to me to make my life any worse. She didn't seem to like that response, and she told me I should call her if he tried anything. She mentioned you, and I asked her to pass on my contact information to you. I wanted a few words." At her request, we provided her with more water. Thanking us, she continued. "I saw some of my fellow jurors on the news the other night. They seemed so certain about that young man's guilt. Not all of them were that positive during deliberations."

"They weren't?" I asked.

"Well, Jurors #1 and #2 were adamant. So was #4. They were convinced of his guilt from the beginning. But #3 and #9 weren't. They were rather on the fence, because they thought that the boy was believable when he alibied his brother. But #1 and #2 snapped and sneered at them, and they changed their tune fairly quickly. It was the same with me." She coughed again. "I thought that the little brother was telling the truth. But I also thought that the witnesses who said the defendant was at the scene of the crime on the night of the murder were also honest people. That was rather a dilemma. So I accepted the forensic evidence and decided that the little boy must have been mistaken somehow. That was stupid of me. But I wasn't at my best. I was quite functional then, even though I had a round of treatment right before the trial. So I had chemo brain. I suppose I didn't process the information correctly. Because I've been thinking about it. I've read the newspaper reports, and now I believe I made a terrible mistake. Do you think that?"

I didn't know how to respond. The thought of adding to this woman's suffering was repugnant to me. Funderburke, though, didn't seem to have any reservations about speaking his mind. "Yes." There was no aggressiveness or condemnation in that single syllable. Just a simple statement that he believed she'd played a role in convicting an innocent man.

Juror #11 nodded. "I should have followed my instincts. My intuition told me that young man didn't do it. But I didn't trust my gut, I just folded to the opinions of the others. And that was very weak of me." She lifted her bony arms a few inches. "I haven't much strength. I was doing so well for a while, but the day after we delivered our verdict I took a downturn. I wonder if God was punishing me for that."

We didn't answer, not knowing how to respond. She continued. "Please, do me a favor. Bring that boy to me. I need to apologize to him. If he wants revenge against me, I'll let him do whatever he wants. If I have to take a little more pain, it'll be worth it to alleviate his." She sank back and groaned. "Please, ring for the nurse. I'm going to have to stop talking. I'm utterly exhausted. Thank you for coming."

Once the nurse arrived, we said our goodbyes and made our way back to the car. "Poor woman," I mumbled.

"Well, if anybody might provoke feelings of sympathy in Volker, she might," Funderburke replied.

We didn't have much appetite for conversation, so the car was silent for nearly half an hour until we made it to a little restaurant on the northwest side of the city. This was the workplace of Juror #5. We'd made an appointment to see her during her break, and we were right on time.

The restaurant was a greasy spoon, a tiny hole in the wall between a bric-a-brac shop and a laundromat. The sign told us to seat ourselves. There were only six other patrons there, so we milled around until we found the cleanest booth. The lighting was poor, and when I mentioned this to Funderburke, he whispered in my ear and suggested that perhaps it was so the customers couldn't get a clear look at their food. I took a glance at the menu, but I didn't pick it up because each of the battered menus in their plastic folders appeared to be spattered with chili or maybe spaghetti sauce. At least, I hoped it was food. After a few moments, a waitress stumbled up to us.

"Are you the Funderburkes?"

"I'm Isaiah Funderburke. This is my girlfriend and investigative partner Nerissa Kaiming."

She identified herself as Juror #5, and asked us if we'd be willing to wait for a few minutes, because the other waitress who was supposed to be on duty was running late. Suggesting that we ought to place an order in case her manager came by, Funderburke asked for a cup of their chicken noodle soup and I ordered a side salad.

They arrived a few minutes later, but we wished they hadn't. The salad had that sickly smell that comes when lettuce is left in a plastic bag for several days too long, and I wasn't sure that it had been washed. As for the soup, the color of the broth wasn't the traditional golden shade associated with chicken. It was more of a pale chartreuse, and after just one spoonful, Funderburke shuddered and pushed the bowl to the far end of the table.

My phone chimed, and when I checked my texts, I saw it was one of my students. Her mother had overdosed again, she and her siblings were now in the E.R. waiting area, and she was asking for an extension on all of her work due Monday. I immediately offered her all the time she needed, and asked if she needed me to come over to provide moral support. Two minutes later, she wrote back to thank me, but she assured me that she and her family were fine for now…although if the situation worsened, she would definitely take me up on my offer.

Before I could tell Funderburke about who had been texting, Juror #5 rushed back to our booth, motioned to ask me to slide over, and sat down, looking around nervously.

"I only have a few minutes. My supervisor just ducked out to buy more cigarettes, and the other waitress can handle the customers." There was a sheaf of papers underneath her arm. "Please, look at these."

We both took a flier. At the top was a picture of Juror #5. It was a very poor photograph, and I wondered if somehow whoever'd created this flier had used the image on her driver's license. Underneath were the words:

THIS WOMAN HAS BLOOD ON HER HANDS!
SHE WAS A JUROR IN THE BENEK BERRCHTWELT TRIAL
SHE SENT AN INNOCENT MAN TO BE RAPED AND
MURDERED.
DO YOU WANT YOUR FOOD SERVED BY SOMEONE
WITH BLOODY HANDS?
<u>**SHAME ON HER!!!**</u>

After we'd finished reading, Funderburke and I locked eyes. "Where did you find these?" I asked.

"They were in the menus. This morning, I handed them out to the customers, and I started getting funny looks. I didn't look inside, so it wasn't until an hour after we opened, when I dropped a menu and the flyer fell out, that I knew what was going on. I didn't receive a single tip during that time, and I *need* gratuities." Her eyes brimmed with tears. "I know what's going on. The prosecutor called me recently and explained that that boy, what is it…Polker?"

"Volker," I corrected.

"Oh. I know he blames me for voting guilty. The guy I convicted, was he really innocent?"

Funderburke nodded. "The evidence strongly suggests that was the case."

Juror #5 sagged. "This is a nightmare. I didn't want to be on that jury, you know."

"Plenty of people don't," Funderburke replied, matter-of-factly and not in a snarky manner.

"Yes, but I actually *couldn't afford* to have jury duty," she moaned. "I'm a single mom. My kids are eight and ten. They both have special needs. Their father ran off halfway across the country, I haven't seen him or received a dime in child support for years. We live in a studio apartment above my sister's garage, I can't afford a car. I work at this crummy restaurant feeding people slop—" An elderly man at the table a few feet from us, who was picking at a plate of pallid-looking French toast, looked up at her with a shocked expression, as if he wasn't able to tell for himself how poorly prepared his meal was. "—because I need to work at a place within walking distance from my apartment, where I can hurry back home to meet my kids as soon as they're done with school. This is the only place that has a shift that matches school hours. My sister's home from work on Sundays; she can watch the kids today so I can work a double shift, just to make enough money to keep us going. If I'm really nice to the customers, I can make just enough in tips to make ends meet. I have twenty-four dollars in an envelope at home. That's all my savings. If I get sick and have to stay home from work, I don't get paid. I'm one bout of flu from being wiped out. And I can't get a better job because I never graduated from high school. I dropped out in the middle of my junior year, so not many places will hire me because I have no skills. And when I got that summons for jury duty…."

Her shoulders sagged and she grabbed a napkin from the dispenser on the table and dabbed her eyes. "I begged the judge to excuse me from jury duty, but nothing I could say made a difference. Do you know how much you make as a juror in Milwaukee?"

Funderburke nodded. "Eight dollars for a morning shift, and the same for the afternoon. Plus nine dollars a day to cover travel expenses."

"Exactly. Even if I didn't have to pay for bus fare, I'd be making less than a quarter of what I make on an average day. It would have been bad enough if I'd only have to show up and wait at the courthouse, like I did the last time I was called up. But then I was seated on the jury, and it lasted so long, and I had to pay for a sitter to watch the kids until my sister came home from work, and then I just had barely enough time to hug my children before I had to rush back here for a seven to ten shift, and then from eight in the morning to ten at night Saturday and Sunday, just to make enough to keep going. And do you know how I got to the courthouse? The nearest bus line is eight blocks away. Every morning I woke up at five, and I had slip out of the apartment while the kids were still sleeping, and walk the eight blocks as quickly as possible, hoping I didn't get mugged. Then I had to switch buses three times in order to make it downtown. It took two hours just to go one way. It was too much. But I know that I made a mistake. You see, I didn't think that boy did it."

"Then why did you vote guilty?" I tried not to sound critical.

"The deliberations were going for days, I had to make them end. When I started the trial, I had five hundred dollars saved up. By the third day of deliberations, it was all gone. No money coming in, and the bills piling up. Serving on the jury was bankrupting me. With the extra work hours and the worry, I was barely getting any sleep. If it had gone on just two more days, I would've been broke. I begged that juror who was holding out to change his vote to guilty so I could go back to my normal routine. You've got to understand, I was desperate. I was afraid that if I didn't end it that night, I'd be wiped out. It's not fair. You shouldn't have to be forced to serve on a jury if it's going to threaten your family's security. That's not right." She started crying again, and we handed her more napkins, which she went through at a rapid rate. They were really flimsy napkins, and they fell apart with only the slightest contact with moisture.

"Is that boy, the little brother, is he really going to try to punish me for my verdict?" she finally asked.

Funderburke and I looked at each other, wordlessly agreeing that we wouldn't say anything that might reflect badly upon Volker.

"Why would you think that?" Funderburke asked. "Because the ADA said so?"

"Well, yes. I know he's just a boy, barely a teenager, but she made it sound like he could destroy me and my children. I don't know, it doesn't make sense when I think about it, but I just…worried. Can't you tell him that I never meant to harm his brother? Please, for my children's sake, can't you convince him to leave us alone? I know he must be furious at me, but if he could only…" Her voice trailed off as her gaze hit the window. "My boss is back. I have to go." She hurried out, leaving the sodden napkins on the tabletop.

The two of us left the rest of our food untouched, and left a ten-dollar bill behind, enough to cover the snack and leave Juror #5 a couple of bucks for a tip. I figured that when we spoke to Volker about this, we needn't mention the gratuity, and Funderburke readily agreed when I suggested this point to him.

"What did you think of her?" Funderburke asked once we had climbed back inside the car.

"I felt sorry for her, and I knew that she was trying to manipulate my emotions to pity her. It worked, but that doesn't mean that my instincts weren't telling me to be suspicious of her."

"And your instincts told you what?"

I deeply appreciate how Funderburke always listens to my gut feelings and respects my reading of a situation, even though he believes in relying solely on logic and observation in order to get a read on someone's character. "My intuition raised a big red flag at the fact that she didn't explain what her kids' special needs are. I would have thought that she wouldn't have spared a single detail if she thought it would've made us feel sympathetic towards her."

"I didn't put it in the dossier because I figured the kids had nothing to do with the case and I didn't want to impose on their privacy, but they both have dyslexia and ADHD. I would not be surprised if Juror #5 has similar conditions, and assuming she never got the assistance she needed when she was supposed to be getting her education, it's more than possible that it played a factor in her dropping out of school."

"I wonder if there's some program she could take in order to get her GED," I mused. "Some program tailored specially for people with issues that might negatively impact their learning abilities."

"You're always looking for single mothers who need a little help bettering their lives with education." Funderburke's voice was warm, and I didn't need to ask for clarification to know that he meant it as a compliment.

Our third visit of the day took us into one of the rougher neighborhoods in town. Graffiti covered most surfaces. Four blocks from our destination, while we were waiting at a red light, a slight person in a ski mask rushed up to the car and attempted to pull open my passenger-side door. Thankfully, I kept it locked. Funderburke honked the horn and sent the would-be thief or carjacker running.

The house we were visiting stood out from the rest of the homes nearby. Given the size, it was more of a mansion than a mere house. It was surrounded by fifteen-foot-tall Cream City brick walls with a spiked iron gate running along the top of the wall. The only way in was through an automated entryway that opened with a goosebump-inducing creak after Funderburke spoke into an intercom, and closed the moment the back bumper of Funderburke's car had crossed the threshold. A security guard in a rumpled uniform led us up the driveway and directed us to park underneath a stone arch.

I'd done a bit of research on the mansion, and I knew that it was built over a century earlier by one of the local ice magnates who'd made his fortune running a company that cut blocks of ice from the river in winter, stored it in warehouses or underground vaults, and then sold it to people during the warmer months to keep their food cool and fresh in the precursor to the refrigerator known as an "icebox."

It was a massive, beautiful home, standing in stark contrast to the homes surrounding it, which were small, dirty, and appeared to be made of corrugated cardboard. A century earlier, this had been one of Milwaukee's more exclusive enclaves, but as the decades passed, the other half-dozen large houses surrounded had all met various ends. Three had been destroyed by a tornado, one had been reduced to ashes in a fire, and the other two had simply fallen into disrepair. These last two large houses had been lost to unpaid taxes and a delinquent mortgage, and eventually sold to a development company that promised to convert them into affordable apartments. Two weeks into the renovations, the company had been hit by a series of lawsuits, and the CEO was drawn into contentious divorce proceedings. That meant that work stopped on the partially gutted houses, and what was supposed to be a week-long break stretched out for months, and after a particularly rainy fall and blustery winter, the new owners of the property visited the once-grand houses in the spring and discovered that the workmen hadn't properly sealed up the structures from the weather, and the stripped-down manors had suffered irreversible damage. Soon afterwards, the company declared bankruptcy, the wrecked mansions were essentially abandoned, and over the years, the city had made some half-hearted attempts at tearing down the buildings and redeveloping the property, but nothing had ever come of it. Dozens of homeless people had taken up residence there, the number increasing every year in the wake of economic decline. After the midpoint of the twentieth century, the demographics and income levels of the neighborhood started changing slowly, and then quickly. Cheaply built houses replaced the destroyed mansions, and the streets that used to be lined with the homes of the city's beer brewers and business magnates were now the residences of drug dealers. The area now was one of Milwaukee's highest-crime areas, and now Juror #4's mansion had become a fortress. As we drove by, I noticed that here and there, the brick wall was scarred with damage that very likely could've been caused by bullets.

When the housekeeper answered the door and let us inside, her greeting was interrupted by the sound of three gunshots. "Hurry, get inside." We didn't need much convincing. "The neighborhood ruffians have taken to using the outer wall for target practice. Don't worry. We've never had a shot hit the house yet, but as a precaution, two years ago the windows were replaced with bullet-proof glass." For some reason, we weren't reassured.

The mansion made Downton Abbey look like a dirt-floored wooden shack. The grand staircase was gray marble, with a veritable Noah's ark of stone carvings of various animals up and down the sides. The paintings on the walls could have made the Louvre jealous. Glass cases were filled with antiquities and collections of natural items, including eggs, butterflies, and geodes. A gigantic statue of Atlas holding up the world filled the far corner. I was afraid to step on the plush carpets out of fear that my foot would sink deep into them and I'd twist an ankle extracting it. And this was just the main hall.

The housekeeper led us down a corridor into what she termed the sitting room. It was stuffed to the gills with more artwork and about fifty gold and silver clocks, ticking loudly enough to make me obsessed with my own mortality. Next to the fireplace, a woman with a facelift that cost as much as my car was wearing a simple-looking black dress that I knew was the work of a leading French fashion designer, as well as a gleaming string of perfectly-matched pearls that I knew weren't cultured, and four of her fingers were encircled by rings, each with a large solitaire diamond, ruby, emerald, and a star sapphire.

"There's no need to sit down, you won't be here long enough for that," Juror #4 informed us. That really didn't bother me. The furniture looked expensive, but far from comfortable. I was afraid that sitting on the embroidered loveseat would depreciate its value. I was even more worried about Funderburke. It was obvious, from the clenching of his jaw and the brooding in his eyes, that he had taken a virulent dislike to this woman. I've seen it before. Funderburke has nothing against people who are rolling in money. If it weren't for wealthy donors, he wouldn't have a job. He bears no ill will towards individuals who have a money bin filled with three cubic acres of cash. It's only when they have an attitude that screams "I'm better than you" with contemptuous hauteur that he becomes overwhelmed with the desire to take them down a peg or two thousand. And at this moment, Juror #4 was radiating an aura that screamed, "Bow and scrape before me, peons!"

"I received a call from that Assistant District Attorney this morning. I'll have you know that the District Attorney is a close personal friend of mine."

"Is that so? When we had dinner with him a few days ago and discussed the case, he didn't mention you." Funderburke's voice was polite, but his eyes were telling Juror #4 to go have Biblical knowledge of herself.

If she saw his attitude through the eyes that plastic surgery had left just far enough apart to be mildly unsettling, she said nothing. "She informed me that the brother of the murderer I helped convict is out for vengeance and that he'll be seeking out a way to aggravate or humiliate me."

Possibly both, I thought but restrained myself from saying.

"I did nothing wrong," she continued, "and I came to the correct verdict. However, if that boy blames me, then I haven't the time or the patience to deal with his juvenile thirst for revenge. I'm willing to offer him a modest settlement if he promises to set aside his puerile desires and leave me alone." She removed a pale blue check from underneath an ebony carving of a rhinoceros. "I believe this will be adequate." She handed the check to Funderburke, who glanced at it and showed it to me. It was for five hundred dollars.

"I'm not sure he can cash this," Funderburke informed her. "You misspelled his last name."

She waved her hand to show how little Funderburke's concerns meant to her, "This is a one-time-only offer. If he declines it, he won't get another chance. And I will not raise the amount, not by a single penny."

I could have told her she ought to have saved the ink and not bothered to write the check, but she seemed so certain a thirteen-year-old boy would leap at the chance to snatch up five Benjamins that I conserved my breath.

"Well?" Juror #4 asked. "Is it a deal?"

"I'll have to speak to my client." With startling speed, Funderburke flopped down on a sofa upholstered in gold silk, which looked like the softest seat in the room. Slipping out of his shoes, he kicked his feet up and rested them upon a teak coffee table. He whipped out his phone and called Volker, surreptitiously looking over at Juror #4 to see the expression on her face. It would have been more satisfying if her stretched skin had been capable of making more expressions.

Funderburke reached Volker fairly quickly, explained the situation, said a few quick "Mm-hmms" in response, and then wished Volker well and told him we'd visit him shortly. With an exaggerated sigh, he rose to his feet, stepped back into his shoes, and walked over to Juror #4. "My client asked me to thank you for your time and consideration, and to do this." He snatched up the check, tore it in half, tore the halves in half, repeated the process one more time, and then dropped the pieces into a cloisonné bowl. "Just so you know, even if you added three zeroes to the end of that amount, the result would've been the same."

Juror #4 stiffened, then jabbed her French-manicured thumb against the wall. What I thought was simply a little decorative rosette on the wainscoting was actually a summoning button. Within moments, the housekeeper appeared. "Show these two out," Juror #4 told her.

As the housekeeper ushered us to the door, Funderburke asked her without bothering to lower his voice. "When she was called for jury duty, did she ask you put on one of her dresses, go downtown to the courthouse, and pretend to be her?"

Much to my surprise, the housekeeper smiled. "Not this time. She ordered me to do that six years ago, when she was last called up. It didn't work out well."

As we pulled out of the gates, two men in tattered army fatigue pants whose chests were covered with enough dirt and grime that I didn't immediately realize they were shirtless jumped out, pounded on the hood of the car, and rushed past us onto the property.

"Don't get out of the car," I told him. "They're her problem."

"Wasn't going to."

We made our way across town, and arrived at Volker's house a half-hour later. Alfie's bike was once again chained to the porch, but the protesters and reporters were gone. Once Otto let us inside, we saw Volker and Alfie sitting at the kitchen table, watching an internet video on Alfie's laptop.

"This started going viral this weekend, so I thought they should see it," Alfie explained.

The video in question was a podcast that came in both video and audio formats, covering various social issues in the Milwaukee area. In the playing video, we saw Juror #2, wearing a moderate-quality suit that probably cost twice what it was worth. The tie was too light in color for the shirt, but once I redirected my focus from his wardrobe, it soon became clear that he was tripling and quadrupling down on his verdict.

"It was obvious to anybody with a clear and logical mind that Benek Berchtwelt was guilty as sin—not that I believe in sin, but you get the idea," Juror #2 said. "There was no evidence that anybody was in the house, other than the inhabitants and Berchtwelt. There was no sign of forced entry. I know that there's a silly theory out there being propagated by that ridiculous private eye for children—" I had my hand on Funderburke's arm, and I felt his muscles clench at that comment. "—but if you look at this as a rational human being rather than as some wannabe Sherlock Holmes, and did a little bit of research, like I have over the last couple of days, you'd realize that if the burglar who had been robbing that neighborhood blind over the past month or so had been jimmying open doors and breaking windows to get inside. There was no sign of that at the victim's home. She'd clearly let her murderer inside herself, which means that it was someone she knew and trusted."

Funderburke leaned forward and paused the video. "He's right, to an extent. It's true that most of the houses the burglar hit showed obvious signs of being broken into, but in at least three cases, the burglary victim simply left the door unlocked or a window open. Lada's back door was unlocked when her mother came home. It's possible that she forgot to lock it for some reason. Veteran burglars know to at least try the doorknob before smashing glass or anything like that."

I reassured him that I knew full well that he knew more about investigating a crime than Juror #2, who might be a competent engineer, but he was a rank amateur as a private investigator. I'd checked his many social media accounts, and his bio read, "Man of Science. Logical Thinker. Smarter Than You." I couldn't know for certain, but my instincts told me this guy had been bullied mercilessly in his youth, and now he was overcompensating with intellectual self-superiority.

Juror #2 spoke for another ten minutes, explaining why he was convinced of Benek's guilt. None of his points had escaped my notice or Funderburke's, but just as it was possible that Lada had left the door unlocked, Juror #2 overlooked all the possible explanations that could discredit his "only Benek could have done it" theory. But it was the oily, supercilious confidence Juror #2 exuded that made me want to punch him in the face through the laptop screen. Just as Juror #4 radiated a belief in her own predominance due to her wealth, Juror #2 created the impression that believed he was the cleverest fellow in the hemisphere by a couple of hundred IQ points. By the time the interview was finished, I couldn't tell who was angrier at Juror #2—Benek or Funderburke.

I was rather relieved that neither of them was the first to speak, otherwise my eardrums might've been damaged. Fortunately, Alfie closed his laptop and slipped it inside his backpack. "I thought you should know what he's saying about the case. I know you don't do much web surfing, especially since your Internet connection is so unreliable."

"Thank you. We appreciate that," Otto replied.

Alfie dragged his left big toe in a semicircle back and forth over the carpet. "You know, graduation is in six days. They're giving Lada an honorary posthumous high school diploma and presenting it to her mother. There's going to be a big picture of her on the stage. I asked if they might honor Benek in some way, I swear I did. I told the principal that since the conviction is being overturned, he should be treated as an innocent man and receive a similar tribute."

"Of course, they said no," Volker scoffed.

"They didn't even take a nanosecond to consider it. They said it would be...inappropriate."

"That's a stupid double standard. They were both murder victims. And Benek suffered far worse than Lada did."

I tried to speak as gently as possible. "None of what you're saying is false, Volker. But—"

"I know, I know. The politics. The public relations logistics. If they even mentioned Benek's name, there'd be an avalanche of angry parents claiming

134

that they were ruining their children's special celebration day. And Benek didn't hurt anybody. I know he didn't kill Lada. He didn't cheat on her and lie like she did to him. But he's the villain, and even if we clear his name, will they even apologize for making the wrong decision? If the real killer gets caught and convicted, are we going to get an honorary diploma? Or are they going to stick with the same old response? "We handled it right, even if it was wrong, and we're not saying it was wrong."

A few moments of silence passed, and then Alfie made his excuses and headed for the door. Picking up his cycling gear from the tabletop, he explained, "I've got my physics exam in the morning. I have to get home and do some last-minute cramming."

"You've got exams too, don't you?" I asked Volker.

"Science Monday, English Tuesday, Spanish Wednesday, Geography Thursday, Math Friday. They'll be a cakewalk. I've got straight A-pluses in all my courses except for gym."

"Well, make sure you get plenty of sleep. Keep up your streak."

"Fine. But you didn't come all this way to talk about my exams. You spoke to three of the jurors, didn't you?"

"We did."

"What did they have to say for themselves?" Volker asked as Otto locked the door behind Alfie.

Funderburke and I looked at each other, and he gave may a little nod, indicating that he thought that I should handle it. So I described our three conversations, doing my best to paint Jurors #11 and #5 in as sympathetic a light as possible without laying it on too thickly. I didn't try to do the same with #4. It wouldn't have done any good anyway.

"So, what do you want me to do?" Volker folded his eyes and a glint of adolescent defiance flashed across his eyes. "Just let it all go?"

"Who put those flyers about Juror #5 in those menus?" I asked. "Was it Alfie…" I turned to my right, "…or was it you, Otto?"

Otto tried to keep a poker face. "Why would I do something like that?"

"Volker's a capable kid, but I don't think you'd let him take a bunch of buses across town to get to the restaurant. Not in that neighborhood. And

Alfie couldn't take his bike that distance. Maybe he borrowed his parents' car, but you...you have your own automobile."

"I admit nothing," Otto said in a voice that failed to make me stop suspecting him.

"But I need to ask you, Volker, what are you going to do to a woman who has terminal cancer? Are you going to cause her more pain than the tumor? Whatever she's done, I don't think you can punish her any more than she's enduring now. And Juror #5...Well, her life's pretty crummy."

"It can get crummier. Trust me."

I didn't like the way Volker stuck out his chin when he said that. Before I could respond, Funderburke said, "But she has two children, kids who need special attention and who are living in a tiny garage apartment."

"Her sister's not going to kick her out. They're not going to be homeless."

"No, but her sister's not that comfortably off herself. She's a blackjack dealer at the Potawatomi Casino. He's a barber. They have six kids of their own, and it really helps them to get a little bit of rent from her sister. They don't want strangers living right next to the yard where their children play. And if Juror #5 loses her waitressing job, then the sister and her husband have three more dependents to feed and clothe and medicate. I know that Juror #5 played a role in what happened to Benek, but those kids didn't. They're innocent, and I don't like it when children who never harmed anybody are drawn into the line of fire because of the mistakes their parents made."

Volker was very still. "Are you saying that if I go after Juror #5 again, I'll lose your support?"

After a pause, Funderburke said, "I don't care to make ultimatums like that. I just want to tell you that I know you believe that you have the right to punish the guilty. But do you have the right to subject the innocent to friendly fire as well? Especially since you've been subjected to so much yourself?"

At least thirty seconds passed, and then Volker rose to his feet. "That's a great question." Without another word, he shuffled off to his room. Having no more to say, we wished Otto a good night and headed to my home.

When we arrived, we found an unexpected guest in the living room. It was Juror #10, the academic. After the standard introductions, she shot us a mildly aggressive look and said, "I received a very interesting phone message today. The ADA said I should talk to you, and I wanted to do it in person."

"Have you been waiting long?"

"Almost an hour. Your family was kind enough to provide me with lunch. That's the best egg salad I've ever had."

That's one of Mom's specialties. "Glad you liked it. Why didn't you text me to let you know you were here?" After a bit of checking, we discovered that after Mom and Dad gave Juror #10 my number, Juror #10 must've hit the wrong key, so the text was off by one digit and went to some stranger. We started talking and it soon became evident that she hadn't read about the evidence Funderburke had found that pointed towards Benek's exoneration, and as we told her about it, she wasn't pleased.

"Do you realize that I've written two articles about the case? They're on my perspectives as a juror and how the case embodies social diseases of domestic violence against women. Because I hear what you're saying, and I still believe that Benek Berchtwelt was guilty."

Another one, I thought, trying not to let it show in my face.

"Those articles were very well-received. And I don't appreciate your trying to clear the name of a clearly guilty and violent man, especially when it could reflect badly upon my judgment and my career. I don't blame you for doing your job for his defense, but now that he's dead…I hope that you'll let the matter rest, otherwise I might have to speak to my lawyers for defamation."

Some people quail at the merest threat of a lawsuit. Funderburke, in contrast, never backs down from a challenge. "I've read your articles, and Volker Berchtwelt was talking about comparable legal action."

"Against me? For what? Jurors are protected from repercussions over their judgments."

"To a certain extent, yes. But your articles made it clear that you believe in Benek's guilt, which means that you believe Volker was lying."

"So what?" Juror #10 was no fool, and it was obvious from the sharp change in posture that she saw where this was going.

"Well, just like you, Volker is very protective of his reputation. So think about that when you speak to your attorneys, who no doubt will bill you for your time."

Her attitude dramatically changed from twenty seconds earlier, Juror #10 rose. "I have to be going. But please, think about what I said."

"And you as well."

She picked up her purse, composed of red and black leather in a checkerboard pattern. I complimented her on it, and she replied, "Thank you. It's a Vera Pelle. I love her work." With that, she walked out of the house.

When Funderburke returned from locking the door, he asked me, "What's up? You look like something's on your mind."

"Did you hear what she said about the purse?"

"Yes, that it was a Vera Pelle."

"Vera Pelle is not a fashion designer."

"She's not?"

"No. She's not a human being, either."

Funderburke thought for a moment. "I don't know Italian, but I know enough Latin to see the root words. 'Vera' means 'truth,' like 'veritas,' right? And 'pelle,' is that like 'pelt'?"

"Exactly. 'Vera Pelle' means 'genuine leather' in Italian. It's actually a lower grade of leather. The best quality is pieno fiore, that's full grain, and cuoio di grano, top-grain, is also pretty good, but vera pelle leather is often pretty cheap and made from treated scraps."

"So she bought a low-end purse..." Funderburke's forehead scrunched. "Wait...Didn't she spend a year teaching in Italy?"

"Unless she associated only with English-speakers, I find it hard to believe that after twelve months, she wouldn't know what "vera pelle" really meant."

Neither of us were sure what to make of that.

My evening was particularly busy, so right after Funderburke and I washed the dinner dishes, I kissed him goodnight. As soon as he left, I shut myself up in my study and finished grading my fourteen remaining pre-exam review quizzes, wrote a page and a half of my dissertation, and drafted the next day's lecture. Before bed, I checked my voicemail and discovered that my student whose mother overdosed had called to let me know her mom was out of danger, but she would need extensions on all of her work. There were thirteen emails from students to answer, mostly simple questions on the homework and exams coming the following week, but another of my scholarship students informed me that her infant daughter was battling a fever, and the baby might have passed the cold onto her. I just managed to slip into my black and gold satin pajamas and get about two-thirds of the way through my regular nighttime prayers before I completely ran out of energy and collapsed.

When I woke up in the morning, I realized that I hadn't shut off my bedroom lights. A moment later, I realized that it was my birthday, and even though I'd only slept for about four hours, I was sufficiently energized to shower, do my hair and makeup, and dress in a midnight-blue silk top and ankle-length black lambskin skirt in less than half an hour. The family had a mildly rushed breakfast at the same place where we'd celebrated Adoption Day, and Dad and I and the older triplets rushed up to Cuthbertson just before the morning bell rang.

That day was way more hectic than I would have liked, but there's no need to list all of the stresses and crises that smacked me upside the head that day. Thanks to about a gallon of iced coffee and a ten-minute nap during my office hours, I made it through classes, Mass, and soccer practice without falling flat on my face, and I was sufficiently energized to wash off the sweat of my workout, redo my hair, and change into a fresh outfit for the family dinner of Caesar salad, cheese tortellini, turkey burgers, and my favorite chocolate pudding cake and frozen custard.

The party on Saturday had technically been for both of us, so it was just extended family and our neighbor Mrs. Stutschewsky, who likes living alone but hates eating by herself, so she joins us for most meals.

Funderburke arrived, with the tight-lipped smile he always has when I tell him what to wear. We have an agreement that he'll wear the outfits I buy him that mirror my own personal fashion tastes when we're at either his home or mine and no one who doesn't know us well can see him and make smart remarks. So he showed up looking sleek, dashing, and sexy in the black leather business suit I'd gifted him for his birthday, with a black silk button-down shirt open at the neck, and a facial expression that said *I must love you a lot if I'm wearing this to please you.* To quasi-match, I was wearing exactly the same outfit, only my suit was scarlet.

I informed him how handsome he looked, and Funderburke simply grunted in reply and pressed my gift into my hands. I tore off the rather asymmetrical wrapping job—Funderburke has many skills, but he's not very talented at making arts and crafts nice and neat. One time, the two of us were frosting cupcakes with the elder triplets, and while mine, forgive my bragging, were bakery quality, Funderburke's looked as if he'd attempted to apply the frosting with a blunderbuss. As he told me then and on many other occasions since, if I want someone with crafting skills, I should call Martha Stewart.

As I was savoring a few tingles of excitement before opening up the blue velvet jewelry case, a quick look of panic flashed across Funderburke's face. "Look, I ought to warn you, those aren't real diamonds. They're rhinestones."

Now, I was less excited. I flicked open the case with my thumb, to reveal a slightly oversized necklace. Even if he hadn't warned me, I would've known immediately that the several dozen gemstones weren't actual diamonds. They didn't sparkle much in the light, and the chestnut-sized centerpiece gem was obviously paste. The design seemed a little old-fashioned. I wouldn't have selected it myself, but I forced myself to give Funderburke a big smile and tell him how much I liked it.

"It's not the gems that provide the value, it's the provenance. Lift up that portion of the box, see what's underneath the necklace."

I did as he said, revealing a photograph and a folded-up piece of paper.

"That's a certificate of authenticity," he informed me.

"What? Does it confirm that they're genuine rhinestones?"

"No. It confirms that was worn by that actress you like on Broadway. In *Follies.*"

I'm a huge fan of musicals, especially Sondheim's. I recognized the woman in the photograph immediately, and confirmed with a glance that the necklace around her neck was the same one I was currently holding.

"There's this prop and costume seller online. I was worried it wouldn't get here in time, but I found it pushed through the mail slot when I got home this afternoon. I hope–" He never got the chance to finish that thought, as my lips were pressed so firmly against his.

I didn't check my watch, but the kiss probably lasted a couple of minutes. It only ended because my little sister Eleanor coughed primly behind me. "I'm going to tell Mom and Dad that you two were making out in the hall."

"Go ahead, you little tattletale," I laughed at her. Handing the necklace to Funderburke, I whirled around and asked him to place it around my neck. My mind was racing, as I had the perfect dress to wear with the necklace. Stephen Sondheim's father was a rather successful fashion designer, and I have one of his vintage gowns. The necklace would pair perfectly with it.

After another long kiss—boyfriends ought to know when they've done well—I pranced around the house, showing each family member my present.

My grandparents—Dad's parents—were uncharacteristically uninterested in my necklace. From their expressions, I figured that something was weighing on their minds. "You know, I won't enjoy my dinner if I'm worrying about what's bothering you two."

Grandma sighed. "Well, dear, it's about your uncle Kesheng."

"Key? What's wrong with him?" Key is much younger than Dad and his sister (who lives halfway across the country), being born when my grandparents were in their mid-forties. He's actually a few years younger than I am.

"You remember how he spent most of Funderburke's party in the basement two days ago? He's back there now."

"Incidents like that have been happening more often lately," Grandpa[1] added. "So we took him to a colleague of ours—" Grandma's a psychologist and Grandpa's a psychiatrist—"and she diagnosed him today."

"What was her diagnosis?" I asked.

"Asperger's Syndrome. A form of autism."

This was at a time when those terms weren't as well-known as they are now, and there were a lot of misconceptions about those diagnoses amongst the broader populace. I asked questions about it, and Grandma and Grandpa

141

explained the details to me. That's when Grandma's voice grew softer, as she was leading into something more serious she was worried about discussing. "It can run in families, though there's no consensus yet on whether there's a genetic link or not. It's possible that Keith has a much milder form of it, and I think it's very likely that Bernard has it as well. I'm going to suggest that they both be evaluated for it soon. And I wouldn't be surprised if Midge has a form of it as well. They all have several characteristics of it, though Key's condition is more severe. But the more I read up on it, the more I realize that quite a few people I know may be on the spectrum, including a lot of students at Cuthbertson. Including…" She looked up at me as if she was nervous about seeing my reaction to what she was going to say next. "Toby. I think she may have it, too."

"What?" That was much louder than I'd expected, and people from other rooms walked in to inquire. After waving them away, Grandma explained further.

"Her mannerisms, her speech patterns, the way she doesn't like being hugged, her insistence on always wearing the same sweater and sweatskirt whenever she can, her extreme interests in manga and anime…." Grandma talked for a while longer, but I didn't really hear anything she was saying. The room started spinning, and I was vaguely aware of the sensation of floating through the air. It wasn't until I was lowered onto a sofa that I realized Funderburke had picked me up like a rag doll and laid me down carefully.

"Are you all right? You were swooning and it looked like you were going to collapse."

A moment later, the three members of the family who were medical doctors rushed up and fretted over me. Funderburke brought me a glass of ice water, and I assured everybody that I was feeling fine, even though I definitely wasn't.

At dinner, everybody was raving about the food, and even though we were having some of my favorites, I didn't taste much of anything. At one point, I dragged my fork along the plate, not realizing that I'd eaten everything. I refused seconds, and I forgot to make a wish when the time came to blow out the candles on my cake.

During the post-dessert conversation that I didn't participate in, the land-line rang. Dad answered, and when he returned, he informed Funderburke it was for him. When Funderburke returned to the dining room, he said, "Please excuse me. I have to go now."

"Where are you going?" Bernard asked.

"It's my...mother. Apparently, she needs my help."

That snapped me out of my daze. "Your mom? What's so serious that it makes you so willing to speak to her again?"

"I didn't say that I was going to *talk* to her, I said she needed me to *help* her. I think I can give her the assistance she needs without actually speaking to her."

I could tell that he didn't want to say too much in front of the others, especially the kids, so I rose from the table and pulled him down the corridor into my study.

"Now that we're alone, spill it."

"She's at an expensive hotel bar downtown. Apparently, she's drunk, belligerent, and threatening to sue the bartender and the hotel if they don't keep serving her favorite expensive vodka. And she's misplaced her purse, so she can't pay for it. She informed them that her son would handle the bill and get her home safely, and fortunately for her she still had her phone in her coat pocket. She told them to make the call on the bar phone because I wouldn't answer if it was her, and to try my cell and my home phone first, and if I didn't respond, I was probably at my girlfriend's house. I don't know how she got your number."

I've been trying to promote a reconciliation between the two of them for quite some time now. A while back, I'd provided Ms. Lilith with my phone and home numbers in case she ever wanted to reach me. But I didn't feel like telling Funderburke that at the moment.

"I'll go with you."

"You can stay and enjoy your birth–"

"I need some air." I grabbed my mocha suede trench coat from the closet, handed Funderburke his walking coat, and led him out the door to his car.

Once we were on our way, he asked me, "Are you going to tell me why you've been so off for the past hour?"

I told him everything, while he drove with a concerned expression. "I can't believe it," I moaned. Why didn't I realize this?"

"You're not a trained mental health professional. Your grandparents are, but they studied long before autism was common knowledge, so they wouldn't have known what to spot either. From what I've read about it, autism spectrum disorder is a fairly new diagnosis."

"I'm always trying to help girls who are in rough situations—"

"Like you were growing up."

"But I couldn't see that my own daughter was struggling. What the hell kind of mother am I?"

"A darned great one."

"That's a nice reflective response, Funderburke, but we both know that's a crock. I had her when I was a dumb and angry kid—"

"And you made sure she wasn't raised in a dangerous situation like you were, and you got the help you needed to raise her, and then you grew up into a responsible adult who devoted her life to protecting and defending girls in similar situations."

"I spend so much time with those girls, I ignore my own daughter."

"You eat breakfast with her every morning and dinner with her every night. You drive her to school and take her home. You go to church with her multiple times a week. You raise her in an environment where she's surrounded by people who adore her. You help her with her homework, you feign interest when she drones on and on about *Death Note* and *One Piece*, you help her brush the knots out of her hair every morning, you make sure she eats well, you remind her to shower regularly, and you never hint that having her when you were barely a teenager did anything other than enhance your life and bring you joy. Now, you're a very giving person, but right now, you're going too far when you're signing up for an organ donation and offering up your own brain. It's your birthday, so I'm going to hold back on further criticisms for the time being. But after midnight, it's not your birthday anymore, so if I hear you taking shots at yourself tomorrow I'm not going to restrain myself from shouting."

I let that soak in for a moment. "The thing is, I've always known Toby was different from other girls, but I never thought she had a neurological condition that mental health professionals are only starting to explore. I just thought she was…I don't know…quirky."

"Well, there's nothing wrong with "different." She's smarter and more interesting than most of the other girls her age, and she's an all-around great kid."

"I know…but…"

"But what?"

"Look at her. She's going to be beautiful. She's just starting puberty now, with each year, she's going to get prettier and get more attention from boys. If she doesn't understand all the social cues and implications properly, who know what sort of danger she could get into? You see what I mean?"

For the first time, a bit of anxiety passed over Funderburke's face. "Well, any guys at Cuthbertson will know if that they cross a line, her stepfather will come after them. And remember, she doesn't like being touched."

"That helps. A little. But Grandma and Grandpa pointed out that Mom and Dad and Bernard might have it too. Isn't that a lot for one family?"

"You know, I vaguely remember reading somewhere that experts aren't certain, but autism can run in families. If your Dad does have a milder form of it, it makes sense that he might have picked a wife who was a lot like him mentally, and some, though not all, of their kids could be autistic as well."

"So maybe some of the younger triplets will have it, too…. I remember Mom telling me once that after getting her law degree, she decided not to become a prosecutor because courtrooms seemed overwhelming to her. And she told me something similar about hospitals, once. Could those have anything to do with autistic reactions?"

Funderburke nodded. "They might."

"But even if it runs through the Kaiming family, it's a huge coincidence that Toby has autism, too."

"Not so big a coincidence as you might think. It's not that uncommon, and besides, haven't you told me on multiple occasions that your Dad reminds you of Toby's biological paternal grandfather? Maybe he was on the spectrum as well, and passed it on to his granddaughter, and part of the reason you connected with Keith in the first place is because there were so many points of similarity with the only other positive male figure you'd ever had in your life."

"Wow. I've gotta unpack all that." I squeezed his right bicep, and we didn't say very much for a while, until we pulled into the hotel parking lot. As we walked towards the door, Funderburke stopped me.

"Wait a sec." He hurried a few yards down the lot to a steel-gray Mercedes-Benz. "This is my mother's car." He peered inside, then pulled out the little flashlight on his key chain. "She's left her purse inside." He tried the door, and when he found it locked, he pulled out his lockpicks and opened the door in less than a minute. Fortunately, it was an older model, not the kind that needed a battery-powered fob to unlock electronically. I'm sure Ms. Lilith could afford a fleet of new cars, but I suppose Funderburke's not the only one with a sentimental attachment to vehicles.

"Lucky for her you're not a burglar," I noted.

"Yeah, unlike my mother, I have principles about taking other people's money when I haven't earned it." He pulled out her purse, re-locked the door, and pushed it shut.

We rode the elevator to the hotel's top floor, and as soon as we passed through the bar's entryway we heard Ms. Lilith arguing with a bartender, threatening the hotel with a lawsuit if they didn't let her go home. Funderburke stepped forward, introduced himself, and pulled out one of his mother's credit cards.

"Where'd you find that?" Ms. Lilith slurred.

Funderburke answered her question while he filled out the charge card slip. Looking over his shoulder, I saw that he was giving the bartender a thousand percent tip. Then the bartender made a crack about Funderburke's suit, and he swiftly reduced the gratuity to a mere two hundred percent.

Ms. Lilith seemed to be under the impression that she was going to be driving herself home, and Funderburke firmly and loudly disabused her of this notion. When it soon became clear that her legs were too wobbly to walk, Funderburke scooped her up and carried her in his arms. "Don't throw up on my coat," he informed her.

In that vein, he buckled his mother into the passenger seat of her Mercedes-Benz, reasoning that if she was going to be sick, he'd rather it was in her car than his. I drove her car to her home, with Funderburke ahead of us. I kept her window open all the way. Fortunately, she held her liquor like a champ.

Once we'd arrived at her palatial house overlooking Lake Michigan, Funderburke carried her inside and set her down on the living room couch. Prudently, I retrieved a stewpot from the kitchen and laid it next to her while Funderburke pulled off her shoes and covered her with an afghan.

"Has she ever gotten drunk like this before?" I whispered in his ear.

"A couple of times, after my evil stepfather left. As far as I know, she nipped the problem in the bud."

Ms. Lilith sat up suddenly. "I haven't gotten drunk in twelve years." She turned the sentence into a single massive word.

"What happened, Mom? Did one of your clients' spouses spend all his money before you could get your hands on it?"

"No." The next words were slurred, but still intelligible. "Your brother cut off all contact with me. He's joined a cult out in Oregon. He says it's a community for recovering addicts like him, but it's a cult."

Funderburke showed no concern whatsoever. "Don't worry. My half-brother's so whiny, they'll kick him out within a week."

"And your sister got kicked out of boarding school."

Funderburke hasn't seen his much younger half-sister since she was a baby, when he was thirteen, and he moved in with his grandparents. "For what reason?"

"She stole the headmistress's car, went on a joyride with two of her friends, and when the headmistress chewed her out, she spat in her face. That's why they expelled her. I don't know what I'm going to do next."

"You'll think of something." Funderburke's face softened. He doesn't know his half-sister, but he doesn't resent her like he does his half-brother, who betrayed him by blaming Funderburke for the crimes of their stepfather. To be fair, the kid was intimidated and bullied into it, but Funderburke's still furious about the treachery.

"All my children hate me," Ms. Lilith moaned. "We used to be so close, Isaiah. Remember when you were six? We went to the grocery store, and you ran ahead of me in the cereal aisle, and when I reached down and picked up a box of my favorite granola, I found the card you'd just placed behind it. I picked it up, and you'd written "I love you, Mommy" on a sheet of construction paper and drawn dinosaurs and flowers. Remember that?" Tears were welling up in her eyes.

Funderburke kept his face impassive. "I remember."

"I still have that card, you know. I framed it, and I keep it in a drawer on my desk at work. I take it out and look at it when I need to be reminded of a time when at least one of my kids didn't despise me." Ms. Lilith hiccuped. "I hear you're squaring off against Tatum Sangster."

"Yes. She interned for you, didn't she?"

"Yeeee-ep! For about two months. Then I fired her."

This was news to us. I beat Funderburke to asking "What happened?"

"You know I hold my employees to very strict standards of professional conduct. I will not allow them to lie to me."

"That's true," Funderburke quipped. "They can drain your clients dry and traumatize the kids, but if they tell a falsehood to your face, they're dead to you."

"Sangster padded her billable hours. She may have been dedicated, but no way was she working twenty hours a day. I considered reporting her to the Bar Association, but given how prominent her parents are, I figured any attempt to punish her might rebound on me. She misrepresented on her résumé, too, you know. She said she won a bunch of awards at law school, but didn't. Stupid of her."

"Why would she do that?"

"She wanted to stand out from the other interns, I suppose. Look better in comparison. She distorted an *ex-parte* conversation with a judge one time in a different courtroom to win a case. That young woman's very ambitious, and she hates to lose."

She sank back onto the couch, and once we thought she'd fallen asleep, we started to leave. When we reached the doorway, she sat up again. "You know Jayna, the private detective at my firm? She's been trailing that fella who was on that jury. The one that comicted—" She hiccuped. "I mean, *convicted* that boy whose brother you're representing. His wife's my client."

"Juror #8?" Funderburke asked, though he used the man's real name.

"That's the one. Jayna saw him stop by a Kinko's the other day, and then he took a sheaf of flyers to this grubby-looking diner. He put fliers in the menus while the waitress was in the kitchen and didn't order anything. Apparently, he's got a grudge against the waitress, who was on the jury with him. You know why he might've done that?"

Funderburke and I said nothing, but we looked at each other with dawning comprehension. Had Juror #8 visited Volker again, asking for forgiveness? And had Volker offered him a chance at redemption, if he helped Volker with his revenge plans, and funded them, too?

If this was the case, what would Volker tell Juror #8 to do next?

---

[1] * I actually call him "Yeh-Yeh," but I'm referring to him as "Grandpa" in this context so as not to confuse him with my great-grandfather.

Chapter Seven: Disrespecting Their Authority

FUNDERBURKE

Prior to the second week of June, the people who had helped wrongly convict Benek thought Volker was either mistaken or a liar. However, as the summer months began, one by one, they all started to fear him.

One reason a lot of adults don't like kids is because they can't control them. I think that the older people get, the more most of them forget what it was like to be a child, especially the intensity of the feelings and frustrations one has when one is quite young. Personally, my early memories remain bright and fresh in my mind, even when I wish I could leave them behind and move on with my life. And I saw a lot of myself in Volker. I was angry with a lot of people at the start of adolescence, particularly my mother and stepfather, and I'm still working through those feelings. When I was Volker's age, I addressed my anger in self-destructive ways until my grandparents, uncle, and Mrs. Zwidecker banded together to provide me with better methods to help me find my way out of the labyrinth of my own emotions. I wonder what might have happened to me if I'd taken Volker's path and sought revenge against everybody who ever wronged me.

As the school year drew to a close, I didn't realize that I'd spend a lot of my summer helping to manage the three-ring circus of vengeance where Volker was playing master of ceremonies. I had hoped that the next three months would be fairly laid-back for me. Since I wasn't going to be as busy with my usual Student Advocate, substitute teaching, and investigative duties (unless a student reached out with an emergency), I planned to get at least ten hours of sleep a night. A few afternoons a week, for a little extra money, I'd help the football team and some other student-athletes train in the weight room. Since Nerissa was trying to complete the second, heavily revised draft of her dissertation, Keith was writing a book on unsolved crimes in Milwaukee, and Midge had her plate full trying to gauge the reliability of some new forensic tests, I planned to spend a lot of time looking after the kids and tutoring them. Keith and Midge had devised a bunch of summer lesson plans, and filling up the elder triplets' brains was now mostly my responsibility. In addition, I'd drawn up a reading list of fifty books I planned to read over the summer.

I did manage to complete all of my goals before school resumed at the end of August (aside from a handful of nights when my sleep wasn't quite as plentiful as I would have preferred), but I didn't have quite as much downtime as I hoped because I frequently had to rush to Volker's defense. The kid did not waste any time. The first day of summer vacation, he launched his all-out attack on everybody on his excrement list.

As the glorious days of summer break began, a young activist's thoughts turned to social change. This was the case of the freshly graduated Juror #12, who had matriculated from college with a 2.8 GPA and an inflated sense of the importance he played in making the world a better place. He moved out of the dorm and into a small apartment with three of his similarly-minded friends, making his money by continuing his reporting jobs at local websites and niche newspapers. Upon inquiry, I learned that most of these writing gigs paid between twenty and fifty dollars per article. Since he and his friends split the rent and could survive on a diet that was sixty percent instant ramen, he was able to make ends meet, once his parents contributed a monthly allowance of five hundred dollars. This allowed Juror #12 to pursue his twin interests of agitating for the causes that he passionately believed in, and making sure that everybody was aware of his moral superiority.

As a graduation present, Juror #12's parents had bought him a brand-new, shiny, turquoise Prius. He never missed an opportunity to inform others of how important it was to switch to hybrid cars, and he took inordinate pride in showing off his recently acquired vehicle.

I should point out that I was not present for the following events. I learned about them afterwards. In any case, on the first day of summer vacation, Juror #12 was leading a rally filled with college students protesting what they perceived to be a terrible injustice. Juror #12 stood on a platform in front of a couple of hundred like-minded activists and railed against what he found morally abhorrent. The crowd seemed to like what he said, and after fifteen minutes of ranting and pumping his fist in the air, Juror #12 had whipped his audience up into a frenzy. They started marching down the street, waving signs, chanting slogans, and leaving a trail of fast-food wrapper litter behind them. A few of them had brought sacks of rotten vegetables at them, and they pelted the windows of businesses that were known to oppose their viewpoints. Some of the business owners rushed out of the shops into the throng, leading to shoving, shouting, and threats of lawsuits.

After the temperature of the protest rose dangerously close to the boiling point, the increasingly angry throng saw something found particularly offensive. A car parked on a corner of the street was decorated with about a dozen bumper stickers that not only opposed their views, but also directly insulted them, their mothers, and certain portions of their anatomy.

It's unclear who was the first to respond violently, but at least two protestors were unable to find a handy dowel or yardstick for their signs, so they duct-taped their cardboard signs to baseball bats. The aforementioned bats may not have been the first objects to strike the heavily decorated car, but they were responsible for reducing the windshield to tiny fragments.

Pretty soon, a couple of dozen protestors sought to join in this particular demonstration, and soon, the bumper-sticker-covered car was surrounded on all sides by protestors who were smacking it with whatever was handy. The outburst of fury didn't last very long, as within three minutes, there was a shapeless, battered mass of metal where the automobile used to be.

As the more perceptive individuals reading this will have already deduced, the car in question was the Prius belonging to Juror #12. But why, these clever readers might very well ask, would a vehicle belonging to Juror #12 be covered in stickers exposing viewpoints utterly opposed to his true opinions? An excellent question and the answer is that Juror #12 did not put them there. It was some other person who printed out the collection of statements the protestors found so offensive, affixed them to flexible magnetic strips, and used these opinions to decorate the car.

When Juror #12 left his podium and returned to his parking space to drive home, his reaction upon seeing what was left of his car was completely predictable. Once his emotions had tempered to the point that he was able to analyze the situation, he called ADA Sangster and named the person who he believed was responsible for placing these messages upon his car.

And so, I was called away from assisting the football team with their bench-pressing in order to come to Volker's defense. At a meeting we attended that evening, ADA Sangster threatened to hit Volker with charges of vandalism and destruction of property. Volker said nothing, he simply sat with a self-satisfied smile while I asked the pertinent question. Did she have any evidence whatsoever that Volker was involved in placing the magnetic bumper stickers on the car? She prevaricated, but it was soon evident that neither witnesses nor surveillance footage featuring Volker would be forthcoming. That should have been enough for me to leave the room with Volker immediately, but I pressed forward, pointing out that had the car been decorated with hard-to-peel-off stickers, that could have been considered malicious vandalism, but the bumper stickers in question were completely magnetic, which means that their application and removal caused no damage to the vehicle whatsoever. The guilt should not lie on the back of the person who applied the magnetic messages. The people responsible for the destruction of the car were the protestors who actually crushed the car like a soda can. "Will the D.A.'s office be prosecuting them?" I asked with the silkiest of tones.

ADA Sangster was either left speechless by my eloquence or muted by rage, possibly a bit of both. She did manage to inform me she'd be warning the other jurors, telling them to be on the lookout for Volker. In any event, despite the howls of protest, which were quite in character for Juror #12, Volker walked out without a single charge filed against him.

I asked him no questions about the event. It is an axiom amongst defense attorneys that one should never ask whether or not the client is guilty, because there's a very strong chance that they'll admit their culpability, and an ethical advocate is therefore hampered in creating a defense. Of course, my gut was darned sure who was responsible, but instincts aren't evidence in a courtroom, and I wasn't about to do anything that could place Volker in a precarious legal position.

So I kept my mouth shut. The magnetic stickers could have been produced at a local printing and copying shop, and I wouldn't be surprised if Volker's new ally, Juror #8, desperate to clear his conscience, had paid for them. Who had placed the stickers on the car? Volker himself? Juror #8? Otto? Alfie? *Never ask a question unless you want to know the answer*, I told myself. I wished Volker a good evening as he climbed into Otto's car, and when I felt the urge to ask a question about the stickers, I resisted and muttered "plausible deniability" to myself a few times.

Briefly flashing forward, several months later I stumbled across an article of supposed urban legends on the Internet on that recounted an incident with some points of similarity to the one I just described, but it was dated a year earlier. Is this where Volker got the idea, much like *Matilda* had inspired him to use superglue on a gravestone? Once again, I chose not to ask.

When I reached the Kaiming house, I picked up the elder triplets and walked them across the street to Lake Park to throw their Aerobie around while dinner was prepared. Midway through our game, I received a text, called a time-out, and checked my phone.

"What is it?" Bernard asked.

"It's…business."

"Can you tell us about it?"

"I'm sorry, but no. I hope you understand, Bernard, but this is the sort of thing I can't discuss."

"Is it client confidentiality, or is it the kind of adult stuff that kids aren't supposed to hear?"

"The latter. Your parents would never forgive me if I told you about this."

"Okay." Bernard and his sisters accepted my explanation as I pocketed my phone. The text was from an administrator at Benek's high school that I'd befriended, telling me that Coach Shencrowe, who'd worked with Lada on her volleyball team, had just been caught in a compromising position in the bedroom of one of his sixteen-year-old liberos. Shencrowe had been arrested, and at Shencrowe's insistence, the father of the libero had been charged with assault, though under the circumstances, it was unlikely that any jury would bring in a guilty verdict.

As Nerissa and I agreed in her study shortly before dinner, if Shencrowe was currently preying upon one of his players, there was no reason to assume that this girl was the first. And if he'd targeted one of his female players in the past, then it was certainly within the realm of possibility that Lada had been the target. Wading more deeply into the hazardous swamp of conjecture, I wondered if a DNA test on Lada's baby might prove anything incriminating.

We both decided to stop theorizing until we received further evidence. No sense in wondering if Shencrowe had knocked on Lada's door on that fatal night, begged her to keep her mouth shut and then strangled her when she threatened to tell the world what he'd done to her. Not without evidence. For all we knew, Shencrowe had a rock-solid alibi. Of course, we didn't know that the authorities would look into his movements that night. Benek was still the perpetrator in their eyes, and I wasn't sure how likely the police were to smear egg on their faces by treating Shencrowe as a homicide suspect in an ostensibly closed case. Still, the force is full of detectives with integrity and curiosity, so I texted a couple of friends of mine, who promised me they'd speak to the people in charge of his case and look into the matter.

I was glad that I kept my phone hidden away while we ate our cottage pie, made with ground turkey and topped with mashed sweet potatoes, with mesclun greens salad with berries and whole wheat biscuits. When I checked my texts after dinner, I was glad that I hadn't spent my meal worrying about the fallout of what just happened at the mansion of Juror #4. Someone had managed to set up a pair of portable fire escape ladders on the side of the wall, one on either side and a thick rubber mat had been thrown over the spikes at the top, allowing anybody to climb up and into Juror #4's enclave. Next to the ladder, on the outer wall, presumably, that same someone had taped a large poster board sign saying, "COME IN—FREE FOOD AND BEER." At first, those who saw the sign had been wary, as there'd been a longstanding rumor that the eccentric wealthy lady who owned the property was in the habit of hunting human beings for sport, but one reckless teenager made the climb, discovered a vast assortment of edible treats and beverages neatly laid out on picnic blankets on the other side, and immediately called for his friends to come over and help themselves to the spread. Several other teenagers joined him, followed by some other residents of the neighborhood, plus a few dozen homeless people. Nearly everybody in the neighborhood had wanted to learn what was on the other side of the wall for years, and Juror #4 had never taken the opportunity to invite her neighbors for an open house.

Within an hour, over a hundred people were eating snacks, drinking, playing music, and generally having a blast. The security guard had been busy chauffeuring Juror #4 to a spa treatment, and the housekeeper's polite requests to ask the guests to leave had been equally politely rebuffed. They'd been invited, the guests informed her. Check the sign. She didn't. The housekeeper didn't like to go on the other side of the wall alone.

She called the police, and when one officer told the revelers, who now totaled one hundred fifty, to leave, one man, who'd watched a lot of legal dramas on television, pointed out that they had every reason to believe that the owner of the property had invited them, so the police had no right to tell them to disperse. When the officer noted that a sign and a ladder was an odd way to throw a block party, the legal drama expert pointed out it seemed unlikely that someone would spend several hundred dollars on food and alcohol just for a prank. As Juror #4 was incommunicado, ensconced in a seaweed wrap and citrus facial, the revelry continued for a couple more hours, until Juror #4 returned and raised precisely the amount of hell that one would have expected.

156

ADA Sangster phoned me and left a voicemail message. When I returned her call, I allowed her to exhaust her plentiful supply of profanities before reminding her that at the time the ladder, sign, and refreshments had been set up, Volker, Otto, and I had been in her office. She hung up on me before I had the opportunity to inquire whether she'd checked the alibis of Juror #8 and Alfie, not that I was going to say anything about those two, anyway.

The following morning, I woke up at nine, which was rather earlier than I would have liked, but I had to take the elder triplets to their allergist appointment across town. As I sat in the waiting room and read Winston Churchill's *The Gathering Storm*, I received another text from a friend of mine in the police department. Apparently, Juror #2, the engineer, was furious, and wanted Volker arrested.

I need to circle around and discuss some background information. Juror #2's principal hobby was his own podcast, where he pontificated on science, politics, and anything else of interest to him. At that time, he had one hundred forty-seven subscribers. In one recent episode, as he was talking to a local physics professor, the professor asked if Juror #2 had any irrational fears. After some prevarication, Juror #2 admitted that he had never gotten over the anxiety that cats provoked in him. As a child, his sister's cats often crept onto his bed, and bit or clawed him in his sleep. So, to this day, whenever he saw a cat, he became very nervous.

Of course, I didn't know for sure that Volker had downloaded this particular podcast, which was labeled as discussing "physics, religion in the public sphere, and our worst fears." But I had to wonder, because that morning, Juror #2 had stepped out of his house to retrieve his paper, and immediately retreated back inside, because about eighty cats were sprawled out on his lawn. When he rushed to his kitchen to pour himself a glass of water, he discovered an approximately equal number of cats in his backyard.

When called, the police politely but firmly directed him to Animal Control. Upon their arrival, they soon discovered that many of the cats were collared and lived in homes throughout the neighborhood. Others were feral street cats who roamed the area. Apparently, large, chopped-up quantities of two plants had been sprinkled all over his lawns: catnip and valerian. Both herbs are particularly beloved by felines. Catnip, for anybody who doesn't know, essentially gets cats stoned. Valerian is similar to catnip, but though its scent attracts cats, it doesn't produce the same effects on them. Most of the cats must have consumed some catnip, because Juror #2 was now host to about one hundred sixty felines that were baked out of their minds.

Animal Control phoned for backup, and Juror #2 called anybody he thought would listen to him and complained. At some point, he theorized that Volker was involved and attempted to swear out a warrant for his arrest. However, since he hadn't witnessed Volker sprinkling the catnip and valerian, and he had no other evidence pointing in Volker's direction, nothing came of it. Volker remained comfortably at home, but Juror #2 was left involuntarily house-bound, because enormous quantities of catnip and valerian were still embedded in his lawns, and no matter how many cats were rounded up and returned to their homes or taken to shelters, new ones arrived and proceeded to trip out in his yards.

No sooner did I apprise myself of Juror #2's situation, when ADA Sangster phoned me. Displaying the charm and friendliness that I had come to expect from her, she informed me that Juror #5, the waitress, had called her to complain. Apparently, forty elderly people she'd never seen before arrived and claimed every table and booth in the diner. They then proceeded to order, taste their food when it arrived, and after a single bite, sent it back with various complaints. The food would be recooked; the new customers would taste it, pronounce it inedible, and send it back again. The process repeated the entire morning, until the cook lost his cool and kicked everybody out of the restaurant, meaning that no one bothered to pay for their food or leave a tip. The result of this was that not only had the diner taken in no money, but it was out a great deal of food as well, as a full restaurant of patrons had sent back each breakfast about ten times, meaning that thousands of dollars of pancakes, eggs, bacon, sausage, and all sorts of other breakfast foods had been wasted. When I asked ADA Sangster if any of the elderly patrons had been Volker in a gray wig, she hung up on me. I wondered if Juror #8's sales connections had led him to be acquainted with a few dozen seniors who were willing to visit a crummy diner and make a fuss for a moderate fee each. I whispered "plausible deniability" to myself and pushed the question from my mind.

Right after I dropped the triplets back off at home, my phone rang again. This time, ADA Sangster asked me if I knew what was going on at the health and wellness store run by Juror #9. I responded with as little testiness as possible, though if pressed, I will reluctantly concede that my attitude may not have been as gracious as it seemed in my head, No, I informed her, I was neither psychic nor was I conducting surveillance on all of the jurors. I was simply going about my business, and not all of my time was devoted to the Berchtwelt family. In retrospect, I might have come across as snarkier than I thought I was being, because Sangster responded with white-hot fury.

Here, I have chosen not to use the ADA's exact words, but instead to use my own descriptive skills to describe the situation that morning. Juror #9's shop, devoted to health, wellness, organic foods, and all manner of holistic healing, whatever that means, had developed a small but fiercely loyal clientele of affluent customers, whose frequent—and rather expensive—purchases had made the business a rousing success. She was now looking for a second location, and possibly a third.

That day, she'd offered a special sale for her best customers, so the shop was busier than usual. It was filled with people, mostly women, who were seizing the opportunity to fill their pantries and cabinets with slightly less pricey items that allegedly made them healthier, closer to nature, and who the heck knows what else. At one point in the morning, sixteen customers were browsing about the store, filling baskets, when a woman with severe, cherry-red blotches and marble-sized acne all over her face walked through the door. She greeted the room loudly, and soon, every eye was upon her. She walked over to a stand full of organic face creams, and picked up a couple of jars, declaring loudly to no one in particular, that she just loved this stuff, and it smelled wonderful, and she'd been smearing it over her face multiple times a day for three weeks. One particularly bold woman dared to ask her if she'd had the blotches and acne for very long. When the response was that she'd had perfectly clear skin since adolescence ended, but those nasty pimples had started coming back, oh, when was it...about three weeks ago. The store's clientele stood still for a moment, carefully placed the cosmetics and lotions they'd selected back upon the shelves, and filed out of the store en masse. The woman with complexion issues placed her loaded-up basket on the counter, announced that she'd left her purse in the car, and said she'd be right back. She did not return.

A short time later, when new customers had refilled the store, a boisterous young woman came in, declaring her intention to purchase some more of the shop's delicious organic foods. She announced at the top of her lungs that she'd never felt better ever since she started eating the shop's food morning, noon, and night. Her rapturous review was interrupted by an eardrum-bursting attack of gastrointestinal disturbance. The woman continued to rhapsodize about the deliciousness of the whole grains, organic green vegetables, and fibrous lentils that were the principal ingredients in the shop's prepared meals. As she spoke, her words were constantly drowned out by less pleasant sounds emanating from a portion of her body that was not her mouth. After a minute or two, the customers lost their appetite for the shop's healthful and sustaining food, and they left without making purchases. Just like the woman with complexion issues, the boisterous young woman placed a basketful of items on the counter and announced that she needed to fetch her wallet from her car, but must have lost her way because she never came back to complete her purchase.

Other women had entered the store periodically throughout the day, with similar conditions, producing comparable results.

ADA Sangster told me that she knew Volker was behind this, and I asked her what crime had been committed. As far as I knew, it was not a crime for someone to rave about the quality of a product, and have zits or indigestion. No one was being threatened, and there was no defamation about the quality of the store's products here. Had Congress passed a law against needing Stridex or Gas-X while I wasn't paying attention? The ADA had no answer to my question, aside from a common obscenity.

That afternoon, after Mass with the Kaimings and a couple of hours' workout, first at the Cuthbertson weight room, then at the local pool, I returned to the Kaiming house, set the dinner table with Bernard's help, and then walked up to Professor Howard Kaiming's bedroom to wake him from his pre-dinner nap.

He was sprawled out in his recliner, with a thin coverlet over his legs and papers covering the curved wooden board he uses as a lap desk. A big sheaf of papers had fallen on the floor, so I bent down and gathered them up, noticing as I did so that all of the papers were connected to Juror #10, the academic. After my movements woke the professor, I told him that dinner (curried chicken, lentils, garlic lemon spinach, and wild rice) would be ready in ten minutes. Rather than let him get up and prepare, I sat down on the edge of the bed and held out the papers, saying nothing, but arching an eyebrow.

The professor didn't show the tiniest scintilla of embarrassment. "I volunteered to help Volker investigate Juror #10."

"Why did you do that?"

Adjusting his glasses upon his wrinkled face, Professor Kaiming said, "I looked up her work and knew at once she was a fraud. And I resent people like her who are ruining the credibility of honest academics."

Here, I need to provide a little more information on the professor's background. An immigrant who earned his doctorate in Chinese history at an American university, temporarily returned to China after WWII to care for dying relatives, and fled with his wife after Mao seized power, Professor Kaiming's career was never as illustrious as he thought he deserved. He managed to land jobs at six colleges and universities of varying levels of prestige over the decades, but was never awarded tenure at any of them. He's very bitter about that. He was wrongly accused of plagiarism by a colleague who actually *was* plagiarizing, which led to a lawsuit. The courts barely awarded him enough money to pay the legal bills, but he was granted the title of professor, without any paying position to go with it. Believing himself to be blacklisted after this, he moved to Milwaukee, where most of his family was already living, and started teaching high school history at Cuthbertson for the last twenty years of his career before retiring. Even though he's had a pretty respectable career, he's always felt like he's been cheated out of the prestige and acclaim he desired.

161

Since his retirement, he's devoted a significant portion of his time and energy to exposing and humiliating academic frauds. The plagiarists, the scientists who make up data, the scholars who draw wild conclusions based on skimpy evidence, and the academicians who let ideology cloud their judgment. At that moment, I realized that the professor and Volker were cut from the same cloth. Both of them were obsessed with getting revenge against people and institutions they felt had wronged them.

"Take a look at this." Professor Kaiming handed me a fistful of printouts. I skimmed through them, paying close attention to the highlighted portions. "Now check out this." He pushed a copy of a dissertation into my arms. It was Juror #10's. As I flipped the pages, checking the portions marked with sticky notes, it became evident very quickly that large portions of the dissertation were almost identical to the passages highlighted on the printouts.

"That woman has stolen eighty percent of her dissertation," the professor snapped.

"How come nobody caught this?" I asked.

"She changes a few words here and there, but this is pretty brazen. Most of the passages she quotes without attribution are taken from authors who are pretty prominent in their field. Her dissertation committee ought to have caught this. But they didn't."

"So, what are you going to do with this information?"

An extremely self-satisfied smile formed on the professor's face. "I'm going to pass it on to several prominent figures at the college where she's set to start work in the fall."

"Anonymously, or under your own name?"

"Anonymously. Though I suppose I've built up a reputation as the unofficial Internal Affairs Department of the academic world. They'll suspect me, especially when they see the Milwaukee postmark. Of course, there's no guarantee they'll do anything with this information. They might sweep it under the rug, possibly because so many of them have crossed that line or some similar line themselves. Or they might like her so much they'll decide to give her a second chance. In any event, I have some friends in higher education-related media who'll break the story. I'll send my files to them as well." Professor Kaiming chuckled. "I don't believe in karma, but I do enjoy comeuppance."

I noticed that he'd left the lid off the jar of balm he uses to ease his sciatica. A friend of his makes it, and it's filled with all sorts of Chinese herbs, and all the writing on the label is in Chinese. As I screwed on the lid, I noticed that the balm smelled like a combination of a freshly mowed lawn and a Thai restaurant.

After dinner, I went over the events of the day with Nerissa as we went for a walk in the park before sunset, and she seemed most interested in the potential implosion of Juror #10's career. "I hope that filthy cheat gets what's coming to her," she snapped.

I was a bit surprised, because Nerissa had been pretty outspoken about her discomfort with Volker's vengeance plan.

"This is different," she explained. "This isn't a case of retaliation against people because they came to the wrong verdict. This is someone who violated all the standards of academic integrity, and has clawed her way into a plum position at the expense of hardworking, honest scholars who are desperate to find a steady, well-paying job. If she ripped off someone else's work, she should never be allowed in a classroom again."

There was genuine fury in Nerissa's eyes. I couldn't explain it, and I knew I couldn't say anything about it to her, but there was something in her attitude that made her even more attractive to me. As I wracked my brain, trying to think of ways to work references to corrupt academics into our date night conversations without being too blatant about it, my phone rang. It was the DA himself on the line.

Politely, without any hint of accusation, he suggested that it might be a sensible idea for me to sit down with Volker and have a conversation with him. He stressed that he knew I was a busy man, but if I could manage to make time in my schedule for tomorrow, he'd be most appreciative. Since he asked so nicely, I felt like I had no option but to agree. Before hanging up, the DA informed me that one of the police officers responsible for arresting Benek was about to retire from the force and planned to start working a six-figure position as chief of security at a major company. But an anonymous person sent his future bosses a letter outlining his alleged failures in investigating Benek's case, and the job offer had been withdrawn.

Nerissa and I visited Volker's house at eleven-thirty the next morning. We'd phoned ahead, and Volker said we could come by at nine, but I wanted more sleep, so I pushed the appointment time forward. Even then, I slept through my multiple alarms, so I only had time for a protein bar for breakfast, and my stomach was already starting to growl.

We sat down with Volker in his living room. He looked tremendously pleased with himself, and I suspected that unless he managed to control emotions, a lot of people would take his triumphant facial expressions as the next best thing to a confession. Nerissa and I agreed that we would be careful not to ask Volker a direct question as to whether or not he was involved in these recent events, but all of our discussion was predicated on the tacit belief that he had planned all of these acts of retribution against the people responsible for convicting Benek, with the help of Otto, Alfie, and Juror #8.

I decided to lead with an oblique statement. "So, have you heard from Juror #8 lately?"

"Why would I?" If Volker's face was testifying against him, his words weren't giving him away.

"He seemed rather upset the last time you spoke to him. Or rather, yelled at him. You were quite upset during that interaction. Do you still feel that way towards Juror #8?"

Volker shrugged. "The guy made a terrible mistake he can never make right. But unlike most of the other jurors and members of the criminal justice system with blood on their hands, he seems repentant, and he wants to do what he can in order to make some form of amends. It's not going to bring Benek back, but it's a start."

After exchanging glances, Nerissa asked, "Just what would it take for you to consider yourself even with the people responsible for Benek's conviction?"

Not a single second of reflection was needed on Benek's part. He'd had his answer prepared for quite some time. "ADA Sangster withheld evidence that could have led to an acquittal. If a prosecutor is guilty of misconduct that leads to an innocent person being convicted, that prosecutor should go to prison for an amount of time equal to the sentence bestowed upon the innocent convicted person. The fact that not all of the sentence was served should not mitigate the guilty prosecutor's sentence. The judge who oversaw the case, I've thought about it, and I accept that he was just the referee. He wasn't responsible for the arrest or the verdict, and I suppose he did a fair job. But he should still be compelled to hang a sign in any courtroom where he works, acknowledging that a terrible miscarriage of justice took place under his watch. Because, at the end of the day, he could have ended the trial or thrown out the verdict, and just because he decided to leave the matter to the appeals courts, which I admit, is standard procedure, doesn't mean he's totally in the clear. The police in charge of the case have to get demoted to traffic cop, and their pensions are forfeited to my family. I don't know for sure what I want from Dr. Albion Suco yet, but he needs to writhe in the muck like a worm. The guards who should have protected Benek in prison? Fired. The prisoners who murdered and raped him? They go into solitary confinement for the rest of their lives, and they get fed Nutraloaf three meals a day."

"What's Nutraloaf?" Nerissa wondered.

"It's special prison food designed to provide sufficient nutrients to survive, but it's excruciatingly tasteless," I explained. "The recipe varies from prison to prison, but it's often made with dough and enough cheap meat and vegetables to provide adequate sustenance. It's designed as a punishment meal."

Volker nodded in agreement with my description. "As for the jurors, they need to all suffer an appropriate amount of public humiliation and personal mortification. I don't want money from them; I want them to go through agony for my amusement."

"You've been taking lessons from the Mikado of Japan?" Nerissa asked.

This confused Volker. "Who?"

"Never mind." Waving away the Gilbert and Sullivan reference, Nerissa continued. "The big question is, how much punishment is going to be enough for them?"

"I don't know. When they've reached the right point, I'll know. Until then, they'll just have to simmer in their own guilt."

After mentally rephrasing my next question several times, I asked, "And what happens if what I suggested earlier happens?"

"What's that?"

"What will happen if they come after you like you went after them?"

Volker set his jaw. "They've already taken away the most important person in my life. What are they going to do next? Take away my scholarship? They'd have to prove wrongdoing, and I don't think they have anything on me. Besides, I'm counting on you to stick up for me like you have in the past. Don't forget, I'm punching up. I'm attacking over a dozen adults who destroyed my family. But if they come after me, they're punching down. They're grown-ups who are trying to crush a kid who they wronged. They called me a liar and charged me with deceit, and they can know themselves Biblically." I might possibly have cleaned up that last comment.

I really wanted to ask him how much of the planning he'd done himself, or if he'd drawn inspiration from some television shows or something like that, or if his associates had contributed to the plans. I could have done a little digging online, but once again, I chose not to pursue that line of inquiry. I wondered how Juror #8 had found the people to sour the customers at Juror #9's shop. Was he friends with members of a local theater troupe? How far ahead had he planned? How many rounds of *Matilda*-inspired revenge might be coming?

As I took a deep breath and imperceptibly whispered "plausible deniability" to myself, seven sharp knocks on the door in rapid succession interrupted our conversation. Otto hobbled over, squinted through the window, and announced. "It's one of the jurors."

"Which one?" I asked, hurrying across the house.

"I don't know. One of the older men."

A glance told me it was Juror #3, the master builder. "Let me in!" he bellowed.

"He looks and sounds upset," I told Otto, indulging in my love for stating the bleeding obvious. "You're under no obligation to open your door to someone in that condition."

"I'm not going anywhere!" Juror #3 howled.

Calling through the door, I replied, "Sir, there is no point in holding a conversation until you can demonstrate that you are calm."

"I need to talk to you right now! If you say no, I'm calling the police!"

Otto reached for the doorknob, but I stopped him. "What should we do?" he asked me.

"He wants to talk, but he doesn't want to moderate his temper. He can talk through the window." I opened up the large window in the living room and motioned Juror #3 over towards me. He could stand amongst the shrubbery and speak through the screen. He wasn't thrilled with this prospect, but he was too wound up to wait any longer.

He pointed an accusatory finger at Volker. "You're a thief."

Volker raised a different finger towards Juror #3. "No, I'm not. What do you think I stole from you? Whatever it is, you're wrong." Volker's hand gesture had the effect of throwing gasoline on the flames.

"I don't know how you did it, but I know it was you. Everybody on the jury knows you've been going after them, so this is how you're trying to get back at me for sending your brother to jail." Juror #3 started spluttering, and for a moment, I thought he was going to spit in the bushes. "You bought a massive five-thousand-dollar television."

"No, I didn't. And if I did, where did I put it?" Volker gestured. "Look at this dump. Our television still has a digital converter box."

"You're gonna pay back every cent you stole, or else I'm calling the police."

Volker started to reply with profanity, and I stepped in to defend him. "Sir, unless you have more evidence than baseless accusations, you're going to need to tone it down a bunch of notches. You made a charge and provided no proof. Volker has denied your allegations. Unless you have something else to add, I'm going to bid you good-day and shut this window."

Juror #3 shook his fist. "I'm leaving, but I'm coming back with the police. And when I bring them here, they're going to arrest you." He stormed away, and we watched him tear off in his car.

For the first time, Volker looked frightened. "Is he really going to have me arrested?"

"If the DA's office thinks there's a case against you, and right now, there's one prosecutor who isn't about to give you the benefit of the doubt, then she can file charges."

"But I didn't do it. You have to believe me! I had nothing to do with this."

Nerissa performed her usual instant judgment of a person. "I believe you. This is theft. It's not your style."

Otto started hyperventilating. "It doesn't matter if he's innocent. They're gonna throw him in jail, and the same thing that happened to Benek's gonna—"

"No, it's not," I interrupted.

"How can you be sure?"

"First of all, Volker doesn't have to wait here to be arrested. Are you hungry? How about we get some lunch?"

The others agreed. Otto had to leave for his shift at work in half an hour, and he liked the thought of Juror #3 and the police arriving to find the house empty. Nerissa, Volker, and I drove away in the opposite direction from Juror #3, with no set plan for where we'd eat.

After about a mile of aimless traveling, Nerissa remembered that we were just a few blocks from a taqueria owned by the family of one of her scholarship girls. Whenever we ate there, we spent the next several hours raving about the meal, so we decided to introduce Volker to the establishment.

Once there, the proprietors ran out from behind the counter and the kitchen, hugged Nerissa, and shook my hand. Nerissa's student took a break from waiting tables to embrace her and then told her she'd be with us as soon as she delivered the next rounds of orders.

As we were being seated, we had a good-natured argument with the proprietors, as they wanted us to have whatever we wanted complements of the house, and Nerissa and I insisted on paying for our meal. Normally, I commit to winning an argument, no matter how trivial, with the determination of General Patton, but when the issue at stake is whether or not I will consume free food, my heart just isn't in it. Nerissa was less willing to concede the point, but I whispered in her ear that we'd leave an absolutely massive tip that would restore parity, and that assuaged her.

After a couple of minutes, Nerissa's student placed a massive basket of homemade tortilla chips and a selection of salsas in front of us. "What can I get you?" she asked.

"Beef tacos and a cola," Volker ordered.

Nerissa took one more glance at the menu and said, "Nopalito salad with the medium spicy chicken and avocado ranch dressing, and an iced tea with lemon, no sugar, please."

"I'll start with the black bean and chicken soup, extra hot, with the avocado added, followed by the ultra spicy grilled chicken burrito, please. And I want that on the house-made whole wheat tortilla, with brown rice, but light on the rice, heavy on the chicken and the pinto beans, drench it in your hottest possible sauce, and just go to town when adding the Oaxaca cheese and guacamole, please. And a large glass of milk and a seltzer water with both lemon and lime, please."

After my order dulled the point of her pencil, Nerissa's student nodded and said, "Your food will be out real soon. Save room for dessert. The special today is plantain cream pie with dulce de leche."

I'd never had that before, but I knew I'd love it.

Our server had left the chips and salsa in front of Nerissa. She was seated next to me at the small rectangular table, and Volker was across from me. She pushed the chips over to our side of the table, saying, "Here, you two. Enjoy."

"Don't you like tortilla chips?" Volker asked as he transferred a handful onto his plate.

"These are amazing. Which is why I can't have any. If I have one, I'll inhale the rest of the basket. So you two eat and enjoy and finish them before my willpower dries up."

Volker didn't need much encouragement, but I waited for my soup to arrive before crumbling some chips into my bowl. Nerissa rarely provokes negative emotions in me, but the looks on her face when I'm enjoying some food that she's denying herself tend to exasperate me. I keep telling her that

I'd feel exactly the same way about her no matter what size she is, and that I like seeing her taking pleasure in a meal. As usual, she told me I was way too sweet, and then continued making the same expressions you see on children from developing nations in charity infomercials narrated by Sally Struthers.

After the basket of chips was empty, with Volker being ninety percent responsible for its destruction, he ignored the dispenser of paper napkins on our table, wiped his lips with the back of his hand, and said, "You've got to believe me, I didn't spoof that guy's credit card. And I didn't ask anybody else to, either. I swear it."

"Then we'll let the police investigate, and even if they don't find the real criminals, they won't find any evidence against you because it doesn't exist," I replied.

"We do believe you," Nerissa added. "I can tell you had nothing to do with the credit card. It's pretty obvious from your tone and posture." I've said it before: Nerissa is great at reading people, especially kids.

Our meals arrived, and we tucked in with a zeal that would have been embarrassing in a public restaurant had not all of the other customers been similarly savoring their food.

After several minutes devoted mainly to chewing, Nerissa set down her fork and said, "Volker, I have to ask something. Are you enjoying all of this? You know what I mean by "this." Don't ask me to specify."

Volker looked up at us. "Neither of you are familiar with *South Park*, right?"

"No, we're not," I replied. "Is there some sort of reference we need to know?"

"Just that it's a recurring theme of the show that the adults are often clueless idiots that leave the kids confused and incredulous. I always related to that, because aside from Grandpa and you two, the adults in my life have always let me down with their denseness. My parents, my pre-Cuthbertson teachers, and everybody connected with the criminal justice system. And yet, I'm always expected to defer to them. There's one episode of *South Park* where Cartman is deputized as a cop. Are you sure you haven't seen that one?"

"No. Neither of us have cable."

"Well, that's the episode that introduced the classic line "Respect mah authori-tay!""

"Oh. That's where that came from." I'd heard the phrase multiple times from classmates and casual conversations, but I never knew the source.

"I keep thinking of that. All these ridiculous people who haven't earned respect demand it. So I think I'm doing them a favor by telling them I don't respect them and I don't recognize their authori-tay over me."

"Do you think that's doing *you* any good?" Nerissa asked.

"You've heard that quote, "Well-behaved women seldom make history," haven't you? Well, I say, "Well-behaved *children* seldom make history." The world's messed up, and if I'm going to be the change I want to see in the world, I have to misbehave."

"That's not the proper context of the line," Nerissa informed him. "The historian Laurel Thatcher Ulrich used it in an article in the 1970s about Puritan funerals, and it wasn't meant to encourage women to misbehave in order to make their mark on the world, but to point out how quiet, conventional women generally don't have their stories told, even though they deserve to have their lives studied."

Volker shrugged. "Well, I like my interpretation better. Because toeing the line isn't going to get justice and punishment and apologies. Kids have no power or money, and normally, the only way they can get what they want is to throw a fit. And that's considered unacceptable behavior, and we get chastised and punished. That's why we have to be strategically sneaky. Otherwise, we become bitter teenagers and adult bullies who repeat the toxic cycle by taking out our aggression on innocent kids. I want to be the change I want to see in the world. So I'm using the *Matilda* method now, but if I don't start seeing some results, I'm sorely tempted to whip up a batch of Mr. and Mrs. Tenorman chili."

"What's that?" Nerissa asked.

Before he could respond, our waitress approached our table and asked us if we were ready for dessert. We all raved about how much we enjoyed the meal, and Volker and I ordered the pie. Nerissa declined, and when two slices arrived at the table, Volker took one bite, and his face lit up in ecstasy. After my first taste, I knew that Nerissa had to try it, and despite her demurrals I pressured her into having a little. As soon the forkful I fed her passed her lips, Nerissa let out a moan that made me feel like I needed to go to confession, and I managed to convince her to try a little more, and her resistance melted until we'd split my slice fairly evenly. The person slicing the pie had been more than generous, so I didn't mind sharing.

After we basked in the afterglow of our dessert for a bit, Nerissa asked, "Volker, is there anything that might make you less angry towards any of the people you're targeting? Is there something that could make you forgive one of them?"

Volker paused. "I'm not admitting to targeting anybody."

Prudent kid, I thought to myself, but didn't say.

"What about Juror #6?" Nerissa continued. "He has dementia. Don't you think that he's being punished enough?"

Volker poked at his plate with his fork as if he tapped it hard enough, another slice of pie would magically appear. "I'd just like a chance to tell him how much he's hurt me. Even if he forgets it an hour later."

I was not sure that this was a smart idea, so I turned to Nerissa and silently asked for her opinion. She gave a little nod, and after a lengthy series of goodbyes and hugs from the store owners, we made our way back to the car. Just as I reached the door, I doubled back and asked for two plantain cream pies to take home for dessert that night at the Kaimings' house. Fortunately, I had an insulated bag in my car to keep them cool, and I asked for a sealable plastic bag of ice to put in the bag with the pies. As we climbed back into my car, Nerissa's student rushed out to us to return the massive tip we gave her. We insisted she keep it all, and the ensuing discussion was extremely civil, but it might have gotten a bit loud, because a police officer walking by on patrol asked us what was going on, and when he learned that we were trying to give our waitress a generous tip and she was resisting, he just stared momentarily and then told us to work it out amongst ourselves.

On our way to the nursing home where Juror #6 lived, I received a text. As I was focused on driving, Nerissa took my phone. "It's an update from one of your sources at Benek and Lada's school. Apparently, two more girls from the volleyball team have accused Coach Shencrowe of grooming them into a sexual relationship."

"That's terrible, but does that help Benek's case at all?" Volker asked.

"Not unless we can somehow find proof that Lada was one of his victims," I responded. "That would give us a motive to advance him as a viable suspect for her murder."

"If we can get his DNA tested, and compare it with Lada's baby, and it matches, that might be exactly the wedge that can be used to extract a confession," Nerissa noted. "Assuming, of course, he's responsible."

"It'd be great if it was him, but there's a good chance it was another guy who knocked her up," Volker sneered. "Alfie was telling me about all the times he saw her hitting on other guys at parties..." He continued to speak ill of the dead for most of the ride, until we arrived at the nursing home.

I'd wondered if anybody would object to our visiting, but the woman at the front desk seemed totally surprised that people were coming to see a resident of the nursing home. "Lemme see if I can find the sign-in sheet somewhere." She rooted around for a couple of minutes, muttering obscenities as her efforts proved fruitless. I would have warned her that there was a young boy present, but thanks to Trey Parker and Matt Stone, he'd heard and said a lot worse on a regular basis, and I didn't feel the need to protect his impressionable ears.

Finally, she dug out a coffee-stained paper on a battered clipboard. I signed us in, noticing that the last visitor on the sheet stopped by two weeks earlier. When I commented on this, she nodded, saying, "Most people dump their relatives and run. Some people have been here for over five years, and no one stops by to see them."

A nurse led us down the corridor. I've heard many retirement homes referred to as God's Waiting Room. This place looked like it was designed to prepare its residents for the first circle of Dante's *Inferno*. This building was the most convincing and least preachy way I've ever seen to convince people to save their money and stay on good enough terms with their family members that their relatives would care for them in their later years.

Finally, we were led into a tiny room, with Juror #6 lying in a hospital bed with a tiny television playing. He didn't seem to be paying attention to it. There were no other decorations or furniture in the room.

"He... seems a lot worse than he was at the trial," Volker commented.

"He's had a series of strokes. He can hear you, but he can't respond. And we don't know how much he understands. I'll leave you alone with him. Ten minutes should be enough for you, right?" I saw the nurse's hand dip into her pocket, and I realized she was ducking out for a cigarette break.

Volker looked down at the man who had covered up his condition in order to serve on the jury and then contributed to his brother's conviction. Finally, he spoke. "I suppose I should feel sorry for you, but I don't. I think you're getting what you deserve, and this feels like justice to me. I have so much to say to you, but even if you can hear me, you're not going to remember it. I just hope you have enough functioning brain cells to realize how much pain you've helped cause."

Nerissa looked disturbed by this. "Volker—"

"What. Am I supposed to tell him I forgive him? Please don't turn me into a filthy hypocrite. This man spent his last days of quasi-lucidity screwing my family over, and I can't lie and tell him that his last major action on this planet was anything but a monstrous injustice. I can't let it go, and I can't move on until I find a way to make this whole mess right. But at least some good has come out of coming here. I don't hate him anymore. I used to despise him and all the other jurors with every fiber of my being. But now this man is getting an adequate punishment. If I believed in divine justice, I'd say that this was God's retribution. I don't believe that's what this is, but it feels right to me. Two of the jurors have gotten what's coming to them. One's dead, and I'm not sure if this is worse than death or not."

Nerissa folded her arms. "There's a third juror who's suffering. Actually, her palliative care facility is just a mile away. I think you should see her."

"Why?" Volker asked.

"I want to see your reaction to what she has to say."

After a bit of discussion, Volker agreed to speak to Juror #11. We phoned ahead to make sure that she was able to receive visitors, and while Volker made a quick trip to the restroom, Nerissa pulled me into a little alcove and whispered to me.

"Volker is starting to scare me. I didn't know it was possible for a kid to have that much anger in him."

I pointed out that when we were his age, we both had more than our share of fury, particularly at the people who had done us wrong during our formative years. She dismissed my retort with a wave of her hand, saying, "Not like this. Not this level of venom. Not this absolute refusal to even consider the possibility of forgiveness. It's almost inhuman."

"I don't think it's inhuman at all. He's thirteen. Prepubescent. You've read the studies on how the brain chemistry of kids this age is so volatile; it's not fair to hold them to the same standards as adults."

"This is something way worse, Funderburke. This is twisted and sick. No matter how much water is poured on the fire, the flames only rise higher. The whole situation is getting out of control. If he had some set endgame, like get Benek's name cleared, and then he's done, that would be a different matter. But Volker's out for revenge, and whether he realizes it or not, his mantra here is *Nothing will ever be enough*."

I agreed with her, which upset me. Not because I mind concurring with her, but because I didn't want to admit that Volker had become a vengeance junkie. "So what do you suggest we do now?"

"I think our top priority is that we have to bring Volker back from the brink. This is more important than finding the real killer; it's even more crucial than getting Benek's conviction posthumously overturned."

"And how do you suppose that we do that?"

Nerissa pouted for a moment, shoving her hands in the pockets of her royal blue lambskin windbreaker. "I don't know. I just had this idea that talking to a terminally ill woman might provoke feelings of pity in him."

"A near-comatose man didn't fill him with sympathy."

"I know. And that gives me chills." To prove her point, she shivered, making her long peach satin sundress shimmer. Normally, when she quivers with cold, it's my signal to slip my coat around her, but it was a warm day (by my standards, at least, not hers), so I'd left my favorite item of clothing at home, and I was only wearing a cotton T-shirt and shorts, so I had nothing to wrap around my perpetually temperature-sensitive girlfriend. Then I realized I had my arms, so I pulled her towards me and felt her press her head against my chest.

"They'll probably let you two borrow a room here if you need it." Volker had slipped behind me without our hearing him.

I grumbled an unintelligible reply, and pretty soon, we'd arrived at Juror #11's room at the hospice. When Volker saw the sign, he recognized the name of the facility immediately. "Alfie's grandmother's in the palliative care wing here."

"Do you want to speak to her?"

"Oh, we've never met. She doesn't know who I am. I just recognized the name of this place."

Juror #11 looked rather better than when we'd seen her last. At our earlier visit, she'd appeared close to death. Today, she still had the pallor of a seriously ill woman, but she was sitting up in a chair, had draped a shawl around her shoulders, and appeared significantly stronger than she had previously.

She greeted us with warmth, and gauged Volker's glare with an appreciative eye. "I know that I failed you and your brother. I told your teachers my instincts were certain your brother was innocent, but I didn't have the strength to stand up to the others who were so certain." She coughed. "That's not a defense. That's an admission of guilt. And a woefully inadequate apology."

"Yes, it is," Volker agreed.

"I know you want retribution. I want to tell you that I've stopped taking painkillers. My doctors think I'm mad, but I have the right to refuse treatment, and I think that I deserve a little suffering. I'm sure you agree. And it makes my mind sharper, so I'm able to reflect on my mistakes with far more focus."

Volker nodded, but the anger didn't seem as strong as it had been with the comatose Juror #6. Perhaps the genuine regret in her eyes was reaching him.

"You don't know anything about my husband, do you?" Juror #11 asked.

We all replied in the negative, so she explained, "He was a cheater and a controller. He never wanted me to have friends, and he wouldn't give up his girlfriends, either. Or admit to having them. I should have left him, but…I had my reasons. You don't need to hear them. But I spent half a century getting back at his little, stupid ways. Dropping his sandwich on the floor when he wasn't looking, then watching him eat it. Hiding his keys and making him search. Ripping the seam in the back of his trousers, knowing he wouldn't notice the damage when he got dressed, knowing he'd never suspect me when people snickered at him in public and he realized the condition of his clothes. Tiny acts of defiance in retribution for a lifetime of thoughtless cruelties. Then, one day, he dropped dead, and I never had the chance to enjoy my freedom because I'd received my diagnosis a couple of months earlier. Not the same kind that took my daughter, but it put everything in perspective. I spent a lifetime afraid to make it on my own, and now I'm dying alone. And what have I done with my life? My only child is dead. I have no grandchildren, my cat is a sociopath who never shows any affection…. Looking back at my life, I have nothing but five decades of resentment and ineffective attempts to get my own back that brought me no happiness and lots of missed opportunities to do something worthwhile."

Volker crossed his arms. "Is this your way of telling me I'm being foolish?"

After more coughing, Juror #11 replied, "It's my way of telling you I wasted my life. Everything I did out of bitterness or fear was time I burnt. I don't want anybody else to make the same mistake." She turned to us. "Could you please leave us alone for a few minutes? I want to tell Volker something privately."

A couple of quick words of agreement, and we were in the corridor. Before we left, I asked what happened to her sociopathic cat, and I was informed it had been adopted by a neighbor with fifteen other felines with comparable mental health issues. We started wondering what Juror #11 was saying to Volker, and then my phone rang. When my caller ID informed me that it was ADA Sangster, I felt the urge to let it go to voice mail, but at Nerissa's encouragement, I decided not to postpone the inevitable. "Tatum, you've got to stop calling me all the time," I told her as I winked at my girlfriend.

"Nerissa's starting to get jealous."

Sangster made a comment that assured me that I wasn't going to be leaving Nerissa for her anytime soon and provided me with the latest news. Upon hearing it, I couldn't muster a snarky remark.

"What's up?" Nerissa asked.

"It's Juror #9. The health and wellness shop owner. She just killed herself."

Chapter Eight: Why Should I Feel Guilty?

NERISSA

"Am I being blamed for this?" Volker asked.

I stared at him for several moments. I saw no remorse in his face, but I did see anxiety. Maybe I was looking for the emotions that I hoped to find, but I had the sense that Volker didn't want any of his victims dead. He wanted them to suffer, certainly, but he wasn't out to put any of them in the ground. At least, I wished to believe he didn't. Hopefully, I wasn't projecting my own preferred reactions upon him.

"How did she do it?" Little tears started forming in the corners of Volker's eyes, and relief rushed into my heart. His voice had grown softer, and perhaps it was my imagination, but he suddenly appeared to be much closer to a little boy than an adolescent. I realized that despite the fact that he had the ability to plot and plan at an adult level, emotionally, he was still a kid. I began to wonder if I'd been too harsh towards him, as the memory of my own unfocused anger at the age of thirteen had faded, but I knew that it had been intense. I was about double Volker's age, so maybe the emotional standards I was holding him to were unfair.

Written down, Funderburke's answer sounds blunt, but he said it in a very gentle manner. "She ran her car in her garage and asphyxiated from the exhaust."

"Did she leave a note, or didn't Sangster say?" I asked.

"Apparently, she must have left behind some sort of message."

It was obvious that Funderburke was holding something back. As the seconds passed, my patience weakened. "Aaaaaannnnddd?"

"She mentioned me, didn't she? Did she blame me?" Volker asked. "Go ahead. Tell me the truth. I want to hear it."

"According to Sangster, she claimed that the stunt that drove away the customers at her store ruined her business. Apparently, her finances were hanging on a razor's edge, and when she didn't get the income boost she was hoping for with that special sale, she realized that she was inexorably headed towards bankruptcy, so...."

Volker and I mentally filled in the rest of that sentence. Eventually, Volker broke the silence. "I never thought this would happen."

"Well, ADA Sangster ended her call with the threat that she didn't know if there was any charge she could file against you, but if there was, she promised to prosecute."

"But I didn't commit a crime. And I'm not admitting to any involvement in whatever happened at her store," Volker added quickly. "What do I do now?"

"She said someone would probably want to speak to you soon. She didn't say if it would be the police or someone from the D.A.'s office..."

Volker seemed to have lost an inch in height and a year in age. "They're going to lock me up, aren't they? Even if they don't have a case, they're going to throw me in a cell as payback for embarrassing them. What are they going to do, tell my parents that if they don't withdraw their lawsuit, they'll prosecute me? Well, the joke's on them. My parents don't care. They'll keep going with their suit even if I spend the rest of my teenage years in solitary."

"That's not going to happen." Funderburke's voice was sharp and certain, but anxiety was cascading into Volker's tone.

"How can you be sure? Sangster's fighting for her professional and maybe political life. Doesn't it make sense that she'd use any weapon at hand to protect her career, even if it means throwing a thirteen-year-old boy in the pen?"

Funderburke stooped down for level eye contact with Volker. "First, remember that we're on excellent terms with the District Attorney. Second, think about the optics. I can call one of my friends at the newspaper. A story about a prosecutor with huge ambitions trying to crush the little boy who might derail her dreams? That's a terrible look for her. As I see it, there's no evidence that you bullied or pressured her into suicide. If someone hired individuals to create the impression that Juror #9's products caused adverse effects, that might be a civil matter, but I doubt it was criminal. But as your legal representative, I would strongly advise you to exercise your right to silence."

"Are you acting as my lawyer?"

"I guess so. And if you wanted to call your grandfather, and Alfie, and Juror #8, and tell them to say nothing without an attorney present, I think that might be a wise idea."

Volker nodded, pulled out his cheap off-brand phone, and hurried off to a corner to make some quick calls.

"Do you think there's any chance he gets arrested?" I asked Funderburke.

"I'm not sure, but I think we should take some steps to let the situation cool down. I don't want him going back home to face not just police investigating the suicide, but also charges connected to Juror #3's credit card being used without his permission."

"Darn it, I forgot about that."

"I'm going to call a friend of mine on the force. If Volker didn't have anything to do with Juror #3's credit card, someone else did. Which means it might be part of a bigger criminal enterprise. I'll call Benny. He usually works on cases like that." Funderburke carried out this action, checked with Volker to make sure he was done talking to his grandfather, and then called Otto to ask him if it was all right if Volker had dinner at the Kaiming house. "He'll be out of the way there for a few hours. We can't duck the authorities forever, but I think it's best he stay at your house for a bit."

"I agree."

Once Volker got off the phone with Juror #8, we climbed back in his car and headed home. We were quiet for a while, and then Funderburke muttered, "That doesn't make sense."

"What doesn't?"

"The alleged statement that the stunt at Juror #9's shop destroyed her business. I don't see how one bad day of sales could destroy her business, especially as not enough time has passed to see if she's lost any customers permanently. Even if she somehow got shut down on Black Friday, it wouldn't be enough to destroy her finances, would it? She could always try something else to stay afloat. And wasn't she thinking of opening new stores?"

I nodded. "You're right. That does not add up. And since she wouldn't lie about her motive for suicide...it makes me wonder, *was* it really suicide?" Actually, I only thought those last eight words. I didn't think it was right to theorize without any solid evidence.

But when we arrived home, it soon became clear that I wasn't the only one with questions about Juror #9's death. Mom had left twenty minutes earlier, and Dad informed us that the authorities asked her to bring her consulting expertise to Juror #9's death. Either there was something obviously wrong, or they were understaffed. Possibly both.

As I walked towards the kitchen to pour myself a glass of water, Dad emerged from the basement, holding four plastic containers filled with homemade pasta sauce. As he set them down in the sink and ran some hot water over the sealed containers to thaw them a bit before transferring them into the gigantic stewpot that the elder triplets could probably use as a Jacuzzi if they threw a handful of Alka-Seltzers into it, I started giving him a summary of the events of the day. Once I got to lunch, I called out to Funderburke, who ran to the car, retrieved the pies, which were still nice and cold, and made room in the fridge for them.

Rally burst into the kitchen just as I was wrapping up my narrative and turned on the television. After setting it to a local news channel, I saw a couple of familiar faces. ADA Sangster was giving another press conference, and Juror #3 was standing next to her.

"—unacceptable that a hard-working, well-respected pillar of the community could be driven to suicide by a vengeful teenager. This kind of harassment is a fundamental threat to the integrity of our justice system, and I will not tolerate this behavior. It sets a precedent that tells jurors that they are not safe if they come to a verdict that someone dislikes. Jurors must be able to perform their civic duty without losing their businesses, or having their credit cards stolen—" Here she gestured towards Juror #3. "—or fearing for their lives. At this moment, I am investigating potential plans for restoring Milwaukeeans' confidence that when they serve as jurors, they will not face any unjust repercussions."

"Unjust!" We turned around and saw Volker, a bit of his former rage returning. "Where does she get off pontificating about justice?"

"I think this is all part of her long-term plan to boost her profile as she prepares to run for one public office or another," Dad commented. "I did some Internet searching on her the other day, and both her parents once clerked for Supreme Court Justices. Did you know that?"

"No."

Volker seemed to be cooling down fast. "I didn't mean for this to happen, you know. I hated her, but I never wanted her to take her own life."

As Dad started shaking out the four glistening ruby bricks of sauce into the stewpot, he asked, "What makes you so sure she did?"

"Well...that's what everybody is saying. Are you telling me that it wasn't suicide?"

"I'm not saying anything about the nature of her death, only that my wife is rarely called out to act as a special consultant when the reasons behind a fatality are obvious."

Volker looked down at his feet, shuffled across the kitchen to the little chair the elder triplets use, and sat down. "I just wanted everybody to admit they'd made a mistake and to feel terrible. And then they doubled down on saying Benek was guilty, and then I wanted them to feel just a little bit of the pain Grandpa and I have been enduring, and then I wanted them to feel a lot of pain. But I didn't want them to die. Why should I feel guilty?"

"Situations can spiral out of control really fast," I told him. "We personify Justice as this blindfolded woman with a sword and scales. It's meant to symbolize that the justice system should be impartial to all who come before it. But there's another twist to the metaphor. When you blindfold a person and give her a sword, and she starts swinging it around, there's no telling

183

what her blade will slice. This is what happens when attempts to get justice aren't carefully controlled. A lot of innocent people can be hurt, and there's no guarantee that the individuals who deserve to feel the sharp edge of Justice's blade are going to get cut." I think I may have taken the metaphor a little too far, but Volker seemed to have tuned out to my little speech at some point.

My attention returned to the television when the husband of Juror #9 appeared on the screen, ranting that his beloved wife was the most wonderful thing that had ever happened to him, and demanding that the authorities arrest the people who had wrecked his wife's previously wildly successful business and crushed her will to live. He pulled out his wallet, opened it up, and removed a photograph, saying, "Take a look at her. She was so beautiful. And now she's gone. There has to be a reckoning for what that little thug did to crush her gorgeous spirit."

"He did it. He killed her." I admit that I had no evidence at all that Juror #9's husband was a murderer. All I had were my instincts, and from the way he was laying his grief on thick and insincere, I was positive he hadn't really cared about his wife, and he didn't really bear any animosity towards the people who had supposedly driven Juror #9 into the grave. So if all of that righteous anger was fake, it stood to reason it was simply a cover for his own culpability.

Dad tapped the sauce blocks with a wooden spoon, though they were still too hard to crack. "Nerissa, what have I told you about accusing strangers of murder without any proof?"

"It's fine when it's in our own home with only family around. And Volker's not going to report me," I added as an afterthought.

"But it sets a bad example for the kids. The other day, Bernard walked into Yeh-Yeh's room while he was watching a *Dateline* mystery, and the first words out of his mouth were, "I think her husband killed her!""

"To be fair, when a woman dies, and her demise is turned into a *Dateline* episode, the killer is the husband ninety-five percent of the time." Upon hearing this, I whirled around. I hadn't noticed Funderburke coming into the kitchen. "Did you get a look at his wallet? He's got the adulterer's circle."

"What's the adulterer's circle?" Bernard asked, displaying his uncanny skill at overhearing things kids his age probably shouldn't.

"I think that's something you can wait to learn," Dad told him.

"I know what adultery is. I've read the Ten Commandments," Bernard replied.

Dad gently but firmly sent Bernard out of the kitchen, and then asked Funderburke to explain the term to him.

"When men cheat and don't want their partner in adultery to know they're married, they often hide their wedding rings in a slot in their wallets. The metal stretches the leather, and when it's done often enough, it leaves a permanent circle in the leather. That's the adulterer's circle. Of course, he could play some sort of sport that requires him to take off his ring beforehand."

"Infidelity is more likely," I asserted. "He's got a physique that doesn't indicate that he's much of an athlete, but it's good enough for him to catch a girlfriend on the side."

After another word from Dad reminding us of the dangers of theorizing based on insufficient evidence, I crossed over to the tiny solarium right off the kitchen and gathered up some heirloom tomatoes and basil to make a Caprese Salad. We had enough fresh mozzarella in the fridge to start our own pizza parlor. Funderburke suggested that Volker join him and the elder triplets in the backyard as they kicked around the soccer ball, and our guest agreed without any sign of enthusiasm. As we prepared the meal, I provided Dad with some more details regarding the events of the day.

When I mentioned my concern over Volker's seemingly unquenchable vehemence, tempered only by the news of Juror #9's death, Dad replied, "If you're an intelligent thirteen-year-old who doesn't just feel, but *knows* that he is the victim of a massive injustice, and you have no faith in the system or anybody else to right the wrongs, it's not surprising that he comes to see himself as the only one pure enough to fix everything. And then when he's confronted with the possibility that he may have caused a destructive act on par with those he condemned others for, it's only logical that a boy with a fully working conscience will have an existential crisis."

I mulled over this for a while. Right after Dad dropped the fresh whole wheat pappardelle—which Great-Aunt Yvonne produces in gargantuan qualities as a hobby and shares with us on a weekly basis—into the water, Funderburke and the kids burst back into the room. "I just heard from Benny. He and his team just made a ton of arrests in a credit card spoofing ring."

"What's that?" Amara asked.

"Apparently, the gangs that used to make their cash selling drugs and extorting local business owners into paying protection have had to get much more technologically savvy in recent years. A number of them have entered the credit card fraud and identity theft rackets. There are these little credit card readers called skimmers that can be ordered online and installed over genuine card scanners, such as at a gas station pump, or any other place where credit and debit cards are used. Also, little cameras can be placed above the keypads to catch the PIN numbers. So some unsuspecting citizen can fill his gas tank and not realize that he's being robbed."

While this was new to Amara, Funderburke had drummed this into my head long ago, instilling in me the habits of tugging the credit card scanner every time I filled up my car and placing my hand over the keypad just in case a tiny camera was watching me type in my code. It came in handy a couple of months ago when a skimmer came off in my hand.

A partially revitalized Volker exclaimed, "So that's what happened to Juror #3!"

"Exactly. Benny and his team tracked down where all these giant TVs and other items were being shipped, and now there's no doubt that Juror #3 was the victim of a professional criminal gang. Of course, I wouldn't put it past Sangster to argue the theory that Volker tracked down some local credit card spoofing gang, asked them very politely to steal Juror #3's information, and they happily obliged. But right now, we've got some pretty promising evidence that Volker has been unjustly accused."

"So what now?" I asked.

Funderburke shrugged. "I asked Benny if I could be the one to pass this information on to Sangster, but apparently, there's some procedural rule and some loose ends to be tied up, so I have to wait for him to take care of everything and pass this news up the chain. It's a pity, because I would've liked to have been there when Sangster heard the news and seen her face. But now that she's made a public accusation on television, Sangster's in a perilous position. Not just professionally, because her boss is going to make sure that all the egg being splattered lands entirely on her face, but also, if she so much as looks at Volker wrong, all he has to do is say the magic words. Slander and defamation of character before witnesses lawsuit."

"No reason why that has to be just an empty threat," Volker murmured. I didn't care for the way he said that. I started getting an odd, chilly, twisted feeling in my stomach.

Funderburke took the kids outside for more soccer, and as Dad finished up the food, Toby and I set the dinner table.

"Are you ready for your doctor's appointment?" Toby and Bernard were going to be evaluated by a specialist in autism in two days.

"Why shouldn't I be ready? I just have to answer the questions he asked me honestly. It's not like I'm going to have to study for them." Toby kept her head turned away from me, and it bugged me that I wasn't able to see her face, but I didn't want to pressure her to make eye contact. I'd read on the Internet that wasn't advisable.

"Well, if you want to talk about it, I'm here for you."

"Thanks. I'm fine." She said nothing else, and I felt like it would do more harm than good to say any more on the subject. It was a struggle keeping it bottled up, because I had so much I wanted to say. I'd done a little of my own Internet searching recently, and I discovered that Juror #2's estranged daughter was a therapist who worked with autistic kids. On her website, she said she got interested in autism care because she had a family member who had undiagnosed autism, and it had really taken a toll on their relationship. Could she have been talking about her father? Could his condition have had anything to do with his adamancy that he was right about Benek's guilt?

Mom called and informed us she wouldn't be home for dinner, so we ate without her. I was still obsessing with autism-related matters. If Rally had autism, would she be able to go off to college? Would she have to stay in

Milwaukee? I'd be fine with that, but would she? What if colleges were scared off by her diagnosis and wouldn't admit her? Then I looked at Mom's empty chair and started worrying. What if she got diagnosed as being on the spectrum, and attorneys tried to use it against her in court? What if autism became just another reason for jurors to dismiss her conclusions? And what if parents didn't think a teacher with autism could properly educate their kids? What would happen to Dad? I was driving myself nuts, but I couldn't stop my anxiety.

At dinner, Yeh-Yeh spent most of the time discussing how he'd found three articles Juror #10 had published in scholarly journals over the last two years and, after fifteen minutes of utilizing a search engine, had found no less than nine examples of plagiarism from other scholars, all multiple paragraphs long, with only minuscule changes, just one word per sentence, at most. He'd reached out to a couple of friends of his who ran academic integrity blogs, and we'd see if the publicity had any impact at all on Juror #10's career.

Time passed. Mom called to say she'd be home at nine, then phoned again to say she'd be back around ten, and the process repeated approximately every sixty minutes. Funderburke wanted to stick around and hear what Mom had discovered, but Volker had to get home, especially now that it didn't appear that the police would be waiting outside his house to interview him. They left around ten-fifteen, and I spent an hour and a half on the basement elliptical machine, did a few dozen crunches, showered, and revised the third chapter of my dissertation until two-thirty in the morning, when Mom staggered into the house.

Having eaten nothing since lunch, she demanded her dinner before providing me and Dad, who had also stayed up, with details. After she'd refueled and had a similar reaction to the plantain cream pie that I did, she confirmed that I should always listen to my instincts. "This wasn't a suicide."

"The husband killed her?"

"He did. The police presented him with the forensic evidence, and he cracked like a murderous egg." Mom leaned back in her chair with a cup of the herbal tea she used to calm down and explained. "The first sign this wasn't a suicide was the bruise on her scalp. She'd been knocked out prior to her death, and one can't climb into a car, attach a long tube to the exhaust pipe, stick in through the window, and lie back and asphyxiate while one's already unconscious. Not only that, but the techs found absolutely no fingerprints anywhere in the car or on the tubing. She should have left them all over if she'd set up the scene herself. Not only that, but her hands were slathered with an herbal cream she sold at her shop, and if she'd pulled the car door shut behind her, she'd have left lotion residue on the door handle."

"Then the suicide note was forged?" Dad asked.

"Actually, it was a suicide text. Obviously, he sent it himself and used the disruption at her store as an excuse."

"He had a girlfriend on the side, of course," I stated rather than asked.

Mom looked surprised at my statement. "Apparently. How did you know?"

"Funderburke saw the Adulterer's Circle in his wallet." It took a minute to explain the term to a confused Mom.

"Was the girlfriend involved?" Dad asked.

"They're still investigating. He denied it in his confession, but he might have been covering for her. He claims she confronted him about his affair, they argued, and he accidentally shoved her, and she knocked herself out on the corner of the end table when she fell. Then he says he panicked and set up the suicide scene. I'll go in tomorrow to double-check the M.E.'s work to see if the head trauma was caused by a fall, like he says. By the way, has that ultraviolet dye I ordered arrived? I need it for an experiment to test the prosecution's theory of that assault case in Madison."

"Yes, it's on the shelf next to your lab," Dad informed her.

"Good, thanks. The paperwork for this murder-made-to-look-like-suicide can wait for tomorrow. And by tomorrow, I mean the upcoming calendar day, because my plate is overflowing with all the work I didn't have the chance to finish today."

"Well, this is going to be a black eye for ADA Sangster," I giggled. "She's going to look pretty silly after blaming this death on Volker."

It just goes to show that I'm not always right. I must've been exhausted, because after I crawled into bed at three-forty, I didn't wake up until after two. Though I slept through it, I learned that around noon, ADA Sangster had held another press conference without the approval of her superiors at the DA's office. Making no mention of either of her previous false allegations against Volker, she announced that newly uncovered evidence would prove beyond a shadow of a doubt that Benek had indeed murdered Lada.

When I checked my messages, I learned that the ADA had invited me, Funderburke, and the Berchtwelts to meet with her that evening. Most of the jurors would be there, too.

Chapter Nine: The Prosecutor Makes an Accusation

FUNDERBURKE

Thisu was one of the rare occasions when I was up earlier than Nerissa, and that day, I slept for eleven glorious hours and woke up at half past noon. Upon struggling out of bed and stumbling through my morning wake-up routine, I picked up my phone and discovered that I had received seven messages from Volker, each left about fifteen minutes apart. I debated whether or not to have some breakfast before calling him back. My planned meal was the low-sugar, high-protein Greek yogurt cheesecake I'd whipped up a couple of nights earlier but hadn't had the chance to eat yet. All I had to do was stir up a couple of cups of Greek yogurt, add an egg and some egg whites, a few spoonfuls of cornstarch, a drizzle of honey from a local farm, and a dollop of vanilla extract, pop it my tiny oven, and by the time I was finished with my home workout of elliptical running and kettlebells, it was ready to be cooled and placed in the refrigerator. Admittedly, it's not as satisfying as actual cheesecake with cream cheese and sugar and chocolate and all the goodies that make life worth living, but it's way better tasting than ninety percent of the allegedly healthy food I eat to keep my muscles firm and my belly flat. The previous day I'd indulged myself with great meals, and today I needed to dine more carefully.

I decided that I'd been giving Volker plenty of attention lately, but I'd been neglecting my cake, but just as I poured a blend of blueberries, strawberries, and raspberries on it and dusted some cinnamon on top, Volker called again. I answered the call by instinct and immediately felt a wave of regret.

"Hi! I finally got through to you. Where were you?"

"In bed."

"You sure do sleep a lot. I thought that adults needed less sleep than kids."

"I thought that too when I was growing up. Maybe that's true for a lot of adults, but I need extra shut-eye. And my breakfast," I added. "Will you be terribly offended if I eat while you talk?"

"Not at all. I'm going to do most of the talking anyway."

I'd already popped the first bite into my mouth, and I felt the first traces of the fog leaving my brain. Caffeine makes my heart skip, so I need a high-protein breakfast as soon as possible, especially if I'm going to get behind the wheel of a car. The thought struck me that it would be even better with hot fudge drizzled over it, but instead of satisfying my sweet tooth, I simply asked Volker why he called.

"Great news! A detective from the D.A.'s office came to our house to search Benek's room an hour ago!"

After using my tongue to extract a raspberry seed from between my teeth, I politely inquired as to why on earth this would be considered a positive development.

"Because if this works out the way I hope it will, then I'm —we're—looking at a major win here."

I wasn't at peak cognitive ability yet. Thanks to the power of breakfast cheesecake, I was regaining my critical thinking skills at a remarkable pace. I knew that something wasn't quite right, but sleep inertia was slowing down my synapses. Anxious to jump-start my mental muscles, I shoved more food into the place where it would do the most good, and upon swallowing, I finally figured out what wasn't making sense to me.

"You sound upbeat. When I last spoke to you, you were pretty down in the dumps over Juror #9's death."

"Well, it's a new day. I wasn't responsible for it at all."

"You weren't so certain of that last night."

"Oh…." His voice trailed off as he demonstrated that his brain was currently nimbler than mine. "Nerissa hasn't told you yet. That makes sense. She didn't get the news until pretty late."

"What news?"

"It's better that she tells you. Call her after I hang up. But first, you need to be prepared. Sangster's almost certainly going to call you later today, and if and when does, she'll invite you to a meeting. I need you to accept. I know you're inclined to be snarky towards her, but please, when she invites you, come. Don't be too willing, that might make her suspicious. Just complain for a little bit, let her be all imperious and order you around for a bit, and then grumble something about doing this because you want to and not because she's telling you to, and then show up with Nerissa."

"How do you know that's going to happen?"

"Because I have a plan for revenge, especially against Sangster." Here, he altered his voice to an unusual cadence, and I didn't learn until much later that he was quoting and imitating. "She is a disease. She is a cold, calculating woman, and I will have revenge!"

"I thought that Juror #9's death put you off vengeance."

"I'm back on the horse. But last night, I realized that of all the people who are responsible for causing Benek's death, Sangster is the worst. She withheld evidence that could have cleared him. She's the one who's led the public smear campaign after his death. She's the one with the most to gain by keeping him branded a murderer. And I realized, I've been foolishly dividing my attention amongst a lot of people of varying degrees of culpability when I should have been directing my focus with laser-like intensity towards the worst of the worst, instead of giving her a chance to regroup and anticipate my plans. If all goes well, this will mark the end of Sangster's legal and political career."

My stomach clenched a bit, even as I remembered that Sangster kept referring to evidence against Benek and proof of passing the video on to Naeem, but she never got around to sharing it with me. I was pretty skeptical about its existence, though instead of voicing these thoughts, I felt the need to point out that there was a very real possibility that his plan might go wrong. "Just how long have you been planning this?" I asked.

"Since nine this morning. It just came to me. I planned it in half an hour, and everything fell into place perfectly. I keep telling you that I don't believe in the Divine Hand of Providence guiding human activity, but if this works out the way I want it to, then I may just have to rethink my entire worldview."

"Are you absolutely certain that this is a good idea? What if something goes horribly amiss?"

"I've thought about that. No guts, no glory. I owe it to Benek's memory. I don't know if I'll ever have another chance to avenge him."

"I thought you never wanted to risk having someone's blood on your hands after last night."

"I don't. But in Sangster's case, I'll make an exception. How about a deal? If this plan doesn't work out exactly as I'd hoped, I will give up all thoughts of revenge and never do anything to get payback ever again. I know you're trying to protect me from legal retributions or save my immortal soul or something silly like that, but please, let me try this."

"I don't think I can stop you."

"That's right, you can't. You've been great to me, Mr. Funderburke. Now I'm staking everything on this last shot. Remember, if, or rather when, Sangster asks for a meeting, you have to grant in to her. Please say "yes.""

I don't know why I said, "Okay." I didn't feel comfortable saying it, but I lost control of my vocal cords.

"Great! Call Miss Kaiming and tell her what I told you and ask her to tell you about last night. Thanks! See you soon!"

I stared at my phone for a few minutes after he hung up, totally nonplussed. For a moment, I thought I'd lost my appetite. Then I glanced at the remains of the cheesecake, realized that I was indeed still hungry, and cleaned my plate and ate another slice with even more berries before calling Nerissa. She didn't answer, and I learned later that she was still asleep.

Fifteen minutes later, I received a call from ADA Sangster, who came just shy of the legal definition of demanding that I attend a meeting she'd be holding at six o'clock that evening. After some feigned reluctance, as Volker requested, I agreed.

Mrs. Zwidecker knocked on my door and informed me that a light bulb in her living room wall sconce had burst this morning when she'd flipped the switch, so I shut off the fuse to the room, picked up a raw potato from her kitchen, chopped it in half, pushed one of the halves over the broken bulb, unscrewed it all, dropped it in an empty cottage cheese container I'd taken from the recycling bin, replaced the bulb, and reactivated the fuse. All was well.

While Mrs. Zwidecker thanked me and pondered different ways to cook the unused potato half for her lunch, my testosterone levels had spiked to dangerously high levels from my little foray into home maintenance, so I decided to jog to the indoor pool down the road and burn off some my pent-up energy. I spent an hour swimming laps, and when I returned to the locker room, I found a text from Nerissa telling me she couldn't believe she'd slept so late and wondered where I was. I replied that I'd be at her house in twenty-five minutes and made it in twenty-three.

Once there, I met Nerissa in her study. She was a bit worried about Yeh-Yeh, who'd left a note saying he'd ordered a rideshare and was running errands. No further specifics had been provided, and since he'd been gone for a few hours and wasn't answering Keith's messages, she was concerned something was wrong. I asked her if Midge had found something to question the supposed suicide of Juror #9, and Nerissa brought me up to speed.

"No wonder Volker's mood changed so dramatically," I noted. I informed her of the details of my conversation with Volker a couple of hours earlier.

"But how did he know about the results of Mom's investigation?" Nerissa asked before I could impress her by regaling her with the story of my potato-wielding skills.

"I don't know. I wondered if he called you, and one of your parents told him."

We checked with Keith and Midge, but both of them denied having spoken to Volker, pointing out that they wouldn't have passed on this information to him even if they had, as it was supposed to be under wraps until the authorities were ready to make a formal announcement.

Then how did he know? I asked myself. I asked where they'd held the conversation, and when they told me the dining room, I performed a quick check, looking for listening devices. Nerissa and her parents checked their phones to see if they'd somehow pocket-dialed Volker without realizing it, and he'd overheard their conversation, but their call histories provided no record of that.

I puzzled over this for the next few hours, as I played board games with the elder triplets, attended afternoon Mass with the Kaimings, and returned home to have a quick late lunch of tuna and spring greens salad before getting dressed for ADA Sangster's little meeting.

As I was buttoning up my shirt, I received a call from my mother.

"Isaiah?"

"What is it?"

"I haven't thanked you yet for helping me the other night. I should have called earlier, but I was too embarrassed."

"That's all right." I was a bit unnerved, because it sounded like she's been crying, which I have rarely known her to do. The woman who strikes fear in every divorce court in Milwaukee is not known for shedding tears. She makes other people sob, especially kids caught up in custody disputes.

"Do you have time to talk?"

"I'm actually on my way to a meeting right now. Is it important? You sound upset."

"I just had an argument over the phone with your sister."

"Half-sister," was my reflexive response.

"She said she hated me, and she never wanted to speak to me again. Isaiah?"

"Yes."

"I know we don't have the best relationship, and I'm not asking you to tell me you love me, but could you please, please just tell me that you don't hate me."

Sighing, I said, "I don't hate you, Mom."

"Because you did once. You did for many years."

"I've been working on that. You know that."

"Yes, thank you. There's something else. I've been speaking to my friends–"

196

I came very close to saying, *You don't have "friends," Mom, you only have colleagues*, but I held my tongue.

"—And one of my old classmates from law school was at that new French restaurant the other day and overheard Tatum dining there with her parents. Apparently, they're not pleased with her. She's an only child, you know, and neither of the Sangsters rose to the career heights they felt they deserved— they both tried to climb the political ladder into elected office and failed miserably, so now they're forcing all their hopes and dreams upon their daughter. They threatened to disinherit her if she let them down. They don't want her to embarrass them. I know you think I'm a terrible mother—"

"I don't—" I lapsed into unintelligible mumbling and hoped that she wouldn't ask me to raise my voice.

"—But as awful a parent as you think I am, take my word on it, the Sangsters are worse. They've put so much pressure on her to become a senator or a governor or even more, and they say that pressure turns coal into diamonds, but sometimes all you get is coal dust. That young woman is all ambition and no ethics. She does not like losing, and her reputation is riding on this case. Remember, animals are the most dangerous when they're cornered. Do not let her scratch you with her claws."

Despite all of my lingering resentments, I was touched, and I said so.

"Well, you'd better get to your meeting. Goodbye." She hung up, leaving me staring at my phone before pulling on my suit.

When I picked up Nerissa and her parents soon afterwards, she commented that this was obviously going to be a confrontational meeting, and in selecting my outfit, I'd been paying attention to her telling me that black and red were dominant power colors. My dress shirt and suit were all black, and as the temperature had dropped twenty degrees since morning as a FROPA passed through and the wind had picked up a dozen or so miles per hour, I'd decided it wasn't time yet for my walking coat to go on summer vacation, though I'd removed the insulated lining. I didn't have the heart to tell her that, as per usual, I'd grabbed my clothes out of my wardrobe without bothering to pay attention to what I was putting on my body, as long as I had one of each necessary garment on me. If I hadn't looked down at my feet,

I wouldn't have been certain that my shoes matched. Incidentally, Nerissa was wearing a crimson-draped satin blouse with a black lambskin skirtsuit, so she'd taken her own "power color" advice. Keith and Midge hadn't gotten the coloring message, as Keith's suit was navy blue and Midge's was tan.[1]

We were the first to arrive at the courthouse, fifteen minutes early, and the security guard showed us into a massive though sparely decorated conference room. Sangster was waiting for us, and she directed us to take chairs on one side of the table next to her. Soon, Juror #2 arrived, though he did not acknowledge our presence. Juror #1 arrived soon afterwards, and greeted us with a similarly frosty reception as she settled down on the opposite side of the table from us. Professor Kaiming arrived next, to our surprise, and sat on the other side of Keith. A nurse wheeled Juror #11 in next, and though she still looked seriously ill, Juror #11 appeared stronger than she had earlier, and she gave us a smile with a twinkle in her eye. Volker, Otto, and Alfie were the next to take their seats at our side of the table, and we exchanged greetings but received no details as to what was happening. The next arrivals were Juror #5 and a woman who I soon learned was the mother of the late Juror #7. Naeem came next, and Sangster's finger pointed to our side of the table. Clotilde Casagrande and Bex Juaquin arrived next and were seated alongside the jurors. Juror #12 came next, but when Juror #8 walked through the door, he was told not to join the other jurors, but to sit alongside us. Juror #3 entered with a very shaky-looking woman clinging to his arm, who I later learned was his wife. At a quarter after six, Juror #4 entered regally, holding onto the District Attorney's arm, not for support, like Mrs. Juror #3, but to indicate how friendly she was with the city's top prosecutor.

The D.A. took the chair at the other end of the table, and Juror #4 sat beside him, smiling as if she were the guest of honor. A young man, presumably a technician, set up a computer screen and a web camera, and after a moment, the face of Juror #10 appeared.

"Well," ADA Sangster beamed with obvious satisfaction. "Everybody's here. I'm so glad that everybody's schedule managed to accommodate this little get-together. This won't take long. I'm here to demonstrate for once and for all that you—" She gestured towards the jurors' side of the table. "—came to the right verdict after all. Benek Berchtwelt was guilty. I now have definite evidence of that."

"Are you certain?" Volker asked with ersatz innocence. "After all, you were pretty certain that Juror #9 committed suicide twenty-four hours ago. And that I'd stolen Juror #3's credit card information."

Juror #3 stared down at his hands and squirmed uncomfortably. ADA Sangster showed no signs of embarrassment.

"Wait, are you saying that wasn't a suicide?" Juror #12 asked. "Because the news said it was."

"It was a murder." Midge's voice was soft, but confident. "Have you made an official arrest yet?" she asked the DA.

He nodded. "Her husband just agreed to a tentative plea deal for twenty years."

Volker smiled at Sangster. "Your allegations record isn't looking too strong at the moment."

Rallying, Sangster replied, "We're not talking about whatever comments I may or may not have made yesterday–"

"Yes, we are," Volker interrupted. "I just did. Pay attention."

Ignoring him, the ADA continued. "–I've called you all here today to clear up some uncertainty and misinformation that has been spread over the last few weeks. When Benek Berchtwelt was convicted of the brutal murder of his estranged girlfriend, Lada Casagrande, the twelve members of the jury considered the evidence and came to a correct and just verdict. Benek. Berchtwelt. Was. Guilty." She punctuated each word with a tap on the table.

Volker imitated her. "No. He. Was. Not."

Jaw clenched, Sangster spoke rigidly. "Could you please show me the respect I deserve and allow me to speak without interruption?"

"People who refuse to show respect don't deserve it in return," he retorted. Volker was deliberately trying to wind her up, and he was succeeding.

"If you don't sit still and be quiet, I'm going to ask you to leave," Sangster snapped.

Juror #2 rose from his chair. "I'm a very busy man, and I had to cancel two appointments to make it here today. I can't stay here all night. Whatever you have to tell us, can you please make it as quick as possible?"

There was a general murmur of agreement amongst the other jurors. Sangster appeared to be a bit annoyed by this response, as she appeared to have prepared a detailed and lengthy presentation. Before she could respond, I contributed my pair of pennies. "Look, I've met most of you. For those of you who haven't spoken to me yet, I'm Isaiah Funderburke. I'm a private detective working for Volker's school This is my girlfriend and partner Nerissa..." From the look on Sangster's face, my window for speaking was narrowing fast, so I decided not to introduce the rest of the Kaimings at the moment. I hoped they didn't feel snubbed. "Over the course of our investigation, we found that there was no reliable evidence connecting Benek to the murder. The witnesses who claimed to have seen him on the night of the murder were mistaken about the day. The bite mark evidence was garbage, the wound on Lada's body was caused by a cat. So if you have any new alleged proof against Benek, I suggest that you bring it up immediately."

"All right!" Sangster snapped. "But first, I want to point out just how wrong you've been with your little theories. Benek Berchtwelt was the only person with the motive and opportunity to commit the murder."

"What about the pervy volleyball coach?" Volker asked.

"He was with his latest underage girlfriend at the time," she replied with a smug smile.

"Do you have any other corroboration besides her word?"

Volker's question erased her smile. "No, but—"

"So you'll accept a groomed girl's word over mine, then? Because when I told the truth about my brother's alibi, you dismissed it out of hand."

"We compared Coach Shencrowe's DNA with that of Lada's baby. He did not father her child. Furthermore, Shencrowe kept a journal of his... conquests. Lada was not mentioned in it."

This was news to me, and I didn't see the point in hiding my surprise and disappointment. "There's still the burglar at large."

Sangster's smug smile returned. "No, he is not "at large." He was arrested last night."

I knew immediately from her face and tone that there had to be some sort of exonerating evidence clearing him, almost certainly an alibi. And as Sangster revealed, the burglar who had been preying upon the neighborhood (his guilt was proven thanks to the stolen goods in his basement, followed by a confession) had celebrated a particularly lucrative heist the afternoon of Lada's murder by going out, getting sloppy drunk, and starting a fight with the bartender. He'd spent the night in a cell, but he'd been released the next morning after the bartender declined to press charges. Bottom line, he had an unshakeable alibi.

"We've checked her two ex-boyfriends, they also alibi out," Sangster continued. "Besides, she was on decent enough terms with both of them. One was still obsessed with her, but not to a homicidal level. The only person with any reason to kill her was the jealous boyfriend who realized she'd cheated on him."

"And the father of the child," Nerissa added.

"My daughter was a good girl!" Mrs. Casagrande shouted at the same time, partially drowning out Nerissa's comment. "She was not the sort of young woman to be unfaithful, and I resent your frequent implications that my daughter was some sort of...slut! Don't you realize that she was a remarkable young woman? Without her comfort, I'd never have made it after my husband's death!"

The ADA mumbled something that was meant to be placating, but it didn't work. "You must have made a mistake at the lab," Mrs. Casagrande insisted. "Benek had to have been my granddaughter's father. There's no other explanation."

"We'll return to that later," Sangster replied. "But the fact remains that he killed her, and thanks to some new information that my investigators uncovered, I'm now able to prove it conclusively." She pointed to Alfie and Juror #8. "These two gentlemen were interviewed this morning in connection to some of the recent attacks on those of you who have only done your civic duty as jurors. During these conversations, Mr. Witteveen mentioned that Benek Berchtwelt was not averse to gaining an unfair advantage at sports."

"He never cheated at athletics!" Volker snapped.

"Oh, yes, he did. Several months before he died, Benek started using a cream made out of a type of naturally occurring steroid found in Chinese herbs. Apparently, he bought it online and had it shipped to his house. Apparently, he'd apply it to his arms and legs to make his muscles grow faster. He didn't tell anyone else about it, because he didn't want any of his teammates using it and challenging him for dominance on the team. Anyway, based on that information, I had an investigator search his room and found *this* hidden in a drawer."

She pulled an evidence bag out of her briefcase. In it was a jar of balm, and the label was written entirely in Chinese characters. I recognized it at once. It wasn't Chinese performance-enhancing herbs. It was Professor Kaiming's sciatica relief cream. Nerissa, Keith, and Midge also knew what it was at a glance, and we all turned towards the professor as one. He covered his smile with his tented hands, and when I caught Volker's eye, I knew that we had to keep this knowledge to ourselves for a bit longer.

"Even if my brother did use Asian herbal performance enhancers, what does that have to do with anything?" Volker scoffed. "Are you suggesting that cream gave him roid rage? Is that what you think? The chemicals he was rubbing all over his body made him snap?"

"You know, that's possible." A surprised yet pleased look spread over Sangster's face as she said that. "I can't rule out the possibility that this crime was fueled in part by the use of illicit substances. If your brother had admitted the fact that he was under the influence when he committed this dastardly crime, I might have been more willing to accept a plea bargain of some kind."

"It wouldn't have done him much good even if he had confessed to a crime he didn't commit," Volker snapped. "After all, it doesn't matter if he was thrown in that filthy jail for five years or five decades. He still would have been stuck with those psychotic degenerates who murdered him a couple of months into his sentence."

If Sangster had grit her teeth any harder, her molars would have been reduced to powder. "The point is, Benek applied these chemicals to his body regularly. Which means that he used his hands to spread the cream over his muscles. Does that sound logical?"

"Well, he wouldn't have used his feet," Juror #12 quipped.

"Exactly. Now, when I saw this lotion, I realized that even if he washed his hands, it was very possible that a significant amount of residue was left on them. And there's no reason to assume that he washed his hands. That's why I had the murder weapon sent up from storage and sent to a laboratory. As you'll recall, Lada Casagrande was strangled with a pair of her own jeans. I wondered if faint but detectable traces of this cream could have been left on the weapon."

I saw Volker quivering, but he didn't appear to be nervous. If anything, he seemed to be trying to restrain his excitement.

Sangster's phone chimed. "That's the lab. They're right outside with the test results." A moment later, a young woman entered the room, carrying a folder with papers in it and a large plastic evidence bag with a pair of jeans inside it. Sangster didn't introduce the lab tech or give her the opportunity to introduce herself. "Well? Did you find anything?"

"I did," the lab tech replied. "After examining the jeans, I discovered some faint, greasy stains near the cuffs of the legs. When I sniffed the stains, I recognized the herbal smell that was present in the sample of lotion I took from the jar you gave me. The tests proved it conclusively. The stains on the jeans were caused by the lotion. They're very faint, so I suppose that explains why no one noticed them before now. Perhaps the person who originally looked over these jeans had a cold, which is why the herbal scent wasn't detected either."

"No one's blaming you," Sangster declared magnanimously. "But Benek Berchtwelt was the only person who used that Chinese herbal steroid cream. The only way the cream could have gotten onto the legs of those jeans is if he handled them. And the only reason why his hands would have touched those jeans there is if he had used them to strangle Lada Casagrande. I believe that this is proof positive that Benek Berchtwelt was guilty all along and that his conviction was just."

I caught a quick exchange of glances between Professor Kaiming and Volker. Volker's head bobbed in a very faint nod, and the Professor cleared his throat. "There's a couple of flaws in your reasoning."

His comments didn't reduce the palpable smugness slathered all over Sangster's face. "Really? What makes you think that?"

"Well, for starters, that jar of cream didn't belong to Benek Berchtwelt."

"It was found in his room."

"Yes, I put it there myself."

"What!" Sangster twisted into a full-body flinch.

"That's right." Professor Kaiming stood up, leaned on his cane, limped down to the head of the table, and picked up the bag containing the jar of balm. "It's not his cream, it's mine. And it's not a steroid cream. It's made by a friend of mine out of herbs he grows in his greenhouse. It's a harmless pain reliever for my sciatica. Works pretty well, I might add. But it certainly doesn't cause my muscles to grow."

After a brief impression of a motorboat running out of gas, Sangster repeated herself. "What?"

"I take it you don't read Chinese characters. If you did, you'd know right away that this doesn't say "Herbal steroid for enhanced athletic performance." It actually says "Leg pain reliever for Professor Howard Kaiming." Take it to someone else who knows the language. They'll tell you." The Professor tossed the bag with the jar to the lab tech. "Run some more tests on its contents. You'll find out pretty fast that no student-athlete would use this to bulk up."

Sangster pointed a quavering finger at Alfie. "But…. He told me this morning."

"I may have been mistaken," Alfie replied with a grin.

"You lied! I'm going to charge you with perjury?"

"Was Alfie under oath?" I asked. "Because if he wasn't—"

"It's still a false statement!"

"I never said that Benek used that jar of cream," Alfie noted. "This morning, I told you that Benek spoke to me once about how he was wondering if he should start using a performance-enhancing drug to ensure he got a college scholarship. I mentioned that he talked about some Chinese herbs that might serve as a natural steroid that were mixed into a cream, and couldn't be detected in a normal blood test. I also mentioned that I'd seen him applying a lotion to his arms one afternoon after practice. That's all I told you. You can't prove that any of that was false. I made simple statements, and I'm the only one alive who can verify them. You jumped to the conclusion that there was a jar of Chinese herbal steroid cream in Benek's room."

We could all see the gears turning in Sangster's head. Before she could respond, the D.A. asked, "But if Benek never used that cream, then how did it get on the jeans?"

"Obviously, someone put it there. The person who had the most to gain by convincing the world that Benek was guilty."

"What are you implying?" Sangster's voice was awkwardly high.

Juror #8 pulled a flashlight out of his pocket and handed it to Volker. "Thanks for getting this for me," Volker said. "Consider the two of us even now. Your debt is paid."

"Just what are you—"

Talking over Sangster, Volker told the lab tech, "You're wearing gloves. Could you please take the jeans out of the bag and hold them up?" As she complied, Volker switched off the room lights. "This isn't a regular flashlight. It's a UV black light." Switching it on, he pointed it at the legs of the jeans. Spots near the cuffs began to glow.

"That shouldn't happen," the lab tech said.

"It should if the cream was mixed with ultraviolet dye," Volker replied.

Midge made a little choking sound, and Keith placed a hand on her shoulder.

"I mixed some in with the cream Professor Kaiming brought to our house this morning." He turned to Sangster. Even in the darkened room, the triumph was plain as day on his face. "Hold out your hands."

"I'm not—"

"Do it, Tatum." The D.A.'s voice was so commanding that she complied instantly.

The black light danced over her palms, which glowed faintly but discernably. "You washed your hands, but you couldn't get rid of all the ultraviolet dye. Your skin absorbed too much of it." Volker gloated. "You tried to frame my brother. But you didn't suspect that I would anticipate your evil plan."

"I don't understand. What's going on?" Juror #5 was twisting her hands with the kind of expression deer make when they're staring into headlights.

"The prosecutor tampered with evidence," Juror #1 explained.

"At the trial, she withheld video proof that my brother did not attack Lada. She placed a mad scientist on the stand to testify to bite mark evidence."

"Even if that's so," Juror #2 snapped, "none of that proves that your brother was innocent!'

"My testimony did!"

"Will you stop with that?" roared Juror #12. "You're a broken record, man! We heard what you said, we figured you were lying–"

"You figured wrong, you filthy hippie!"

Nerissa tapped Volker on the shoulder. "Volker, maybe you should concentrate on your case against ADA Sangster right now. Remember what you said yourself about targeting your focus."

A fraction of a second's annoyance in Volker's expression shifted immediately to agreement. "You're right, Miss Kaiming. I'll deal with *them*—" He stabbed his thumb in the jurors' direction. "—later. Right now, I'm going to ask you—" He turned towards the DA. "What are you going to do about your miscreant prosecutor?"

"We'll launch a formal investigation," the DA replied. "Not just into your brother's case, but into every case she's ever touched."

"You'll never do that." Some of Sangster's former defiance returned. "Hundreds of convictions could be overturned. The lawsuits and settlements could bankrupt the city. Even the state. If any dangerous men get released from prison and rape or kill someone else, then it's on you. You'd better be looking for another job."

"I didn't become a prosecutor because I wanted to parlay it into a political career, like you," the DA responded with equal asperity. "I got into this branch of law because I believe that decent, law-abiding people need to be protected from dangerous, cruel people. And when I find one of those individuals working in my office, I consider that both a personal and a professional betrayal. If the voters believe that I should be held accountable for your actions that occurred under my watch, then I'll abide by their judgment. I love this job because I love what it stands for to me. An ideal to be lived up to, not a position of power to maintain. And if I sell out one innocent person because I want to keep my title or save a budget, then I will twist the most important aspect of my professional life into something vile and unrecognizable."

Sangster wasn't finished yet. "My parents will crush your career."

"I am not devoid of powerful friends either." The DA turned to Keith and Midge. "Please don't go home just yet. If you could stick around downtown for a couple of hours, I will meet you wherever you wish. There's a great deal to discuss. There may be a lot of work for you, Midge. I'm going to need to work with people I can trust, and maybe I might be able to convince your uncle to come out of retirement for a bit."

"It may not be that difficult," Midge replies. "He keeps telling me how bored he is."

Before I could respond, Sangster leapt forward and wrapped her hands around Volker's neck. I managed to pull her off without any difficulty, and Midge quickly examined the discolorations on the boy's throat.

His voice was croaky and distorted, but his words were still clear. "And now you've committed assault and battery on a minor before witnesses. You'd better believe you're going to face criminal and civil penalties now."

Sangster's face paled, and she flounced out of the room, slamming the door behind her. "I need to take care of her," The D.A. told us. "Please excuse me."

After he left, the rest of us were silent for a few moments. I was going to say a few words about the situation, but the lab tech beat me to it. "Am I in trouble? Because I swear, I didn't know that anything unethical was happening."

I assured her that she'd be all right, and she didn't seem to believe me, but then Nerissa said exactly what I did using slightly different words and arguably a more soothing tone, and the lab tech seemed to find Nerissa more convincing than me, because she hugged her and then hurried away.

Juror #4 was the next to leave, without a word or a glance to anybody else in the room. Jurors #2 and #12 were right behind her. "Don't you have anything you have to say to me?" Volker shouted to their backs. They didn't.

Juror #1, who has played very little part in the narrative so far, looked at us. "You may think that this is a victory. But it isn't. When you bend the rules, you compromise your integrity." Volker started to reply, but she flounced out of the room.

Juror #5 was next to rise. "I have to get back to my kids," she informed us apologetically. "My sister's going to kill me if I'm not back by seven-thirty. I'm sorry. I know I messed up. But they should never have let someone like me on a jury. I'm just not smart enough. It's their fault, really." She hurried out the door.

Nerissa nudged me and pointed. Juror #10, the academic fraud, had logged out of her video connection. I didn't know how long she'd been gone. Not wanting to waste the power, I shut down the computer.

The mother of Juror #7 was next. "I know you're upset about what happened to your brother. You have every right to be. But my baby girl did not deserve to have her headstone desecrated. That just wasn't right." She hurried away before Volker could say anything.

Juror #3 rose and placed his hands on his wife's shoulders. "Come on, honey, let's go home."

"No, we're not leaving," she told him.

"Honey, please."

"You know that you can't just leave. Speak to him."

Juror #3 moved reluctantly, robotically. "I...should not have accused you of stealing my credit card information," he told Volker.

"No, you shouldn't have. That is why I am going to sue you for slander and collect ten million dollars."

Juror #3's eyes bulged, and his face reddened. "I don't have ten million dollars."

"Then I will just have to be content with everything you do have."

"That's ridiculous."

"You went on television and made a criminally false statement smearing me. I'm going to have ambulance chasers lined up around the block, desperate for a piece of you. And when we're finished, maybe there'll be enough for you and your wife to have a cardboard box under the freeway. But not much more than that."

The knees of Juror #3 started sagging. "Please. My wife's got serious mobility issues. I just sank half of my savings into building a special house for her so she can move around comfortably. I need to work for another ten years just to have enough to retire."

"Watch how hard I cry. My lawyers will be in touch with you shortly."

"Volker!" Nerissa and Midge spoke at once. The message in that single word was unmistakable.

He whirled around at them. "Do NOT tell me to let this go! I have the chance to punish, really punish, one of the people who sent Benek to his death. Leaving this man bankrupt is how I'm going to honor my brother's memory."

"Do you want to know how you can hurt my husband? I mean really, really hurt him? Put him through so much pain that he won't be able to stand it? Absolutely gut him? Tear away at his insides? Hurt him more than any loss of money could possibly do?" Mrs. Juror #3 slowly rose to her feet and hobbled towards Volker. "Hurt me. He cares about my comfort and well-being more than his own. You can clean out his bank account, but that won't cause him anguish more than damage to me will. I know him so well, you see. He loves me too much, really."

"Honey, what are you–"

"This is between me and the boy, dear. He wants revenge, and I'm going to give it to him. Look at this." She pulled a slip of paper out of purse, fumbled around, found a pen, and then scribbled *I give permission for Volker Berchtwelt to inflict any sort of physical harm he desires upon me, and I hereby hold him harmless for any criminal or civil penalties.* Signing her name, she pressed the paper into Volker's hand. "Go ahead. Pull back and give me a black eye. Or better yet, let's go out into the hall. You can push me down a flight of stairs. When my husband sees me lying there, bleeding, bones broken, he'll be devastated. You can still sue us, if you like. No reason you can't have both the money and the satisfaction of seeing my husband in agony." She took Volker's hand. "Come on. Let's go to the staircase."

"I don't want to."

"But you want justice for your brother, don't you? All you have to do is give me a tiny little shove, and you can know that you've done right by your brother. We won't be able to afford proper reconstructive surgery after the fall, you know. My husband will have to devote himself to my care full-time, so he won't be able to earn more money to help us. We'll be completely and utterly ruined, just like you want. Let's go, dear." She tugged his arm. "This is the revenge you want. The revenge you need. I'm giving it to you on a silver platter. Come with me to the stairwell and push me."

"You're crazy!"

He didn't come with her, but Mrs. Juror #3 limped out of the room and dragged herself a couple of yards down the corridor to the big stone stairwell. The rest of us joined her in the corridor. "I'm right here. You just have to give a tiny little shove."

Volker's expression was rather like a goldfish that had been lifted out of its bowl, and was now flopping and gasping about on a dry surface. "Lady, there's something messed up with you."

"More than you know, dear." She gestured for him to come forward. He didn't want to at first, and then, to my surprise, Otto gave him a little push, causing him to stumble forward. Mrs. Juror #3 nodded. "Go on, shove me."

"I'm not going to do that."

"Don't you want vengeance?"

"I...I want it my way!" Without warning, Volker burst away from us and sprinted for the restroom.

"What the heck was that, honey?" Juror #3 looked dazed.

"We've raised three kids together, dear. I know how to deal with an angry child. When they want something, sometimes the best way to lance the boil is to offer them more than they're asking. Take it to the extreme. When my daughter wanted a tattoo, I said she could, as long as she got two, and I got to pick the other and place it wherever I want. Her skin is unblemished to this day. As far as I know." This last bit was added a few moments later as an afterthought.

"You took a crazy risk there, honey." Juror #3 shook his head. "That kid's a psycho."

"No, he's not," his wife replied before I could come to his defense. "He's a good boy. I know that when it comes right down to it, he'd never seriously harm anybody in any way. And now that he's passed up on a free offer to cause serious harm, he'll know he doesn't have it in him to go through with the lawsuit. That's lucky for us, because once the lawyers get involved, there's no stopping—" Her legs buckled, and she went flailing backwards. Her right hand gripped the banister tenuously, but fortunately, Nerissa and I were on her in half a second, pulling her back up, and Midge and Keith were there a moment later to assist.

While Juror #3 chastised his wife to be more careful, she muttered, "Knees aren't what they used to be. Thanks for the help."

A moment later, Volker exited the bathroom. He looked pale, and from the faint odor on his breath, I could tell that he'd been violently ill. Midge rummaged through her gigantic purse, pulled out a mint, and handed it to him, which he accepted with a silent nod and a barely perceptible smile.

"Look, kid..." Juror #3 stammered. "I know I made mistakes. I really messed up. I can't bring back your brother, but there's got to be something I can do to make amends, something short of handing over all my worldly goods to you."

"I don't see how," Volker's voice, so resonant a few minutes earlier, was now barely a whisper.

"I could...I'm a master builder, you know that. Is there anything you need done around your house? Any remodeling you need, I could do for free."

"The place is a dump," Otto informed him. "Whenever we use the shower, it leaks through the floor into the basement. And I keep tripping when I'm climbing into the tub."

"I could redo your bathroom, give you a walk-in shower." The two men talked for a bit. Juror #3 handed Otto a business card and told him to call him sometime in the next few days to schedule a consultation. His wife's legs wobbled rapidly as she tried to walk, and he scooped her up in his arms and carried her down the stairs.

"May I have that, please?" I pointed to the little permission slip Mrs. Juror #3 had written for Volker. It was sticking out of his pocket. He handed it to me, and I took it and tore it into confetti over the garbage can. Documents like that are dangerous.

Juror #11 cleared her throat and pushed her wheelchair up to Volker. "I'm fully aware that I owe you a massive debt. I don't have much time to repay it, but if you can think of anything it's in my power to do, please tell me sooner rather than later." She shook hands with all of us, and her nurse wheeled her down the corridor.

Volker dragged his toe along the floor. "You know, I learned something today. Multiple things."

"Oh? Like what?" Nerissa asked.

"That you can think you want something, even believe with every fiber of your being that the only way you can ever be happy again is to make someone else feel as awful as they made you feel. And then, when it's in your power to mete out that punishment…you start having second thoughts, and you don't know if it's because your conscience is holding you back, or if you're just too weak to seize your opportunity."

Nerissa patted him on the shoulder. "It's the former. Believe that."

Volker's face darkened. "I also learned that a good way to tell the difference between fundamentally decent and totally crummy people is to see which of them is willing to admit a mistake and make amends and which scatter like cockroaches when confronted with their culpability."

None of us had a ready response to that.

Midge wiped her glasses on her handkerchief and replaced them on her face. "Is anybody else hungry? I only had fruit and cottage cheese for lunch because I was short on time."

The rest of us chimed in our agreement, and Keith said, "I have a lot of questions about how you set up your little trap. Will you mind providing us with some details in a few minutes?"

Volker smiled. "Not at all. I'm very proud of my plan."

212

Clotilde Casagrande and Bex Juaquin came up to us. I'd thought they'd left while we weren't looking. "Please excuse us, but may we join you?"

"Because if Benek didn't kill Lada," Bex continued, "I think we know who really did."

---

[1] * I did not write these last two sentences myself. Nerissa added them when she was proofing my manuscript, apparently believing my attention to sartorial details was lacking. –Funderburke.

Chapter Ten: What Do We Tell Volker?

NERISSA

After some discussion on the best place to eat, we decided to drive down to the edge of downtown to a little Irish restaurant and inn. The manager was a friend of mine, and when I called, she kindly set aside a little private dining room for our meeting. Five minutes later, Funderburke, Mom, Dad, Yeh-Yeh, Volker, Otto, Juror #8, Naeem, Mrs. Casagrande, Bex, and I were seated around a circular table. Once we placed our orders, Funderburke made sure the door was securely shut and then asked Mrs. Casagrande to provide her theory of the case.

"It was Dalton Blencowe. I suspected him before, but I'm certain of it now."

Several people at the table were unfamiliar with his name, so Funderburke took a moment to explain that Dalton was a former boyfriend of Lada's. In response to my question as to what made her so sure, she answered, "He broke into my house yesterday." She hesitated for a moment. "I suppose that's not quite accurate. He didn't actually smash a window or pick the lock or anything. I left the door unlocked. I was gardening, and he must have waited until I started planting tomatoes around the other side of the house, and slipped inside."

"What did he do?" I asked.

"I went into the house to use the bathroom, and I nearly bumped into him. He had his hands full of some of Lada's things. I've left her room just as it was. He'd taken a framed picture of her, and a stuffed animal she'd had since she was a child, and most of her...underthings."

I found myself wishing Funderburke had spent more time investigating this guy. "How did he respond when you confronted him?"

"He begged me to let him keep what he was holding. He said he wanted some mementos to remind him of her. Of course, I absolutely lost it. I told him I'd call the police if he didn't put down all of her stuff and get out of my house immediately. He dropped what was in his arms onto the carpet and sprinted out the door, and after I'd put away my gardening tools and triple-locked my home, I put back everything he'd taken and scrubbed down her room to get rid of every trace of him. I knew that the ADA was full of it when she said he wasn't dangerous."

I pushed a strand of hair out of my eyes. "The guy sounds like a creep, but is he a killer?"

"He raided her room! Doesn't that scream guilt?"

"Of theft, yes. But all you had to do was shout at him and he skedaddled. I'm just wondering, if he was a strangler, why didn't he attack you when you caught him?"

Mrs. Casagrande didn't have an instant answer to that. "I suppose my guardian angel was looking out for me," she finally replied. "But what am I going to do about him?"

"You could file a police report," Funderburke informed her, "but it would've helped if you still had his fingerprints on Lada's possessions, and you said you wiped down everything. Is he going away to college?"

"No," Bex told us. "He doesn't have the grades for it and he didn't get a sports scholarship. He's working at his aunt's restaurant now busing tables, and frankly, I think he's going stay there until she retires."

"I thought Sangster said he had an alibi," I remembered.

"She said a lot of things, like there was forensic evidence not brought up at trial that proved Benek's guilt," Funderburke noted. "As far as I can tell, that was a lie. Until I see proof, I'm assuming her claims of the other suspects having alibis is pure piffle."

"What do you think, Bex?" Mom asked. "Is he a killer?"

215

"If it wasn't Benek, then I wouldn't mind Dalton being the guy. He always creeped me out. He was just totally obsessed with her, and it only got worse after they split up. Like on Black Friday, when my parents were visiting friends of theirs, I don't know for a second Thanksgiving dinner, a few months before Lada dropped out of school—"

"She didn't drop out, she transferred to online learning because of her condition," Mrs. Casagrande snapped.

"Right, sorry. Before she *transferred*, six, no, seven of us were hanging out, having a good time at my house. I was there with my then-boyfriend, Benek and Lada were, there, and so were Tessie and Pete, two other friends from school. Plus Alfie. I remember, Lada was singing Taylor Swift on the karaoke machine. She loved karaoke. Anyway, my parents were out of town, so we were all sitting around, drinking hunch punch, when Dalton pounded on the door. I didn't want to let him in the house, so I kept the screen door locked. He screamed out at Lada, begging her to take him back, and she just turned her back on him and told me to slam the door in his face. He kept pounding for another fifteen minutes, but finally, he gave up and went away. Then he came back an hour later." Bex shuddered. "The guy has crazy stalker issues. I do not trust him."

"What happened when he came back?" Nerissa asked.

"He just kept ringing the bell, shouting, "Lada! Lada! Lada!" By that time, we'd all paired up and gone off to...." Bex's voice trailed off as she decided not to finish that sentence. "When I heard him pounding, I jumped out of bed, opened my window, and told him to beat it. He swore at me, but then my neighbor came out with his gun and told him to shut up and get the hell out of the neighborhood, or he'd shoot him, stuff him, and mount his head. Dalton ran out into the night."

"Did Lada hear him the second time?"

"I don't know. She and Benek didn't leave my parents' bedroom until noon the next day. Man, were they hungover. And normally neither of them drank very much. I think the hunch punch was a little strong. I only had a sip because I didn't like the taste."

Yeh-Yeh wanted to know what hunch punch was, and I informed him that it was a mixture of strong hard liquors and fruit juices, often served at teen and frat parties. Not that I consumed any of it in my college days. I just knew what it was from people who did drink it.

"Everybody got up late the next day, actually. I tried to wake up my then-boyfriend at eleven, because I didn't know when my parents would be back, but I couldn't even shake him awake. Tessie and Pete were absolutely wasted, too—"

"Was Dalton ever violent?" Funderburke asked.

"No, just weird. But he could've hit his breaking point or something."

"It would've helped if I'd known about Dalton during the trial," muttered Naeem.

Bex squirmed but had no response.

Mrs. Casagrande rose from her chair. "I'm sorry, I have to head home. I have a migraine coming on. Can they cancel my order?" We assured her that we'd pay for her meal and Bex's, Bex promised she'd get Mrs. Casagrande home safely, and the two of them rose to leave. As they reached the door, Mrs. Casagrande turned around, took a long, deep breath, and said, "My daughter was a good girl. She wasn't perfect, but she wasn't promiscuous and she wasn't a liar. She was a treasure, and she deserves to be remembered as more than just some…slut who cheated on her boyfriend, had a baby by an unknown father, and then got murdered. She brought me so much joy, and…." Tears welled up in her eyes, and she dabbed at her eyes and hurried out the doorway.

"What do you think?" Naeem asked us after we sat quietly for a few moments. "Is Dalton the guy?"

"I'd need to meet him before coming to an opinion," Funderburke replied.

There was silence for a while, and then Dad asked, "So, Volker, would you mind telling us about how you set up your plan, please?"

Mom nodded. "Yes, how did you know all those details about the death of Juror #9?"

Volker looked down at his hands. "I don't want to get him in trouble."

"*Bernard,*" Mom, Dad, Funderburke, and I said simultaneously.

"He must've woken up in the night, didn't he? He went to the bathroom

217

or something like that, and he overheard us talking and listened in on the whole conversation," Dad deduced.

"Exactly," confessed Volker. "He heard Dr. Kaiming come home, and after he couldn't fall back to sleep right away he went down to greet her, but then he started hearing what you were saying and didn't want to miss it. I called the house around ten, and he was the one who answered the phone. He told me everything. Please don't be mad at him."

"We're not." Mom looked at Dad. "From now on, if there's ever anything we don't want that boy to overhear, we'll communicate in sign language." That wasn't a joke. Midge's grandmother went deaf a decade earlier, so Keith and Midge learned ASL.

"Well, Bernard caught all the details and passed them on to me. I don't need to repeat them, but the point you mentioned about Juror #9 using hand cream that should have left traces on the car door handle got me thinking. And I knew that detail would stick in Sangster's mind as well.

You see, I knew that Sangster was hurting. She'd gone on television and made two demonstrably false accusations against me. Her credibility was shot. If an official investigation proved my brother innocent, in the world's eyes, she wouldn't just be involved in a miscarriage of justice, she'd be a killer. Goodbye, political ambitions. So, what to do? I knew that someone as obsessed with her personal image and future as she was would be desperate to salvage her reputation. And I knew for someone who couldn't admit being wrong ever, the easiest road to public rehabilitation was to prove she was right in the first place. Which means that she had to demonstrate that Benek was guilty, and since he was innocent and she couldn't possibly uncover any real evidence against him, she'd have to manufacture some. Are you all following me here?"

We were.

"At first, I thought she might bribe a witness or something like that, but then I realized, the safest way for her to frame Benek would be to create physical evidence against him. I figured the original crime scene had been cleaned, Lada's body was buried, and about the only existing piece of evidence that could be tampered with was the murder weapon. But it was a pair of jeans. She couldn't plant fingerprints or hair or DNA on it, since Benek was also in his grave. Maybe they had a sample of Benek's hair or something somewhere, but I was betting that it might look too suspicious if she sent for his hair, and then later that day one of his hairs was miraculously discovered in the cuffs of the jeans or something like that. So I figured it had to be something else that wasn't from Benek's body, but was Benek-adjacent. And that's when I thought of Juror #9's hand lotion not being found on the car door handle.

Well, I'd heard Professor Kaiming complaining about his sciatica at dinner, and I'd seen his jar of Chinese herbal cream when I spoke to him one time at the house. And that's when I got the idea. A unique brand of hand cream that only Benek could've used. At least, in the story Sangster would be told. I'd heard about steroid creams, and off the top of my head, I came up with the idea of a special Chinese herbal steroid lotion. I saw the label was in Chinese, I was willing to gamble that Sangster wasn't sufficiently multilingual to read it. Then I got a text from Alfie telling me that he'd been called to the DA's office to talk to Sangster about his involvement in my revenge plan. I mean, my *alleged* revenge plan. It was kismet! He was in the right place at the right time. I texted him and told him what to say and how to say it. I needed him to protect himself, so I told him to be vague and not force the issue. Sangster had to think that using the cream as evidence was *her* idea. I calculated that if Volker subtly stressed that Benek was the only guy at school who used the Chinese cream, and with the mention of Juror #9's absent lotion residue fresh in her mind, she'd make the connection. Hand cream residue could easily be left on denim and go unnoticed at first. So I called the Professor and begged him to sacrifice a jar of his balm and to take a little of Dr. Kaiming's—Dr. Midge Kaiming's UV dye. Bernard mentioned you mentioning it, too."

"That stuff's not exactly cheap, you know," Midge noted.

"If you'd let me sue the pants off Juror #3 I could've bought you enough UV dye to paint your house. There's still time, you know. Anyway, the Professor loved my idea—"

"I did." Yeh-Yeh chuckled.

"—and he grabbed a rideshare and dropped off the lotion and dye. I had just enough time to mix the dye into the cream and hide it in Benek's room before the investigators arrived. After they left, I called Juror #8 and told him he'd nearly done enough to make everything right, and I'd forgive him if he bought me a black light flashlight. The rest you know. I assumed she'd apply the cream to her own hands and grab hold of the legs of the jeans, too excited about clearing her name to worry about absorbing any steroids into her own system. Everything went exactly as planned, and Sangster's tears of unfathomable sadness were so yummy and sweet!"

I couldn't speak for anybody else, but I was glad I was on Volker's side.

Mom looked skeptical. "There was a lot of supposition and blind luck in your plan. What would you have done if ADA Sangster had sensed a trap?"

"I wouldn't have been any worse off than I was before. Anyway, I figured that with her paying close attention to Juror #9's death, she wouldn't have gotten much sleep at all last night. I was counting on her not being in prime critical thinking mode."

Mom nodded. "I've had my I.Q. drop forty or fifty points on occasions when three babies have kept us up all night. Changing the subject a bit, did you notice the reporters waiting outside when we left?" I had, as did Funderburke and Dad. Nobody else saw them. "I'll bet she called them, expecting a triumphant vindication to make up for last night. The sight of all the surviving jurors behind her as she announced Benek's supposedly incontrovertible guilt would make for impressive optics. I wonder if she's thought to call them in order to let them know she won't be holding a press conference and they can go home?"

I didn't know, but I hoped those members of the press either gave up and left, or took some initiative and started to dig around and discover the major story that had just broken in the courthouse.

Funderburke leaned back in his chair and folded his arms. "When I think about it, I suspect that she planned to parlay the false evidence into a full victory."

"What do you mean?" Volker asked.

"You're not the only one trying to play 3-D chess with this case, Volker.

220

Think about it. Last night turned into a black eye for her. Does she aim for a total victory in the hopes that the brightness of her triumph will lead everybody to forget about her previous mistakes, or does she actually rewrite the past? Suppose, armed with the balm evidence on the murder jeans, Sangster declares that this is proof positive that your brother was guilty. If he did it, then you lied on the stand when you gave him an alibi. So what happens if Sangster threatens to prosecute you for perjury, armed with this new evidence that supposedly proves your story was false?"

"Do you think she would really have tried to throw him in jail?" Otto looked shocked.

"More likely juvie. She might have gone for a brief sentence, just to get her own back, but if she was being pragmatic, she might have offered a bright, shiny deal. Volker confesses to stealing Juror #3's credit card info and passing it on to the gang. He also admits to leading a harassment campaign against all of the other jurors, especially Juror #9. Volker admits that Juror #8 helped him hire actors to storm Juror #9's store, Juror #5's rotten restaurant, and everything else. Maybe she negotiates with Juror #9's husband, tells him she's willing to offer him some perks in prison, maybe a few candy bars a week and a little portable TV, *if* he states that his wife was so distraught due to Volker's actions that she spoke of taking her own life, even though he got to her first. That means Volker's reputation is shattered, and the previous night's press conference was correct after all. She was right all along, and she can ride the groundswell of support and sympathy to any public office she wants."

"Do you really think she'd think of that?" Otto asked.

"I do," Naeem nodded his head. "I'm sure of it. A couple of my clients in the past have swallowed their pride and confessed to crimes they swear they didn't commit—and I believe them, because they admitted to other infractions—when Tatum offered them a plea deal. I can't prove it, but in one case, there was this guy who was one of her political donors. His garage burned to the ground, and the insurance didn't want to pay, because they said it was negligence on the owner's part for smoking around a leaky gasoline can. He denied he'd had anything to do with it, but the insurance company wouldn't budge. Then I had a teenaged boy for a client, charged with setting off fireworks around the neighborhood. He admitted it, but swore that he'd never caused any damage to property. Tatum swooped in and offered him probation *if* he admitted to setting her friend's garage on fire with a careless firework. He didn't want to lie, but he was facing jail time, so he went with his common sense instead of his conscience and confessed to burning down the garage accidentally with his fireworks. My client kept his freedom, and Tatum's donor got a fat, juicy insurance check. Yay, criminal justice system?"

Our meal arrived at that moment, and soon the table was covered with Irish root soup, corned beef and cabbage, Reuben sandwiches, shepherd's pie, pot roast braised in Guinness, smoked salmon salad, Cobb salad, and meatloaf. As our appetites were fierce, the males at the table divided up the grilled cheese and chicken & biscuits Mrs. Casagrande and Bex had ordered amongst ourselves. Afterwards, the adults decided against dessert, while Volker and Alfie shared a celebratory slice of cheesecake with both caramel and chocolate sauce.

"I have to get going. I've got work in an hour," Otto rose from the table, and Volker and Alfie joined him. A brief discussion followed over who would pay for the check, and Mom and Dad won, if winning meant that they paid for everybody.

Volker shook hands with Juror #8. "I appreciate all you've done the last several days."

"Are you sure we're okay?"

"Yes. The slate is cleared. You've made amends and helped to clear my brother's name."

"It's not clear yet," I reminded him. "It won't be until Lada's real killer is caught."

Volker nodded. "Do you think the authorities will keep looking?"

"I don't know, but I will," Funderburke assured him. "Mrs. Casagrande has me wondering about that Dalton kid. I think I'm going to ask a few questions, see if I can figure out where he was that night."

"And I'm going to think about how those other unrepentant jurors can be made to see the error of their ways," Volker smiled. I didn't care for that grin and decided to wipe it off his face.

"Volker, maybe you can take a little time off from that. Remember, Sangster just tried to strike back at you. You don't know what'll happen if one or more of the jurors decide to get their own revenge. Don't play *Matilda* unless you have telekinetic powers."

Mutiny was slathered all over Volker's face, but he mumbled something placating.

"By the way," Funderburke asked as they were heading for the door. "I've noticed that there hasn't been any retribution against Juror #1. Is there a reason for that?"

Volker shrugged and forgot to maintain plausible deniability. "I was going to get around to her eventually. I just couldn't find anything I could leverage against her. Nothing that would hurt her or embarrass her. All I could find were some threads on an online forum by some of her students that called her a fixer."

"A fixer?" Funderburke's eyebrows pushed together. "What was the context?"

"I don't know. She's worked at a lot of different schools in the system. A different one every semester. All over Milwaukee. One of the posters on the forum said the schools use her to hush up scandals, but it wasn't clear what."

"Huh." Funderburke reflected on this, then we said our goodbyes as the others left, leaving just the four Kaimings and Funderburke. Yeh-Yeh was leaning back in his chair, snoring. He often does that after meals.

The waitress brought us the check, and Mom and Dad looked over the bill. "Are you sure I can't pay for part of that?" Funderburke asked.

Mom's phone chimed, and she read a text. "This is from the DA. Apparently, he's too busy to meet with us tonight, but he wants to talk later in the week. And he figured we'd gotten dinner downtown. He's offered to reimburse us if we send him the receipt." She looked up. "If I'd have known he would do that, we'd have eaten somewhere a lot fancier. Lucky I didn't accept Otto's suggestion to split up the check evenly five minutes ago."

"Split evenly...." Dad's voice trailed away.

"Something wrong?" I asked.

"It's what Bex was telling us about that party she held. About the teens splitting up into pairs."

"What about it?" I thought it was odd Dad was thinking about that. Usually, he goes out of his way not to know what teens are up to in their free time.

"She said there were seven of them at the party. That's an odd number."

"I suppose Alfie was left on his own," I shrugged. I didn't say it, but I figured that with his looks, he didn't have much luck with girls.

"What do you think he did? Went home? Sat alone in the living room and watched television?"

"I don't know," I told Dad. "Should I call and ask him? Or Bex?"

"I just wonder…And I was thinking about the baby."

"Lada's daughter?"

"Right. I know we've had our own issues with bite mark analysts lately, but we don't think all lab techs are incompetent, do we? Mrs. Casagrande's theory that they messed up and Benek really was the baby's father doesn't hold water, does it?"

"No. It doesn't." All of a sudden, my instincts were on fire. "Something's bugging me. I spoke to every one of Lada's friends who'd speak to me. And they made it clear, they were sure Lada was one hundred percent faithful to Benek. She hadn't been with anybody else since she started dating him."

"The only person who insisted that Lada was a promiscuous cheater was Alfie," Funderburke mused. "Was he mistaken? Did he dislike her for some reason and allow his prejudices to warp his view of her?"

"Or was he lying?" Funderburke and I said together.

"Look, Lada seemed stunned to learn Benek wasn't the baby's father," I said. "If she'd been sleeping around or even if she'd knowingly been assaulted, she'd have been aware of the possibility. But what if she *didn't know* about another potential father to her child? What if she was drugged and raped and had no idea?"

"The party Bex told us about tonight…." Mom whispered.

"Bex said everybody was drunk and overslept except for her, because she barely touched the hunch punch. But everybody else was really messed up the next morning, or rather afternoon. But I don't think she mentioned

Alfie's condition."

"She didn't," Funderburke insisted.

"So are we all now thinking the same theory?" I asked.

"Maybe, but we shouldn't," Dad said. "Not without evidence."

"And I know where to start looking." Funderburke picked a fork up off the cheesecake plate. He slipped it into one of the little plastic bags he carries with him and asked the waitress if he could borrow it for a few days.

"I can give you some plastic utensils to take home," she told him, leading to explain his actual reasons for wanting the fork. After hearing his explanation, she told him to keep it.

Two days later, we called Alfie and asked him if he was free for a meetup. He said he'd be on our side of town, meeting some friends at a lakefront festival, so he agreed to meet us across from my house in Lake Park. Funderburke and I were seated at a picnic bench in the shade of some tall trees when Alfie arrived on his bike.

Funderburke was dressed a little more casually than I thought was appropriate for this meeting, wearing a black T-shirt and matching athletic shorts. Granted, the T-shirt accentuated his muscles to impressive effect, but I wished he'd thought to wear one of the seersucker suits I'd bought him. Even though the temperature was back up in the low-eighties, I was comfortable in my pearl-colored seersucker pantsuit and white asymmetric cotton blouse.

"See that tree?" Funderburke pointed. "When I was a kid, and I was playing in this park, there used to be a real long branch the kids would use as a natural see-saw. Then the Parks Department sawed it off because they were afraid someone would get hurt. Killjoys."

Alfie waved as he walked up to us after locking his bike to a rack, and we returned the gesture, even though our hearts weren't in the greeting. "Hi!" He told us as he swung his cutoff jean-wearing legs over the opposite side of the picnic bench. "So what's up? You said you had news on the case that you wanted to tell me in person?"

"We do," I said, trying to decrease the level of grimness that was seeping into my tone.

"Any news on Sangster?"

"The D.A. told us there'd be a formal announcement later tonight. He's deliberately scheduling it too late for the six o'clock news." After a moment's pause, I added, "I understand his motives even if I don't agree with his tactics."

"I hope she's arrested and convicted," Alfie replied.

"With luck, more than one person will be," Funderburke said.

Alfie knit his eyebrows. "You mean one of her assistants?"

"No." Funderburke pulled out a file he'd been holding under the table. "I mean the real killer of Lada Casagrande. And her rapist. They're the same person."

"Wait, Lada was raped?" Alfie overdid the level of surprise he was trying to convey.

"Yes. That was the motive." I crossed my arms and pointed my sharpest stare into his eyes. "For a long time, she didn't know what had happened to her. She thought the only guy she'd been sleeping with was Benek. Because she wasn't promiscuous, like you said she was. She told her female friends, like Bex, all about her love life. And she'd only been with three men. Her boyfriends. She was a serial monogamist, and she honestly believed that Benek was her daughter's father."

"Wait, are you saying she didn't know she'd been...raped?"

"She did not. I don't know if she was drugged at Bex's house, or if she was just affected by an extremely strong hunch punch, but whatever happened, she was taken advantage of while she was unconscious. Benek and other kids at the party were affected as well."

"Hang on, are you saying that someone doped the punch that night? Was it Dalton? Did he find a way into the house, spike it, and then when everybody was asleep—"

"It wasn't Dalton, Alfie. Because the person who drugged and violated her that night...or maybe he didn't need to drug her due to the deceptively high alcohol content of the hunch punch, I don't know, was the one who impregnated her. And thanks to one of Midge's friends doing a rush job at her lab, we have a DNA profile matched with the baby." Funderburke pulled out the report and held it out to Alfie. He didn't take it. "I hope you understand why I'm not offering you a cigar."

"What are you saying?"

"That party at Bex's house was on the Thanksgiving long weekend. Lada announced her pregnancy a little over a month afterwards. She figured out that if Benek wasn't the baby's father, then she had to have been assaulted sometime in late November, maybe early December. And since she didn't remember being attacked, she realized that it had to have been done when she was unconscious. And I suppose there was only one instance during that time frame when she knew she'd passed out and had no memory of what happened. So she thought about that night and realized that only three other boys were in the house that night. Maybe you said or did something that awakened her suspicions. Maybe she saw some of you in Aurelia. I don't know. But she suspected you, though she wasn't sure. So she invited you to her house that night to confront you." I took a deep breath. "I bet she didn't want it to be true. You were her boyfriend's best friend. You hung out with them all the time. She considered you a friend–"

"We were never really friends." Alfie's face soured. "She never particularly liked me, and she kept telling Benek to hang out with other guys."

"So you resented her," I continued. "She thought you weren't good enough to be her boyfriend's best pal. And you were jealous of Benek. He was handsome, popular, a top athlete, dating a gorgeous young woman…And you…were just his much less attractive buddy."

"Hey! Don't insult me."

"Don't insult me by denying it!" I retorted. "This DNA test proves that you got her pregnant. And since she didn't cheat on Volker—"

"She did! She came on to me one night. I'd been drinking, my defenses were weak, and afterwards, I was afraid that I'd lose my best friend—"

"No! No! No!" I slammed my hand down on the table with each word. "Do. Not. Lie! Don't make me sit through your cowardly little attempt to distort the truth to try to wriggle your way out of trouble!" People at nearby tables were looking at us with quizzical looks, but I didn't care. "What happened? Did you spend all those months Lada and Benek were dating resenting her?

Did she make you feel small and ugly and inadequate? Did you vow to get revenge? Did you get your hands on some Rohypnol or something—"

"I didn't drug her! I swear!"

"So it was just the punch, then?" Funderburke asked. "Whoever made it loaded it up with hard liquor, and the fruit juice disguised it, so everybody who drank it got a much stronger dose of than they were prepared for, is that it?"

"I got really drunk too, that night," Alfie mumbled.

"Is that your excuse, then? The liquor made you do it?" I felt myself growing so angry, my face felt like someone threw kerosene on it and touched it with a lit match. "You're trying to tell me it's nobody's fault? You couldn't control yourself? Huh? That makes everything okay, then? You're telling me you're a victim, too? A poor misunderstood victim who couldn't stop himself from attacking a helpless woman because he couldn't hold his liquor and keep his pants up? Huh? Is that what you're saying?" I started hyperventilating, and Funderburke put an arm around my shoulder. His touch had a calming effect on me, and I curled up against him and nestled my head on his shoulder, waiting for my heartbeat to slow down to a normal rate.

"You know, Alfie," Funderburke said with preternatural calmness, "The reason I thought Lada's killer absolutely had to be a burglar was because of the absence of fingerprints. It was too warm that night for most people to wear a coat, let alone gloves. And if someone had wiped off surfaces, there would've been evidence of that, and there wasn't. So I theorized that a burglar wearing gloves was the most likely killer. I didn't realize until recently that there was someone else who'd been wearing gloves that night. You wore your cycling gloves when you rode your bike to Lada's house." Funderburke nodded down at Alfie's hands, which were encased in blue and black gloves. "If you'd used fingerless gloves when riding, we'd be having a very different conversation now."

My pulse was still throbbing at a rate so fast I was starting to feel dizzy, but I regained my voice. "She suspected you, but she wasn't sure. So she invited you to her home, and you pedaled down there, not knowing what to expect.

228

When she confronted you, you must have given yourself away somehow. Maybe she saw the guilt in your eyes, perhaps you said something...it doesn't matter. She knew, and she was about to tell the world what you did. Why did you choose the jeans, Alfie? Did you just grab the first item that came to hand and use it to kill her? It doesn't matter. She knew what you did, and you murdered her to escape punishment. I bet you freaked out when you realized what you did. Of course, you already freaked out when she figured out what you'd done to her. And then you ran home, leaving her body lying there like a piece of garbage. Because you couldn't show her any respect or dignity, could you? You couldn't find a girlfriend of your own, so you acted out your sick desires on the woman who was dating your best friend."

"Yes, and when the police focused on Benek, you didn't say a word to help him, did you?" Funderburke added. "Throughout the investigation, the trial, after he was sent to prison, you could have saved him. All you had to do was tell the truth. But you couldn't do that, could you? Benek loved you like a brother, and you sat back and let him suffer for your crime."

"I was positive they'd acquit him," Alfie stammered.

A thunderstorm settled over Funderburke's face. "Well, they didn't. They voted for conviction, and soon afterwards, he suffered a terrible assault and death. And you let it happen. You killed him too, you know. Volker accused the jurors and the investigating officers and Sangster of being responsible for Benek's rape and murder, but you were guiltier than any of them."

"Did you resent Benek, too?" I asked. "Were you tired of always being in his shadow? Did you keep your trap shut as another twisted act of revenge?"

"I never wanted anything bad to happen to Benek!" Tears began streaming down Alfie's face, but he wasn't going to get a tissue from me.

"I know you felt guilty, Alfie," Funderburke told him. "That's why you've been helping Volker with his revenge plan. You're handing out pennies in an attempt to pay off a multi-billion-dollar debt."

Between sobs, Alfie whispered, "What do you want me to say?"

Gathering up every atom of strength and control I possessed, I made my voice as soft and calm as possible. "I want you to tell the world what you've done. What you did to Lada, both that night in November and eleven months later. How you sat back and allowed the criminal justice system to pulverize your buddy. You let your best friend pay for your crime. Now you have the opportunity to start making amends." I pulled my phone from my purse, pulled up a number from my contacts, and set it in front of him. "Call the DA right now. Tell him everything. If you want to be able to live with yourself ever again, here's your chance."

Alfie stared at my phone for over a minute. Finally, he looked up and said, "I can't."

"The DA's going to learn what happened in the next few minutes," I pointed out. "It's either going to be from us or from you. And you'll have a much better chance at negotiating a deal if you're honest and helpful."

The tears dried up, and a new steeliness slipped into his demeanor. It provoked a wave of nausea in me. "I can't do that."

"I say you can."

"You know what happened to Benek. He was stronger than I was. I'm not letting that happen to me. I can't change the past, and I'm not sacrificing my future. None of this was my fault. It wasn't!" Alfie leapt up from the bench and sprinted towards his bike. Before we could climb out from the bench, he was forty yards away from us, and before we could catch up with him he'd pulled on his helmet, unlocked and mounted his bike, and sped away out of the park.

I glowered at his shrinking back as he vanished down the road. I'd grabbed my phone from the table as we'd run after Alfie, and now I was squeezing it so hard it was starting to hurt. "I want to be the one to tell the DA everything, please."

"That's fine by me." Funderburke ran his hand over his forehead. "Now, what do we tell Volker? And when?"

Epilogue: I'm Still Angry

FUNDERBURKE & NERISSA

FUNDERBURKE

As if we didn't have enough on our plates, now we had to prevent Volker from becoming a murderer. We tried to keep the truth from Volker for a while until we knew the DA's plans, but somehow Sangster heard about it, and the day after we confronted Alfie, after a press conference where she blamed "a power-hungry District Attorney and institutional sexism" for her firing and pending criminal charges, she mocked the new theory accusing Alfie. So we had to tell Volker everything. To say he took it badly was the understatement of the millennium.

After a couple of hours of talking, we thought we'd managed to get him calmed down, but we had to leave his house eventually, and then Otto went to work, and as soon as he was on his own, Volker slipped out of the house, hurried through the neighborhood to Alfie's house, and confronted Alfie just as he was returning from his summer job at a car wash.

At some point, Alfie's mother looked out the window and phoned the police, because "that crazy Berchtwelt boy is beating up my son." As a point of fact, Volker had pushed the backs of Alfie's knees, climbed atop the prone teenager, and landed two blows that barely left a bruise before Alfie pushed him off and rose to his feet. She rushed out at the shouting boys, and when a police car that had been on patrol only two blocks away pulled up in front of the house, the arriving officers were met with two very different stories.

Volker announced that he'd demanded to know why Alfie had killed Lada, and that Alfie had confessed in his mother's presence that he hadn't meant to do it; it was all an accident. Alfie and his mother declared that Alfie had said nothing of the kind and that Volker was clearly disturbed. We learned all this when Otto telephoned, interrupting our dinner and asking us to come across town to pick up Volker from the local station, as Otto would get fired if he left work. Given the circumstances, they didn't want to file charges against anybody at the moment, so Volker wasn't under arrest.

The moment Volker was in our car, he was breathing fire. "He confessed to me! He admitted he killed her!"

"What did he say? I asked. "His exact words, as closely as you remember."

"He said, 'I didn't mean to kill her. It was an accident.' That's an admission of guilt, isn't it? Even if it doesn't make much sense. Did those jeans wrap themselves around her neck purely by chance?"

"Tomorrow, we can take you to make an official statement of what you heard." I hesitated, knowing he wouldn't like what I had to say, but I continued. "But I'm afraid that it may not be enough to get a conviction."

"Why not?"

"Because it's your word against his. And if his mother protects her son by declaring that he didn't say anything incriminating, well, then..."

"But we've got him for raping Lada, don't we?"

"No," Nerissa answered with obvious disgust. "He definitely fathered her baby, but with Lada unable to tell her story, all Alfie has to do is declare that it was consensual, and no one can prove otherwise. It's a classic case of "he said, she's dead." And there's no forensic evidence, no witnesses—"

Volker swore. "Are you saying he's going to get away with it?"

Neither of us said anything because we didn't want to inflame the situation. Pointless, really, because the situation was already a three-alarm fire.

"I'm going to kill him," Volker muttered.

"No, you're not! You're not going to destroy your life to get revenge!"

My words did nothing to calm him, and Volker kept ranting about Alfie's betrayal.

We couldn't leave him alone. I had the sense that the moment we left,

Volker would grab a steak knife from the kitchen and head for Alfie's house. We waited until three A.M. for Otto to return, Volker throwing a tantrum the entire time. Before we left, we managed to extract a promise from Volker that he would wait until we heard from the DA before he tried anything.

Unfortunately, the DA confirmed that we didn't have enough evidence to take Alfie to trial. Even with Volker's sworn statement, the testimony of Alfie and his mother would cancel it out. As Volker would later rage, "Incredible! First, they don't believe me when I testify to Benek's alibi; now they say I'm not convincing enough when I tell them the killer confessed right in front of me!"

Otto lied to his grandson, telling him that the authorities needed two weeks to run some tests that might prove Alfie was at the Casagrande house, but I doubted that Alfie believed it. I could see it in his eyes. The same young brain that had recently plotted more benign forms of revenge was now trying to develop a plan to get away with cold-blooded murder.

Since their visit, Volker had formed a surprising friendship with Juror #11, and the two of them talked on the phone almost every day. I don't know the substance of their conversations, although Volker did inform me that he'd told her that Alfie was the real killer.

Once again, I need to stress the focus on Volker in this narrative is not fully representative of our schedules that summer. Aside from my summer work (including unexpected investigations for fourteen other students), Nerissa's dissertation and constantly being called upon to assist her scholarship students, family issues, and actually having a life outside of school, there was no possible way that we could watch him every second. Admittedly, we cared more about keeping Volker out of prison than keeping Alfie out of the ground.

Perhaps Alfie's parents sensed what Volker was planning, because they abruptly left for a family vacation in an undisclosed location. Alfie didn't even bother to tender his resignation to the car wash.

NERISSA

But it wasn't just Alfie who was getting away with his crimes. Sangster and her parents pulled out all the stops and exploited every connection they had to get her out from under the pending charges.

First, she gathered her own legal team and filed suit against the D.A., claiming that he had created a hostile work environment and was retaliating against her for complaining. The DA was forced to recuse himself from Sangster's case due to the conflict of interest, and an outside party was brought in to handle the situation. Turns out, the woman chosen to negotiate the lawsuit was a college friend of Sangster's mother.

We were told we'd be called in a week to be interviewed, and then, a couple days later, the DA called, fury in his voice. The matter had all been settled without his input, and the deal had already been approved by a judge. To summarize the situation, Sangster's attorneys agreed to withdraw the lawsuit in exchange for no criminal charges being filed against her, and a settlement of over a quarter million taxpayer dollars. Additionally, she'd resign from her position. A lot of bureaucrats thoughts this was a neat, cost-effective solution that would prevent a scandal and keep a bunch of convicted felons from being released and filing lawsuits of their own. As the DA fumed when he came to our house for dinner, the deal was signed and a lot of influential people were backing it. He was so angry he only ate three servings of brisket and roasted potatoes.

I honestly thought that Volker was going to fall victim to spontaneous human combustion when I next saw him. "So that's it, then? She's just going to walk? A lot richer than she was a week ago?"

"She's walking all the way to Washington, D.C.," I mourned. "I hear she's landed a job at a consulting firm for a six-figure salary."

"Then that's it? There's nothing we can do?" From the fire in his eyes, I could tell Volker was plotting a second murder.

"No, this time, you have options within the law," Funderburke assured him.

"Like what? Her lawyer definitely made sure her deal is ironclad."

"Have you forgotten already? You mentioned it yourself not long ago. You can't send her to prison for tampering with evidence, no, but you can sue her for assault and battery. She choked you, remember? You have about twenty witnesses, many of which are hostile against you, but...."

Volker loved that idea. "I was so angry that it slipped my mind." The prospect of litigation got his mind off killing Alfie for much too short a while. This is because the consulting firm that hired Sangster didn't want the publicity of a trial affecting their reputation, so they advised Sangster to settle the matter immediately. Her lawyers offered ten thousand dollars, and Volker's lawyer, a friend of Funderburke's from law school who never liked Sangster and was taking the case *pro bono*, made it clear that he wouldn't accept anything less than the amount of the settlement Sangster received from her own settled lawsuit. In fact, Volker's payout had to be *more* than Sangster's.

Her lawyers pointed out that a hefty percentage of that money had gone to her attorneys for legal fees, and Volker's advocate countered by observing that was not his problem.

Normally, a lawsuit like this would last for months, possibly years. But for reasons I couldn't understand, the consulting firm considered Sangster one of their new stars, and they didn't want a lawsuit casting a shadow over her work and the reputation of the firm, so they must've said something to convince Sangster to end it quickly and quietly.

So the lawyers shut themselves inside a conference room and launched negotiations, and after a couple of hours, they agreed upon a number that essentially left Sangster in essentially the same financial position she was in before her own lawsuit was settled, because Mommy and Daddy were coming to her rescue by writing a check. For some reason, Sangster and Volker were in the same room when the final details were settled, and Funderburke and I were there to witness Volker's triumph.

Sangster signed more papers than a Hollywood starlet does when greeting a throng of her fans and then threw down the pen. "You're pretty pleased with yourself, aren't you, you little brat? Just remember, I still know you lied to shield your brother the strangler."

Until that moment, I assumed that Sangster was aware that she'd prosecuted an innocent man and that she was willing to sacrifice him to protect her career. *She* was more of a strangler than Benek. As I observed the fire blazing in her eyes, I realized that while she certainly was sensitive to any potential threat to her personal reputation, she genuinely believed that Benek was guilty, and no amount of evidence, even a signed confession from Alfie, would convince her otherwise. I couldn't decide which possibility made me dislike her more: whether she was deliberately malicious or just a true believer in her case against Benek.

Volker's face displayed an equal amount of loathing for her as she had for him, and I saw his fist clench. I almost screamed out, *No! Don't hit her! She'll countersue and take the money back!*

But Volker didn't throw a punch. He simply held his hand up to her eye level and extended his middle finger.

Sangster offered us expletives for goodbyes and stomped out of the room towards the next plane to Washington, D.C.

That night, Volker and Otto joined us for dinner, and Mom pointed out that his new windfall was essentially taxpayer money twice removed.

"I'm not turning it back over to the city government," Volker snorted. "They'd just pay it out to some other grifter who claimed he twisted his ankle in a pothole."

"Can't argue with that," Mom sighed as she speared another bite of her curried chicken.

"Besides, it's not like I'm going to get a dime of the money from my parents' wrongful death lawsuit." He didn't. A couple of years later, they finally settled their litigation and received four and a half million dollars. That was the price of Benek's life. By that time, the legal fees ate up seventy percent of that sum, and Volker's parents individually managed to burn through their shares of the remaining amount in record time, buying cars, taking trips, and throwing parties to impress friends, both eventually winding up in even more debt than they'd been in before they filed the lawsuit.

Mrs. Gastrell hated to lose, and she bided her time before attempting to have Volker's scholarship revoked again, this time buying the school a new field hockey field (named after herself, of course) to bolster her case. This time, she was successful, but that's because we decided the scholarship should go to someone who needed it more. There was just enough money in Volker's settlement to cover his tuition for his remaining years at Cuthbertson, plus college as well, depending on which school he chose.

FUNDERBURKE

I knew that Alfie couldn't stay away for too much longer. His parents couldn't afford to go away on vacation for more than a week or two. But I was surprised when Juror #11 called me a mere five days after the Witteveens left town. She'd just seen Alfie walking down the hall of the hospice with his parents. Apparently, his grandmother had taken a turn for the worse, so the Witteveens had surreptitiously returned to Milwaukee to say goodbye. I phoned Otto, told him to keep Volker in the house for as long as possible, and Nerissa and I drove across town.

It's important to remember that nobody knew about Alfie's culpability except for a select few individuals. Alfie wasn't under police surveillance or anything like that. He was just avoiding us.

When we arrived, Juror #11 was waiting for us in the main atrium in her wheelchair.

"You arrived in time. They're still here, but they won't be for much longer. I just heard from the nurse's station intercom that his grandmother passed away fifteen minutes ago."

I considered that it was probably for the best that Alfie's grandmother never learned that her grandson was a rapist and a strangler.

"What do we do now?" Nerissa asked.

As I tried to answer this question, a familiar figure stumbled into the atrium and collapsed into a chair. Alfie's face was redder than usual, but it was due to crying, not acne. He grabbed a handful of tissues from a box on a table next to him. After he dried his eyes and looked up at us, he recoiled.

"Can't you leave me be? My grandmother just died."

"Relax," Nerissa sniffed. "We don't have the authority to arrest you. We don't have the evidence for it, anyway. All we're here to do is warn you that you'd best stay out of Volker's way."

"Our condolences on your grandmother's passing, by the way," I told him, even though I didn't want to provide him with any comfort whatsoever.

"Well, tonight I'm loading up all my possessions, and then I'm never coming back to Milwaukee again. I'm going to college in Ohio, and I'm moving there as soon as possible. I'll stay in a motel until the dorms open. So just keep Volker occupied for a few more hours, and then I'll be gone."

"Do you feel any guilt at all?" Nerissa asked.

"Why should I? I mean, I'm not admitting to anything, but…my going to prison isn't going to bring Lada or Benek back."

"Is that supposed to erase any calls for justice?" I asked. "The inability to resurrect the dead means that all murderers should walk free?"

"Look, I know what you want from me, but I'm not going to give it to you. I screwed up—that's not a confession, teens screw up all the time—but college is a fresh start. I'm starting my life over with a clean slate."

"When people call college "starting over," it usually means escaping the nasty nicknames and rumors that dogged them in high school," I noted. "It's not a get-out-of-jail-free card."

"Well, didn't you say there's no evidence against me?"

I had, and I affirmed that point.

"Then I'm going to pick up some food for my parents while they make the arrangements for my grandmother's funeral, then, like I said, I'm leaving."

"Aren't you going to stick around to pay your respects at her memorial service?" Nerissa asked.

"Why should I? I don't owe the dead anything. I'm sad she's gone, but my sticking around won't help anybody. I just want to live my life, and I'm not going to let you or anybody else stop me. Goodbye. Don't ever try to talk to me again." Alfie leapt out of his chair and sprinted out the front door.

"That little turd's going to get away with it, isn't he?" Nerissa grumbled.

"Do you have any ideas on how to trick him into confessing?"

"No. But the thought of him suffering no consequences for what he did makes me sick."

"Me, too." I looked around the atrium.

"What's the matter?"

"Where's Juror #11? She was here a minute—"

The sound of screeching tires and a stomach-clenching thud pierced the walls of the hospice. The receptionist at the front desk screamed and dialed the phone while the two of us hurried outside. Alfie was lying motionless on the ground of the parking lot, bleeding, The back tire of a car rested atop his stomach. A moment later, the frail figure of Juror #11 pushed open the driver's door and wobbled out of the automobile.

"Oh, dear me," she gasped. "What a terrible accident."

Well, of course, we all knew what had really happened. It turned out the car had belonged to the receptionist, who'd been focused on a *Glamour* magazine article, and Juror #11 had managed to swipe her keys off the desk and hurry outside unnoticed while we spoke to Alfie.

I phoned 911, but after failing to find Alfie's pulse, I informed the dispatcher that there was no need for the ambulance to run any red lights. When the police arrived, Juror #11 played the "dotty, dying old woman" card, blaming chemo brain for her belief she had to rush to a job she'd retired from years earlier. I don't think anybody believed that she wasn't aware of what she was doing, but the woman was obviously in terrible health, so no one wished to throw her into prison. Luckily for us, no one seemed to think we'd encouraged Juror #11 to do what she did, which we definitely hadn't. She came up with this plan all on her own, and as she assured us later, Volker knew nothing of her intentions.

As we waited for the authorities to let us leave, an older, heavier, less hirsute version of Alfie walked up to us. I assumed that this was Alfie's father, about to blame us for what happened to his son. I was only half right.

"I know who you are," he informed us.

"I'm sorry for your double loss," I spoke automatically.

"Save it. I know you don't mean it. Well, perhaps you do for my mother-in-law. But I've known for a long time that there was something not quite right about my son. Ever since he was thirteen, and I caught him with his six-year-old cousin. He didn't get the chance to do anything to her; I walked in on them in the nick of time, but…I knew from that moment my son was a ticking bomb." He looked up at us. "What would you have done? Institutionalize him? That would've killed his mother. Anyway, I'm not sure what'll happen to her, losing her mother and son in the same day." Indeed, that night, Mrs. Witteveen had a breakdown and never fully recovered. She spent the rest of her life—a little under five years—in and out of mental hospitals. As far as I was concerned, she was Alfie's third victim, along with Lada and Benek.

Mr. Witteveen pulled out his phone. "After Volker came to the house, I confronted Alfie. He denied it at first, but I knew he was lying and pressured him until he told me everything. I recorded it." After asking for our information, he sent the video to us. "Watch it. He confesses to everything. The rape, the murder, all of it. I told him that if he ever took the tiniest step off the straight and narrow again, I'd send it to the police. I don't know if that makes me an accessory after the fact or not, but I couldn't send my boy to prison, unless I knew he was going to hurt some other girl. Anyway, I don't care what you do to me now. Just use this to help Benek's family."

We spoke to the DA, showed him the video, and he agreed that Mr. Witteveen shouldn't face criminal charges. He'd had the video for five days, but the argument that he was trying to spare Alfie's dying grandmother in her final moments was enough to give him a pass. The next morning, the DA announced that Benek was officially cleared of all wrongdoing and that the conviction would be vacated as soon as possible, and he made a formal apology to the Berchtwelt family. But before the DA did so, that evening, we arrived at Volker's house and told him everything.

And for the first time since I'd known him, Volker cried. He bawled uncontrollably and didn't stop for almost two hours.

NERISSA

Toby and Bernard saw the specialist, and just as Key had, both received an unequivocal diagnosis of Asperger's Syndrome. Mom and Dad were also examined, and were deemed to have a milder case of the same condition. Other members of the family received similar examinations, but were judged to be essentially neurotypical.

I set aside the history books I was reading for my dissertation and focused on reading everything I could find about autism. After poring through fifty books in two weeks, Dad suggested that maybe I should take a break.

"I don't want to. All these years, I've felt that there was a gulf between me and Toby that I couldn't cross. Now, if I understand her mind better, maybe it'll bring us closer together."

"First of all, she adores you. She just shows her affection in a different way from how you expect."

"Huh. You know, I see a lot of you in these descriptions of autistic people in these books. A lot of them don't care about what other people think about them. I was thinking, if you'd cared about most people's opinions, you'd never have taken us in. So maybe I have Asperger's Syndrome to thank for having a home and a family."

"That's one way of looking at it, I suppose."

I dropped the book on my desk. "This says that the common belief that people on the spectrum can't feel empathy is a misconception. I believe that. But what about me? I don't have autism. And a teenaged boy just got flattened in a parking lot, and I couldn't care less. I feel nothing. I feel worse for the woman who ran him over. What does that mean? Am I a sociopath?"

"You know you're not. I told you once that there are no stupid questions, but I was wrong. Asking if you're a sociopath is an idiotic question."

"Then why am I not upset that a dying woman decided to commit an act of vigilante justice in her final days?"

"I think you are. It's just that your emotions aren't what you think they ought to be. But from what I can see, your feelings about this case are very powerful, though they're mixed with frustration that the justice system doesn't come out looking too effective in this case."

"Part of me feels like justice was done in that parking lot. And that frightens me."

"I think that shows that your conscience is working. Just like Volker, you hate it when something doesn't feel morally right to you."

Dad summarized my feelings pretty well. Often, when a case ends, I feel pretty satisfied. But at that moment, I just felt empty.

FUNDERBURKE

Armed with the recent exoneration of Benek, Volker and I spoke to the authorities at his former high school, and after a surprisingly civil discussion, they agreed to grant Benek a posthumous honorary diploma, as well as an award for his outstanding athletic achievements.

Two memorial plaques were commissioned, one in honor of Lada, one commemorating Benek. Featuring their photographs, brief biographical statements, and information on how they died, these plaques were installed in the library of their former high school at the start of July. A reading room was named in their honor. A handful of teachers and friends of Benek and Lada's attended, including Mrs. Casagrande and Bex. Volker found it ironic that the school had chosen to name a part of the library after Benek, as his brother had hardly spent any time at all in that area of the school. Lada, in contrast, had borrowed over six dozen teen vampire romance novels from the library over the three years she attended school in-person. It suddenly struck me that if Naeem had made the argument at the initial trial that Lada's bite mark was just a bit of vampire roleplay gone wrong, the verdict might have gone the other way. Then, I decided there was no point in theorizing about that possibility.

As he looked at the plaques, Volker ran his fingers over the part of Benek's plaque that said VICTIM OF A TERRIBLE MISCARRIAGE OF JUSTICE. "It feels wonderful to see that, but it would be better if everybody at this school who assumed Benek's guilt were compelled to stand here and make a public apology," he declared.

"We need to celebrate the triumphs we've achieved," I told Volker. "We've found out who really killed Lada, and we cleared Benek's name. That's leaps and bounds ahead of where we were a few months ago."

"I know," Volker nodded. "But I'm still angry."

"Do you still want revenge?"

"Yes. And I'm still going to get it, *Matilda*-style. But not through superglue in hats or peroxide in hair tonic. Do you remember how Matilda finally triumphed at the end, aside from the telekinetic powers?"

"Yes. She terrified her antagonist."

"By revealing that person's wrongdoing to the world in the most dramatic manner possible. I'm going to do that, even if I can't make objects levitate. There's nothing wrong with that, is there?'

I shrugged. "I don't believe that anybody should ever be able to punish you for telling the truth."

A huge smile spread across Volker's face. "Exactly."

NERISSA

As for the jurors, they all went on with their lives, some more happily than others. For the purposes of conveying information, I'm going to break the chronological narrative flow and jump back and forth over the events of the next few years.

My instincts pushed me to encourage Funderburke to look into Juror #1, and after a few days of P.I. work, Funderburke discovered that Juror #1 was a well-known "fixer" in the public school system. One of the dirty so-called "secrets" that everybody knows but few people mention is that the rate of inappropriate conduct between teachers and students is frighteningly high. But the media rarely covers it, and in the tiny fraction of cases that make the news, it's treated as an unfortunate isolated incident rather than as a symptom of a widespread epidemic, or adolescent boys living out their fantasies rather than being exploited. So, as an administrator, Juror #1 moved from school to school, transferring miscreant teachers from one school to the next, finding ways to convince students and parents to stay quiet, and basically keeping a lid on any potential scandals before they rose to public prominence.

Funderburke and I were not inclined to keep matters like this hushed up, and we started bringing these matters to the attention of prominent people. Pretty soon, individuals I won't mention started attacking us as out-of-touch employees of an elitist private school, but then students who had been victimized started speaking up, and pretty soon, the situation exploded, though you wouldn't know it if you only watched the local news on television. I could fill another book with the fallout of what happened over the next couple of years, but for the purposes of focus and brevity, I'll just focus on the fact that Juror #1 quietly resigned from her position and then moved to Illinois, where she started a similar job with comparable duties. Volker immediately sent out emails to as many students as he could find, telling them about the dirty laundry of her past career.

Our paths crossed with Juror #1's again soon afterwards, but that's another story. We'll tell it in the near future.

Juror #2 continued his job as engineer, while running his own podcast and appearing on other people's during his spare time. He kept bloviating on every possible topic, as was his First Amendment right, and at least once a week, he'd mention his time on the Berchtwelt jury. He remained adamant that he'd reached the correct verdict.

"I still don't believe Witteveen's supposed deathbed confession," he insisted. "I believe he knew he was dying, and he wanted to clear the name of his dead friend and probably help the Berchtwelt family receive a massive settlement. If you look at the forensic evidence intelligently and impartially...."

Of course, Alfie's confession wasn't on his deathbed. That was just one of the many details Juror #2 got wrong.

Every week, Volker posts on Juror #2's social media pages and asks to be invited onto his podcast to discuss the case. To date, Juror #2 has never agreed. Other local podcasters and vloggers have allowed Volker to defend Benek on their shows, and so far, the reactions have been overwhelmingly, though not completely, in Volker's favor.

Juror #2 and his daughter are still estranged, though we got in touch with his daughter, and she has been really helpful in assisting the Kaimings to navigate the world of autism.

As far as I know, Juror #2 still hasn't gotten over his fear of cats.

Over the course of the next year, Juror #3 remodeled the Berchtwelts' bathroom and added a second half-bathroom as well. He also fixed up the kitchen and oversaw the long-overdue repair of the Berchtwelt roof. Otto and Mr. and Mrs. Juror #3 have become friends, and they socialize frequently. Volker doesn't attend these get-togethers, but he has informed us on multiple occasions that Juror #3 is no longer on his excrement list.

Juror #4, we would learn several months later, was no longer content with being extremely rich. Instead, she wished to become jaw-droppingly, earth-shakingly, mind-bogglingly wealthy. I don't know if she actually wished to build a gigantic money bin and swim around in it, but apparently she'd steadily grown dissatisfied with all of her millions and decided that they just weren't enough for her anymore.

Around the time of Benek's death, she learned about a major investment opportunity, and she instructed her legions of accountants to sink the lion's share of her fortune into it.

Her top financial advisor warned her that this was an extremely risky move, for if the deal she was anticipating didn't go through, she could lose her investment, and though she'd still be far from poor, she might have to start selling artwork if she wanted to keep up her current lifestyle. According to rumor, Juror #4 told him to shut up and do as he was told. Worrying that the worst was likely to happen, her financial advisor put the investment in motion with extreme trepidation.

The feared disaster never occurred, and Juror #4's investment recouped more than ninefold. She went from being a mere multi-millionaire to a bona fide billionaire and soon set about achieving her long-held goals.

Not surprisingly, Juror #4 was frustrated by how her neighborhood had changed over the decades, and she decided to alter the situation by buying up as much of it as she could. Pretty soon, she owned most of the land surrounding her mansion, and after evicting the individuals she could and luring away all the homeless people from the derelict structures for a day, a demolition crew razed the battered buildings and a construction crew started work on a massive iron gate meant to keep out anybody she considered undesirable, which was pretty much everybody.

Over the next couple of years, she purchased as many plots of land as possible, tore down the buildings on them, and started building luxury condos, office space, and storefronts in the area. Little by little, the demographics and income levels of the area changed, and not everybody was pleased with this. People who'd lived in the area started protesting, arguing that their cost of living was skyrocketing with higher rents and all the other costs that come with gentrification. None of this had any effect on Juror #4, and her plans for the neighborhood continued, and she started hosting increasing numbers of wealthy and prominent people at her home to raise her social profile.

Benek has made sure that all of the members of her newly expanded coterie are aware of her role in sending his brother to an undeserved death in prison, and I understand that this is a major topic of gossip behind Juror #4's back, though never to her face.

The restaurant where Juror #5 worked shut down six months after Alfie's death, when a listeria outbreak sent eighteen customers to the hospital and two unfortunate individuals to the morgue. After a couple of months on unemployment relief, which wasn't enough to make ends meet and required a further strain on her sister's family's finances, Juror #5 managed to land a work-from-home position in telephone customer service. It paid slightly better than her waitressing job, and it allowed her to spend more time with her two kids…three kids, after a brief, disastrous relationship left her with a new baby. The father vanished without paying a cent of child support.

Volker still despised her, but he had nothing against her children, so when Funderburke and I advised him to consider their feelings, he decided to leave Juror #5 be.

Juror #6's dementia progressed for another twenty months from the time we visited him in his care facility, until he developed pneumonia and his children decided that it was in his best interests to withhold treatment. He passed away six days later and was cremated.

Juror #7's mother threatened the cemetery where her daughter was buried with a lawsuit, saying that they were negligent in allowing her baby girl's headstone to be vandalized, leading the cemetery to pay for a replacement.

Volker mentioned that there was nothing stopping him from buying the plot next to where Juror #7 was buried and erecting a gravestone with an arrow on it and the message "THIS WOMAN SENT MY INNOCENT BROTHER TO DIE IN PRISON." We reminded him that Juror #7 left behind a young son who only had forty thousand dollars left in the settlement with the supermarket, after the lawyers pocketed most of the negotiated sum. Reflecting on how death erased his animosity towards Juror #6, Volker eventually conceded that his beef with Juror #7 should have died when she did.

Juror #8's kids weren't handling the divorce well. His son was arrested for shoplifting hundreds of dollars of merchandise from a big box store, and his daughter spent several days in the hospital after a fentanyl overdose, which she later swore was due to recreational drug use and not a suicide attempt.

After a long talk, Juror #8 managed to convince his estranged wife that the divorce was taking its toll on the kids, and eventually, she became amenable to a reconciliation in the interests of their family. They are still together. Volker and Juror #8 send each other cards every Christmas. If Funderburke's mother had any resentment over losing a client, she never shared her feelings with us.

Juror #9's husband's plea deal was approved, and he will rot in prison for a long time. His girlfriend was not charged as an accessory.

Juror #10 began teaching at her new job that fall, but Yeh-Yeh's investigation, publicized online by Volker, proved that her M.A. thesis and Ph.D. dissertation were full of plagiarism. The universities she attended were reluctant to take any steps, but widespread outrage from various quarters led to her degrees being rescinded. My observation of her "Vera Pelle" gaffe led to Funderburke discovering that her claims of teaching in Italy were bologna, and that, in fact, several details on her CV were pure fabrications. It's unclear whether Juror #10 left voluntarily or if she was discreetly forced out, but in any event, she was out of academia after Thanksgiving. She is currently working in retail.

The authorities decided not to charge Juror #11, especially because her condition took a downturn a few days after she ran down Alfie. After one last round of questioning at the police station, she returned to the nursing home and never left. Volker visited her at least four times a week for the rest of the summer, often with us.

"You came through for me," Volker told her when she was fading fast in late August. "You made it right."

"No, I didn't," she gasped. "Don't think that. What I did, I did to save you from the consequences of what you might have done to him if he'd continued to walk free. But don't think what I did made anything right. Not really. Don't think that for a second."

I don't know if she convinced Volker, but when she passed away on the last Thursday before school started, he cried for the rest of the night.

Juror #11 amended her will three weeks before she died, leaving everything to Volker. She didn't have very much in her estate, especially after she'd bought the hospice receptionist a brand-new car, but now, in addition to his settlement with Sangster that covered the next nine years of his education, Volker had more than enough to pay for a master's degree.

Juror #12 tried to sue Volker over his car, but since he had no evidence pointing towards Volker's involvement and anyway it was his fellow activists who smashed it up, the suit never went anywhere. He continued to advocate for the causes he believed in and eventually ran for public office. Volker launched a mudslinging campaign against him, bombarding the candidate's social media pages with messages that boiled down to "Juror #12 wrongly convicted my brother. Why would you trust his judgment?" He starred with Juror #12's opponent in a series of attack ads as well. Juror #12 lost the election by over forty thousand votes.

FUNDERBURKE

Five days after Alfie's death, Otto came to me asking for suggestions on how to improve his diet and start an exercise routine. "I've been in denial," he informed me, "but if I don't start making changes soon, my diabetes is going to take me out in less than two years. Volker's parents aren't gonna raise him. It's all on me to last another five years at least to look after him. I can't let him wind up in foster care."

So I provided some tips on what to eat and invited him to exercise with me, and by Christmas, he'd dropped thirty pounds, and his A1C was a dozen points lower. He still wasn't in peak health, but he claimed to be feeling stronger than he had in decades.

None of the police or corrections officers involved in the case suffered any career setbacks due to their involvement in Benek's arrest and death. The prisoners who'd violated and beaten Benek were stripped of certain privileges and comforts, but as we suspected, the powers that be decided that they were already serving life, so there was no point in charging them with another murder. After all, they couldn't let their corpses lie in a cell for another eighty years. Volker continues to name names on social media, and I have no insight into the state of any of their consciences.

Dr. Albion Suco continued to stand by every pronouncement he ever made in court, but as the years passed and forensic dentistry fell into disrepute, he was called fewer and fewer times as an expert witness. As of these writings, nineteen people who were convicted in part on his testimony had their convictions overturned, including Benek, whose exoneration was the only one of the nineteen to occur too late to help. When Suco came to Milwaukee to give a lecture at a conference a year later, Volker sat in the front row and booed him throughout the entire speech. Midge sat next to him, booing as well.

All the focus on the Berchtwelt case took my mind off my mother. Uncle Francis spoke to me again after Sunday Mass the week after Alfie's death. Apparently, my mother had gone on another bender and had run over her patio furniture when she'd arrived home blotto.

"She's really upset about your sister, Funderburke. From what I hear, that girl's spiraling out of control, and so is your mother."

"What do you want me to do about it?"

"Be the son the mother you wish you had deserves."

So I thought about what he said for a while, and I put my P.I. skills to the test and did a little reconnaissance on her normal routine. I reflected on what my mother had said the last time we'd met and an idea formed.

Mom was going through a small bottle of ludicrously expensive vodka every other day. I'm not sure if she was drinking it all—maybe she was pouring some of it down the sink and regretting it afterwards, but every evening, right after she left her office, she stopped by the upscale liquor store three blocks down the road, bought a half-pint bottle of her favorite vodka, and took it home.

After a few days of watching her habits, she showed up at the liquor store around six that evening and headed straight for the vodka section. As she pulled a bottle off the shelf, a piece of paper stuck behind it fluttered towards her chest. She caught it before it fell to the ground and saw that it was a handmade card with the words "I love you, Mommy" written in crayon. My art skills in drawing dinosaurs and flowers had improved dramatically over the past two decades.

She stared at the card for what seemed like half an hour and then slowly turned around to see me standing at the end of the aisle. Shoving the bottle back onto the shelf, she ran forward into my arms.

I'm not saying that evening completely fixed our relationship. Not by a long shot. The old resentments came back regularly, and Mom and I continued to clash more often than we got along. We continued to have a few ups and a ton of downs, and several dozen downs were coming over the next few months. But after half a lifetime of estrangement, I'd made a grand gesture of reconciliation, and I didn't regret it. I was still furious with her, but I was trying harder not to be.

NERISSA

As I wrap up this account of the Berchtwelt case, I think that the best place to finish it is on a very pleasant cookout in the Kaiming backyard towards the end of July. A handful of guests attended, including Volker, Otto, Mrs. Casagrande, her son, daughter-in-law, and Aurelia. Mrs. Casagrande's opinion of us had risen dramatically since we'd identified her daughter's true killer, and as she told us on multiple occasions, she now considered us family. Michelle Lilith also attended. For some time, she'd been angling for an invitation to a Kaiming family meal, and after a bit of prodding, Funderburke made the offer.

"Do you want to come to the Kaiming house for dinner?" he asked her in my presence.

"You don't really look like you want to ask that."

"Yes, I do."

"Your face doesn't show it."

"This invitation will be withdrawn in five...four...three...two..."

"All right, I'll come." And she did. I wound up talking to her more than Funderburke did, and she spent most of her time worrying about Funderburke's little half-sister, who was now living with an aunt in Chicago and was rebelling in every way possible. Ms. Lilith suggested that it might help if Funderburke sat down with his sibling and tried to set her back on the right path, and I promised to coax Funderburke into meeting his half-sister.

The dining fare was mostly calzones and strombolis, cooked in the new outdoor pizza oven Dad bought and installed for Mom. It was a beautiful night, and as we cleared up the food at dusk, the yard filled with fireflies, zooming through the air and flashing in the grass. The kids ran around, catching them and setting them free.

After releasing a jarful of fireflies he and Bernard had caught together, Benek picked up a slice of strawberry pie, sat next to me, and started venting.

"You know, I'm sick and tired of people telling me that I've finally gotten closure, and I can "let it go." I can't. Not completely. I've tried, honestly I have. But every day, I tell myself that I should move on with my life and stop thinking of ways to humiliate and shame the people who played a role in Benek's death. All those jurors, how often do they think about Benek?"

"Do you still want revenge against them?" I asked.

"Sometimes. Every time I start plotting something, I think about that night I believed I drove Juror #9 to suicide, and I know I don't want anything like that. I want them to live with crushing guilt, not die. Is that so wrong?"

I shrugged in a non-committal manner.

"This whole forgiveness thing," Volker continued. "What good is it really? If someone does you wrong and you sue them, you get money. You can hold it in your hands, put it in your wallet. It's there for you until you spend it. But if you forgive someone, they never know for sure if it's genuine, and when all of a sudden you don't feel like forgiving them anymore, they don't know it. They think the slate is clear, when you still know everything isn't right. What's the point?"

"If you bake a pie, it can last for an hour until it's eaten. If you build a house, it can last for centuries before it burns down or collapses. Nothing lasts forever, but what is important is that something's there for the time it's needed."

Volker nodded. I couldn't tell how deeply my little speech had permeated his psyche, but I'd tried. Based on personal experience, I knew the anger would come flowing back at inopportune times, but what was important was that he kept fighting against it. As Funderburke's uncle told me once, forgiveness is a lifestyle choice, not flipping a switch. Volker would almost certainly be struggling with his anger for a long time to come.

Just because you learn something one day, it doesn't mean that you retain that lesson for the rest of your life.

252

Acknowledgements

My deepest thanks to Shawn Simmons, Deb Well, and everybody at Level Best Books. Thanks for believing in me, Funderburke, Nerissa, and all of the Kaiming family.

About the Author

Chris Chan is a writer, educator, and historian. He works as a researcher and "International Goodwill Ambassador" for Agatha Christie Ltd. His true crime articles, reviews, and short fiction have appeared in *The Strand, The Wisconsin Magazine of History, Mystery Weekly, Gilbert!,* Nerd HQ, Akashic Books' *Mondays are Murder* webseries, *The Baker Street Journal, The MX Book of New Sherlock Holmes Stories, Masthead: The Best New England Crime Stories, Sherlock Holmes Mystery Magazine,* and multipleBelanger Books anthologies. He is the creator of the Funderburke and Kaiming mysteries, a series featuring private investigators who work for a school and help students during times of crisis. The Funderburke short story "The Six-Year-Old Serial Killer" was nominated for a Derringer Award. His first book, *Sherlock & Irene: The Secret Truth Behind "A Scandal in Bohemia,"* was published in 2020 by MX Publishing, and he is also the author of the comedic novels *Sherlock's Secretary* and its sequel *Nessie's Nemesis.* His book *Murder Most Grotesque: The Comedic Crime Fiction of Joyce Porter* (Level Best Books) was nominated for the 2022 Agatha Award for Best Non-Fiction. *Murder Most Grotesque, Sherlock's Secretary,* and his anthology *Of Course He Pushed Him & Other Sherlock Holmes Stories: The Complete Collection* were all nominated for Silver Falchion Awards. He is also the author of *The Autistic Sleuth* (MX Publishing) and *Some of My Best Friends Are Murderers: Critiquing the Columbo Killers* (Level Best Books), the latter being nominated for the 2025 Agatha Award for Best Non-Fiction.

AUTHOR WEBSITE (live link):

https://www.levelbestbooks.us/chris-chan.html

https://chrischancrimeandcriticism.blogspot.com

SOCIAL MEDIA HANDLES (live links):

@GKCfan

https://www.instagram.com/chan3589/

https://www.facebook.com/chrischanauthorpage/

Also by Chris Chan

Full-Length Novels

Sherlock's Secretary, published by MX Publishing (November 2021)

Ghosting My Friend, published by Level Best Books (March 2023)

Nessie's Nemesis, published by MX Publishing (September 2023)

She Ruined Our Lives, published by Level Best Books (February 2023)

Full-Length Non-Fiction Books

Sherlock & Irene: The Secret Truth Behind "A Scandal in Bohemia," published by MX Publishing (August 2020)

Murder Most Grotesque: The Comedic Crime Fiction of Joyce Porter, published by Level Best Books (September 2021)

The Autistic Sleuth: Screen Portrayals of Detectives on the Spectrum in Sherlock Holmes Adaptations, The Millennium Trilogy, The Bridge, Death Note, The Curious Incident of the Dog in the Night-Time, and Other Productions, withn Patricia Meyer Chan, Ph.D., published by MX Publishing (September 2024)

Some of My Best Friends Are Murderers: Critiquing the Columbo Killers, published by Level Best Books (September 2024)

Anthologies

Of Course He Pushed Him and Other Sherlock Holmes Stories: Volumes One & Two, published by MX Publishing (June 2022– Volume One published separately in September 2022, Volume Two published separately, in November 2022)

Additionally, numerous short stories, reviews, and non-fiction essays

www.ingramcontent.com/pod-product-compliance
Lightning Source LLC
Chambersburg PA
CBHW020055301225
37489CB00041B/318